DLY.

ASS

JORDAN BOYD
colorist

RUS WOOTON
letterer • logo design

SEBASTIAN GIRNER &
BRIAH SKELLY
editors

IMAGE COMICS, INC.

Robert Kirkman • Chief Operating Officer
Erik Larsen • Chief Financial Officer
Todd McFarlane • President
Marc Silvestri • Chief Executive Officer
Jim Valentino • Vice President

Eric Stephenson • Publisher/Chief Creative Officer
Jeff Boison • Director of Publishing Planning & Book Trade Sales
Chris Ross • Director of Digital Sales
Jeff Stang • Director of Direct Market Sales
Kat Salazar • Director of PR & Marketing
Drew Gill • Art Director
Heather Doornink • Production Director
Nicole Lapalme • Controller

imagecomics.com

ERIKA SCHNATZ
production design

DEADLY CLASS VOLUME 8: NEVER GO BACK. First printing. July 2019. Published by Image Comics, Inc. Office of publication: 2701 NW Vaughn St., Suite 780, Portland, OR 97210. Copyright © 2019 Rick Remender & Wes Craig. All rights reserved. Contains material originally published in single magazine form as DEADLY CLASS #36-39 and DEADLY CLASS: KILLER SET, FCBD SPECIAL. DEADLY CLASS™ (including all prominent characters featured herein), its logo and all character likenesses are trademarks of Rick Remender & Wes Craig, unless otherwise noted. Image Comics® and its logos are registered trademarks of Image Comics, Inc. No part of this publication may be reproduced or transmitted, in any form or by any means (except for short excerpts for journalistic or review purposes), without the express written permission of Rick Remender & Wes Craig, or Image Comics, Inc. All names, characters, events, and locales in this publication are entirely fictional. Any resemblance to actual persons (living or dead), events, or places, without satirical intent, is coincidental. **PRINTED IN THE USA.** For information regarding the CPSIA on this printed material call: 203-595-3636. For international rights, contact: foreignlicensing@imagecomics.com. ISBN: 978-1-5343-1063-6

EST
1637

IN VITAM MORTEM

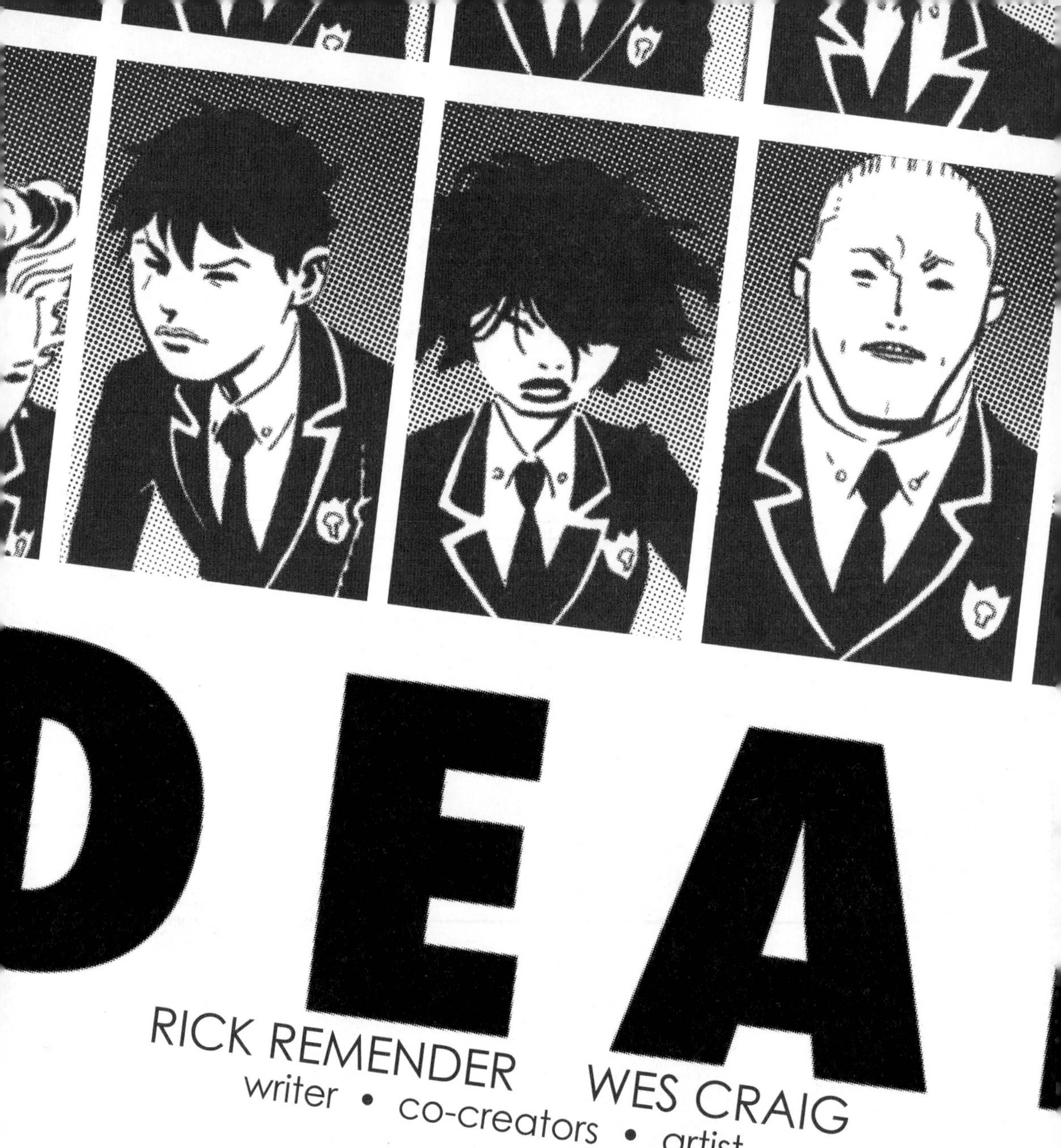

RICK REMENDER WES CRAIG

writer • co-creators • artist

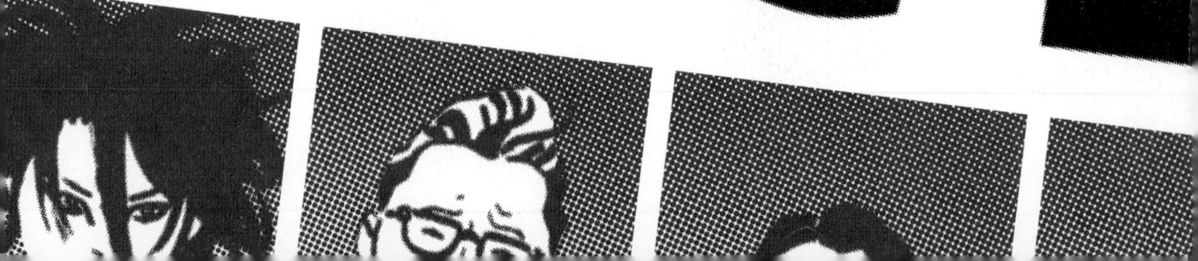

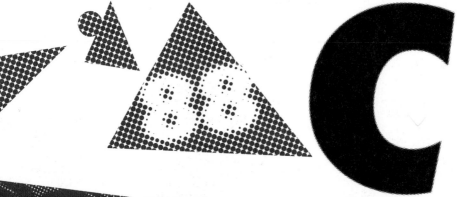

MARCUS: EVERYONE HE LOVES DIES.

DAYS FLIP BY LIKE AN OLD CALENDAR IN A BLACK AND WHITE MONTAGE.

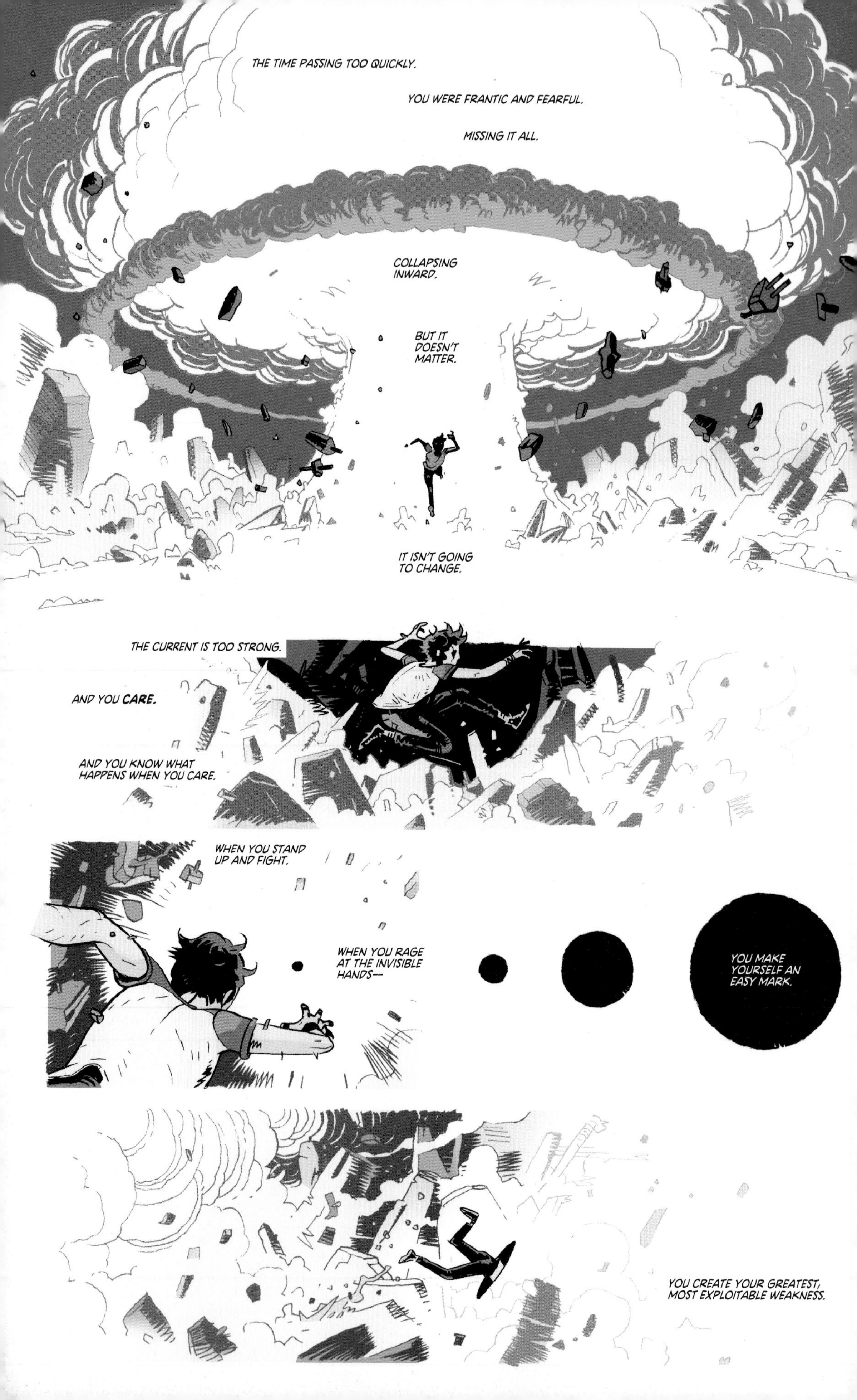
THE TIME PASSING TOO QUICKLY.
YOU WERE FRANTIC AND FEARFUL.
MISSING IT ALL.
COLLAPSING INWARD.
BUT IT DOESN'T MATTER.
IT ISN'T GOING TO CHANGE.
THE CURRENT IS TOO STRONG.
AND YOU CARE.
AND YOU KNOW WHAT HAPPENS WHEN YOU CARE.
WHEN YOU STAND UP AND FIGHT.
WHEN YOU RAGE AT THE INVISIBLE HANDS--
YOU MAKE YOURSELF AN EASY MARK.
YOU CREATE YOUR GREATEST, MOST EXPLOITABLE WEAKNESS.

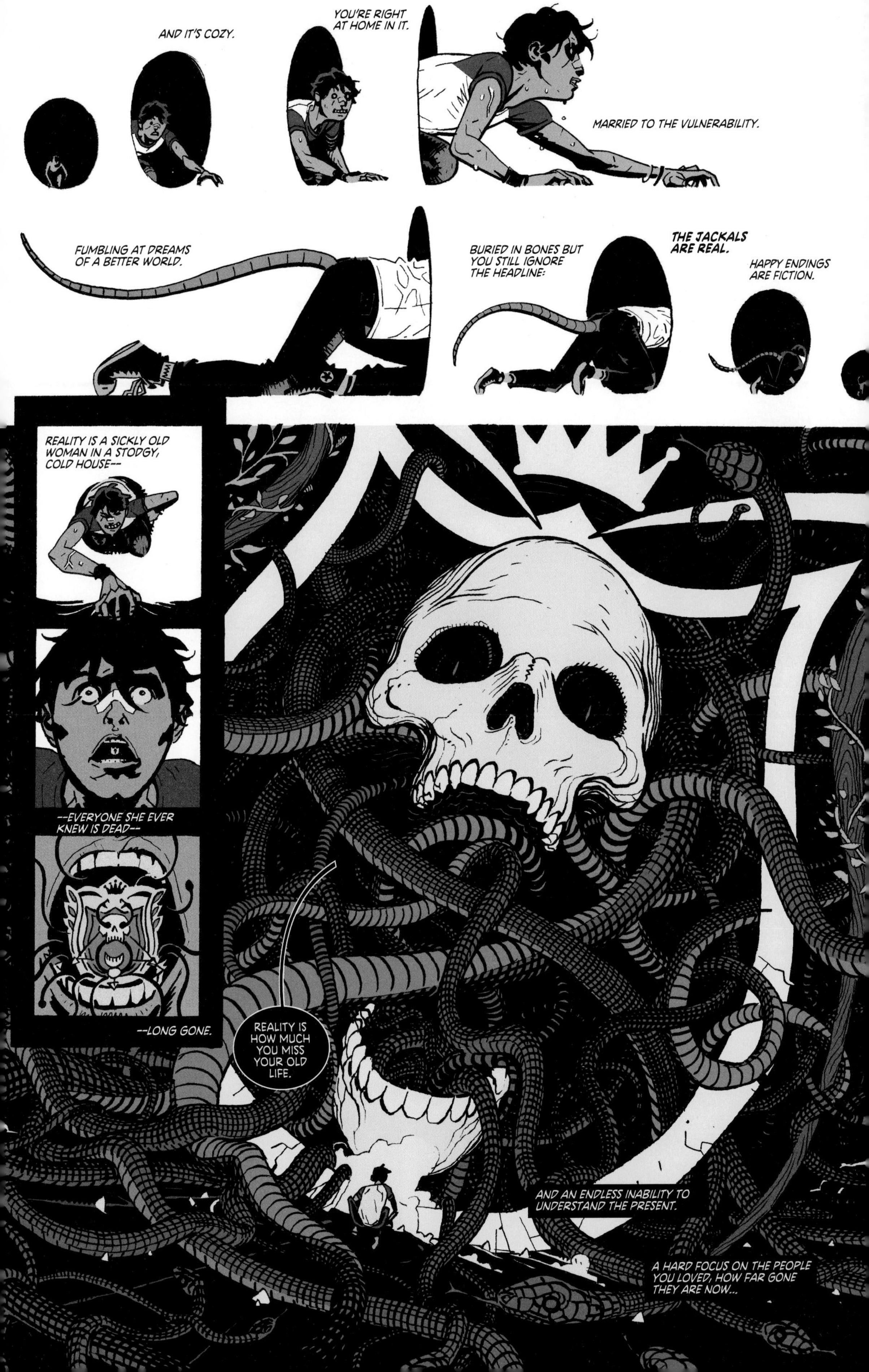
AND IT'S COZY.
YOU'RE RIGHT AT HOME IN IT.
MARRIED TO THE VULNERABILITY.
FUMBLING AT DREAMS OF A BETTER WORLD.
BURIED IN BONES BUT YOU STILL IGNORE THE HEADLINE:
THE JACKALS ARE REAL.
HAPPY ENDINGS ARE FICTION.
REALITY IS A SICKLY OLD WOMAN IN A STODGY, COLD HOUSE--
--EVERYONE SHE EVER KNEW IS DEAD--
--LONG GONE.
REALITY IS HOW MUCH YOU MISS YOUR OLD LIFE.
AND AN ENDLESS INABILITY TO UNDERSTAND THE PRESENT.
A HARD FOCUS ON THE PEOPLE YOU LOVED, HOW FAR GONE THEY ARE NOW...

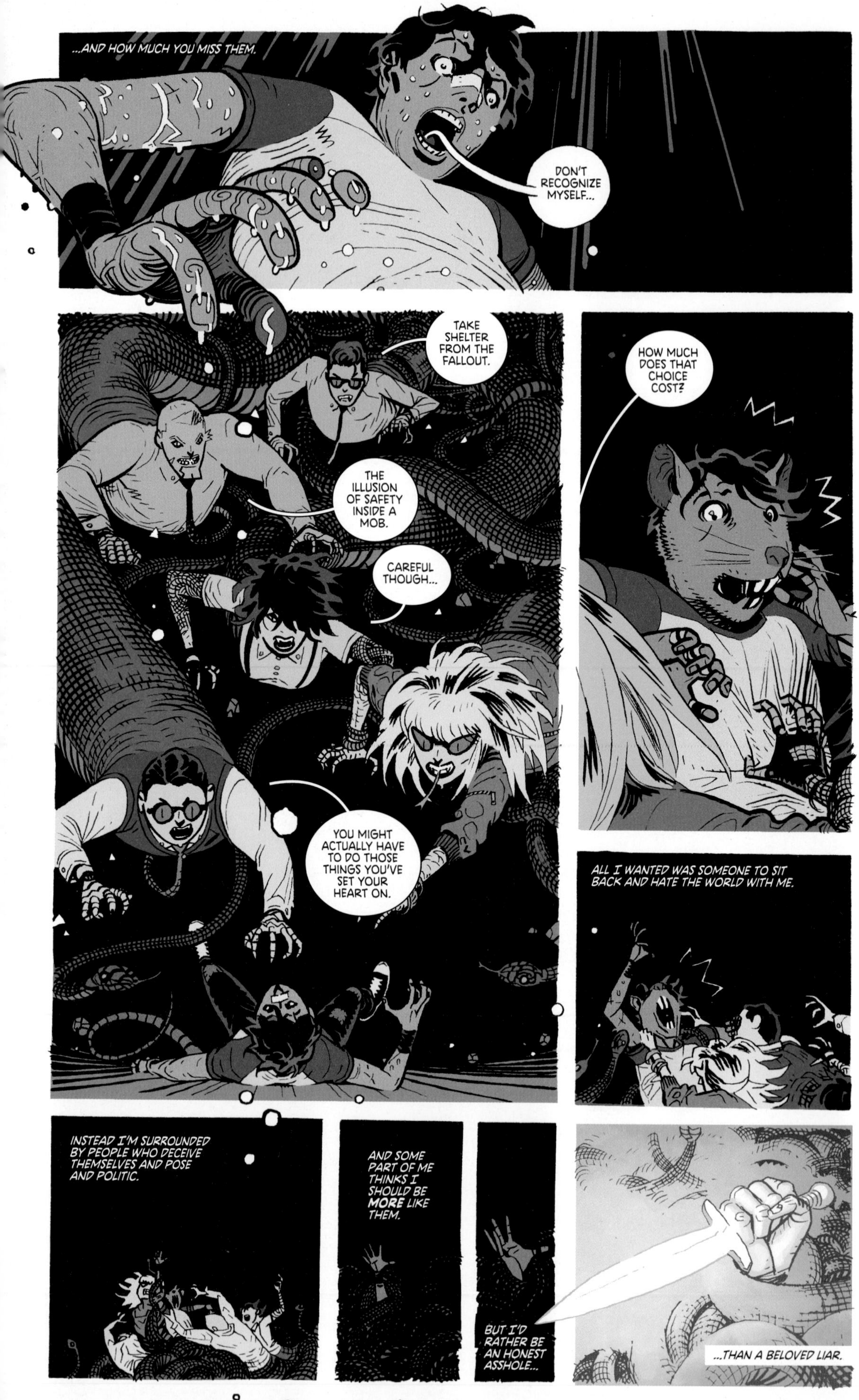
...AND HOW MUCH YOU MISS THEM.
DON'T RECOGNIZE MYSELF...
TAKE SHELTER FROM THE FALLOUT.
THE ILLUSION OF SAFETY INSIDE A MOB.
CAREFUL THOUGH...
YOU MIGHT ACTUALLY HAVE TO DO THOSE THINGS YOU'VE SET YOUR HEART ON.
HOW MUCH DOES THAT CHOICE COST?
ALL I WANTED WAS SOMEONE TO SIT BACK AND HATE THE WORLD WITH ME.
INSTEAD I'M SURROUNDED BY PEOPLE WHO DECEIVE THEMSELVES AND POSE AND POLITIC.
AND SOME PART OF ME THINKS I SHOULD BE **MORE** LIKE THEM.
BUT I'D RATHER BE AN HONEST ASSHOLE...
...THAN A BELOVED LIAR.

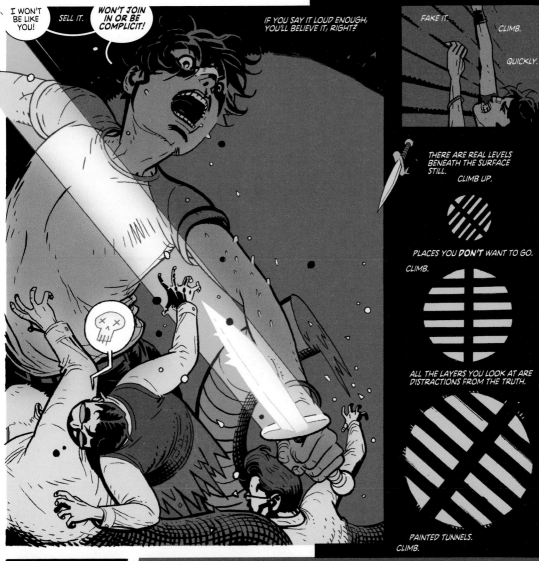

I WON'T BE LIKE YOU!

SELL IT.

WON'T JOIN IN OR BE COMPLICIT!

IF YOU SAY IT LOUD ENOUGH, YOU'LL BELIEVE IT, RIGHT?

FAKE IT.

CLIMB.

QUICKLY.

THERE ARE REAL LEVELS BENEATH THE SURFACE STILL.

CLIMB UP.

PLACES YOU **DON'T** WANT TO GO.

CLIMB.

ALL THE LAYERS YOU LOOK AT ARE DISTRACTIONS FROM THE TRUTH.

PAINTED TUNNELS.

CLIMB.

FALSE DOORS.

MANNEQUIN PROPS.

EVERYTHING YOU THINK YOU KNOW ABOUT YOURSELF:

A FAKE SUBURB BUILT FOR NUCLEAR TESTING.

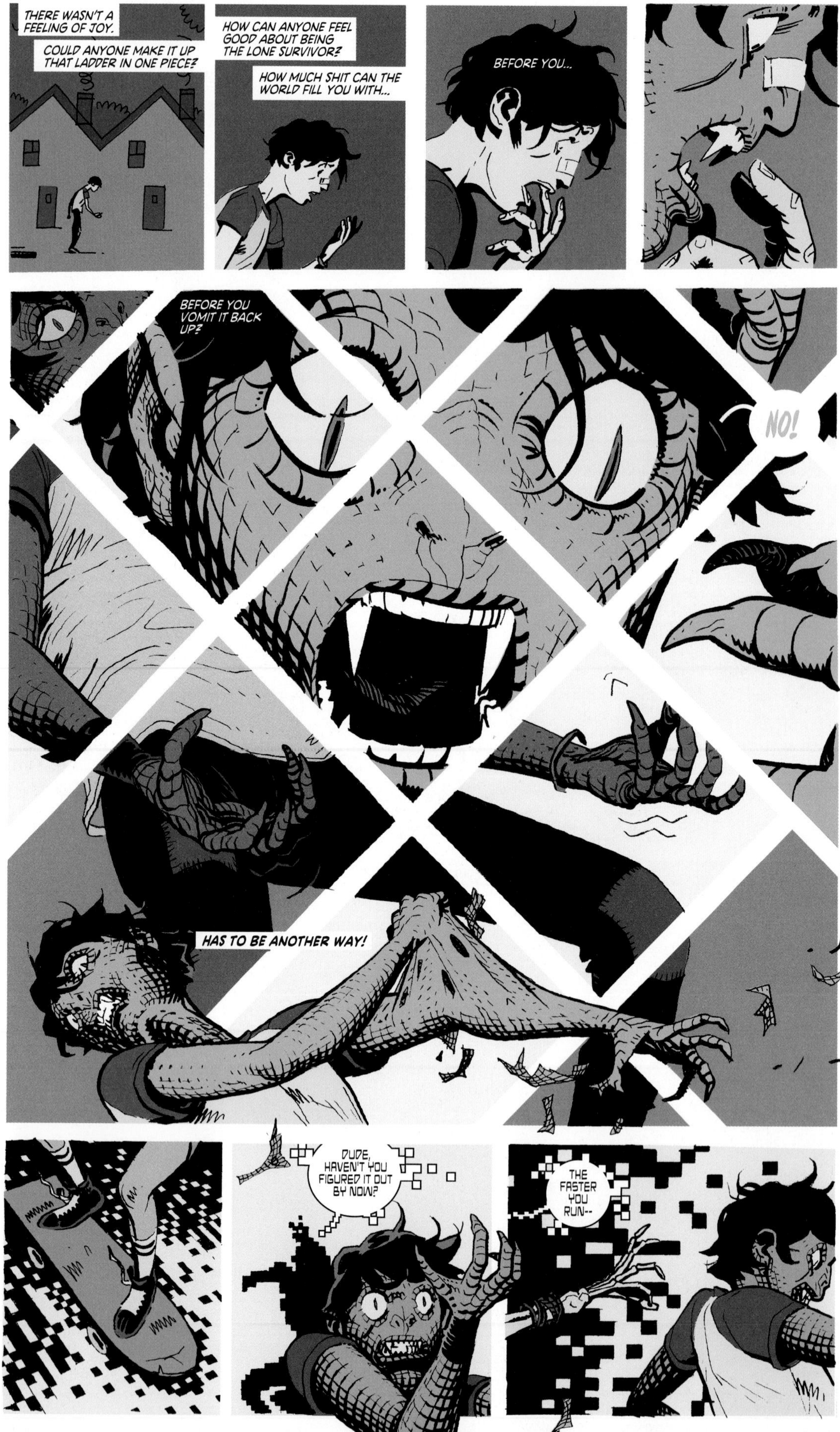
THERE WASN'T A FEELING OF JOY.
COULD ANYONE MAKE IT UP THAT LADDER IN ONE PIECE?
HOW CAN ANYONE FEEL GOOD ABOUT BEING THE LONE SURVIVOR?
HOW MUCH SHIT CAN THE WORLD FILL YOU WITH...
BEFORE YOU...
BEFORE YOU VOMIT IT BACK UP?
NO!
HAS TO BE ANOTHER WAY!
DUDE, HAVEN'T YOU FIGURED IT OUT BY NOW?
THE FASTER YOU RUN--

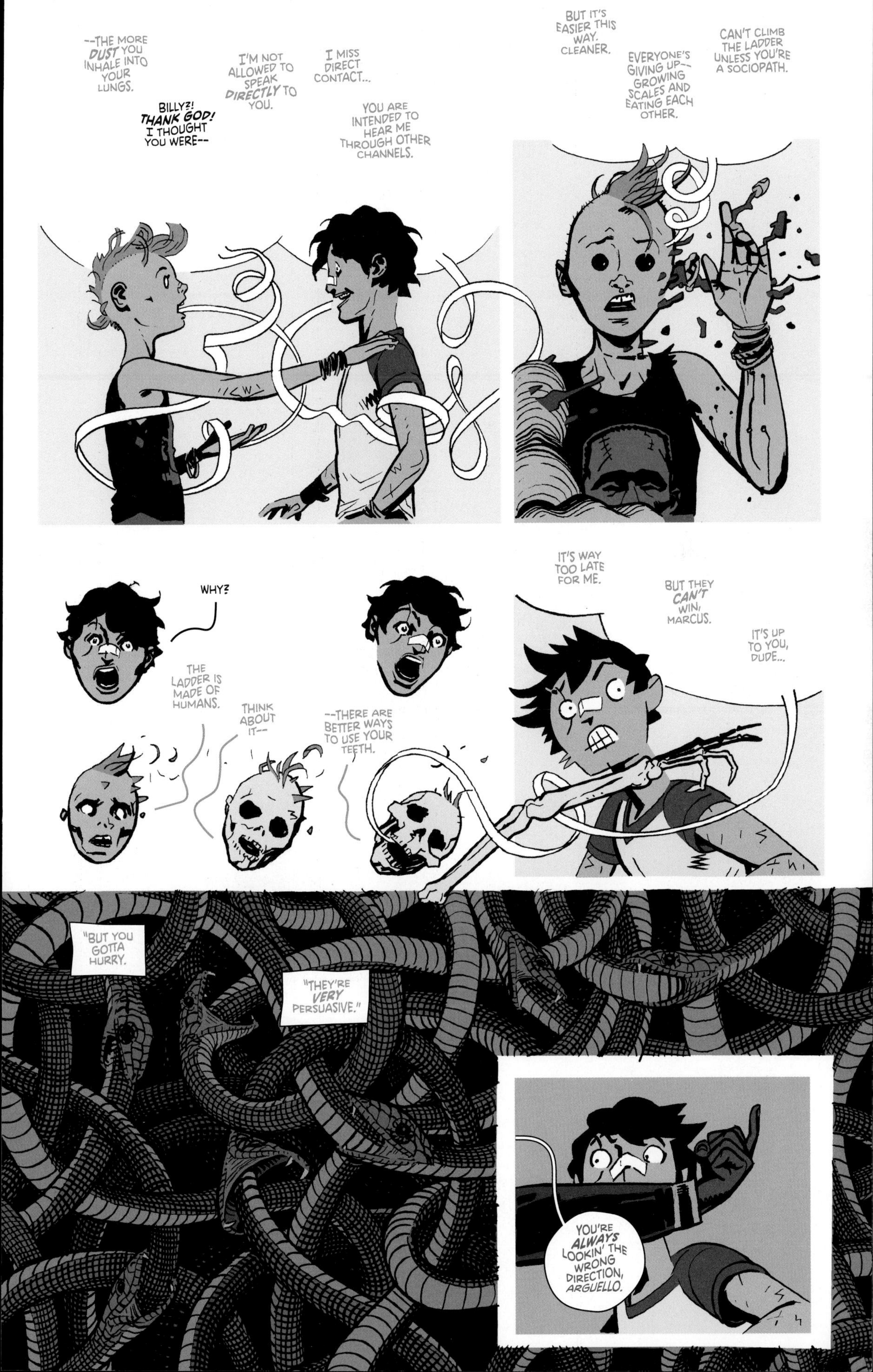
--THE MORE DUST YOU INHALE INTO YOUR LUNGS.
BILLY?! THANK GOD! I THOUGHT YOU WERE--
I'M NOT ALLOWED TO SPEAK DIRECTLY TO YOU.
I MISS DIRECT CONTACT...
YOU ARE INTENDED TO HEAR ME THROUGH OTHER CHANNELS.
BUT IT'S EASIER THIS WAY. CLEANER.
EVERYONE'S GIVING UP-- GROWING SCALES AND EATING EACH OTHER.
CAN'T CLIMB THE LADDER UNLESS YOU'RE A SOCIOPATH.
WHY?
THE LADDER IS MADE OF HUMANS.
THINK ABOUT IT--
--THERE ARE BETTER WAYS TO USE YOUR TEETH.
IT'S WAY TOO LATE FOR ME.
BUT THEY CAN'T WIN, MARCUS.
IT'S UP TO YOU, DUDE...
"BUT YOU GOTTA HURRY.
"THEY'RE VERY PERSUASIVE."
YOU'RE ALWAYS LOOKIN' THE WRONG DIRECTION, ARGUELLO.

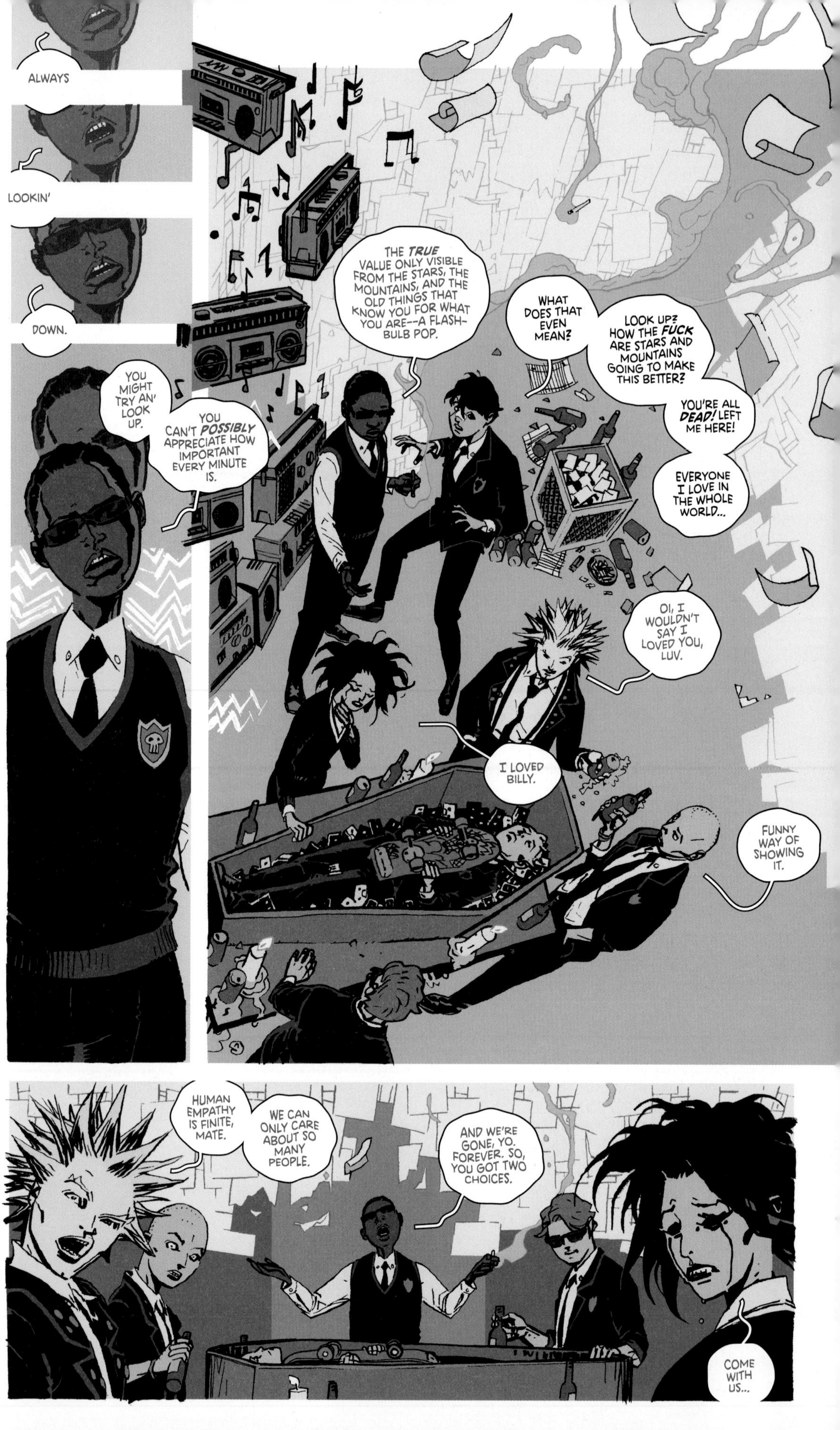
ALWAYS
LOOKIN'
DOWN.
YOU MIGHT TRY AN' LOOK UP.
YOU CAN'T **POSSIBLY** APPRECIATE HOW IMPORTANT EVERY MINUTE IS.
THE **TRUE** VALUE ONLY VISIBLE FROM THE STARS, THE MOUNTAINS, AND THE OLD THINGS THAT KNOW YOU FOR WHAT YOU ARE--A FLASH-BULB POP.
WHAT DOES THAT EVEN MEAN?
LOOK UP? HOW THE **FUCK** ARE STARS AND MOUNTAINS GOING TO MAKE THIS BETTER?
YOU'RE ALL **DEAD!** LEFT ME HERE!
EVERYONE I LOVE IN THE WHOLE WORLD...
OI, I WOULDN'T SAY I LOVED YOU, LUV.
I LOVED BILLY.
FUNNY WAY OF SHOWING IT.
HUMAN EMPATHY IS FINITE, MATE.
WE CAN ONLY CARE ABOUT SO MANY PEOPLE.
AND WE'RE GONE, YO. FOREVER. SO, YOU GOT TWO CHOICES.
COME WITH US...

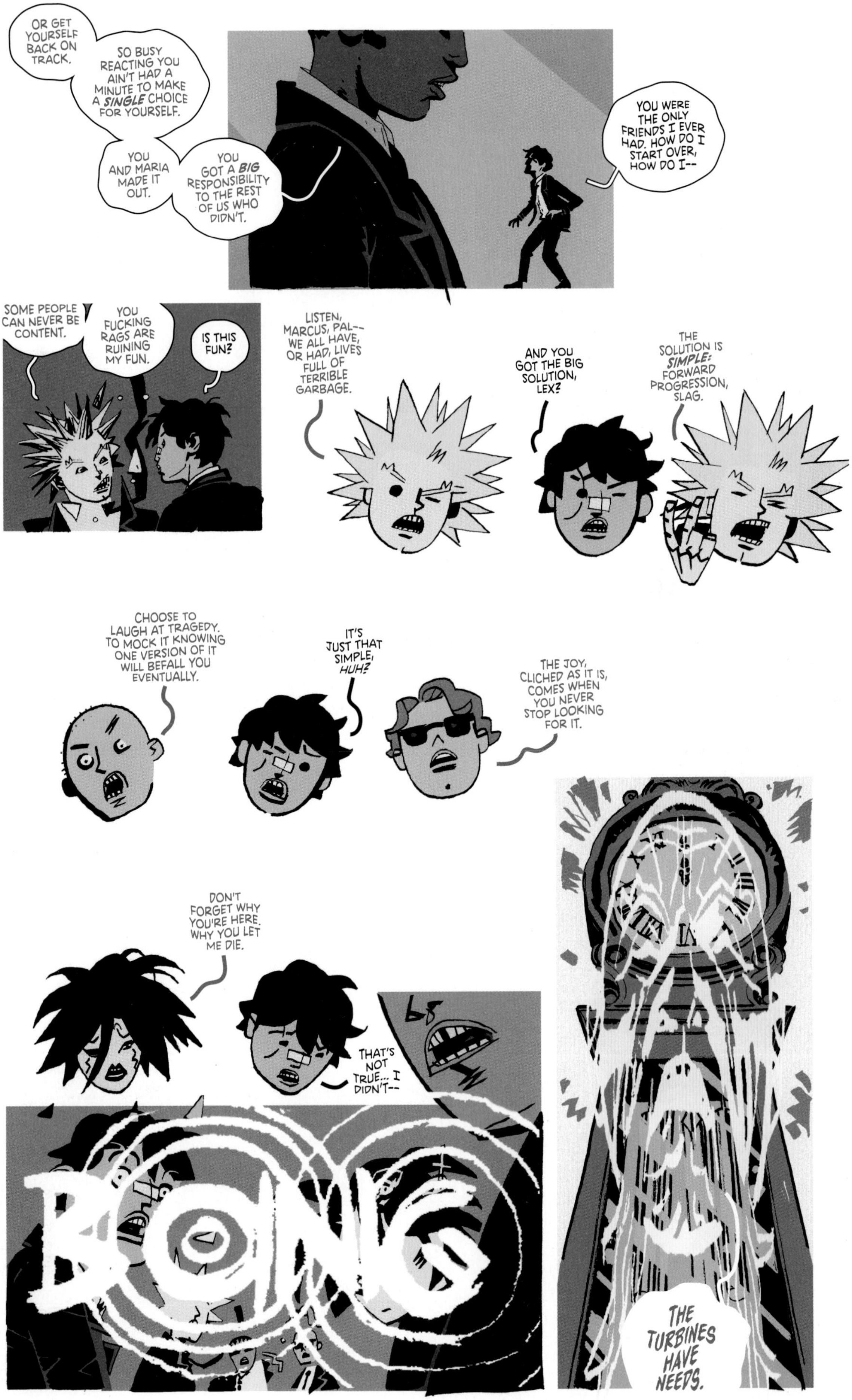
OR GET YOURSELF BACK ON TRACK.
SO BUSY REACTING YOU AIN'T HAD A MINUTE TO MAKE A SINGLE CHOICE FOR YOURSELF.
YOU AND MARIA MADE IT OUT.
YOU GOT A BIG RESPONSIBILITY TO THE REST OF US WHO DIDN'T.
YOU WERE THE ONLY FRIENDS I EVER HAD. HOW DO I START OVER, HOW DO I--
SOME PEOPLE CAN NEVER BE CONTENT.
YOU FUCKING RAGS ARE RUINING MY FUN.
IS THIS FUN?
LISTEN, MARCUS, PAL-- WE ALL HAVE, OR HAD, LIVES FULL OF TERRIBLE GARBAGE.
AND YOU GOT THE BIG SOLUTION, LEX?
THE SOLUTION IS SIMPLE: FORWARD PROGRESSION, SLAG.
CHOOSE TO LAUGH AT TRAGEDY. TO MOCK IT KNOWING ONE VERSION OF IT WILL BEFALL YOU EVENTUALLY.
IT'S JUST THAT SIMPLE, HUH?
THE JOY, CLICHED AS IT IS, COMES WHEN YOU NEVER STOP LOOKING FOR IT.
DON'T FORGET WHY YOU'RE HERE. WHY YOU LET ME DIE.
THAT'S NOT TRUE... I DIDN'T--
BONG
THE TURBINES HAVE NEEDS.

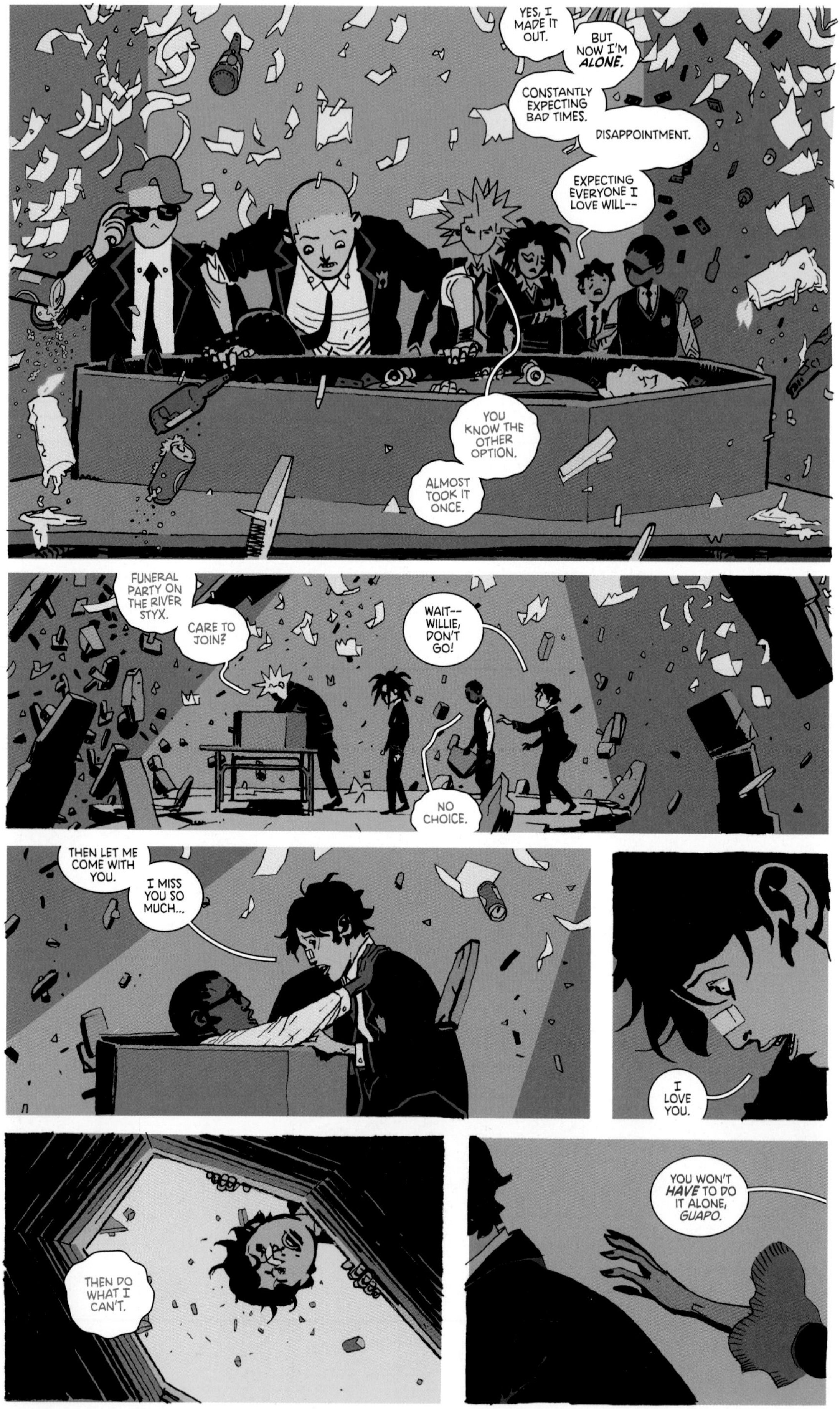

YES, I MADE IT OUT.
BUT NOW I'M ***ALONE.***
CONSTANTLY EXPECTING BAD TIMES.
DISAPPOINTMENT.
EXPECTING EVERYONE I LOVE WILL--
YOU KNOW THE OTHER OPTION.
ALMOST TOOK IT ONCE.
FUNERAL PARTY ON THE RIVER STYX.
CARE TO JOIN?
WAIT-- WILLIE, DON'T GO!
NO CHOICE.
THEN LET ME COME WITH YOU.
I MISS YOU SO MUCH...
I LOVE YOU.
THEN DO WHAT I CAN'T.
YOU WON'T ***HAVE*** TO DO IT ALONE, *GUAPO.*

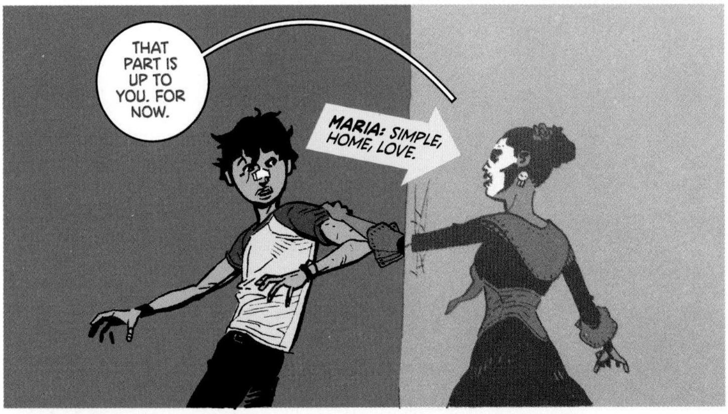
THAT PART IS UP TO YOU. FOR NOW.
MARIA: SIMPLE, HOME, LOVE.

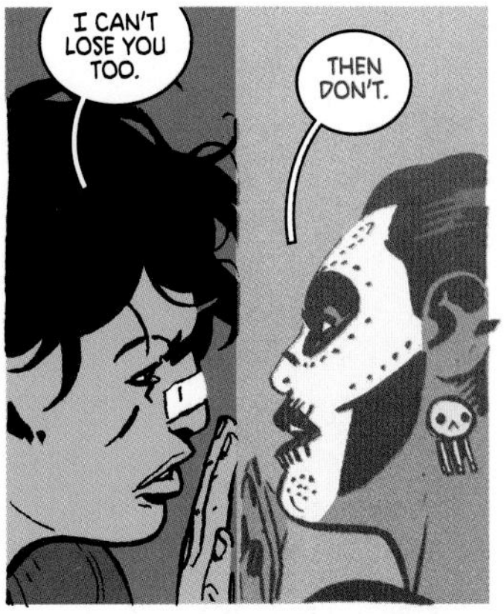
I CAN'T LOSE YOU TOO.
THEN DON'T.

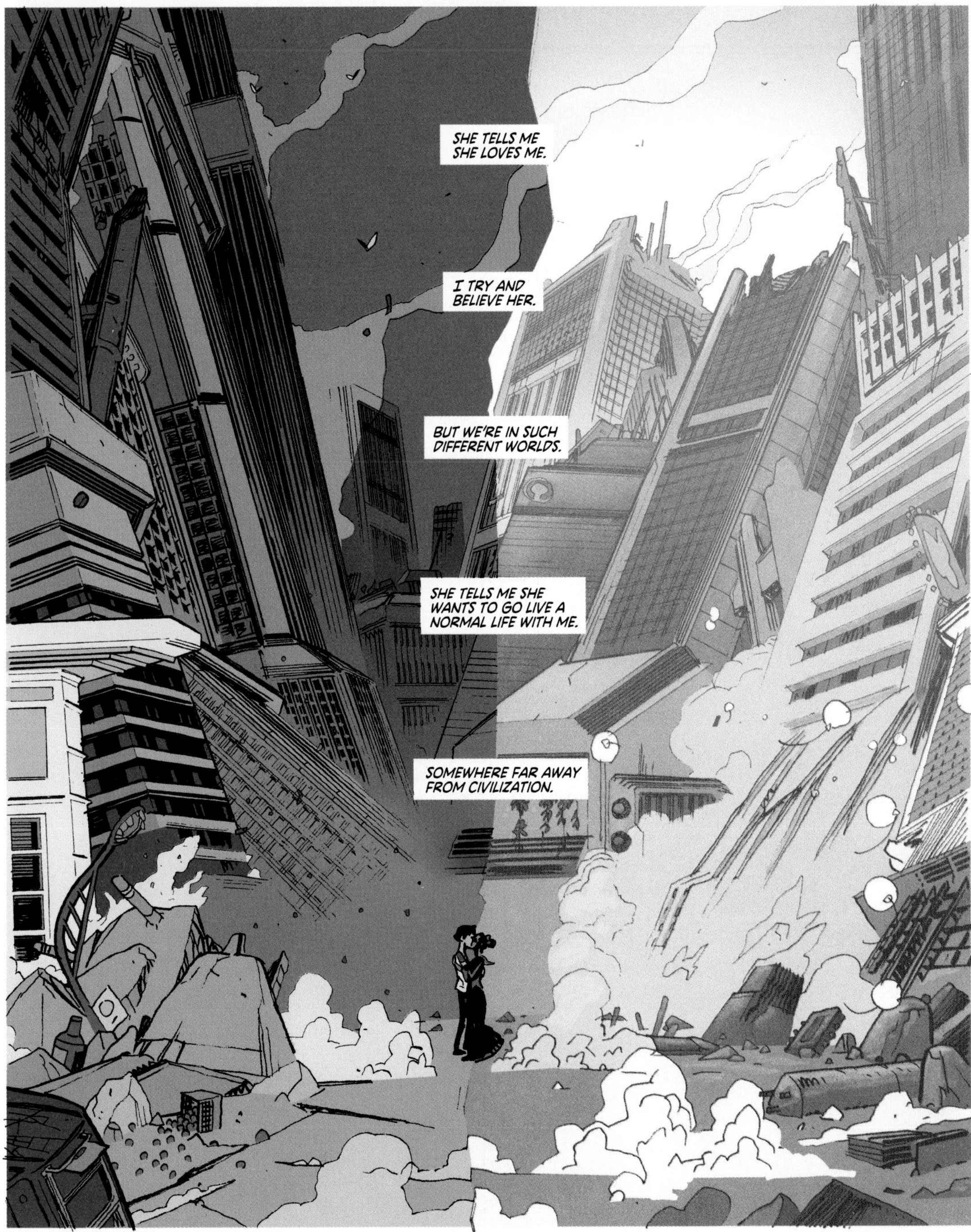
SHE TELLS ME SHE LOVES ME.
I TRY AND BELIEVE HER.
BUT WE'RE IN SUCH DIFFERENT WORLDS.
SHE TELLS ME SHE WANTS TO GO LIVE A NORMAL LIFE WITH ME.
SOMEWHERE FAR AWAY FROM CIVILIZATION.

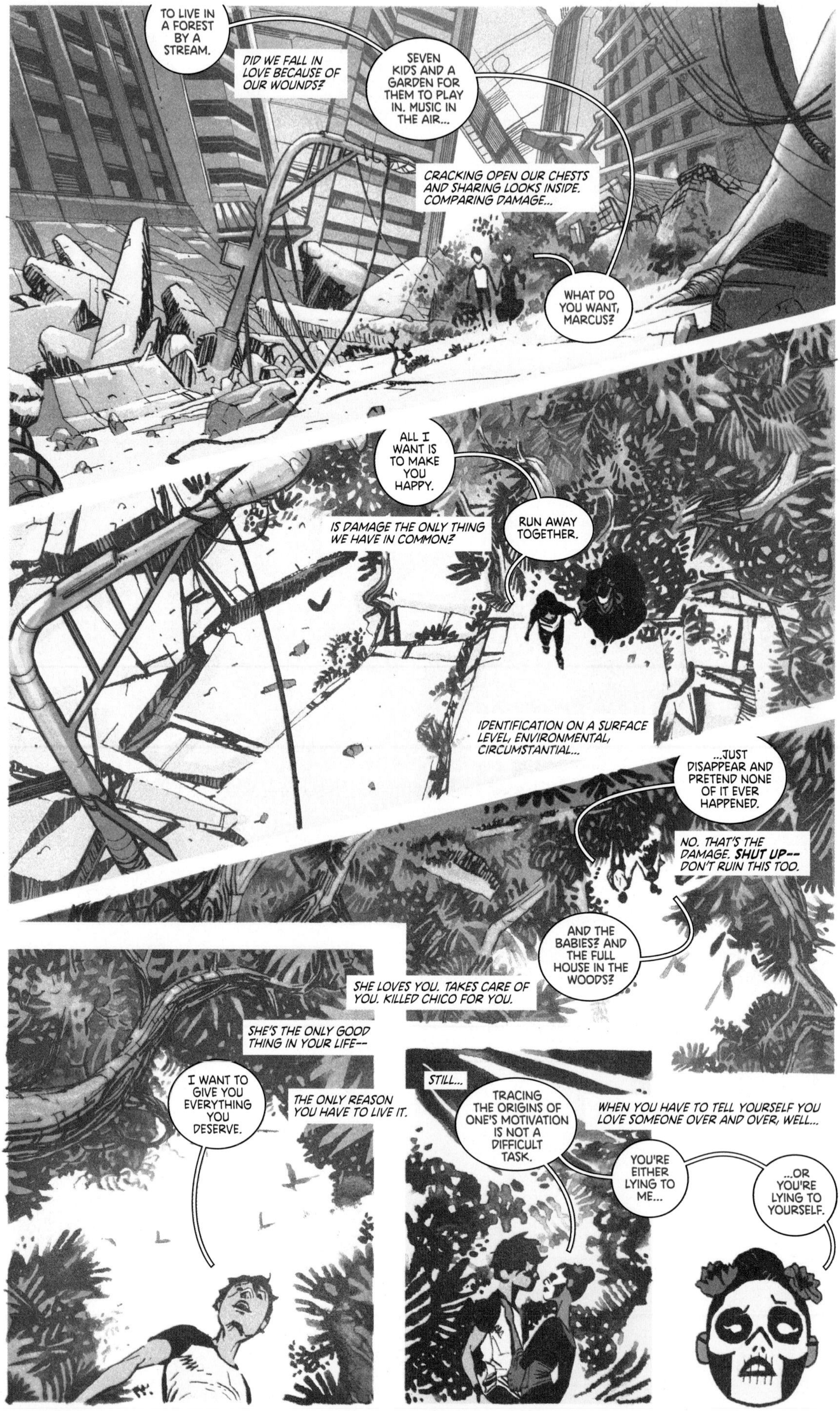
TO LIVE IN A FOREST BY A STREAM.
DID WE FALL IN LOVE BECAUSE OF OUR WOUNDS?
SEVEN KIDS AND A GARDEN FOR THEM TO PLAY IN. MUSIC IN THE AIR...
CRACKING OPEN OUR CHESTS AND SHARING LOOKS INSIDE. COMPARING DAMAGE...
WHAT DO YOU WANT, MARCUS?
ALL I WANT IS TO MAKE YOU HAPPY.
IS DAMAGE THE ONLY THING WE HAVE IN COMMON?
RUN AWAY TOGETHER.
IDENTIFICATION ON A SURFACE LEVEL, ENVIRONMENTAL, CIRCUMSTANTIAL...
...JUST DISAPPEAR AND PRETEND NONE OF IT EVER HAPPENED.
NO. THAT'S THE DAMAGE. **SHUT UP--** DON'T RUIN THIS TOO.
AND THE BABIES? AND THE FULL HOUSE IN THE WOODS?
SHE LOVES YOU. TAKES CARE OF YOU. KILLED CHICO FOR YOU.
SHE'S THE ONLY GOOD THING IN YOUR LIFE--
I WANT TO GIVE YOU EVERYTHING YOU DESERVE.
THE ONLY REASON YOU HAVE TO LIVE IT.
STILL...
TRACING THE ORIGINS OF ONE'S MOTIVATION IS NOT A DIFFICULT TASK.
WHEN YOU HAVE TO TELL YOURSELF YOU LOVE SOMEONE OVER AND OVER, WELL...
YOU'RE EITHER LYING TO ME...
...OR YOU'RE LYING TO YOURSELF.

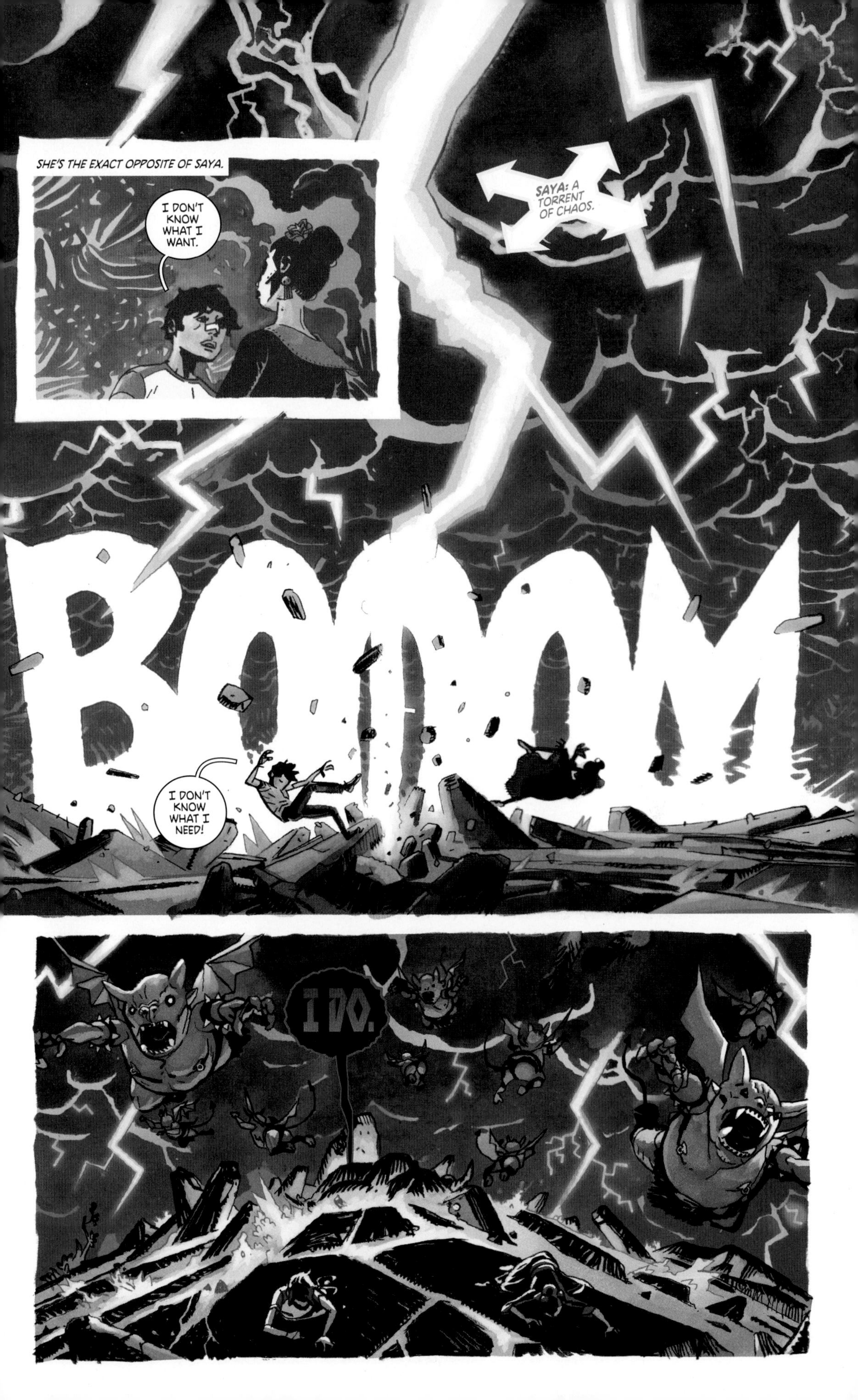
SHE'S THE EXACT OPPOSITE OF SAYA.
I DON'T KNOW WHAT I WANT.
SAYA: A TORRENT OF CHAOS.
BOOOM
I DON'T KNOW WHAT I NEED!
I DO.

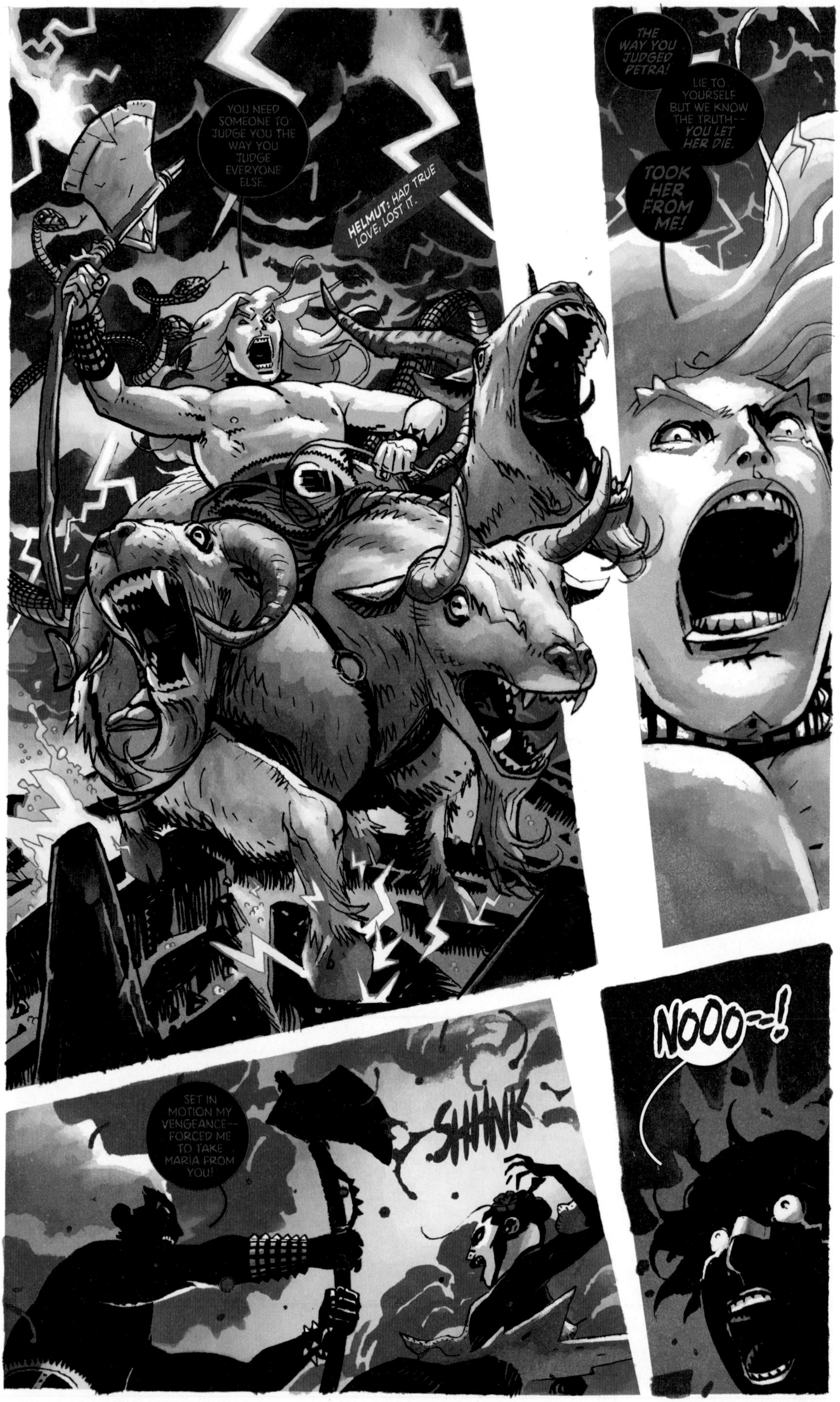
YOU NEED SOMEONE TO JUDGE YOU THE WAY YOU JUDGE EVERYONE ELSE...
HELMUT: HAD TRUE LOVE, LOST IT.
THE WAY YOU JUDGED PETRA!
LIE TO YOURSELF BUT WE KNOW THE TRUTH-- YOU LET HER DIE.
TOOK HER FROM ME!
SET IN MOTION MY VENGEANCE-- FORCED ME TO TAKE MARIA FROM YOU!
SHHNK
NOOO--!

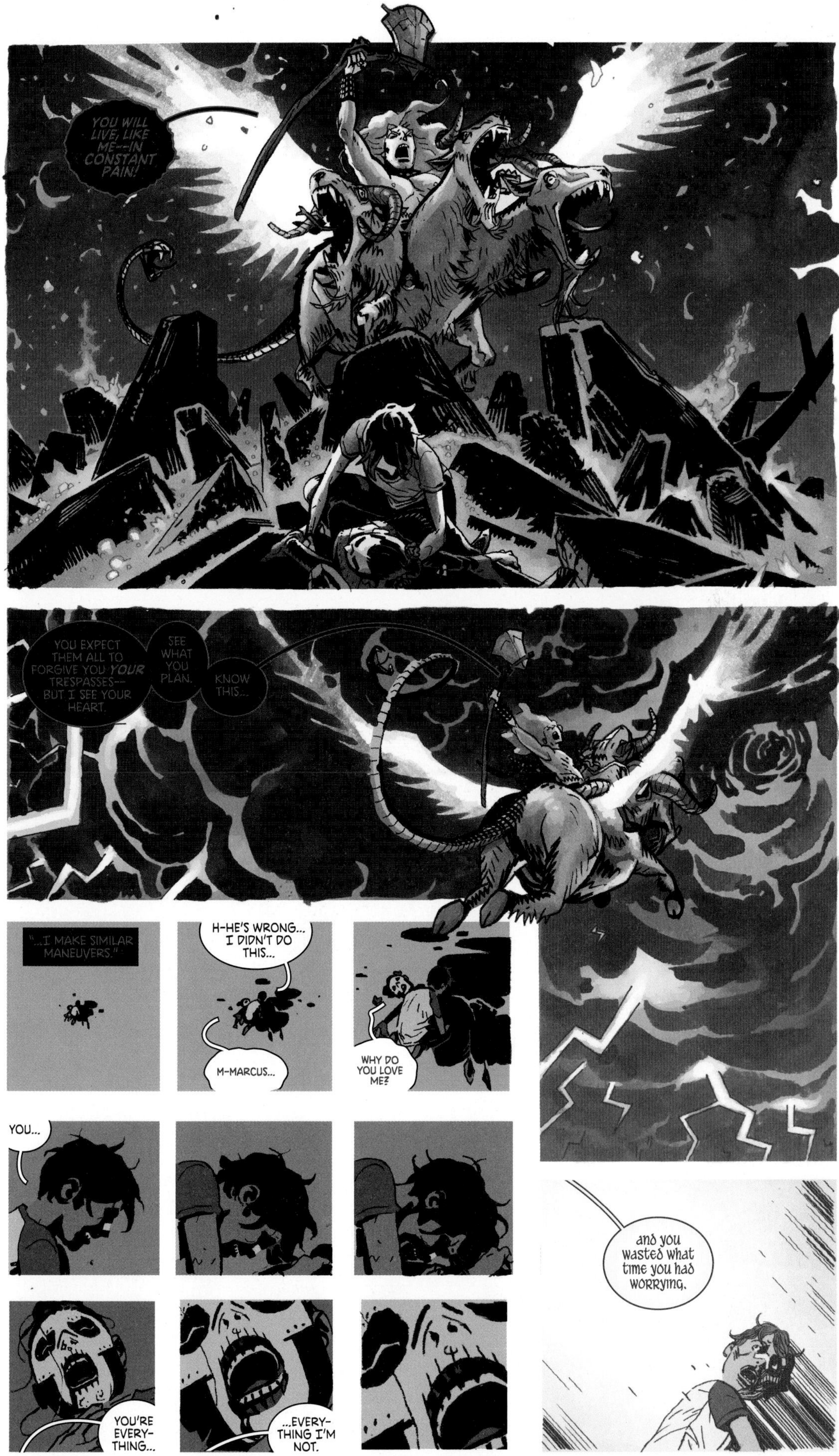
YOU WILL LIVE, LIKE ME--IN CONSTANT PAIN!
YOU EXPECT THEM ALL TO FORGIVE YOU YOUR TRESPASSES--BUT I SEE YOUR HEART.
SEE WHAT YOU PLAN.
KNOW THIS...
"...I MAKE SIMILAR MANEUVERS."
H-HE'S WRONG... I DIDN'T DO THIS...
M-MARCUS...
WHY DO YOU LOVE ME?
YOU...
YOU'RE EVERY-THING...
...EVERY-THING I'M NOT.
and you wasted what time you had worrying.

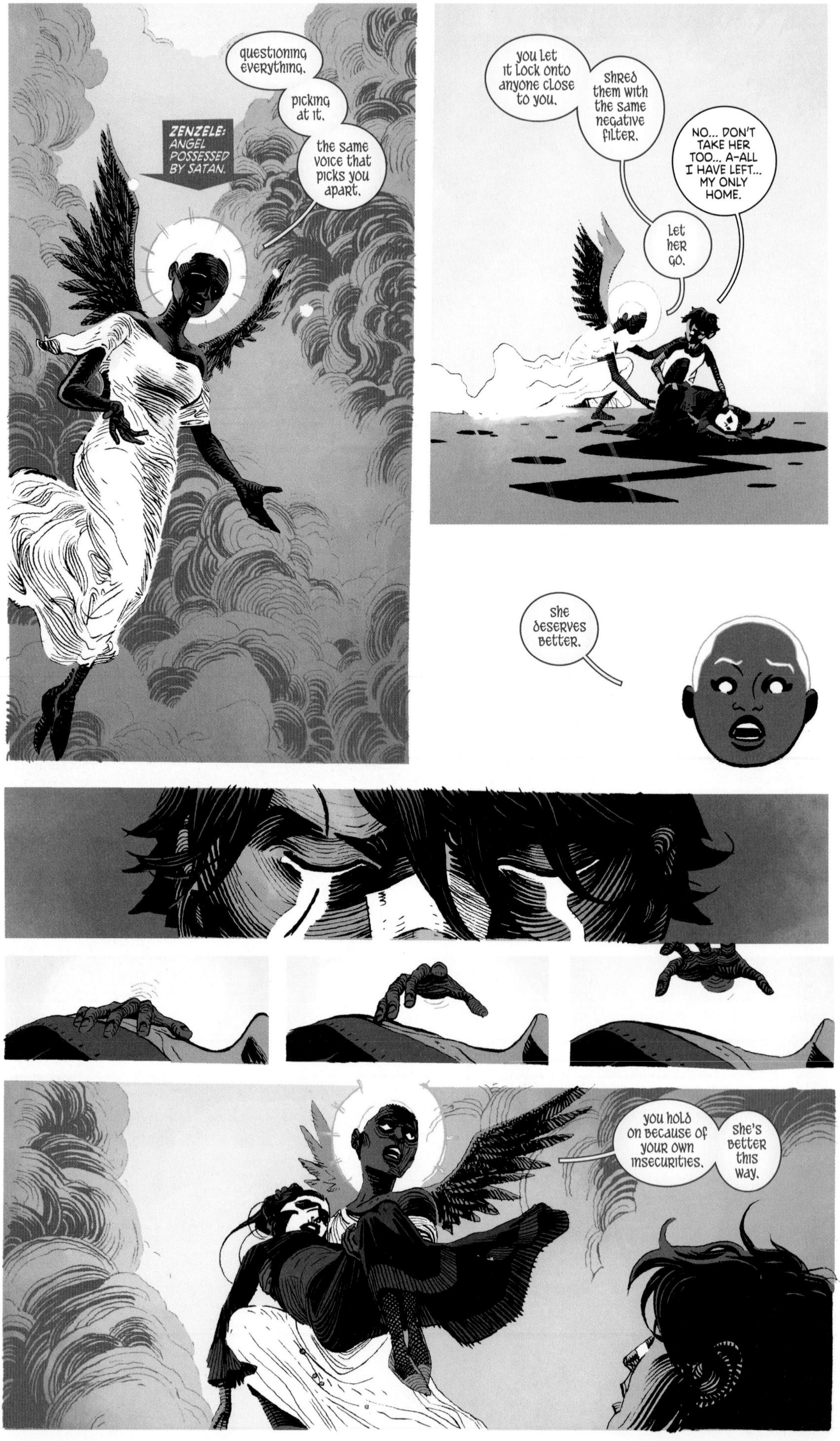
questioning everything,
picking at it,
ZENZELE: ANGEL POSSESSED BY SATAN.
the same voice that picks you apart,
you let it lock onto anyone close to you,
shred them with the same negative filter,
NO... DON'T TAKE HER TOO... A-ALL I HAVE LEFT... MY ONLY HOME.
let her go,
she deserves better,
you hold on because of your own insecurities,
she's better this way,

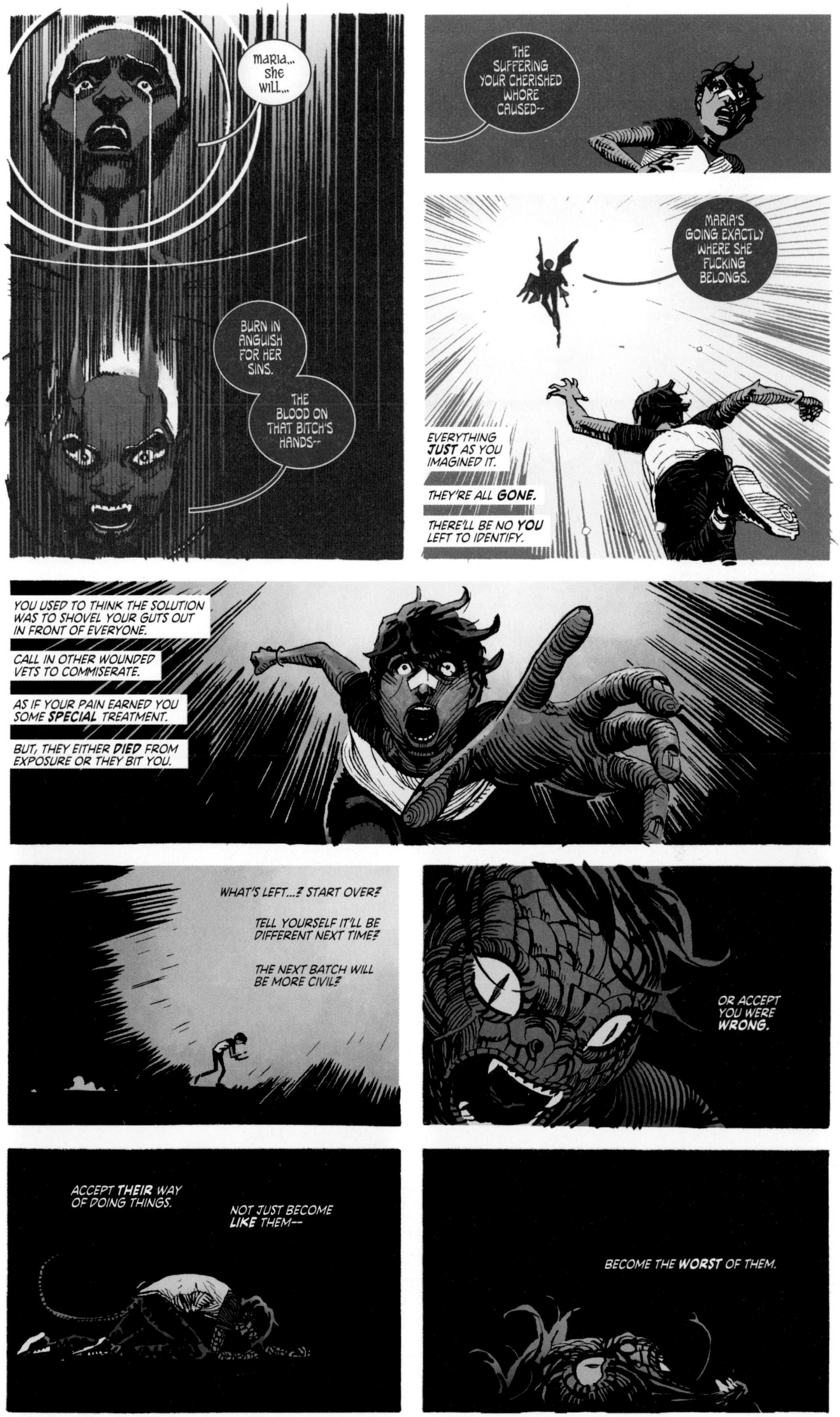
MARIA... SHE WILL...
BURN IN ANGUISH FOR HER SINS.
THE BLOOD ON THAT BITCH'S HANDS--
THE SUFFERING YOUR CHERISHED WHORE CAUSED--
MARIA'S GOING EXACTLY WHERE SHE FUCKING BELONGS.
EVERYTHING JUST AS YOU IMAGINED IT.
THEY'RE ALL GONE.
THERE'LL BE NO YOU LEFT TO IDENTIFY.
YOU USED TO THINK THE SOLUTION WAS TO SHOVEL YOUR GUTS OUT IN FRONT OF EVERYONE.
CALL IN OTHER WOUNDED VETS TO COMMISERATE.
AS IF YOUR PAIN EARNED YOU SOME SPECIAL TREATMENT.
BUT, THEY EITHER DIED FROM EXPOSURE OR THEY BIT YOU.
WHAT'S LEFT...? START OVER?
TELL YOURSELF IT'LL BE DIFFERENT NEXT TIME?
THE NEXT BATCH WILL BE MORE CIVIL?
OR ACCEPT YOU WERE WRONG.
ACCEPT THEIR WAY OF DOING THINGS.
NOT JUST BECOME LIKE THEM--
BECOME THE WORST OF THEM.

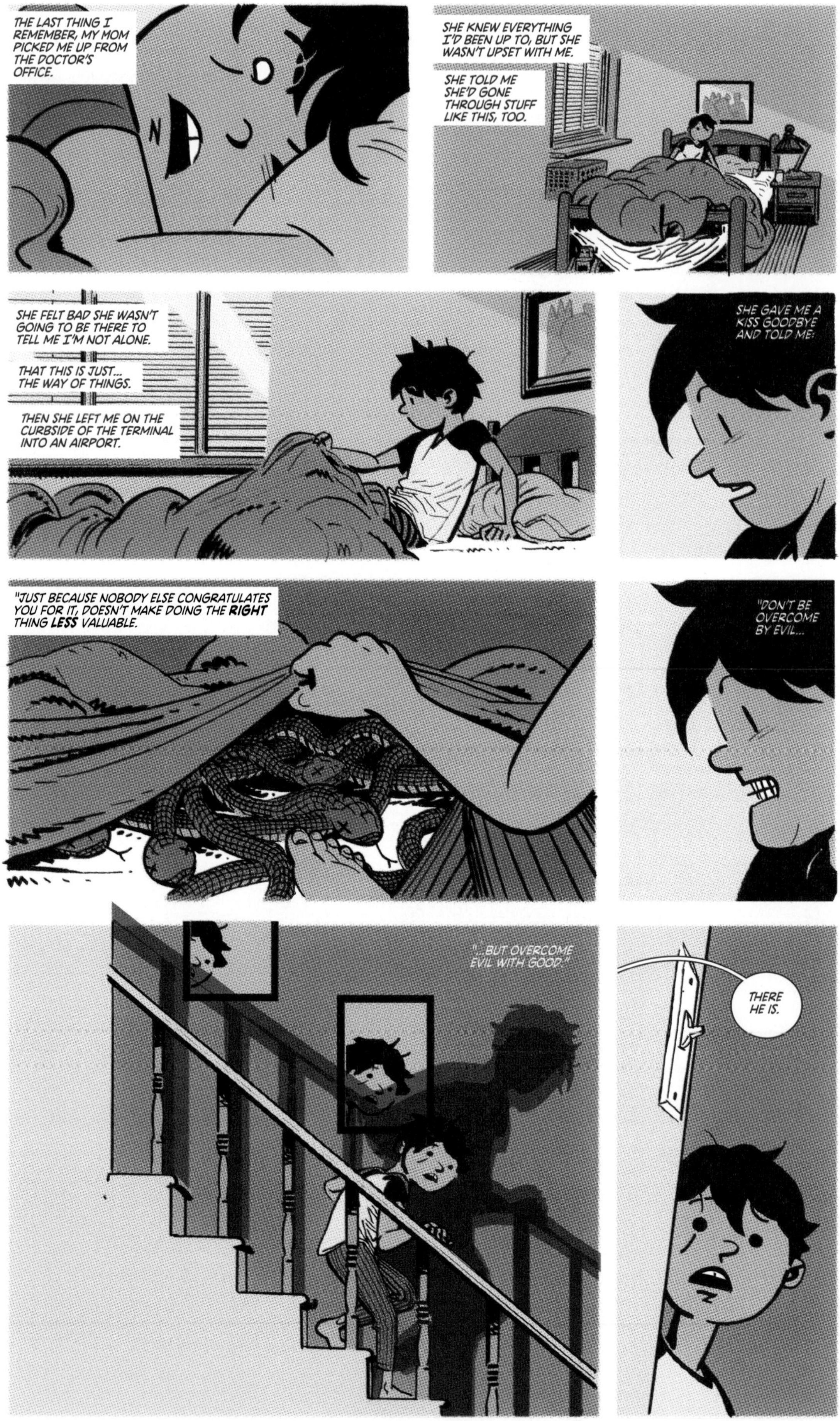
THE LAST THING I REMEMBER, MY MOM PICKED ME UP FROM THE DOCTOR'S OFFICE.
SHE KNEW EVERYTHING I'D BEEN UP TO, BUT SHE WASN'T UPSET WITH ME.
SHE TOLD ME SHE'D GONE THROUGH STUFF LIKE THIS, TOO.
SHE FELT BAD SHE WASN'T GOING TO BE THERE TO TELL ME I'M NOT ALONE.
THAT THIS IS JUST... THE WAY OF THINGS.
THEN SHE LEFT ME ON THE CURBSIDE OF THE TERMINAL INTO AN AIRPORT.
SHE GAVE ME A KISS GOODBYE AND TOLD ME:
"JUST BECAUSE NOBODY ELSE CONGRATULATES YOU FOR IT, DOESN'T MAKE DOING THE **RIGHT** THING **LESS** VALUABLE.
"DON'T BE OVERCOME BY EVIL...
"...BUT OVERCOME EVIL WITH GOOD."
THERE HE IS.

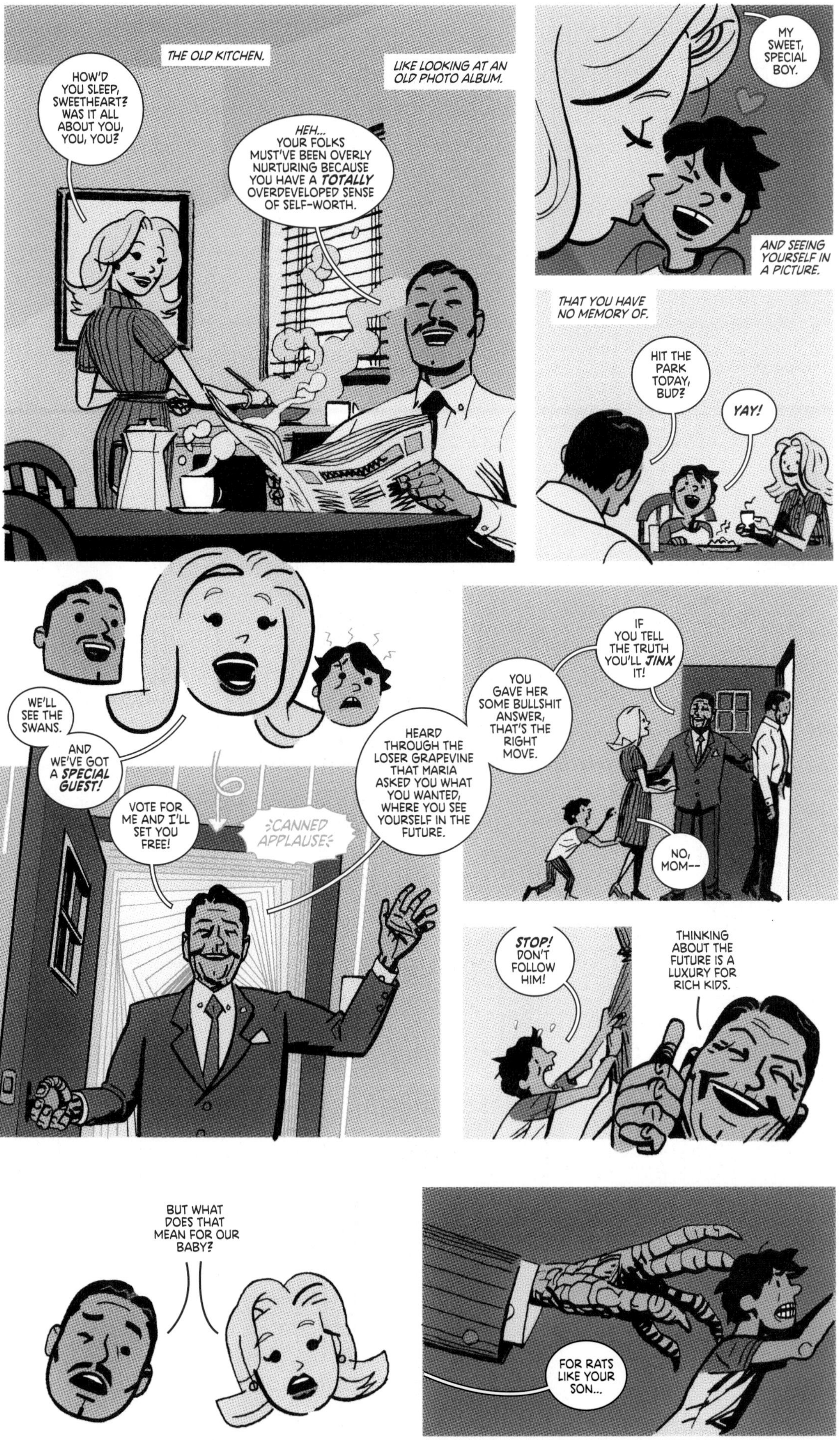
THE OLD KITCHEN.
HOW'D YOU SLEEP, SWEETHEART? WAS IT ALL ABOUT YOU, YOU, YOU?
LIKE LOOKING AT AN OLD PHOTO ALBUM.
HEH... YOUR FOLKS MUST'VE BEEN OVERLY NURTURING BECAUSE YOU HAVE A TOTALLY OVERDEVELOPED SENSE OF SELF-WORTH.
MY SWEET, SPECIAL BOY.
AND SEEING YOURSELF IN A PICTURE.
THAT YOU HAVE NO MEMORY OF.
HIT THE PARK TODAY, BUD?
YAY!
WE'LL SEE THE SWANS.
AND WE'VE GOT A SPECIAL GUEST!
VOTE FOR ME AND I'LL SET YOU FREE!
CANNED APPLAUSE
HEARD THROUGH THE LOSER GRAPEVINE THAT MARIA ASKED YOU WHAT YOU WANTED, WHERE YOU SEE YOURSELF IN THE FUTURE.
YOU GAVE HER SOME BULLSHIT ANSWER, THAT'S THE RIGHT MOVE.
IF YOU TELL THE TRUTH YOU'LL JINX IT!
NO, MOM--
STOP! DON'T FOLLOW HIM!
THINKING ABOUT THE FUTURE IS A LUXURY FOR RICH KIDS.
BUT WHAT DOES THAT MEAN FOR OUR BABY?
FOR RATS LIKE YOUR SON...

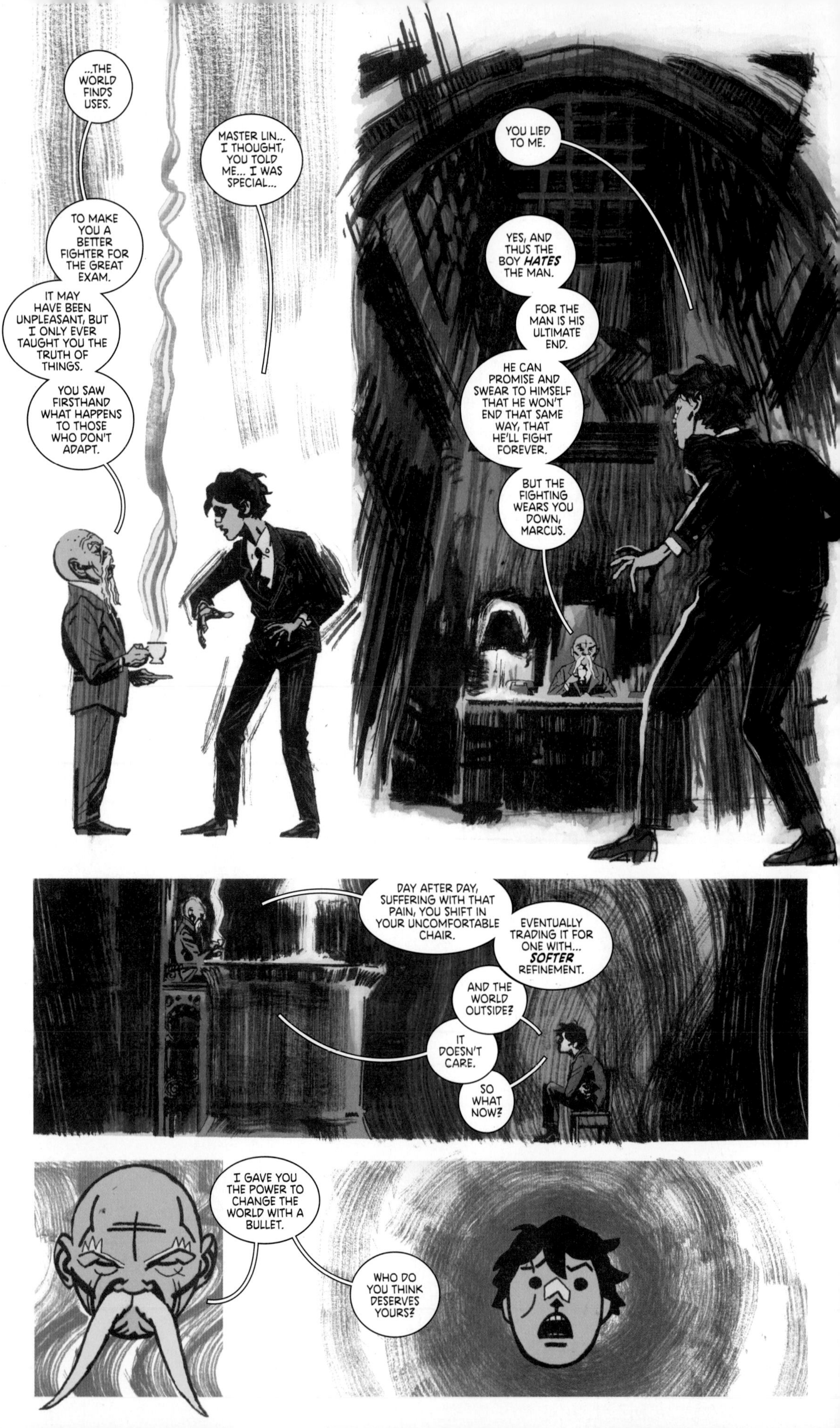
...THE WORLD FINDS USES.
TO MAKE YOU A BETTER FIGHTER FOR THE GREAT EXAM.
IT MAY HAVE BEEN UNPLEASANT, BUT I ONLY EVER TAUGHT YOU THE TRUTH OF THINGS.
YOU SAW FIRSTHAND WHAT HAPPENS TO THOSE WHO DON'T ADAPT.
MASTER LIN... I THOUGHT, YOU TOLD ME... I WAS SPECIAL...
YOU LIED TO ME.
YES, AND THUS THE BOY **HATES** THE MAN.
FOR THE MAN IS HIS ULTIMATE END.
HE CAN PROMISE AND SWEAR TO HIMSELF THAT HE WON'T END THAT SAME WAY, THAT HE'LL FIGHT FOREVER.
BUT THE FIGHTING WEARS YOU DOWN, MARCUS.
DAY AFTER DAY, SUFFERING WITH THAT PAIN, YOU SHIFT IN YOUR UNCOMFORTABLE CHAIR.
EVENTUALLY TRADING IT FOR ONE WITH... **SOFTER** REFINEMENT.
AND THE WORLD OUTSIDE?
IT DOESN'T CARE.
SO WHAT NOW?
I GAVE YOU THE POWER TO CHANGE THE WORLD WITH A BULLET.
WHO DO YOU THINK DESERVES YOURS?

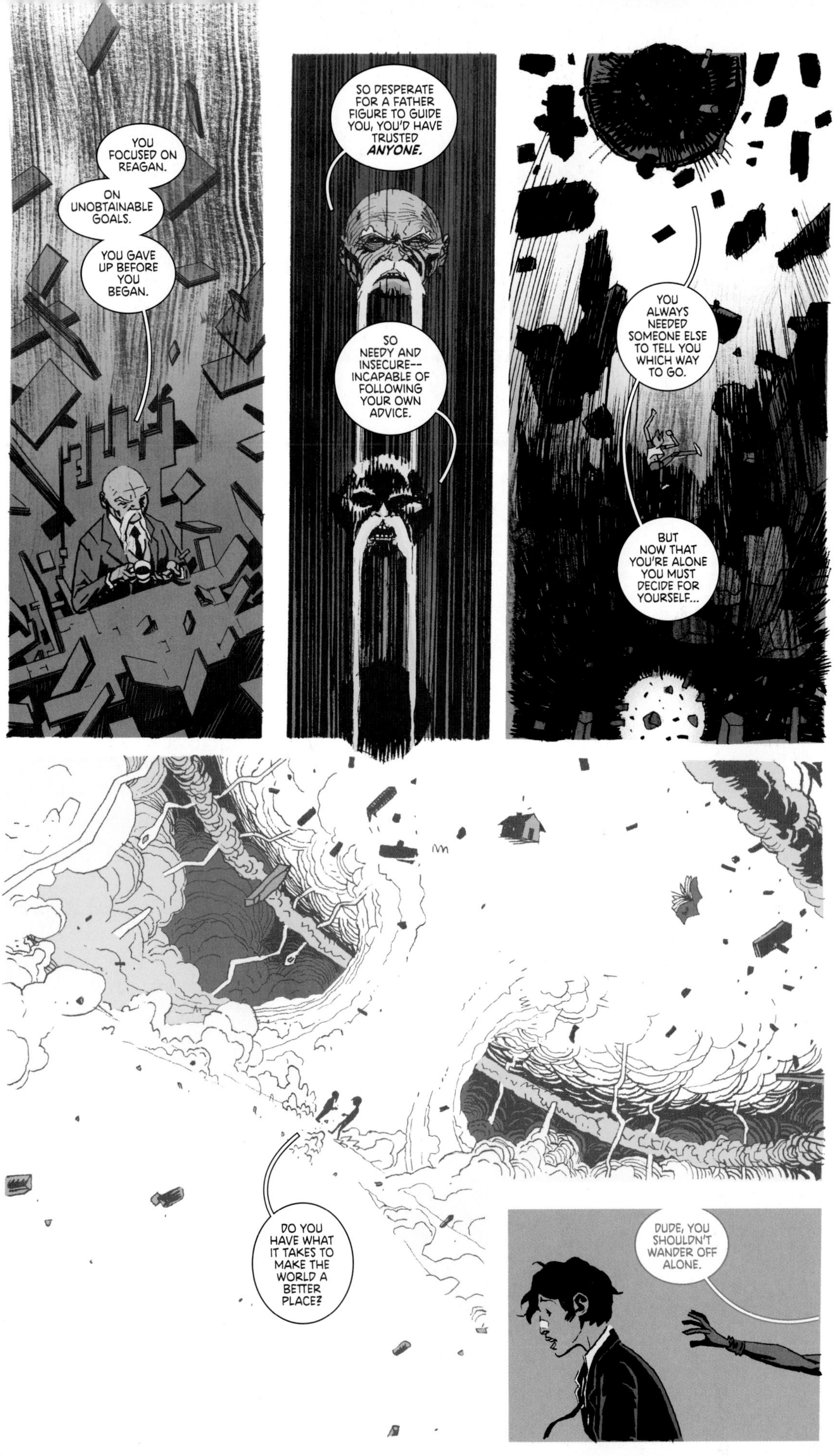
YOU FOCUSED ON REAGAN.
ON UNOBTAINABLE GOALS.
YOU GAVE UP BEFORE YOU BEGAN.
SO DESPERATE FOR A FATHER FIGURE TO GUIDE YOU, YOU'D HAVE TRUSTED *ANYONE.*
SO NEEDY AND INSECURE-- INCAPABLE OF FOLLOWING YOUR OWN ADVICE.
YOU ALWAYS NEEDED SOMEONE ELSE TO TELL YOU WHICH WAY TO GO.
BUT NOW THAT YOU'RE ALONE YOU MUST DECIDE FOR YOURSELF...
DO YOU HAVE WHAT IT TAKES TO MAKE THE WORLD A BETTER PLACE?
DUDE, YOU SHOULDN'T WANDER OFF ALONE.

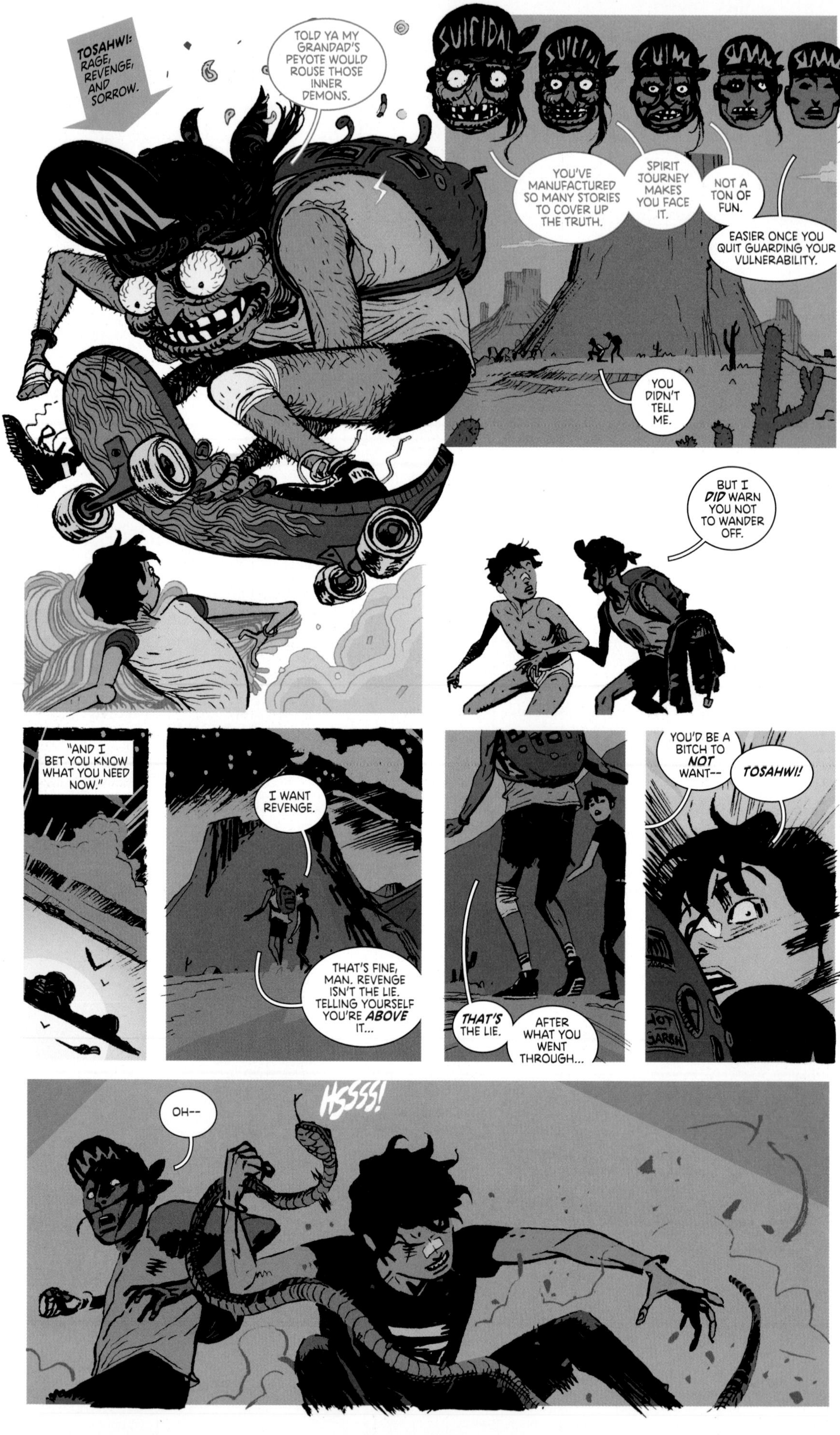

TOSAHWI: RAGE, REVENGE, AND SORROW.
TOLD YA MY GRANDAD'S PEYOTE WOULD ROUSE THOSE INNER DEMONS.
SUICIDAL
YOU'VE MANUFACTURED SO MANY STORIES TO COVER UP THE TRUTH.
SPIRIT JOURNEY MAKES YOU FACE IT.
NOT A TON OF FUN.
EASIER ONCE YOU QUIT GUARDING YOUR VULNERABILITY.
YOU DIDN'T TELL ME.
BUT I *DID* WARN YOU NOT TO WANDER OFF.
"AND I BET YOU KNOW WHAT YOU NEED NOW."
I WANT REVENGE.
THAT'S FINE, MAN. REVENGE ISN'T THE LIE. TELLING YOURSELF YOU'RE *ABOVE* IT...
THAT'S THE LIE.
AFTER WHAT YOU WENT THROUGH...
YOU'D BE A BITCH TO *NOT* WANT--
TOSAHWI!
OH--
HSSSS!

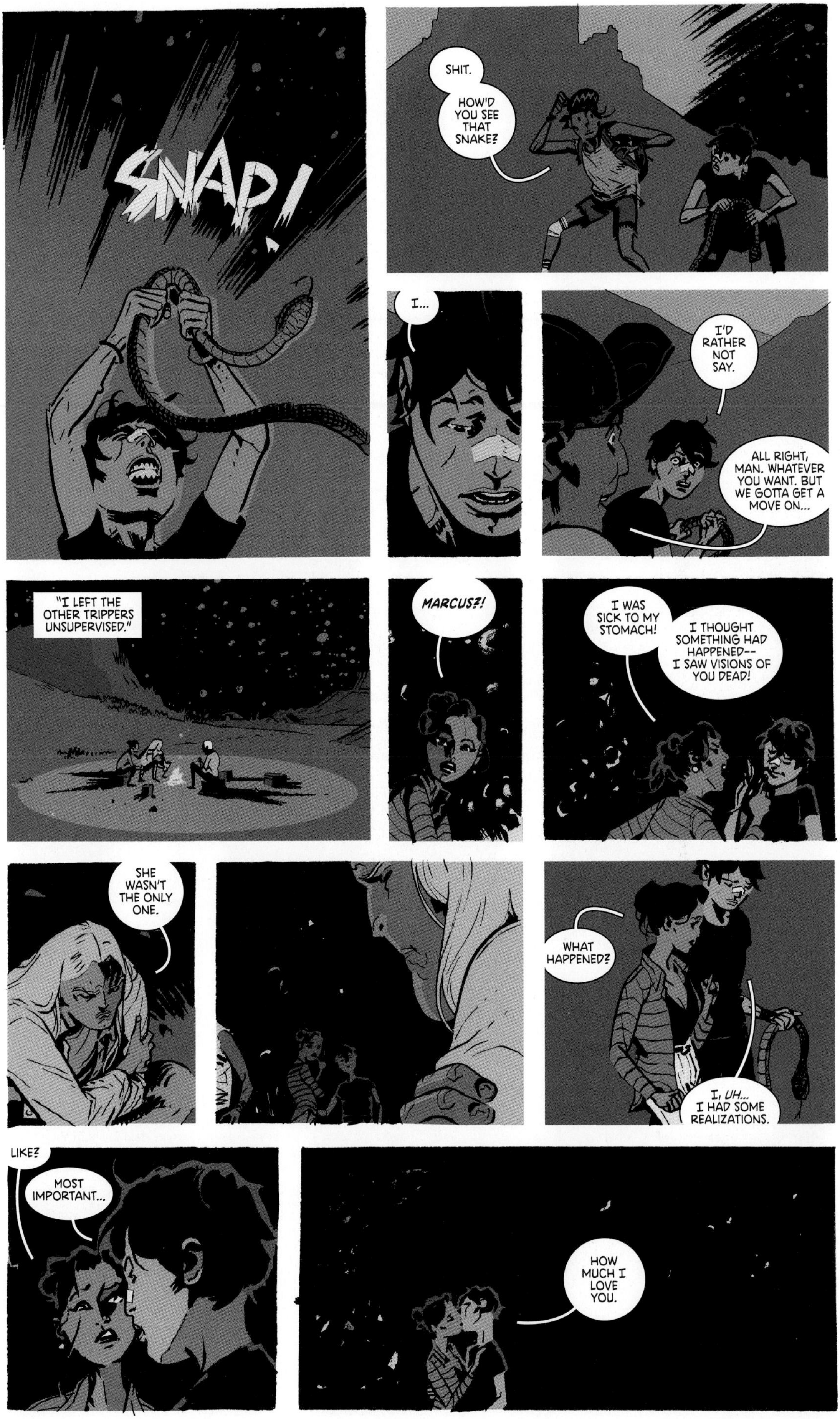
SNAP!
SHIT.
HOW'D YOU SEE THAT SNAKE?
I...
I'D RATHER NOT SAY.
ALL RIGHT, MAN. WHATEVER YOU WANT. BUT WE GOTTA GET A MOVE ON...
"I LEFT THE OTHER TRIPPERS UNSUPERVISED."
MARCUS?!
I WAS SICK TO MY STOMACH!
I THOUGHT SOMETHING HAD HAPPENED-- I SAW VISIONS OF YOU DEAD!
SHE WASN'T THE ONLY ONE.
WHAT HAPPENED?
I, UH... I HAD SOME REALIZATIONS.
LIKE?
MOST IMPORTANT...
HOW MUCH I LOVE YOU.

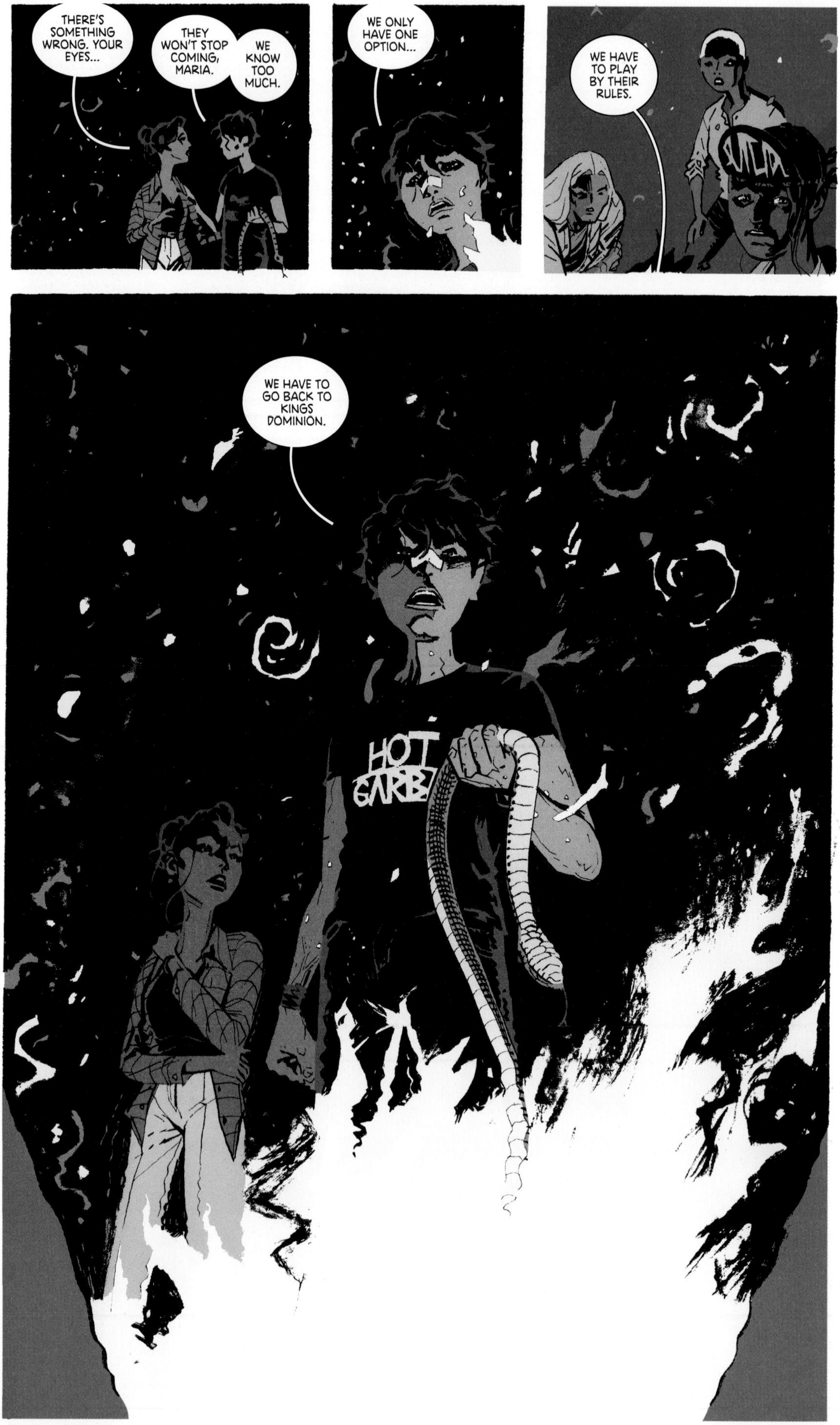
THERE'S SOMETHING WRONG. YOUR EYES...
THEY WON'T STOP COMING, MARIA.
WE KNOW TOO MUCH.
WE ONLY HAVE ONE OPTION...
WE HAVE TO PLAY BY THEIR RULES.
WE HAVE TO GO BACK TO KINGS DOMINION.
HOT GARB

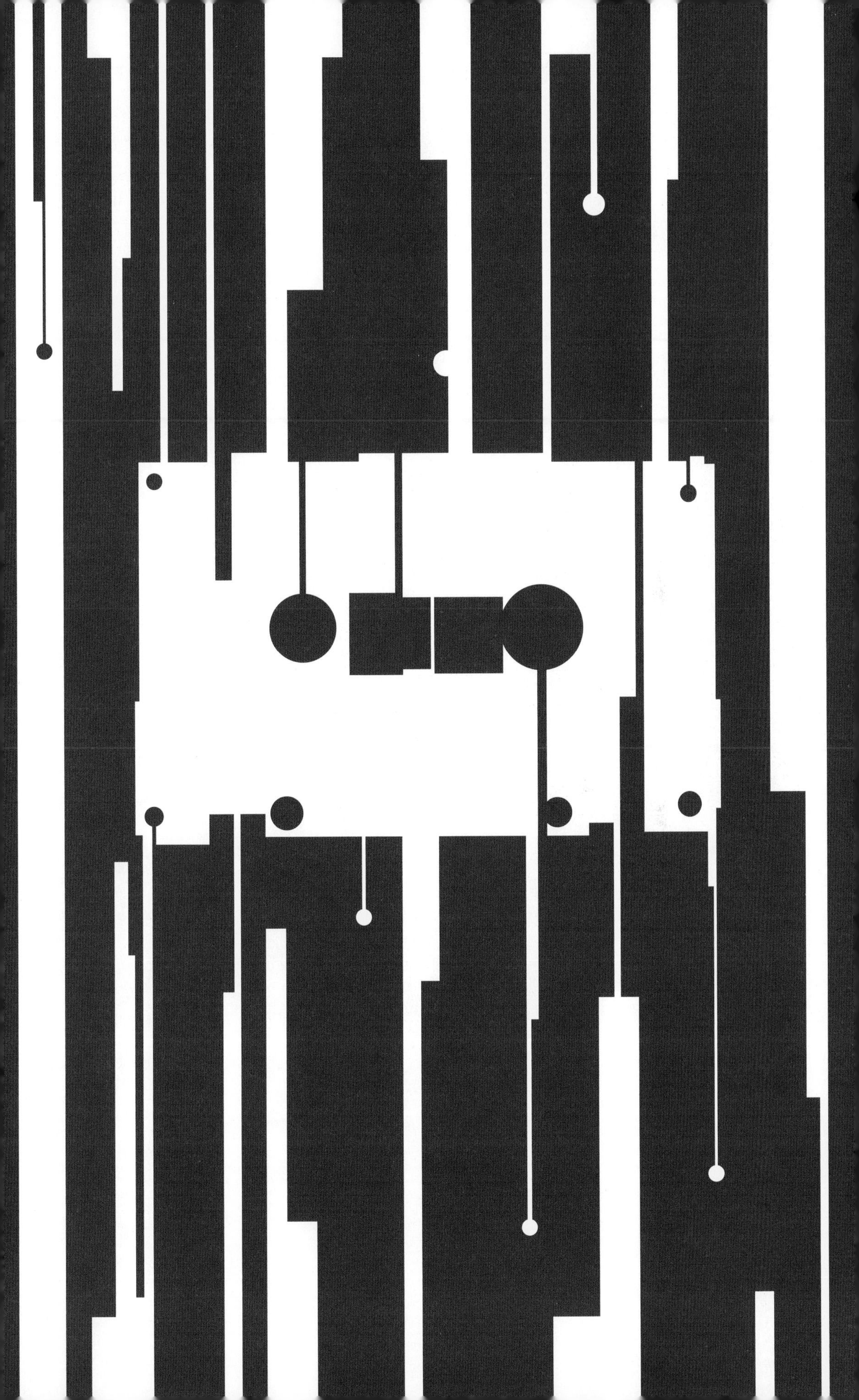

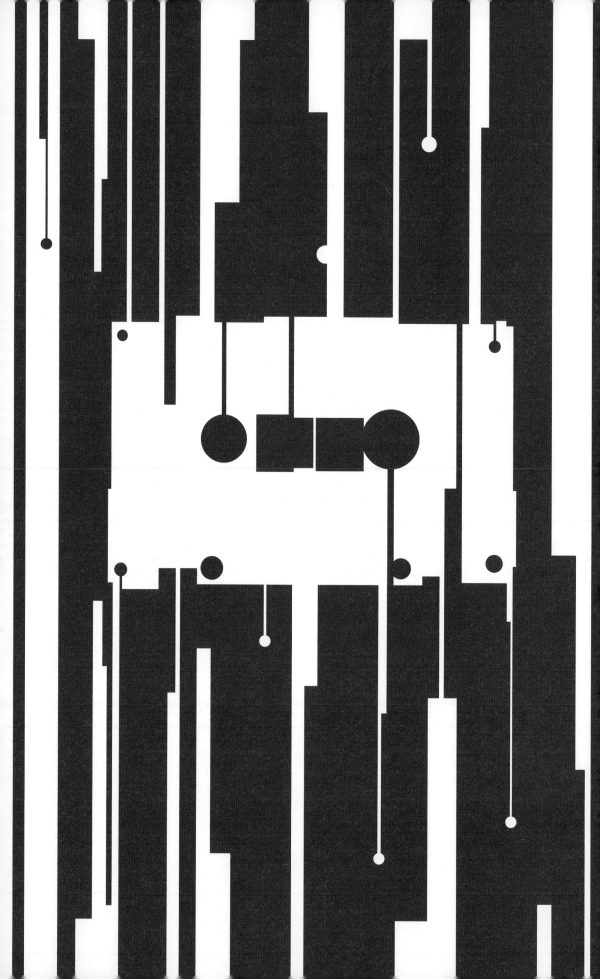

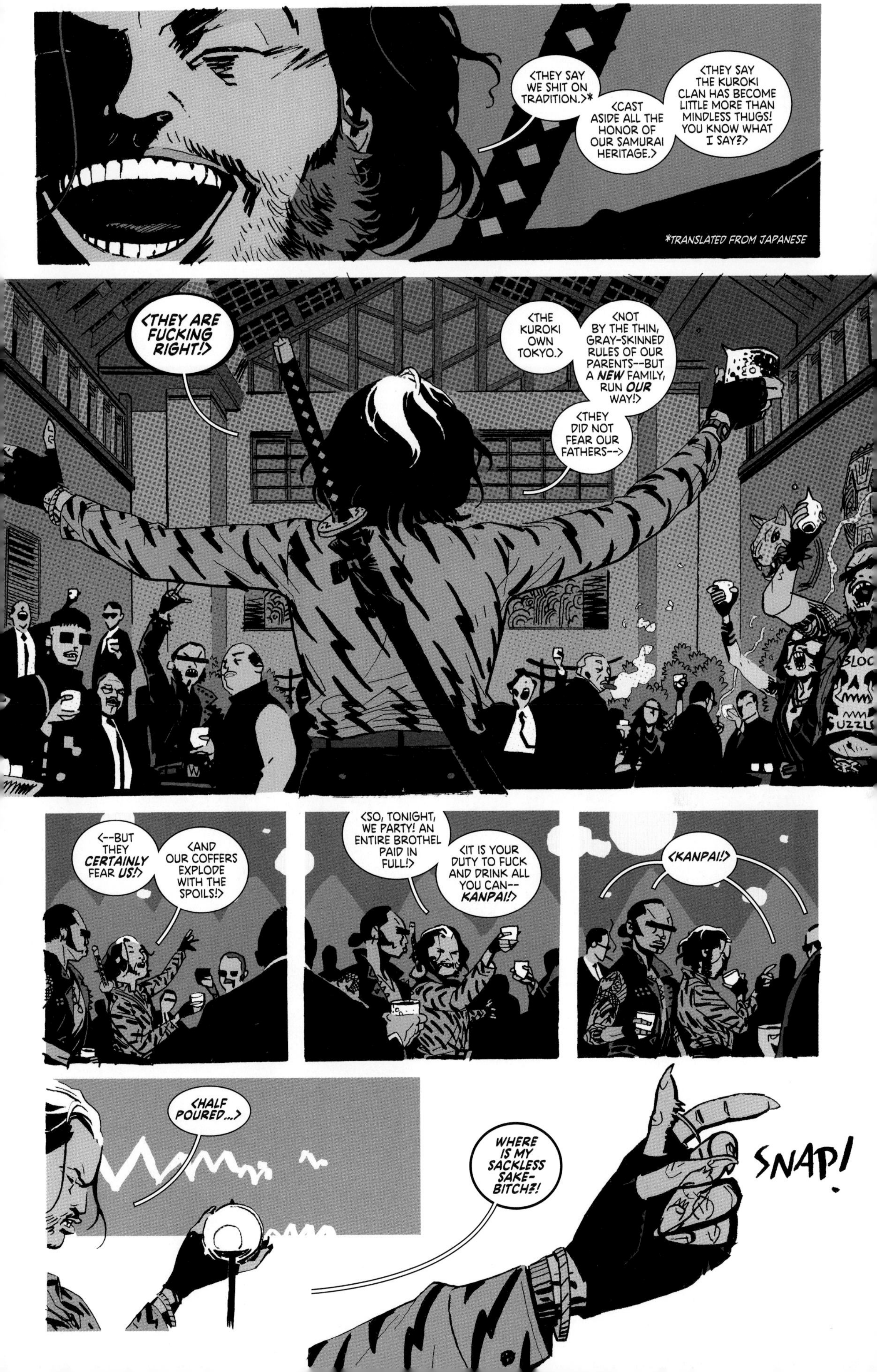

<THEY SAY WE SHIT ON TRADITION.>*
<CAST ASIDE ALL THE HONOR OF OUR SAMURAI HERITAGE.>
<THEY SAY THE KUROKI CLAN HAS BECOME LITTLE MORE THAN MINDLESS THUGS! YOU KNOW WHAT I SAY?>
*TRANSLATED FROM JAPANESE
<THEY ARE FUCKING RIGHT!>
<THE KUROKI OWN TOKYO.>
<NOT BY THE THIN, GRAY-SKINNED RULES OF OUR PARENTS--BUT A NEW FAMILY, RUN OUR WAY!>
<THEY DID NOT FEAR OUR FATHERS-->
<--BUT THEY CERTAINLY FEAR US!>
<AND OUR COFFERS EXPLODE WITH THE SPOILS!>
<SO, TONIGHT, WE PARTY! AN ENTIRE BROTHEL PAID IN FULL!>
<IT IS YOUR DUTY TO FUCK AND DRINK ALL YOU CAN--KANPAI!>
<KANPAI!>
<HALF POURED...>
WHERE IS MY SACKLESS SAKE-BITCH?!
SNAP!

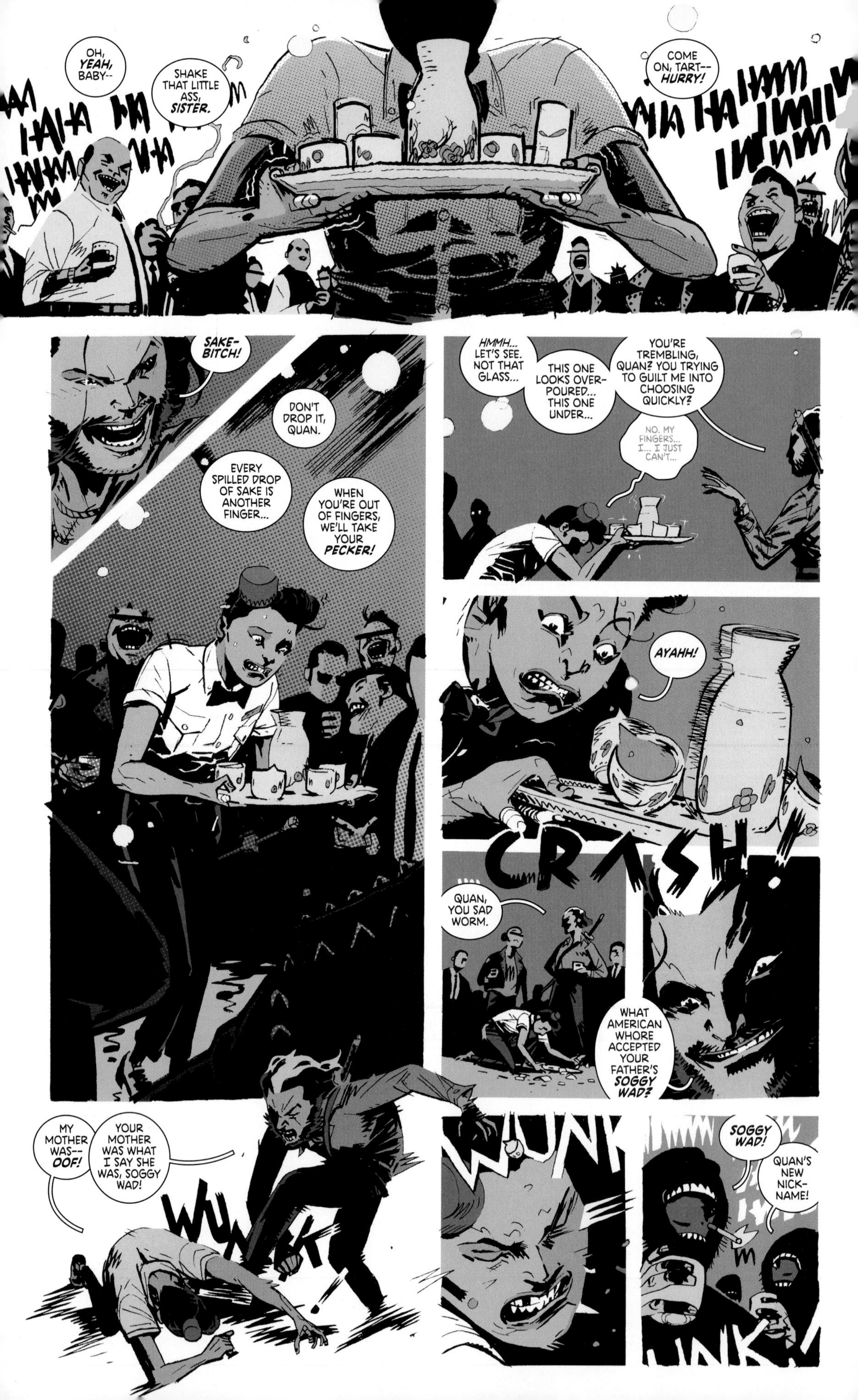
OH, YEAH, BABY--
SHAKE THAT LITTLE ASS, SISTER.
COME ON, TART-- HURRY!
SAKE-BITCH!
DON'T DROP IT, QUAN.
EVERY SPILLED DROP OF SAKE IS ANOTHER FINGER...
WHEN YOU'RE OUT OF FINGERS, WE'LL TAKE YOUR PECKER!
HMMH... LET'S SEE. NOT THAT GLASS...
THIS ONE LOOKS OVER-POURED... THIS ONE UNDER...
YOU'RE TREMBLING, QUAN? YOU TRYING TO GUILT ME INTO CHOOSING QUICKLY?
NO. MY FINGERS... I... I JUST CAN'T...
AYAHH!
CRASH!
QUAN, YOU SAD WORM.
WHAT AMERICAN WHORE ACCEPTED YOUR FATHER'S SOGGY WAD?
MY MOTHER WAS-- OOF!
YOUR MOTHER WAS WHAT I SAY SHE WAS, SOGGY WAD!
WUNK
WUNK
SOGGY WAD!
QUAN'S NEW NICK-NAME!

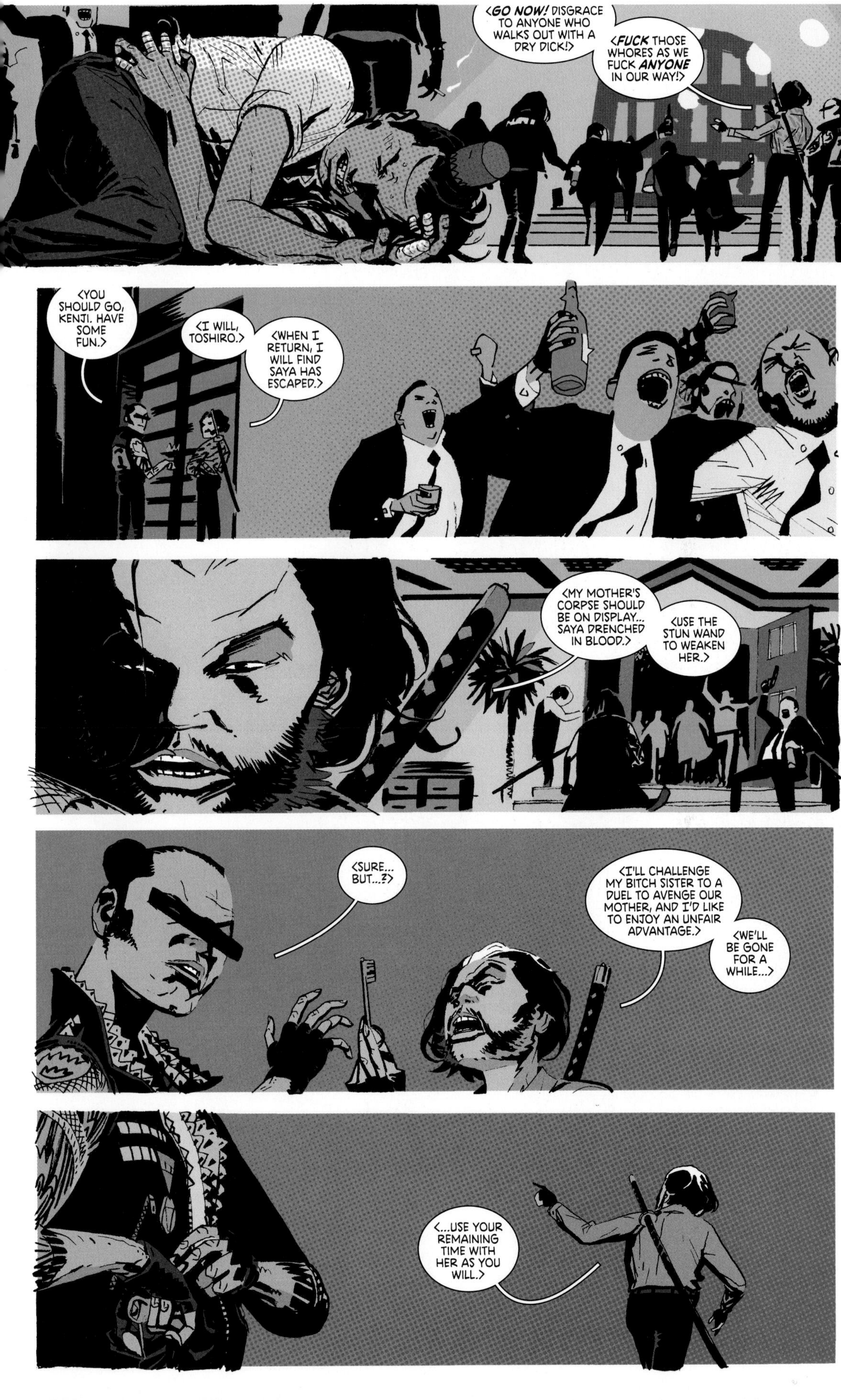
<GO NOW! DISGRACE TO ANYONE WHO WALKS OUT WITH A DRY DICK!>
<FUCK THOSE WHORES AS WE FUCK ANYONE IN OUR WAY!>
<YOU SHOULD GO, KENJI. HAVE SOME FUN.>
<I WILL, TOSHIRO.>
<WHEN I RETURN, I WILL FIND SAYA HAS ESCAPED.>
<MY MOTHER'S CORPSE SHOULD BE ON DISPLAY... SAYA DRENCHED IN BLOOD.>
<USE THE STUN WAND TO WEAKEN HER.>
<SURE... BUT...?>
<I'LL CHALLENGE MY BITCH SISTER TO A DUEL TO AVENGE OUR MOTHER, AND I'D LIKE TO ENJOY AN UNFAIR ADVANTAGE.>
<WE'LL BE GONE FOR A WHILE...>
<...USE YOUR REMAINING TIME WITH HER AS YOU WILL.>

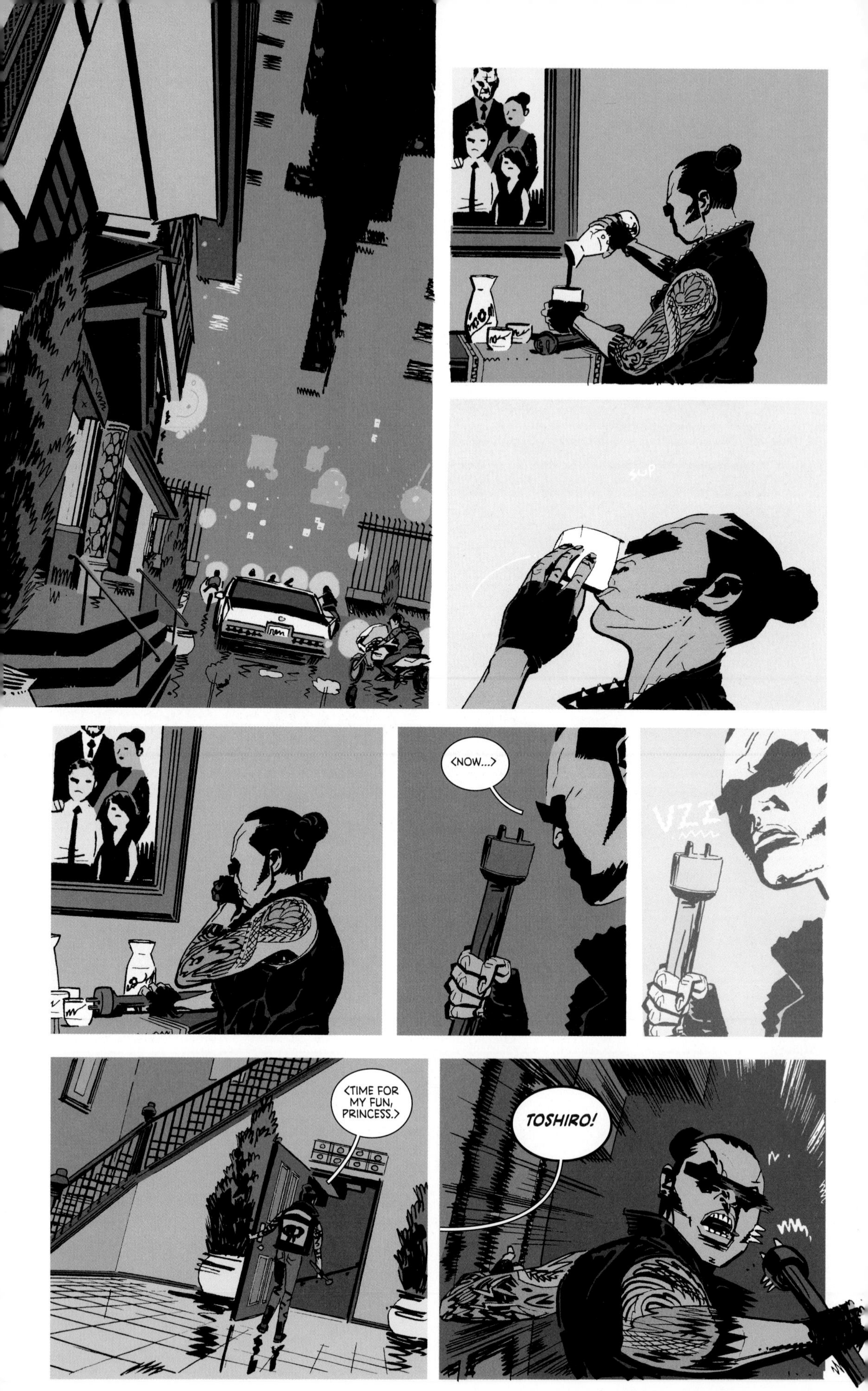
SLIP
<NOW...>
VZZ
<TIME FOR MY FUN, PRINCESS.>
TOSHIRO!

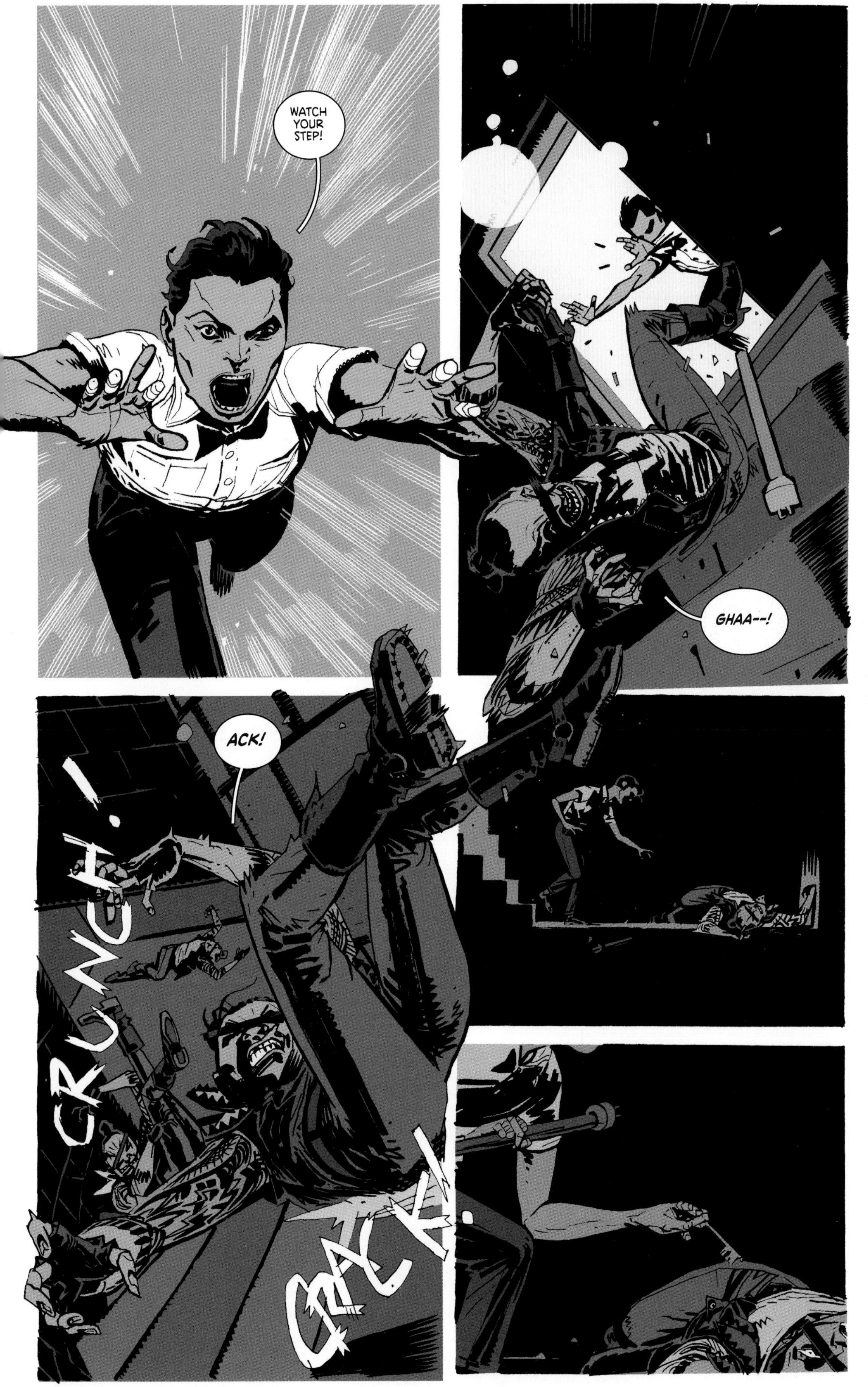
WATCH YOUR STEP!
GHAA--!
ACK!
CRUNCH!
CRACK!

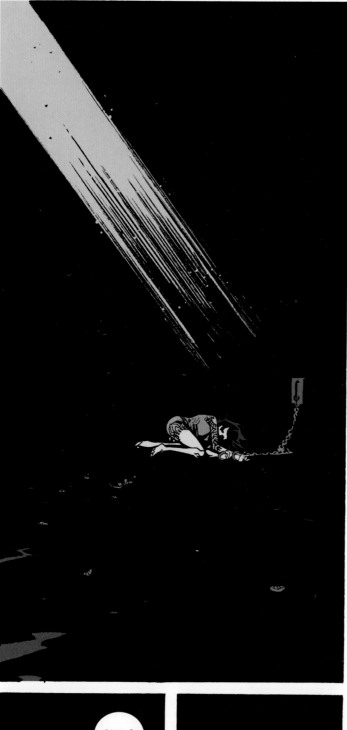

click

SAYA...?

I-I BROUGHT THE KEY...

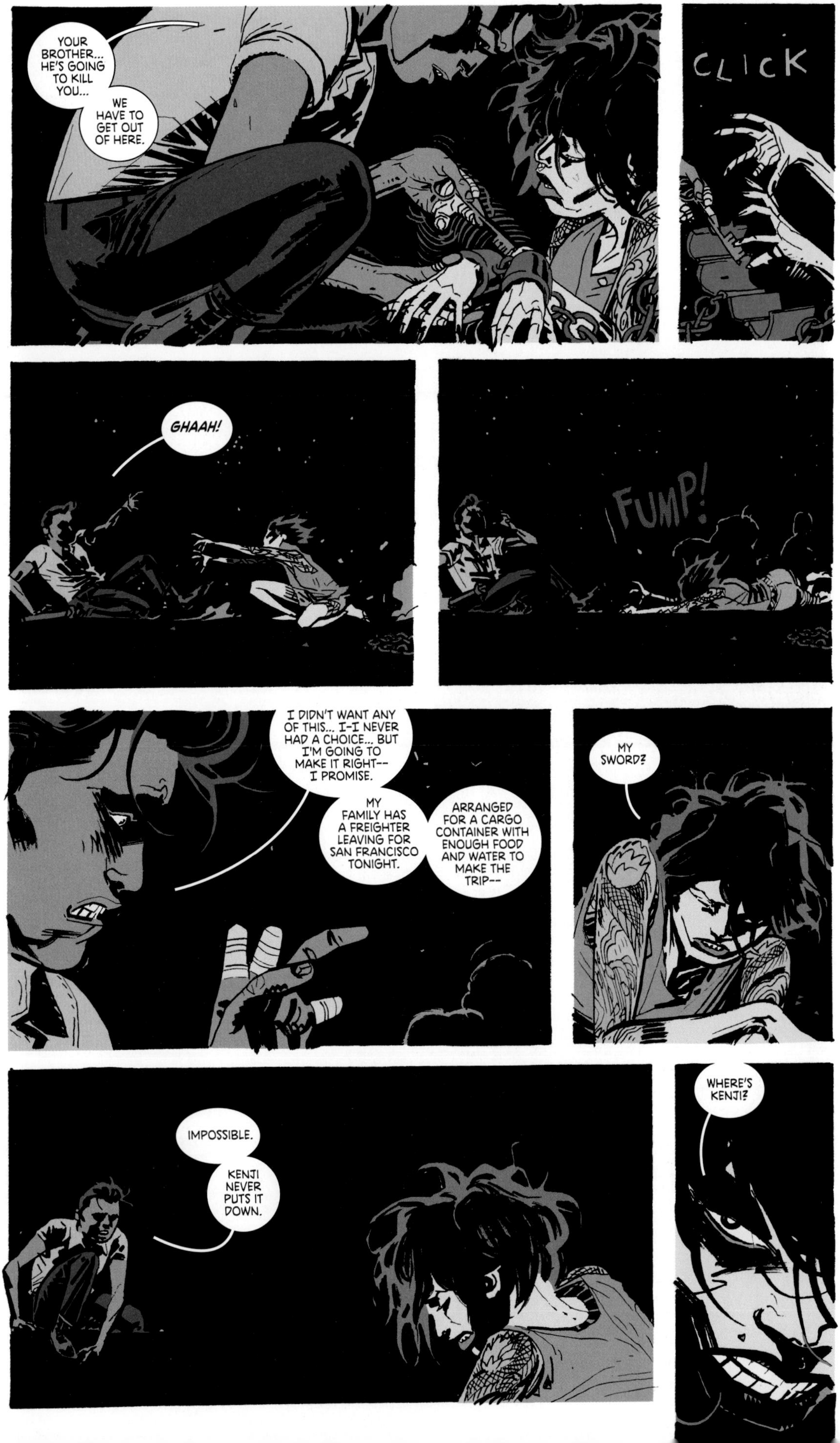

YOUR BROTHER... HE'S GOING TO KILL YOU...
WE HAVE TO GET OUT OF HERE.
CLICK
GHAAH!
FUMP!
I DIDN'T WANT ANY OF THIS... I-I NEVER HAD A CHOICE... BUT I'M GOING TO MAKE IT RIGHT-- I PROMISE.
MY FAMILY HAS A FREIGHTER LEAVING FOR SAN FRANCISCO TONIGHT.
ARRANGED FOR A CARGO CONTAINER WITH ENOUGH FOOD AND WATER TO MAKE THE TRIP--
MY SWORD?
IMPOSSIBLE.
KENJI NEVER PUTS IT DOWN.
WHERE'S KENJI?

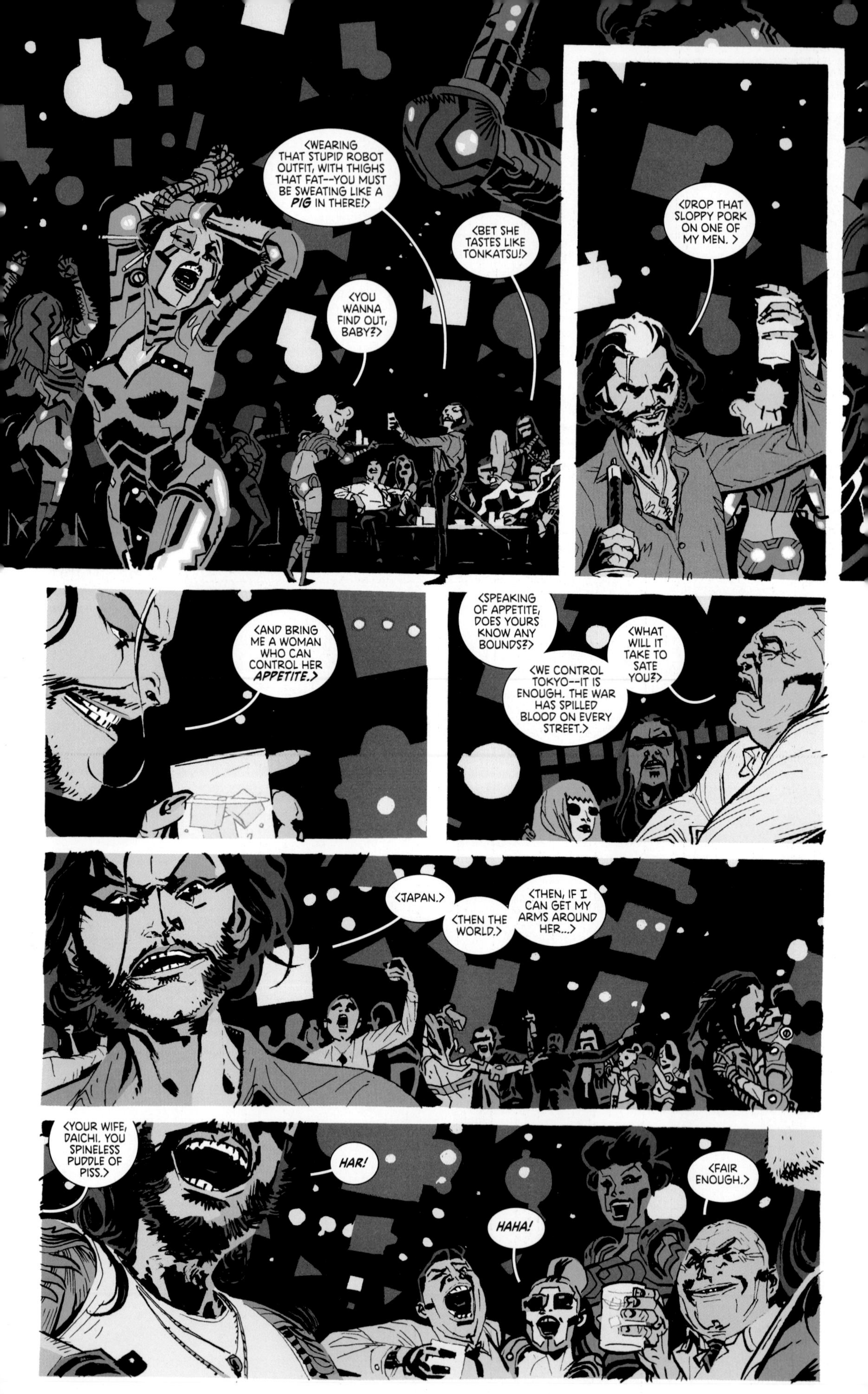
<WEARING THAT STUPID ROBOT OUTFIT, WITH THIGHS THAT FAT--YOU MUST BE SWEATING LIKE A *PIG* IN THERE!>
<YOU WANNA FIND OUT, BABY?>
<BET SHE TASTES LIKE TONKATSU!>
<DROP THAT SLOPPY PORK ON ONE OF MY MEN. >
<AND BRING ME A WOMAN WHO CAN CONTROL HER *APPETITE.*>
<SPEAKING OF APPETITE, DOES YOURS KNOW ANY BOUNDS?>
<WE CONTROL TOKYO--IT IS ENOUGH. THE WAR HAS SPILLED BLOOD ON EVERY STREET.>
<WHAT WILL IT TAKE TO SATE YOU?>
<JAPAN.>
<THEN THE WORLD.>
<THEN, IF I CAN GET MY ARMS AROUND HER...>
<YOUR WIFE, DAICHI. YOU SPINELESS PUDDLE OF PISS.>
HAR!
HAHA!
<FAIR ENOUGH.>

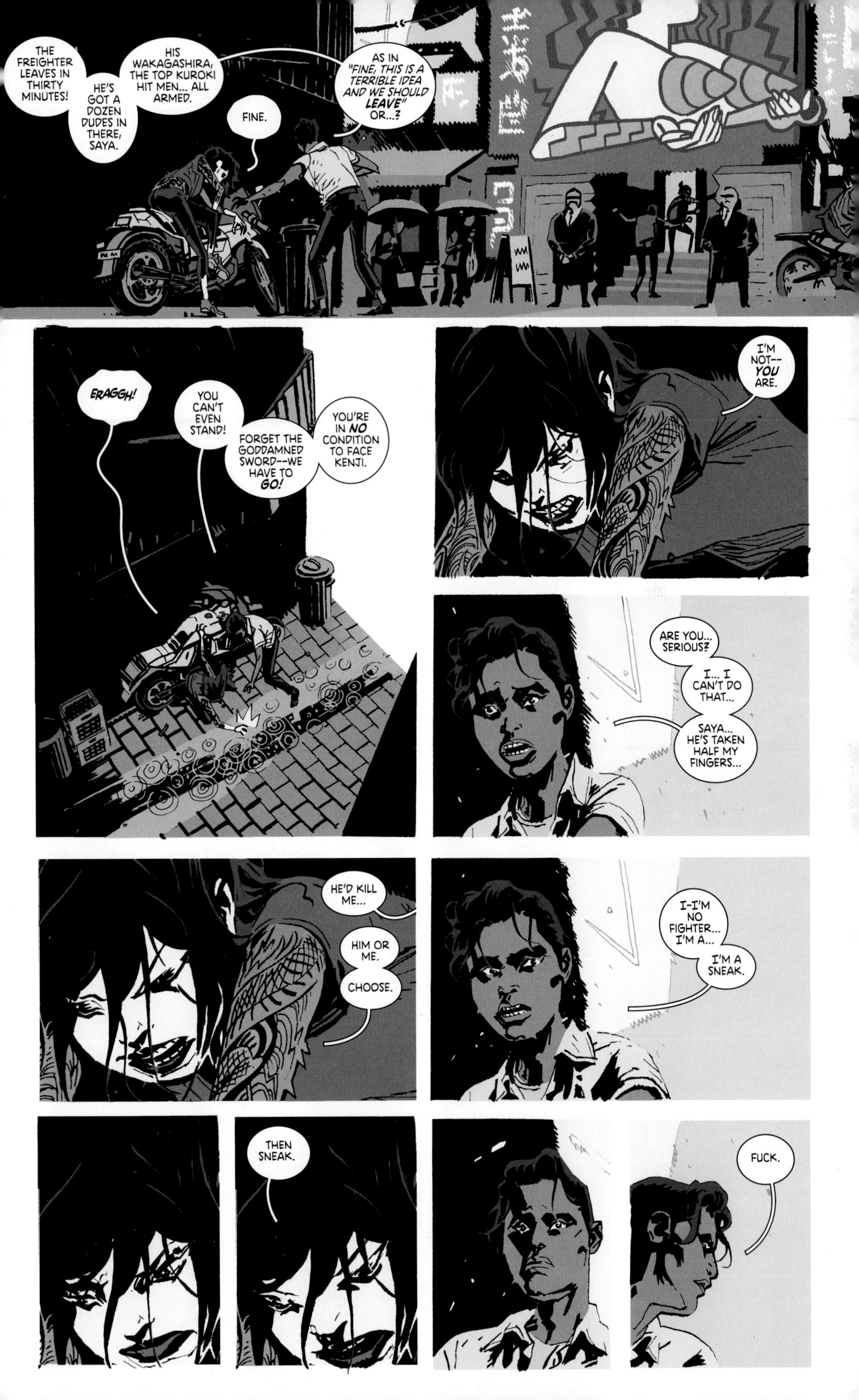

THE FREIGHTER LEAVES IN THIRTY MINUTES!
HE'S GOT A DOZEN DUDES IN THERE, SAYA.
HIS WAKAGASHIRA, THE TOP KUROKI HIT MEN... ALL ARMED.
FINE.
AS IN "FINE, THIS IS A TERRIBLE IDEA AND WE SHOULD LEAVE" OR...?
ERAGGH!
YOU CAN'T EVEN STAND!
FORGET THE GODDAMNED SWORD--WE HAVE TO GO!
YOU'RE IN NO CONDITION TO FACE KENJI.
I'M NOT-- YOU ARE.
ARE YOU... SERIOUS?
I... I CAN'T DO THAT...
SAYA... HE'S TAKEN HALF MY FINGERS...
HE'D KILL ME...
HIM OR ME.
CHOOSE.
I-I'M NO FIGHTER... I'M A...
I'M A SNEAK.
THEN SNEAK.
FUCK.

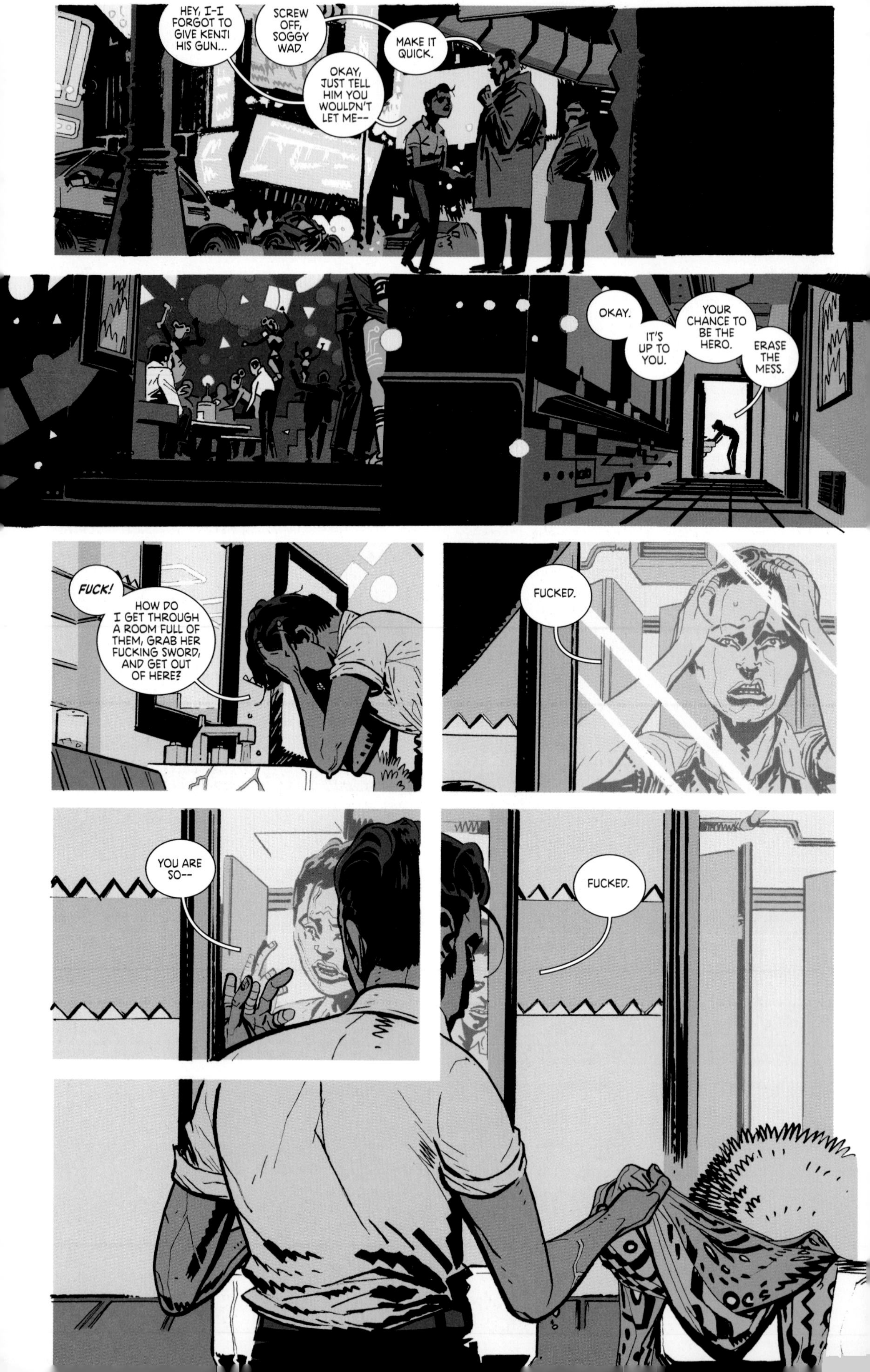
HEY, I-I FORGOT TO GIVE KENJI HIS GUN...
SCREW OFF, SOGGY WAD.
OKAY, JUST TELL HIM YOU WOULDN'T LET ME--
MAKE IT QUICK.
OKAY.
IT'S UP TO YOU.
YOUR CHANCE TO BE THE HERO.
ERASE THE MESS.
FUCK!
HOW DO I GET THROUGH A ROOM FULL OF THEM, GRAB HER FUCKING SWORD, AND GET OUT OF HERE?
FUCKED.
YOU ARE SO--
FUCKED.

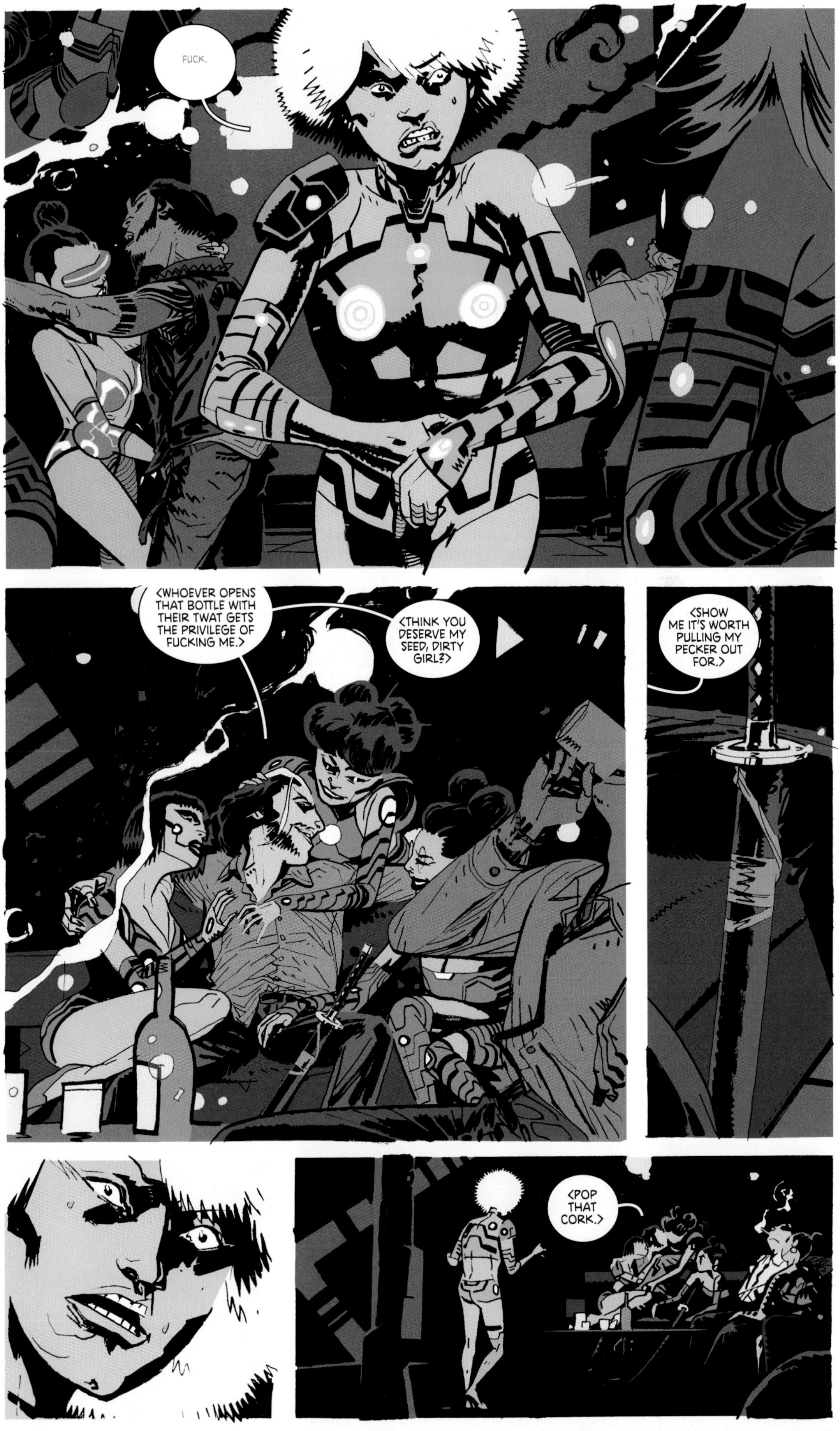
FUCK.
<WHOEVER OPENS THAT BOTTLE WITH THEIR TWAT GETS THE PRIVILEGE OF FUCKING ME.>
<THINK YOU DESERVE MY SEED, DIRTY GIRL?>
<SHOW ME IT'S WORTH PULLING MY PECKER OUT FOR.>
<POP THAT CORK.>

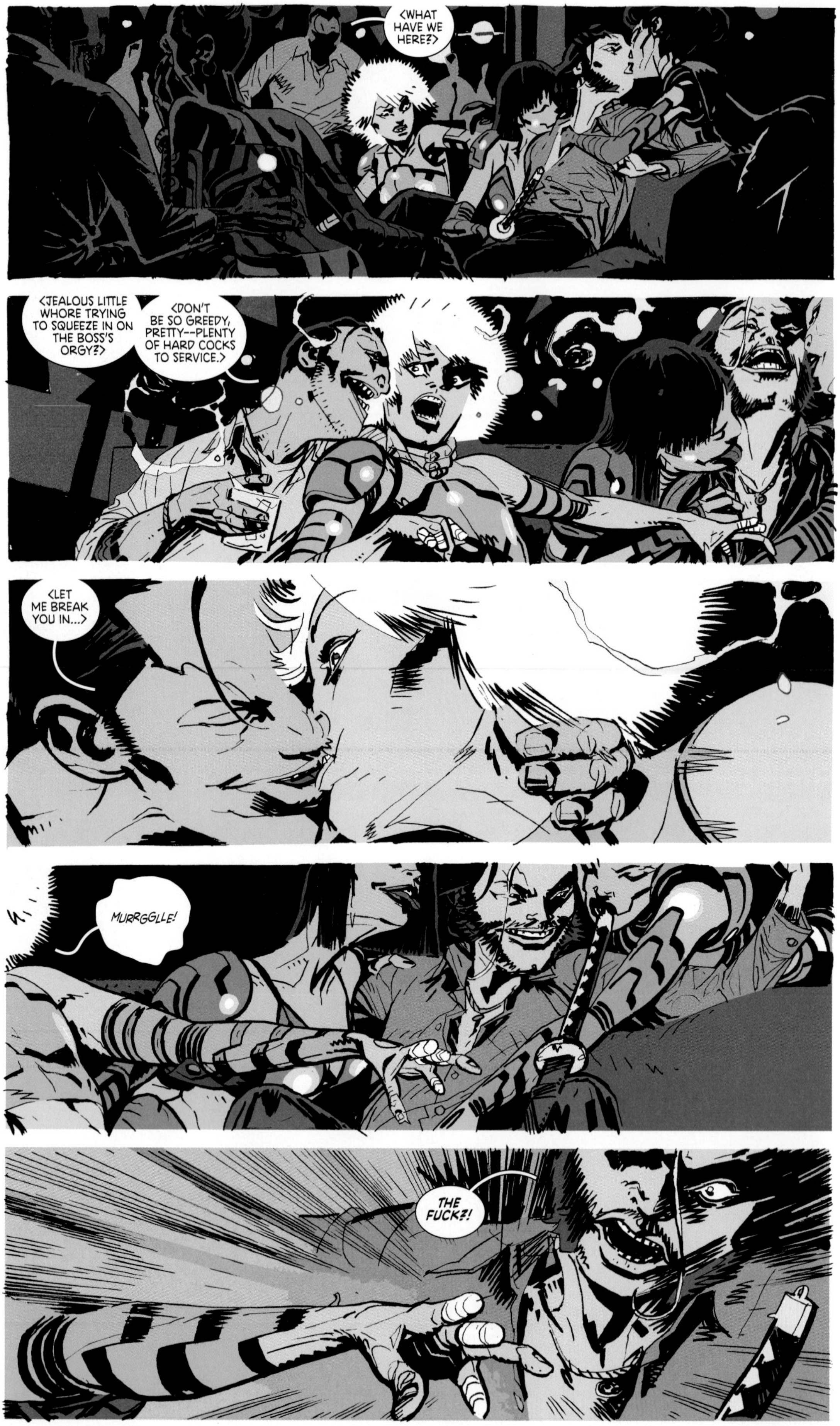
<WHAT HAVE WE HERE?>
<JEALOUS LITTLE WHORE TRYING TO SQUEEZE IN ON THE BOSS'S ORGY?>
<DON'T BE SO GREEDY, PRETTY--PLENTY OF HARD COCKS TO SERVICE.>
<LET ME BREAK YOU IN...>
MURRGGLLE!
THE FUCK?!

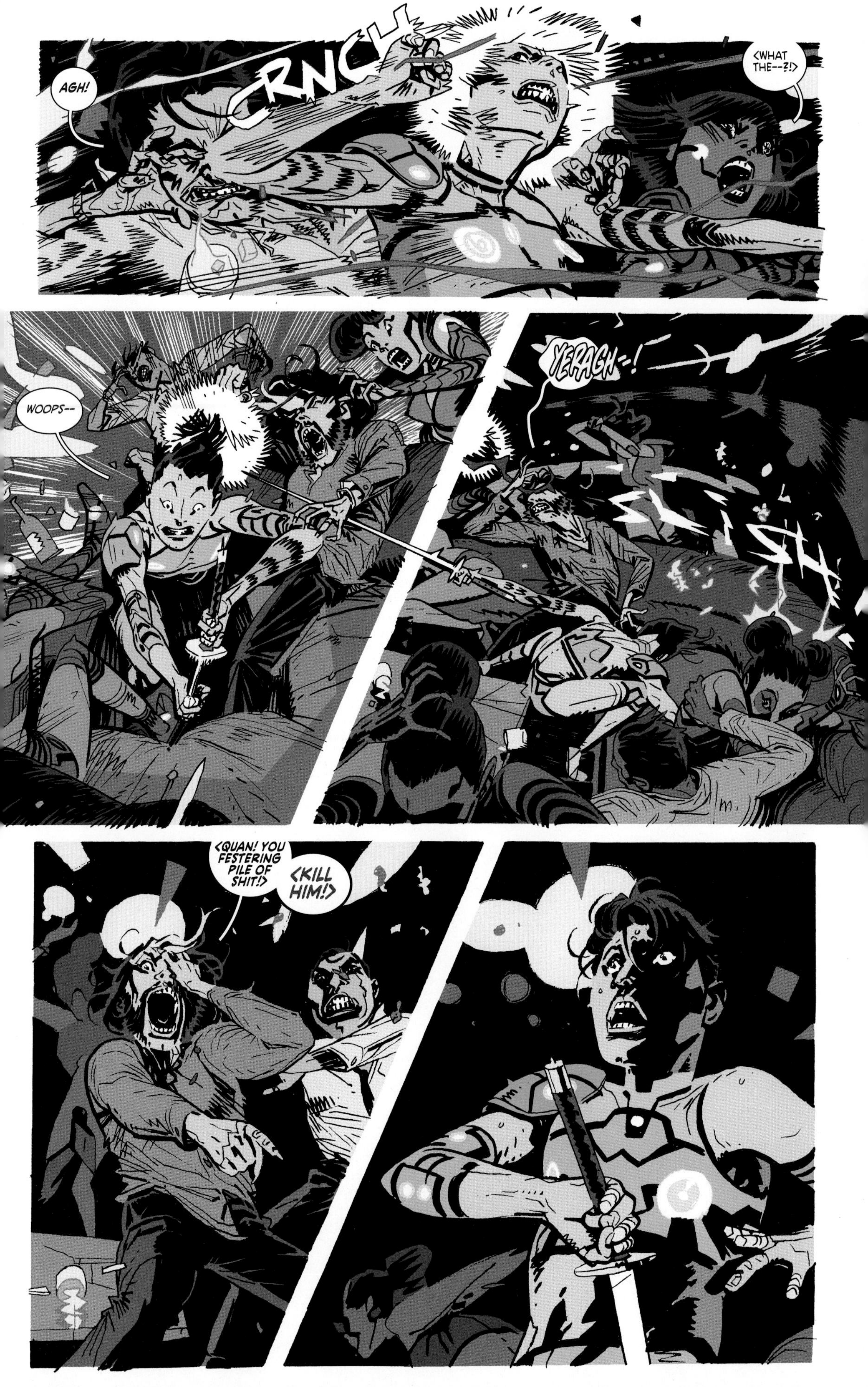
AGH!
CRNCH
<WHAT THE--?!>
WOOPS--
YERAGH--!
<QUAN! YOU FESTERING PILE OF SHIT!>
<KILL HIM!>

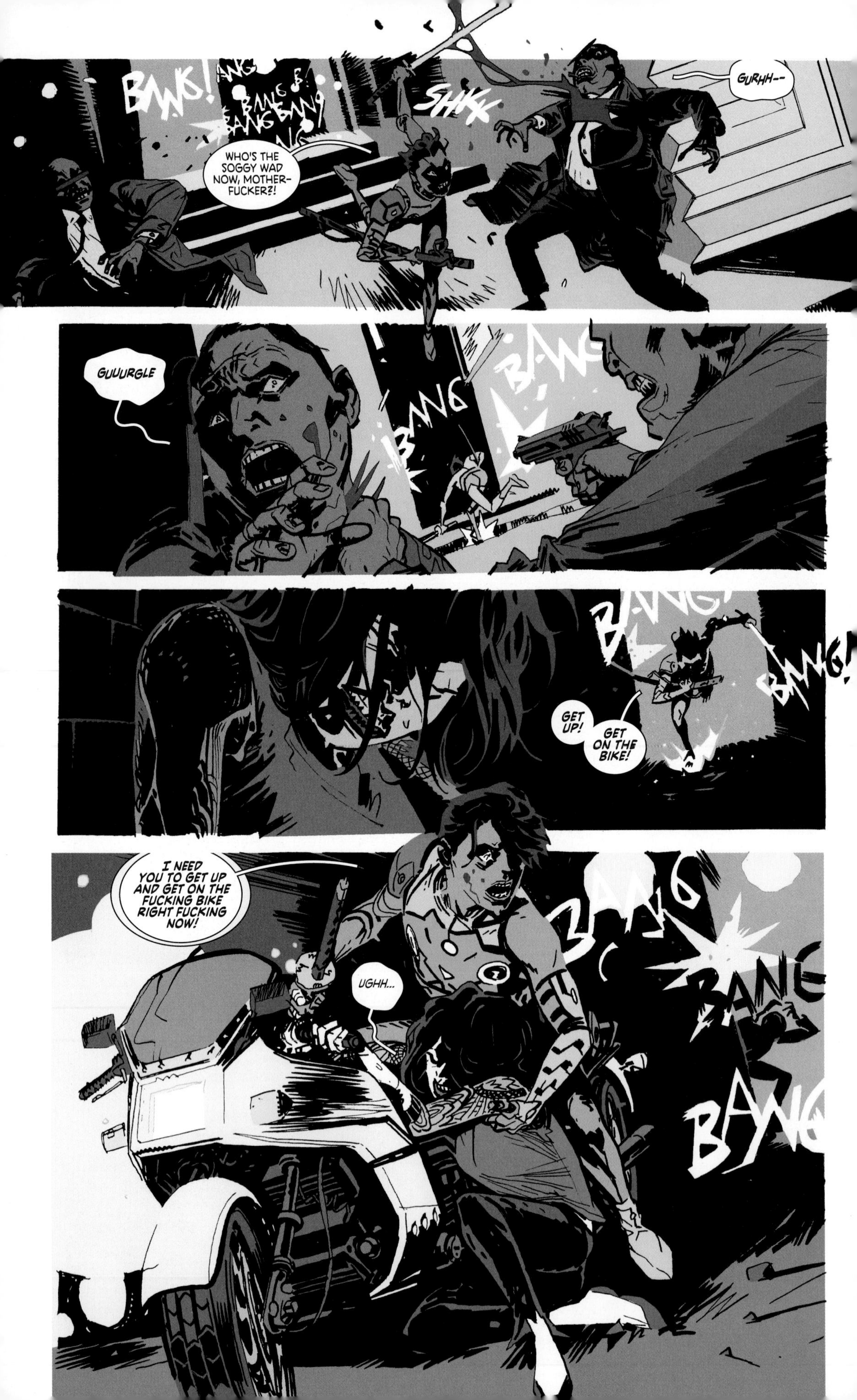
BANG!
BANG BANG
SHKK
GURHH--
WHO'S THE SOGGY WAD NOW, MOTHER-FUCKER?!
GUUURGLE
BANG
BANG
BANG!
BANG!
GET UP!
GET ON THE BIKE!
I NEED YOU TO GET UP AND GET ON THE FUCKING BIKE RIGHT FUCKING NOW!
UGHH...
BANG
BANG
BANG

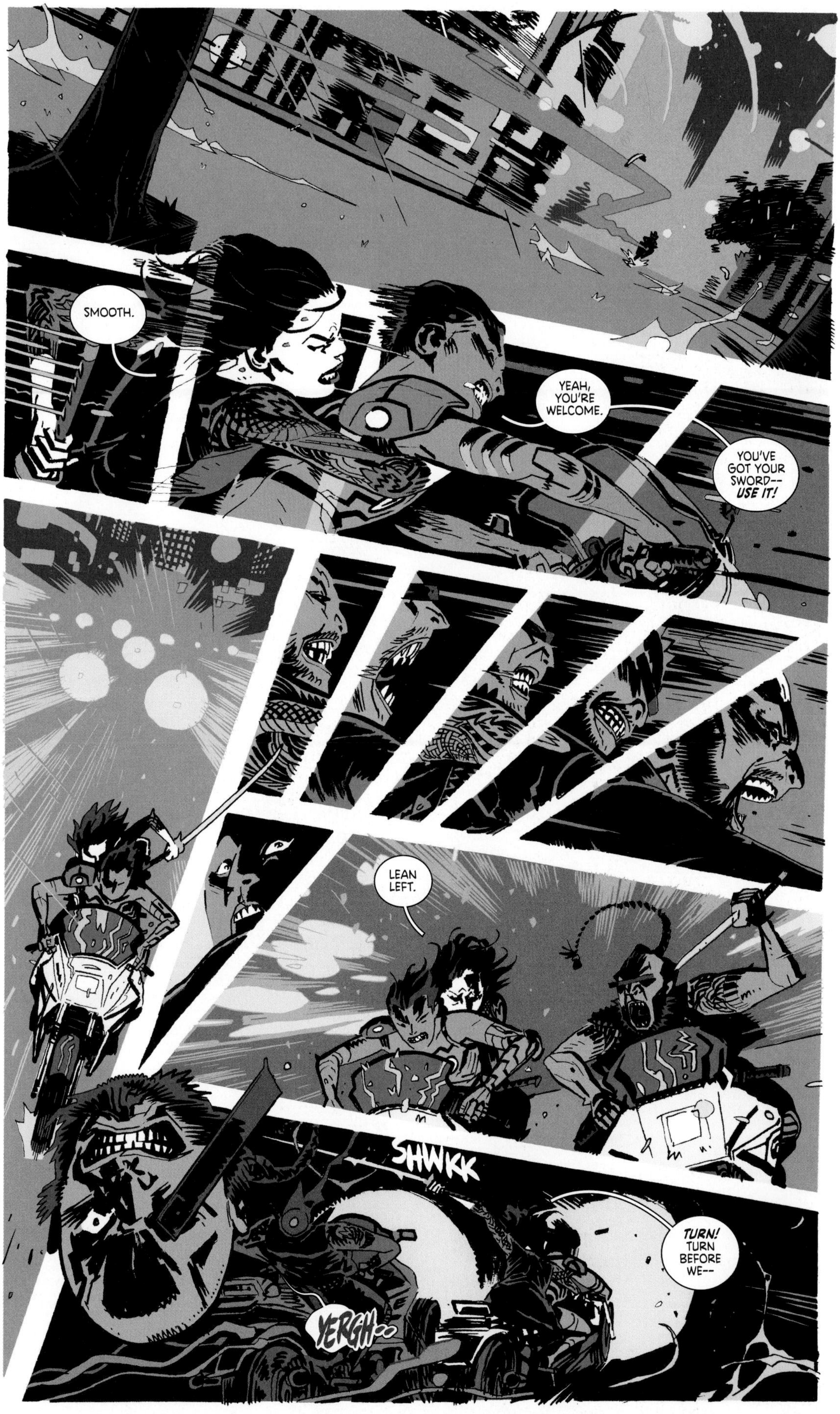
SMOOTH.
YEAH, YOU'RE WELCOME.
YOU'VE GOT YOUR SWORD-- USE IT!
LEAN LEFT.
SHWKK
TURN! TURN BEFORE WE--
YERGH--

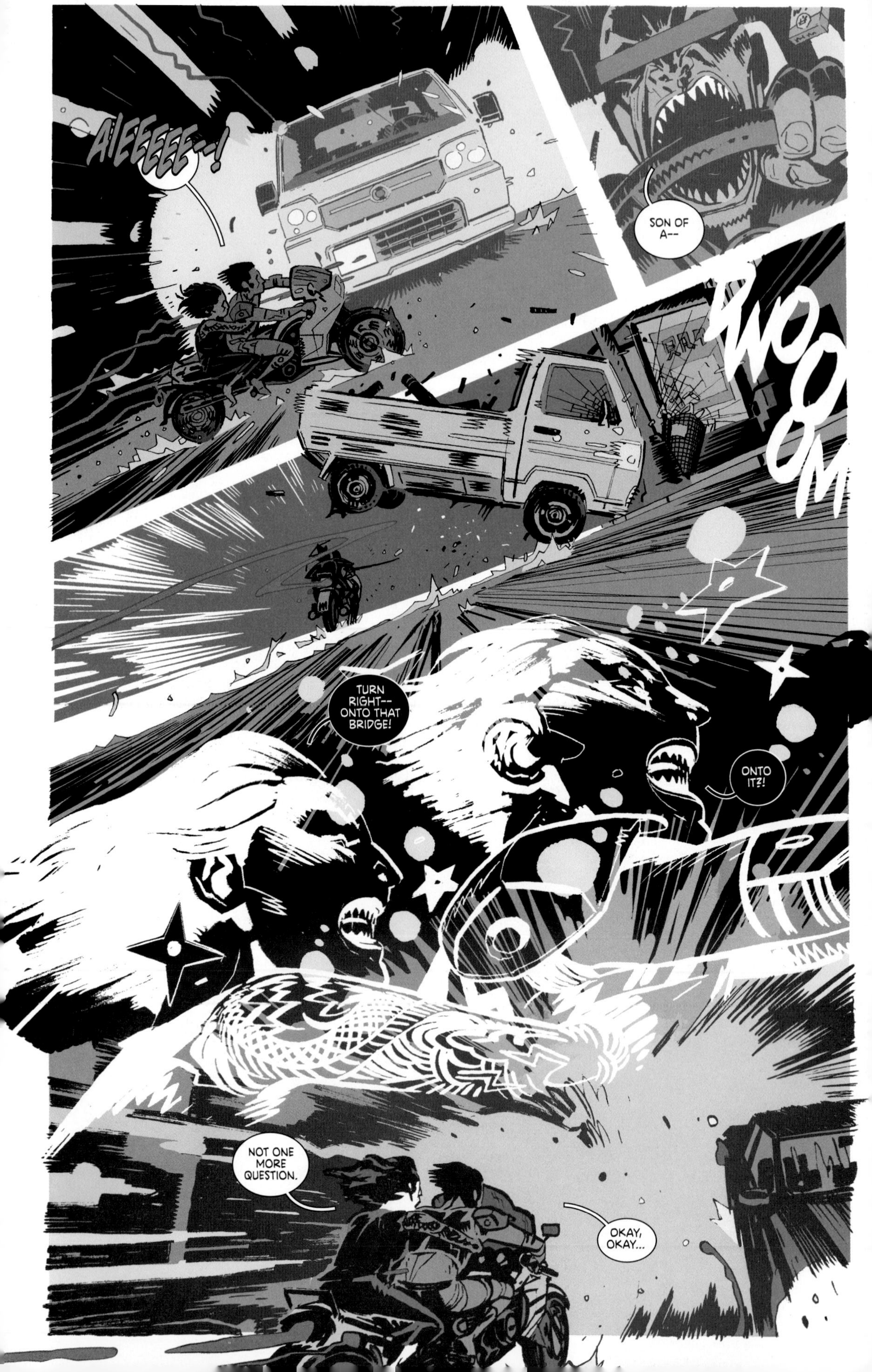
AIEEEEEE--!
SON OF A--
VROOOM
TURN RIGHT--ONTO THAT BRIDGE!
ONTO IT?!
NOT ONE MORE QUESTION.
OKAY, OKAY...

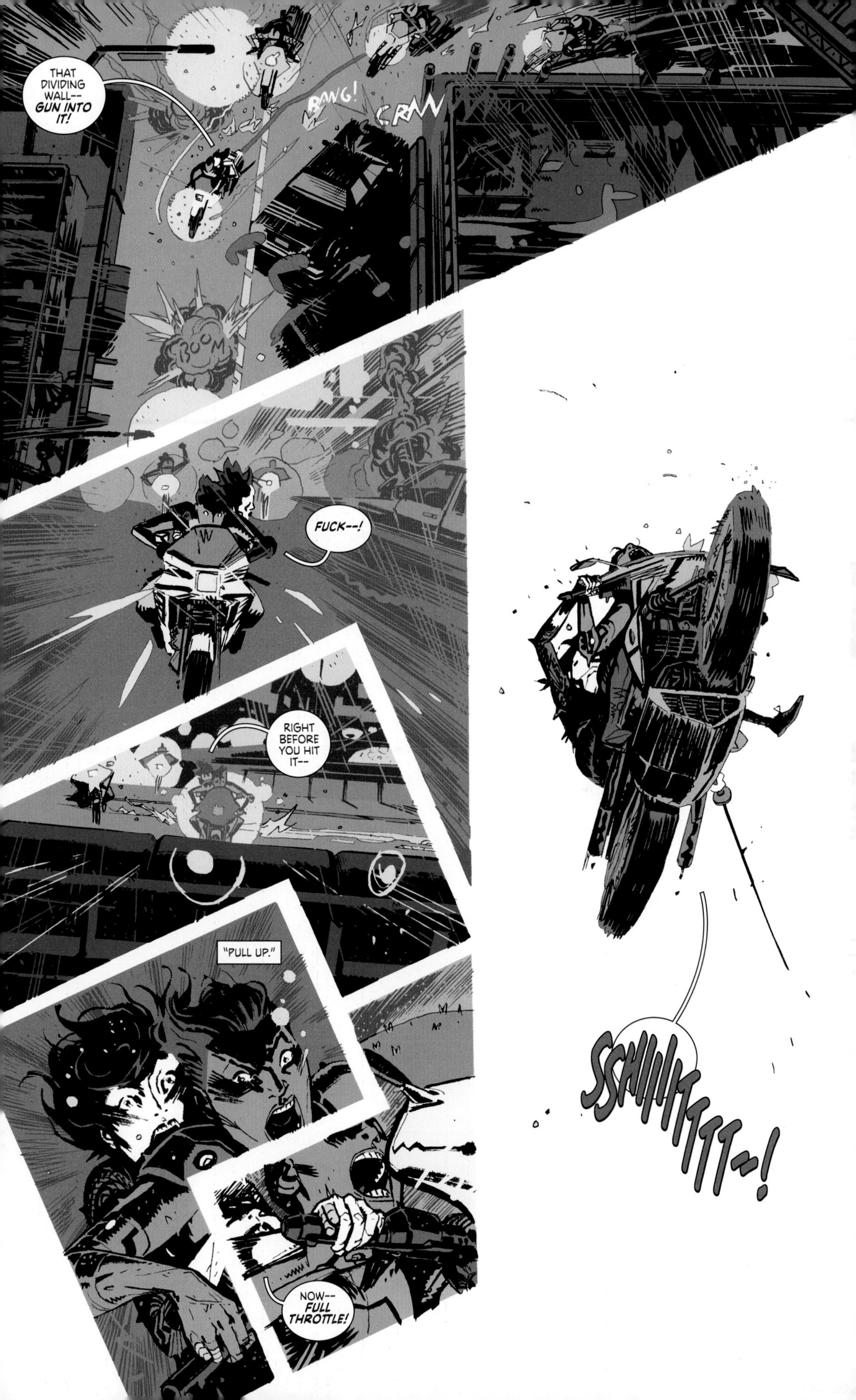
THAT DIVIDING WALL-- GUN INTO IT!
BANG!
CRAN
BOOM
FUCK--!
RIGHT BEFORE YOU HIT IT--
"PULL UP."
NOW-- FULL THROTTLE!
SSHIIIIITTTT--!

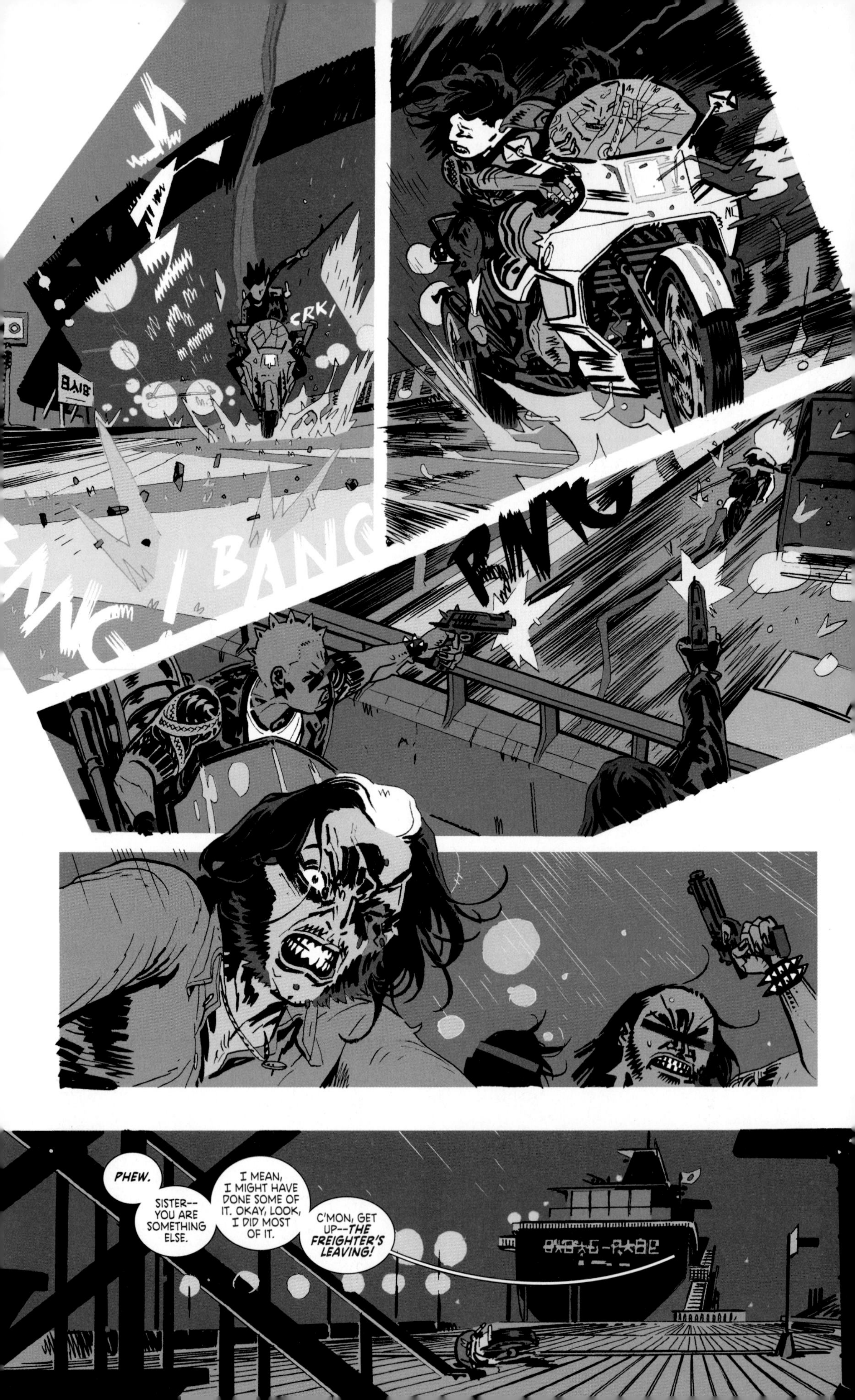
CRK!
BANG
BANG
PHEW.
SISTER-- YOU ARE SOMETHING ELSE.
I MEAN, I MIGHT HAVE DONE SOME OF IT. OKAY, LOOK, I DID MOST OF IT.
C'MON, GET UP--THE FREIGHTER'S LEAVING!

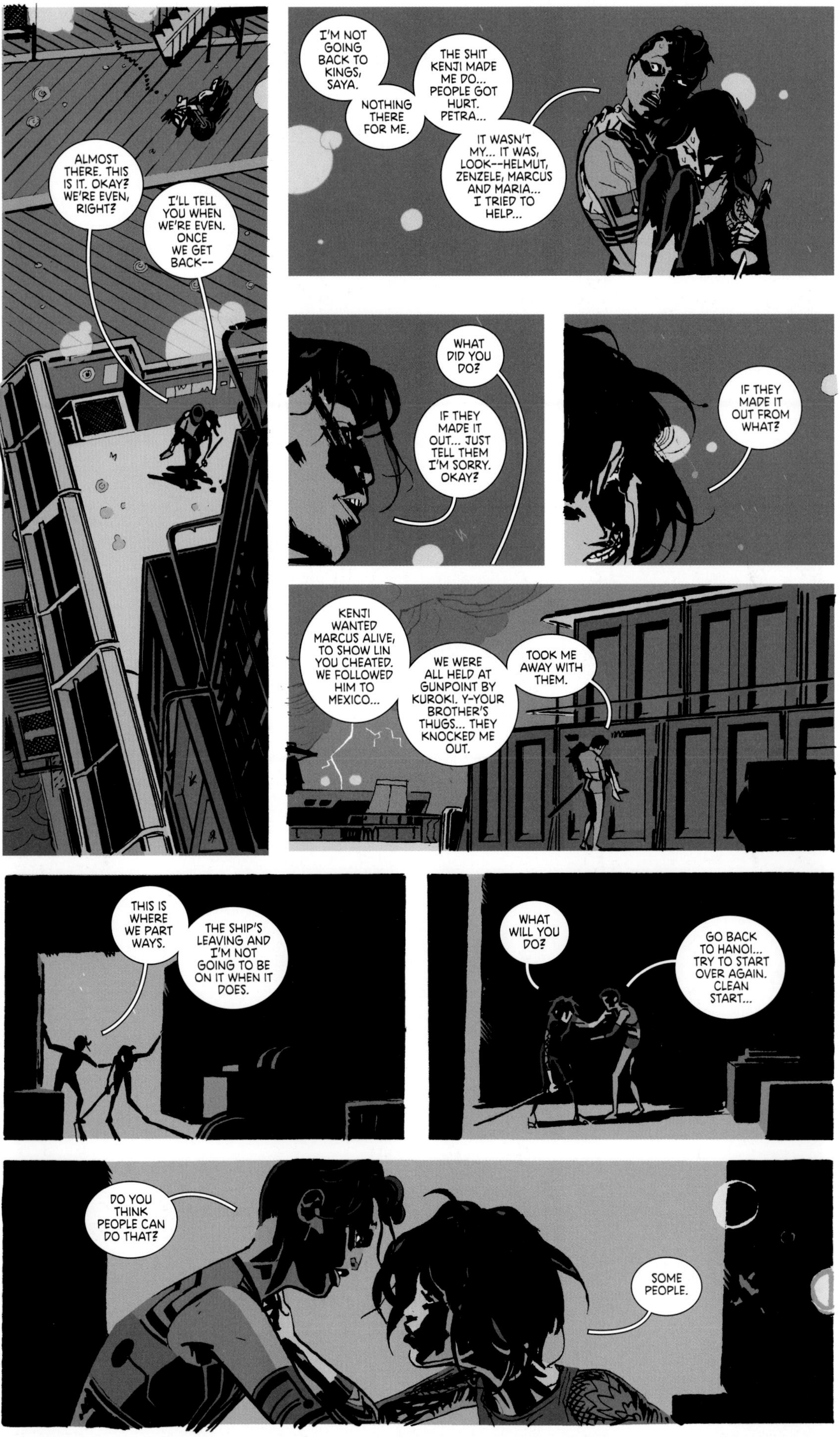
ALMOST THERE. THIS IS IT. OKAY? WE'RE EVEN, RIGHT?
I'LL TELL YOU WHEN WE'RE EVEN. ONCE WE GET BACK--
I'M NOT GOING BACK TO KINGS, SAYA.
NOTHING THERE FOR ME.
THE SHIT KENJI MADE ME DO... PEOPLE GOT HURT. PETRA...
IT WASN'T MY... IT WAS, LOOK--HELMUT, ZENZELE, MARCUS AND MARIA... I TRIED TO HELP...
WHAT DID YOU DO?
IF THEY MADE IT OUT... JUST TELL THEM I'M SORRY. OKAY?
IF THEY MADE IT OUT FROM WHAT?
KENJI WANTED MARCUS ALIVE, TO SHOW LIN YOU CHEATED. WE FOLLOWED HIM TO MEXICO...
WE WERE ALL HELD AT GUNPOINT BY KUROKI. Y-YOUR BROTHER'S THUGS... THEY KNOCKED ME OUT.
TOOK ME AWAY WITH THEM.
THIS IS WHERE WE PART WAYS.
THE SHIP'S LEAVING AND I'M NOT GOING TO BE ON IT WHEN IT DOES.
WHAT WILL YOU DO?
GO BACK TO HANOI... TRY TO START OVER AGAIN. CLEAN START...
DO YOU THINK PEOPLE CAN DO THAT?
SOME PEOPLE.

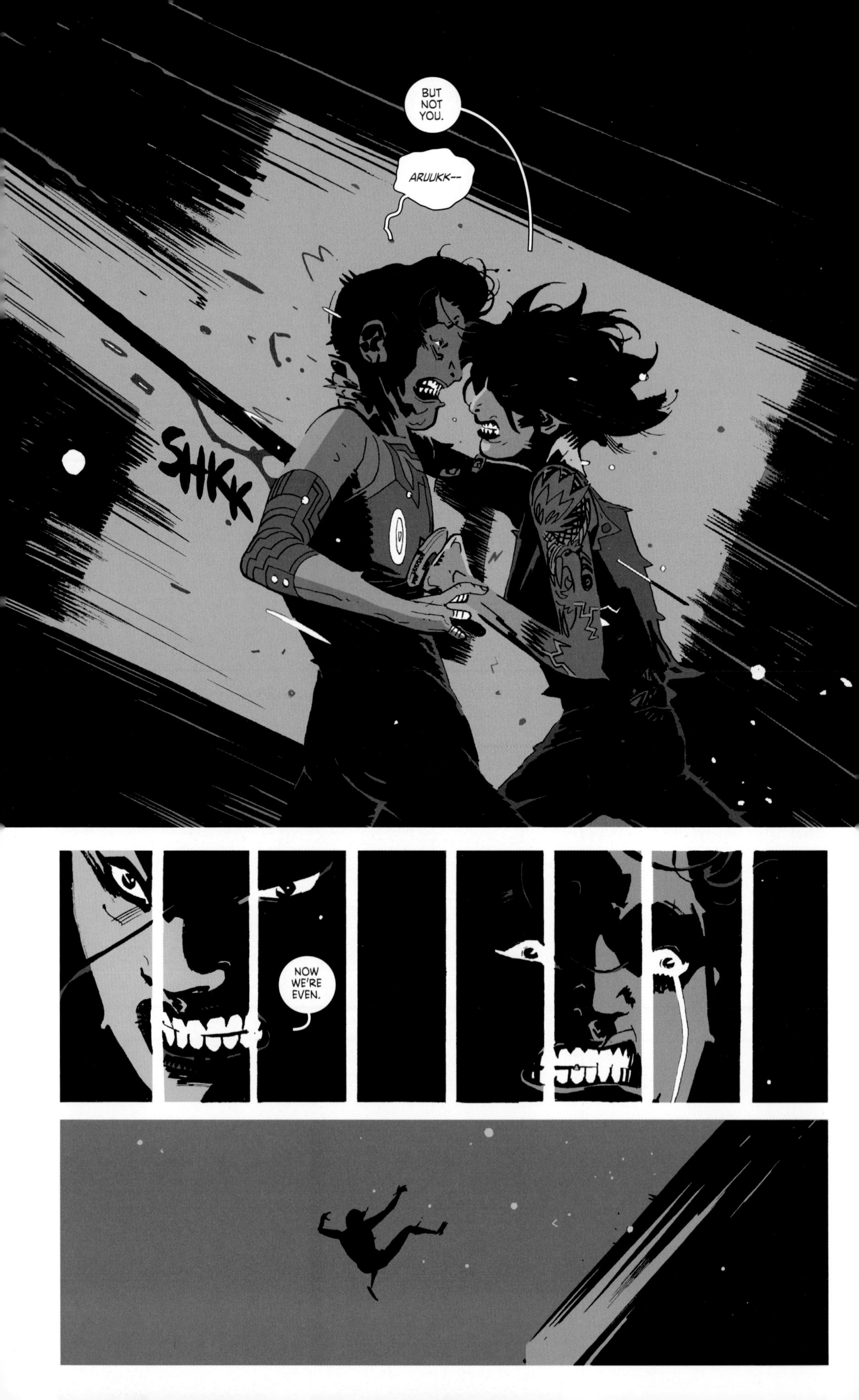
BUT NOT YOU.
ARUUKK--
SHKK
NOW WE'RE EVEN.

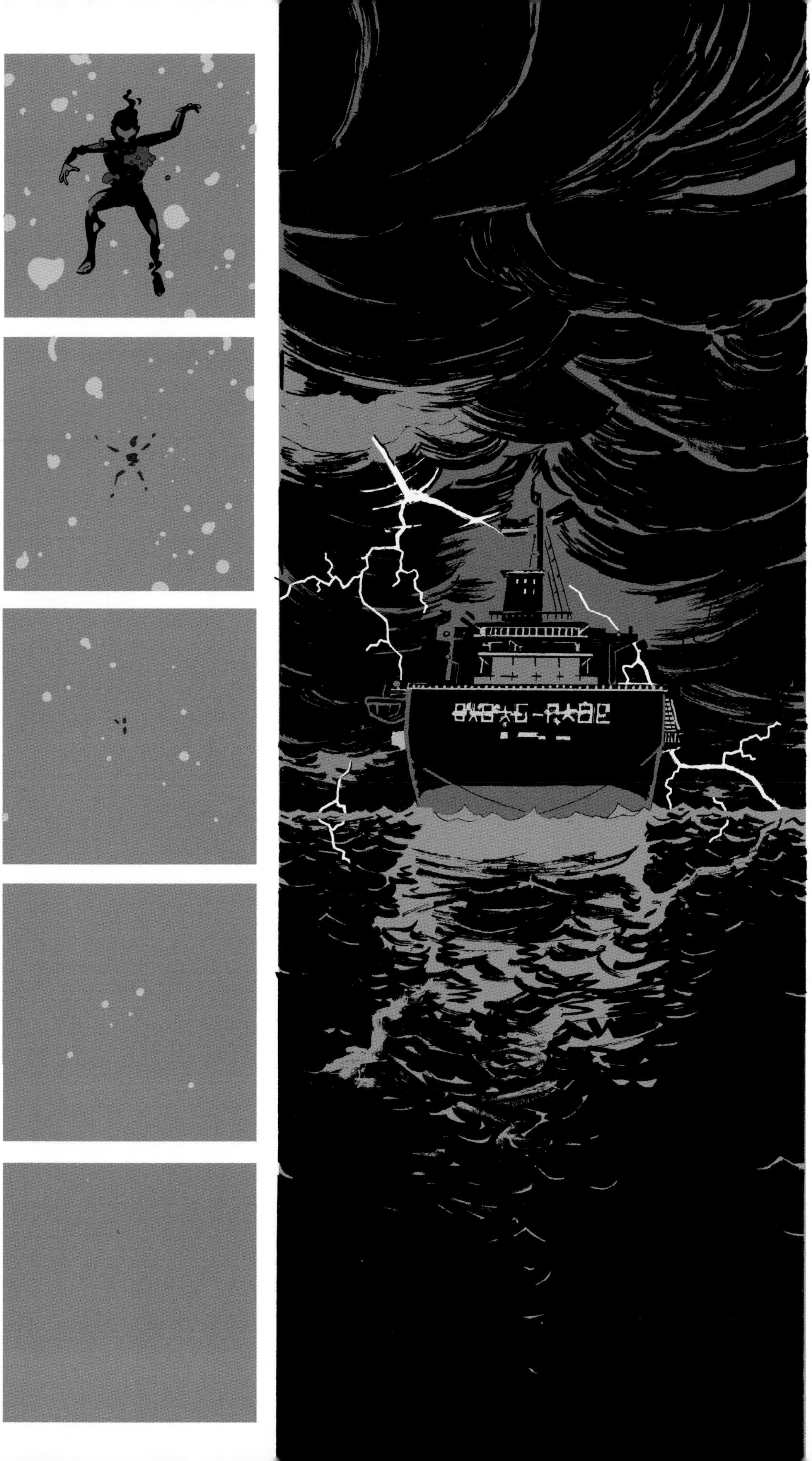

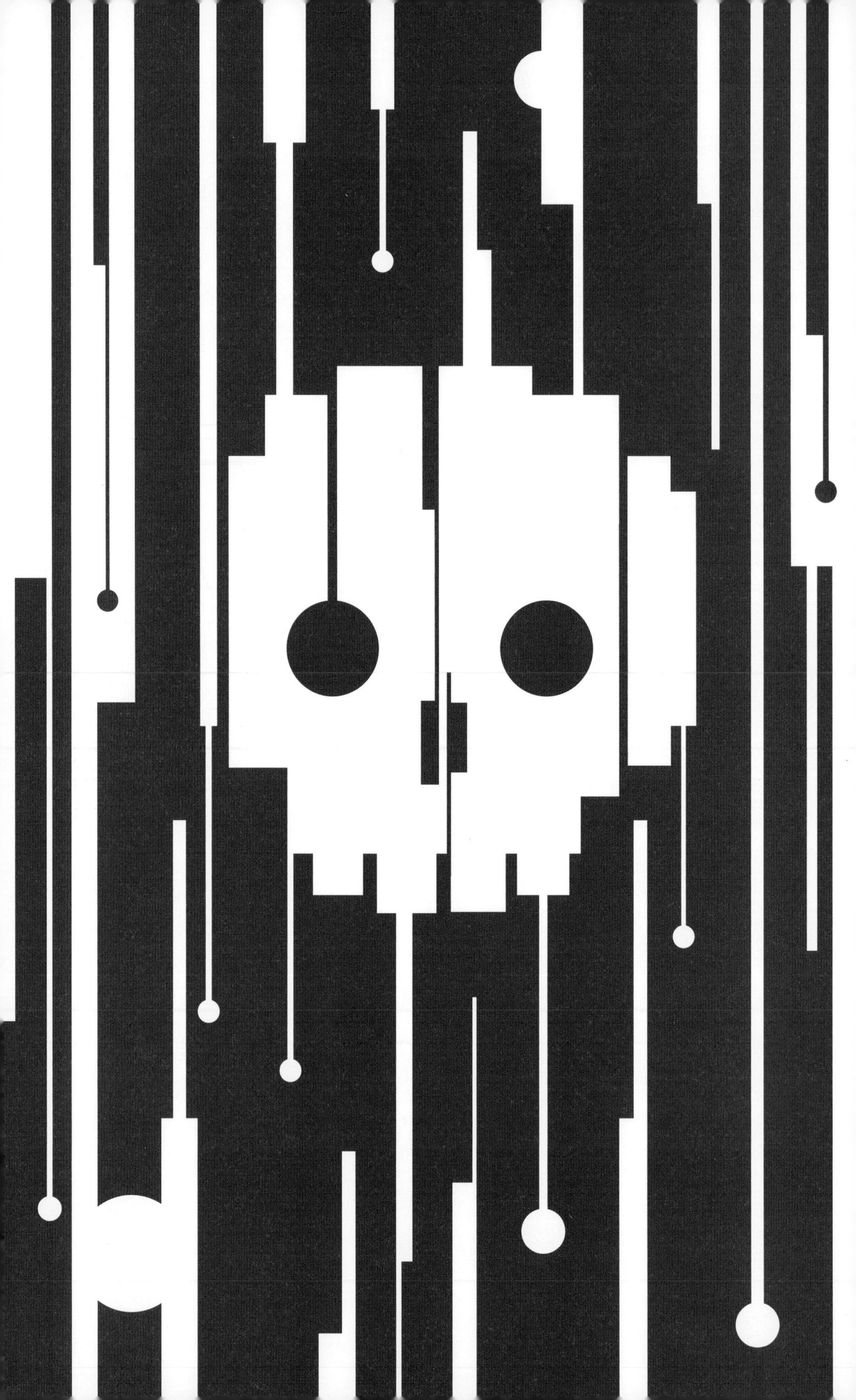

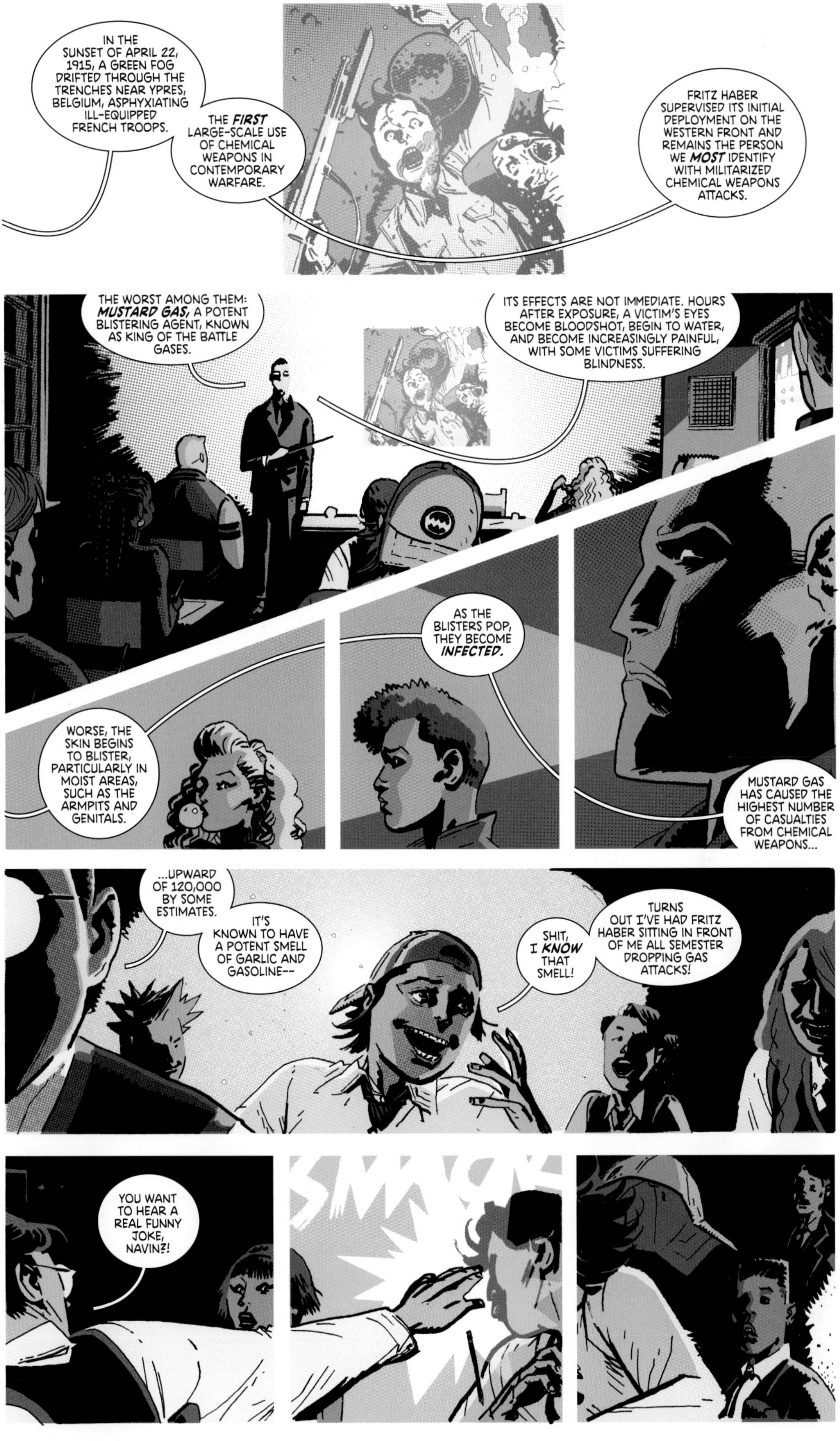
IN THE SUNSET OF APRIL 22, 1915, A GREEN FOG DRIFTED THROUGH THE TRENCHES NEAR YPRES, BELGIUM, ASPHYXIATING ILL-EQUIPPED FRENCH TROOPS.
THE FIRST LARGE-SCALE USE OF CHEMICAL WEAPONS IN CONTEMPORARY WARFARE.
FRITZ HABER SUPERVISED ITS INITIAL DEPLOYMENT ON THE WESTERN FRONT AND REMAINS THE PERSON WE MOST IDENTIFY WITH MILITARIZED CHEMICAL WEAPONS ATTACKS.
THE WORST AMONG THEM: MUSTARD GAS, A POTENT BLISTERING AGENT, KNOWN AS KING OF THE BATTLE GASES.
ITS EFFECTS ARE NOT IMMEDIATE. HOURS AFTER EXPOSURE, A VICTIM'S EYES BECOME BLOODSHOT, BEGIN TO WATER, AND BECOME INCREASINGLY PAINFUL, WITH SOME VICTIMS SUFFERING BLINDNESS.
WORSE, THE SKIN BEGINS TO BLISTER, PARTICULARLY IN MOIST AREAS, SUCH AS THE ARMPITS AND GENITALS.
AS THE BLISTERS POP, THEY BECOME INFECTED.
MUSTARD GAS HAS CAUSED THE HIGHEST NUMBER OF CASUALTIES FROM CHEMICAL WEAPONS...
...UPWARD OF 120,000 BY SOME ESTIMATES.
IT'S KNOWN TO HAVE A POTENT SMELL OF GARLIC AND GASOLINE--
SHIT, I KNOW THAT SMELL!
TURNS OUT I'VE HAD FRITZ HABER SITTING IN FRONT OF ME ALL SEMESTER DROPPING GAS ATTACKS!
YOU WANT TO HEAR A REAL FUNNY JOKE, NAVIN?!

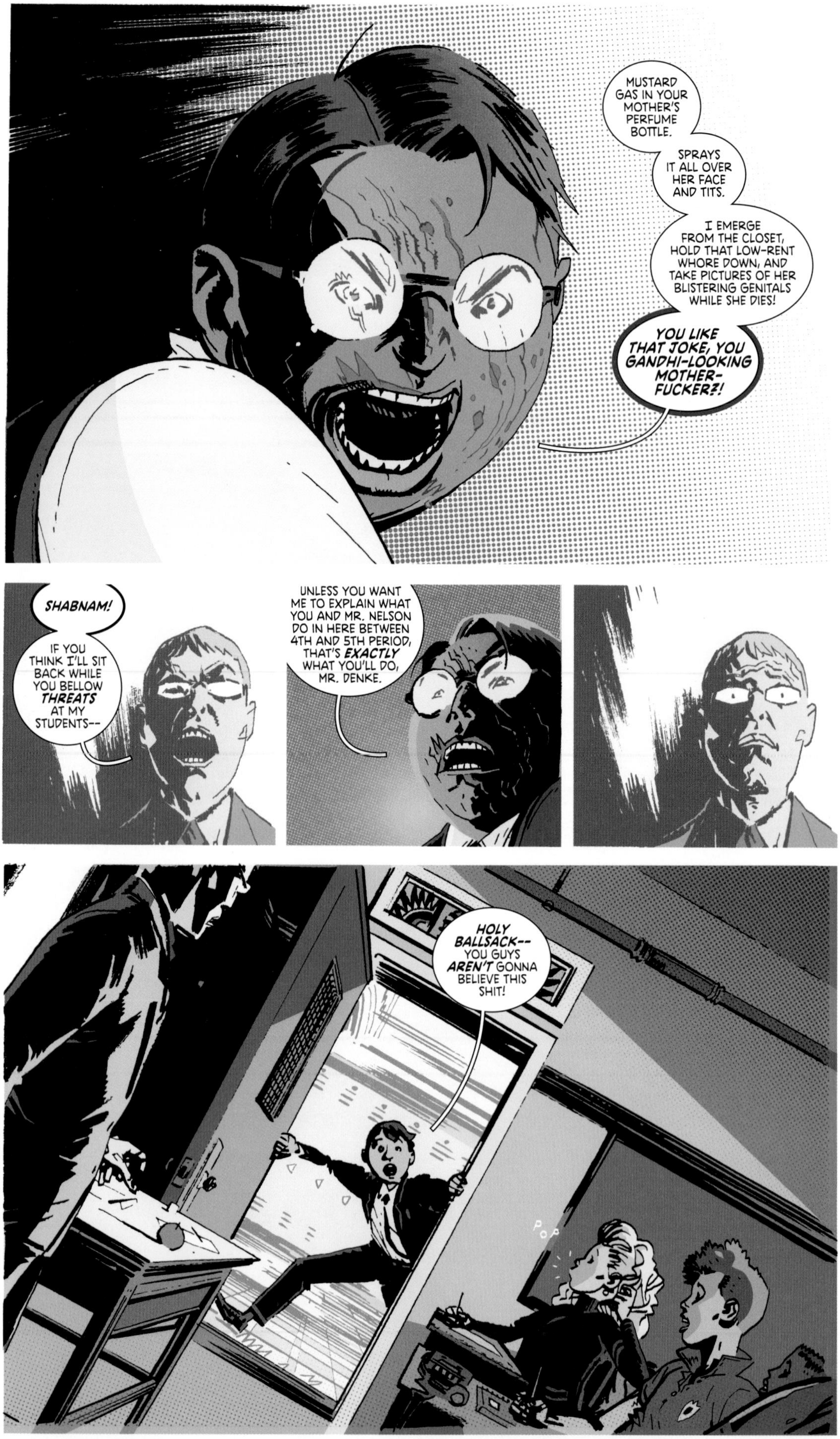

MUSTARD GAS IN YOUR MOTHER'S PERFUME BOTTLE.
SPRAYS IT ALL OVER HER FACE AND TITS.
I EMERGE FROM THE CLOSET, HOLD THAT LOW-RENT WHORE DOWN, AND TAKE PICTURES OF HER BLISTERING GENITALS WHILE SHE DIES!
YOU LIKE THAT JOKE, YOU GANDHI-LOOKING MOTHER-FUCKER?!
SHABNAM!
IF YOU THINK I'LL SIT BACK WHILE YOU BELLOW THREATS AT MY STUDENTS--
UNLESS YOU WANT ME TO EXPLAIN WHAT YOU AND MR. NELSON DO IN HERE BETWEEN 4TH AND 5TH PERIOD, THAT'S EXACTLY WHAT YOU'LL DO, MR. DENKE.
HOLY BALLSACK-- YOU GUYS AREN'T GONNA BELIEVE THIS SHIT!
POP

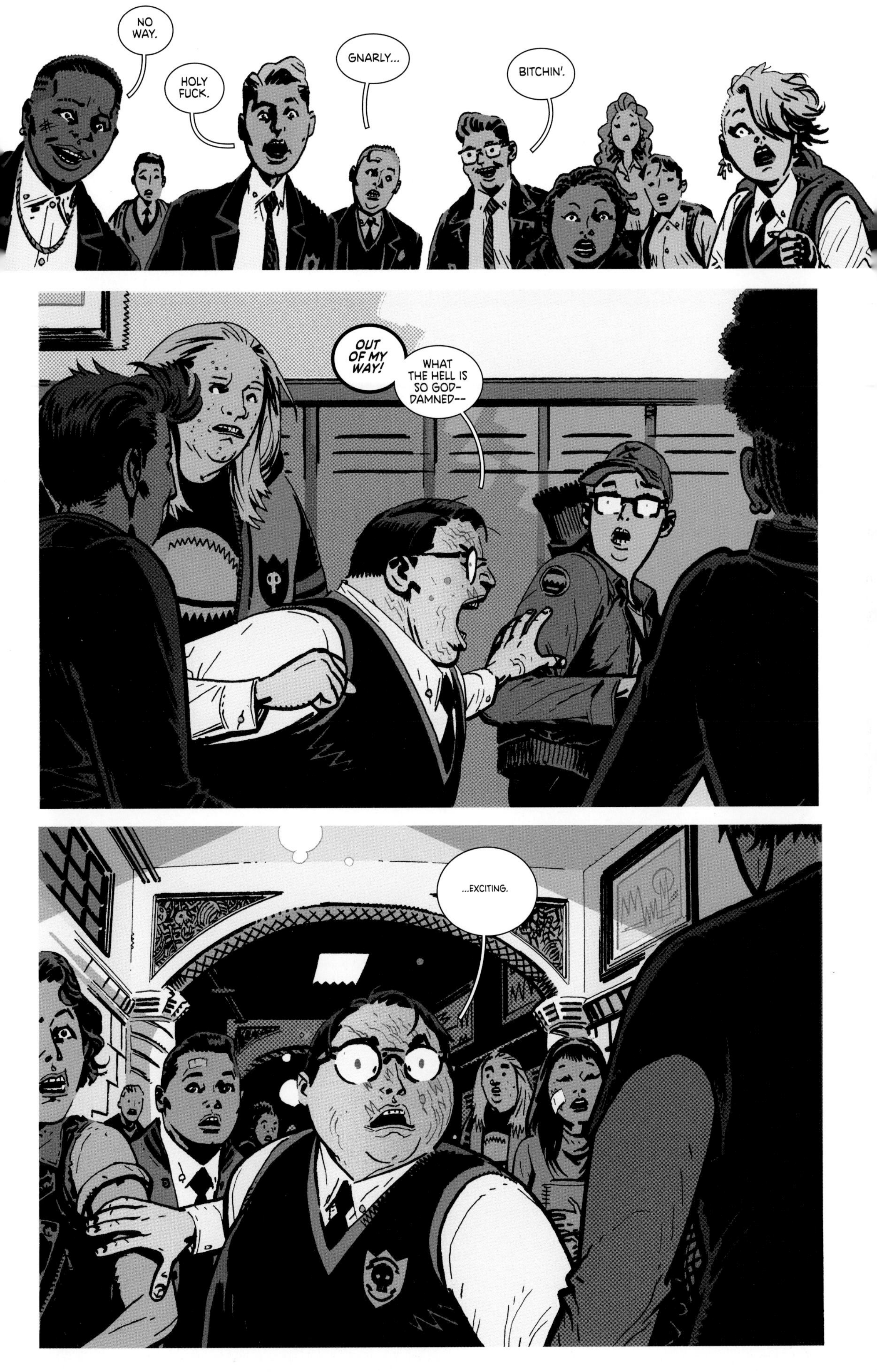
NO WAY.
HOLY FUCK.
GNARLY...
BITCHIN'.
OUT OF MY WAY!
WHAT THE HELL IS SO GOD-DAMNED--
...EXCITING.

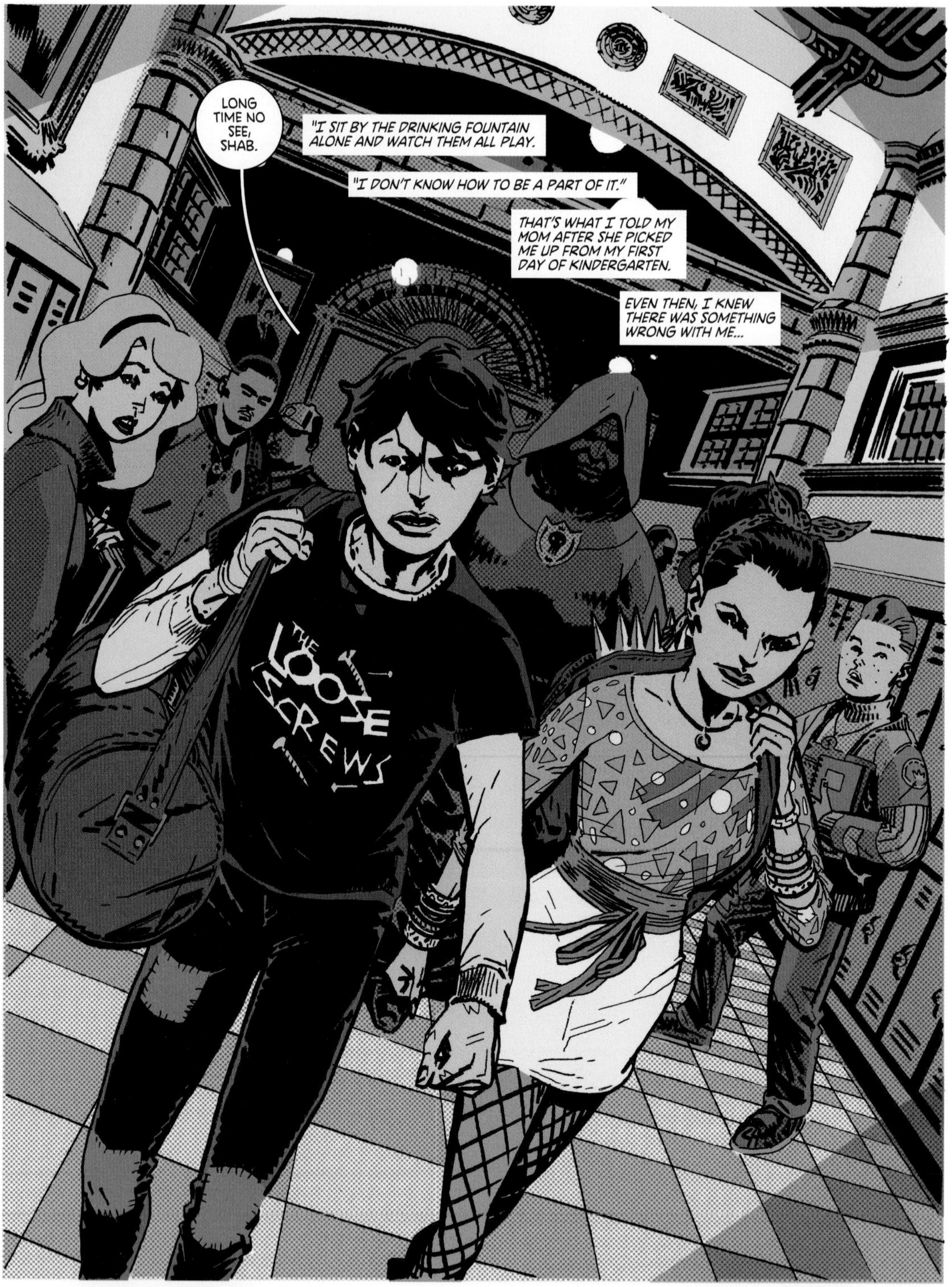
LONG TIME NO SEE, SHAB.
"I SIT BY THE DRINKING FOUNTAIN ALONE AND WATCH THEM ALL PLAY.
"I DON'T KNOW HOW TO BE A PART OF IT."
THAT'S WHAT I TOLD MY MOM AFTER SHE PICKED ME UP FROM MY FIRST DAY OF KINDERGARTEN.
EVEN THEN, I KNEW THERE WAS SOMETHING WRONG WITH ME...
THE LOOSE SCREWS

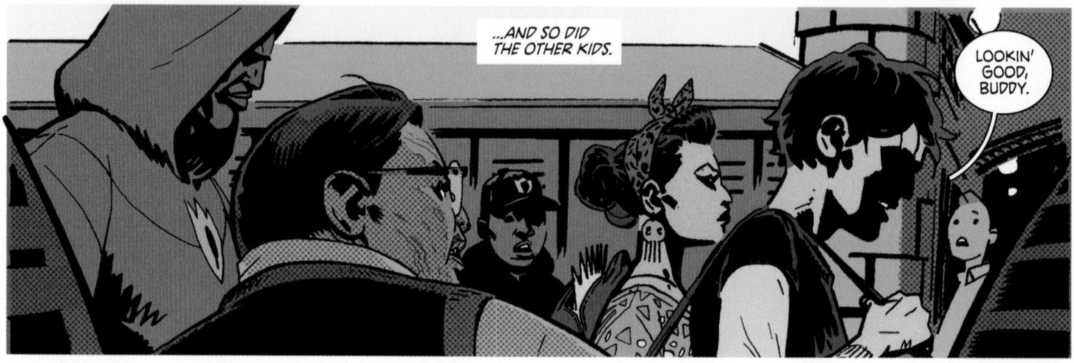
...AND SO DID THE OTHER KIDS.
LOOKIN' GOOD, BUDDY.

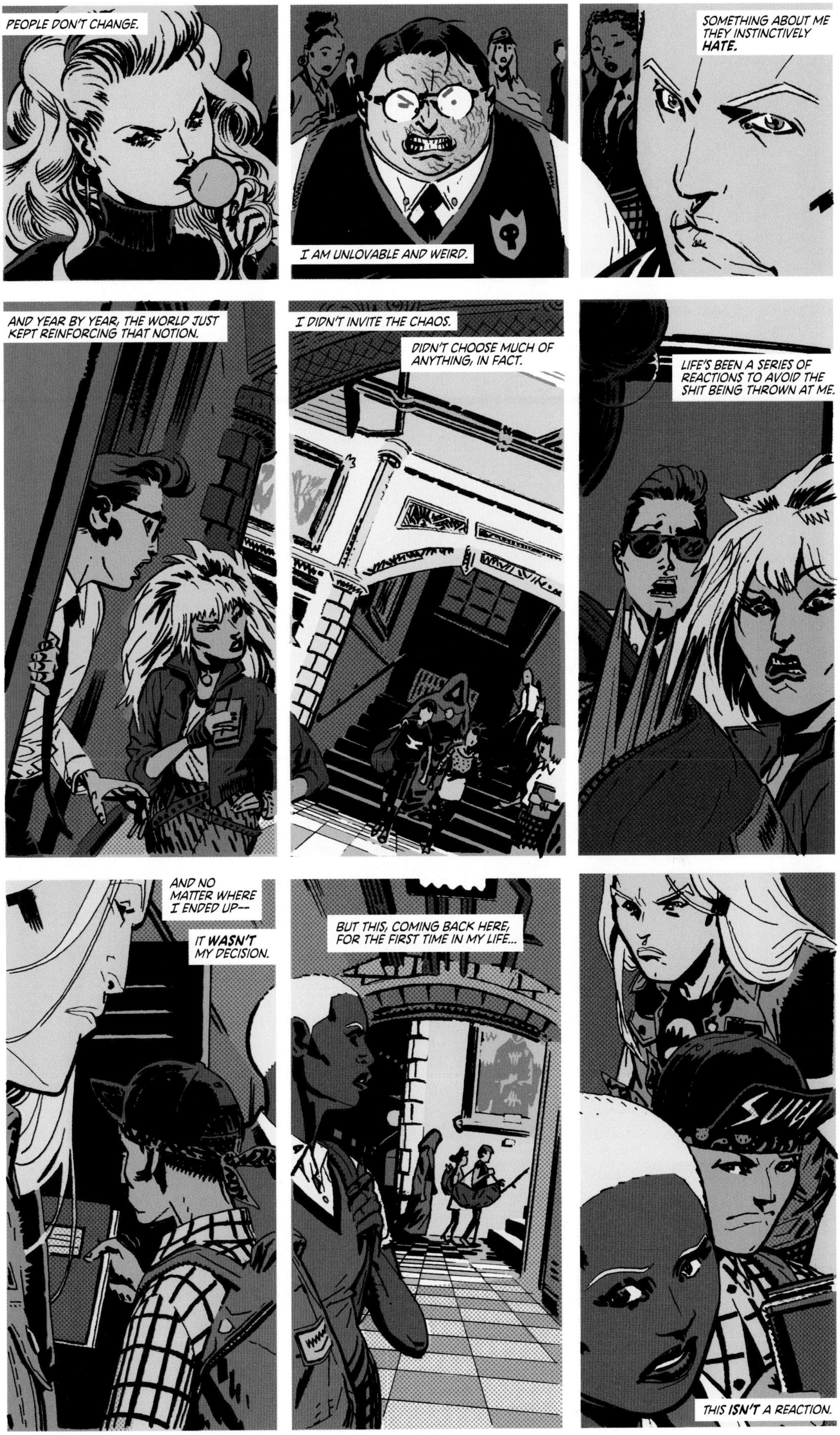
PEOPLE DON'T CHANGE.
I AM UNLOVABLE AND WEIRD.
SOMETHING ABOUT ME THEY INSTINCTIVELY **HATE.**
AND YEAR BY YEAR, THE WORLD JUST KEPT REINFORCING THAT NOTION.
I DIDN'T INVITE THE CHAOS.
DIDN'T CHOOSE MUCH OF ANYTHING, IN FACT.
LIFE'S BEEN A SERIES OF REACTIONS TO AVOID THE SHIT BEING THROWN AT ME.
AND NO MATTER WHERE I ENDED UP--
IT **WASN'T** MY DECISION.
BUT THIS, COMING BACK HERE, FOR THE FIRST TIME IN MY LIFE...
SUIC
THIS **ISN'T** A REACTION.

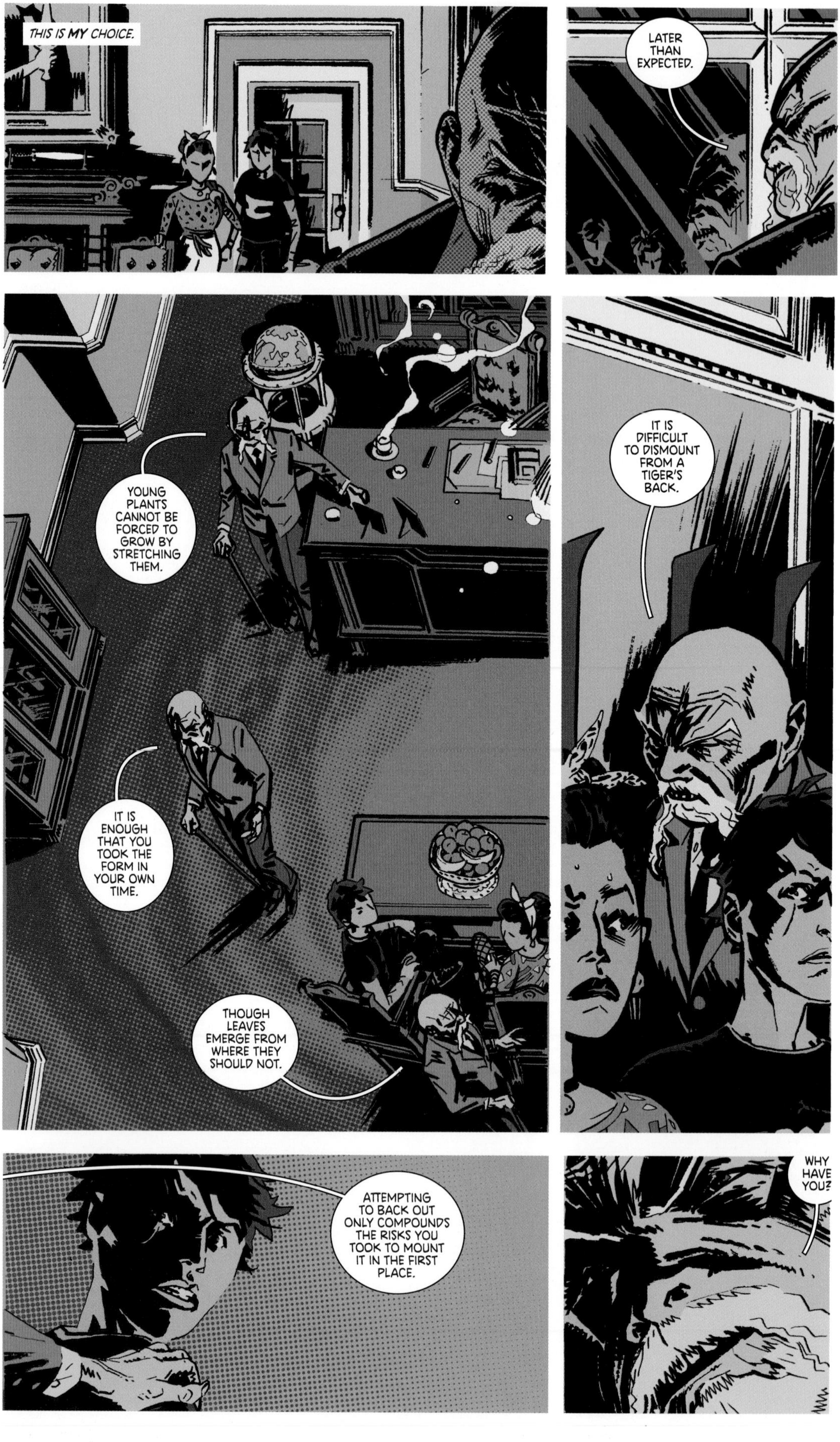
THIS IS MY CHOICE.
LATER THAN EXPECTED.
YOUNG PLANTS CANNOT BE FORCED TO GROW BY STRETCHING THEM.
IT IS ENOUGH THAT YOU TOOK THE FORM IN YOUR OWN TIME.
THOUGH LEAVES EMERGE FROM WHERE THEY SHOULD NOT.
IT IS DIFFICULT TO DISMOUNT FROM A TIGER'S BACK.
ATTEMPTING TO BACK OUT ONLY COMPOUNDS THE RISKS YOU TOOK TO MOUNT IT IN THE FIRST PLACE.
WHY HAVE YOU?

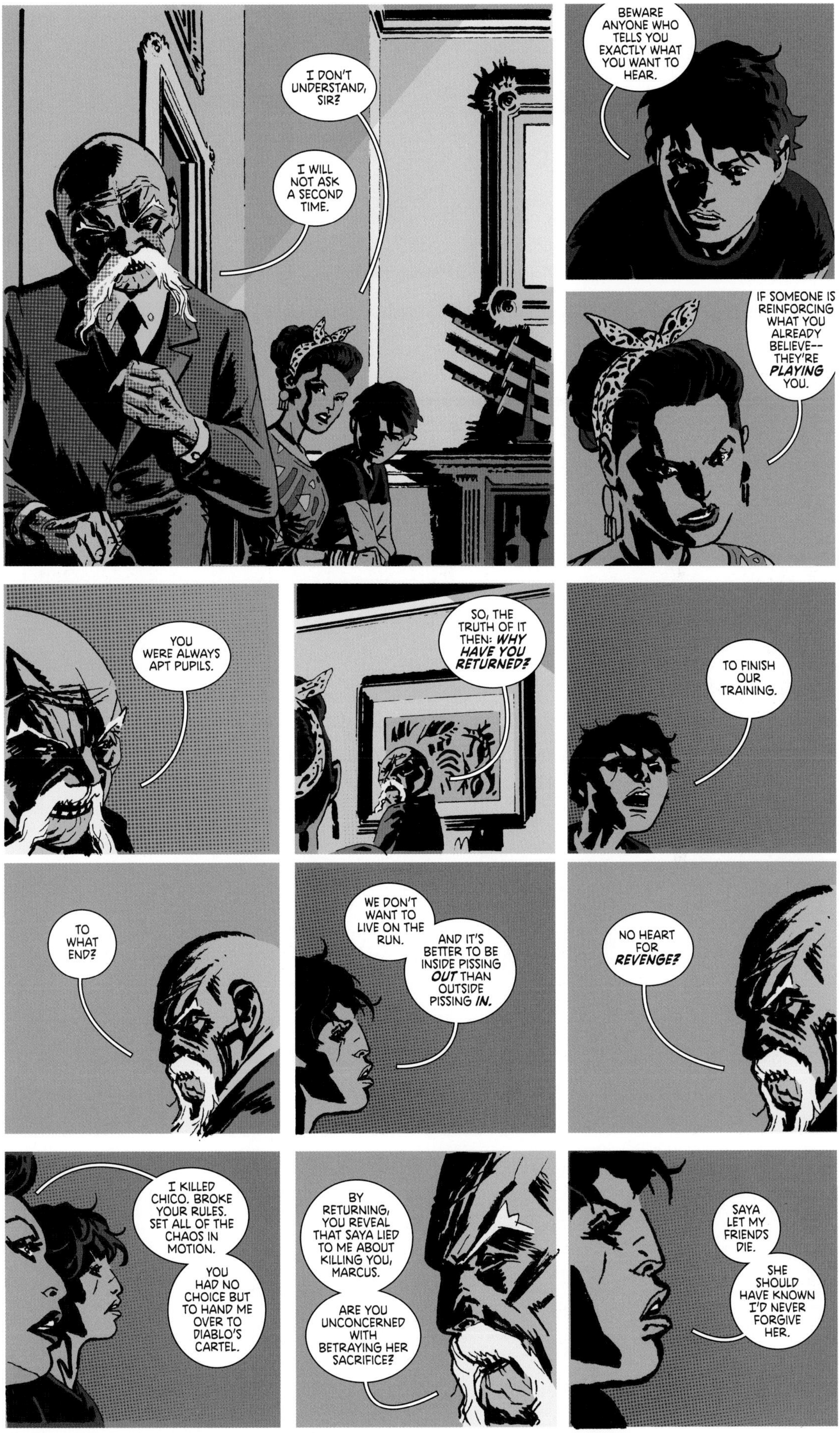
I DON'T UNDERSTAND, SIR?
I WILL NOT ASK A SECOND TIME.
BEWARE ANYONE WHO TELLS YOU EXACTLY WHAT YOU WANT TO HEAR.
IF SOMEONE IS REINFORCING WHAT YOU ALREADY BELIEVE-- THEY'RE PLAYING YOU.
YOU WERE ALWAYS APT PUPILS.
SO, THE TRUTH OF IT THEN: WHY HAVE YOU RETURNED?
TO FINISH OUR TRAINING.
TO WHAT END?
WE DON'T WANT TO LIVE ON THE RUN.
AND IT'S BETTER TO BE INSIDE PISSING OUT THAN OUTSIDE PISSING IN.
NO HEART FOR REVENGE?
I KILLED CHICO. BROKE YOUR RULES. SET ALL OF THE CHAOS IN MOTION.
YOU HAD NO CHOICE BUT TO HAND ME OVER TO DIABLO'S CARTEL.
BY RETURNING, YOU REVEAL THAT SAYA LIED TO ME ABOUT KILLING YOU, MARCUS.
ARE YOU UNCONCERNED WITH BETRAYING HER SACRIFICE?
SAYA LET MY FRIENDS DIE.
SHE SHOULD HAVE KNOWN I'D NEVER FORGIVE HER.

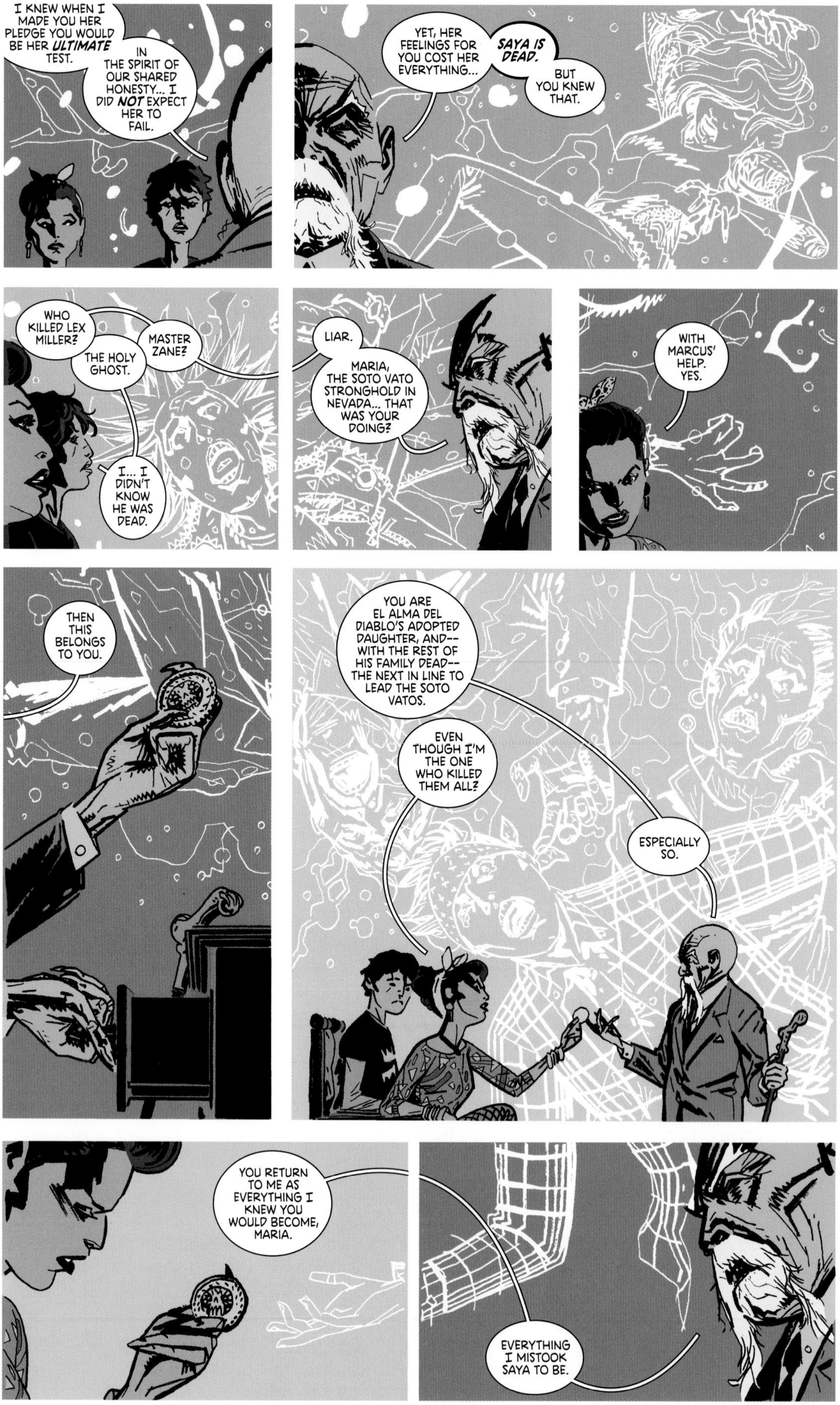
I KNEW WHEN I MADE YOU HER PLEDGE YOU WOULD BE HER *ULTIMATE* TEST.
IN THE SPIRIT OF OUR SHARED HONESTY... I DID *NOT* EXPECT HER TO FAIL.
YET, HER FEELINGS FOR YOU COST HER EVERYTHING...
SAYA IS DEAD.
BUT YOU KNEW THAT.
WHO KILLED LEX MILLER?
THE HOLY GHOST.
MASTER ZANE?
I... I DIDN'T KNOW HE WAS DEAD.
LIAR.
MARIA, THE SOTO VATO STRONGHOLD IN NEVADA... THAT WAS YOUR DOING?
WITH MARCUS' HELP. YES.
THEN THIS BELONGS TO YOU.
YOU ARE EL ALMA DEL DIABLO'S ADOPTED DAUGHTER, AND-- WITH THE REST OF HIS FAMILY DEAD-- THE NEXT IN LINE TO LEAD THE SOTO VATOS.
EVEN THOUGH I'M THE ONE WHO KILLED THEM ALL?
ESPECIALLY SO.
YOU RETURN TO ME AS EVERYTHING I KNEW YOU WOULD BECOME, MARIA.
EVERYTHING I MISTOOK SAYA TO BE.

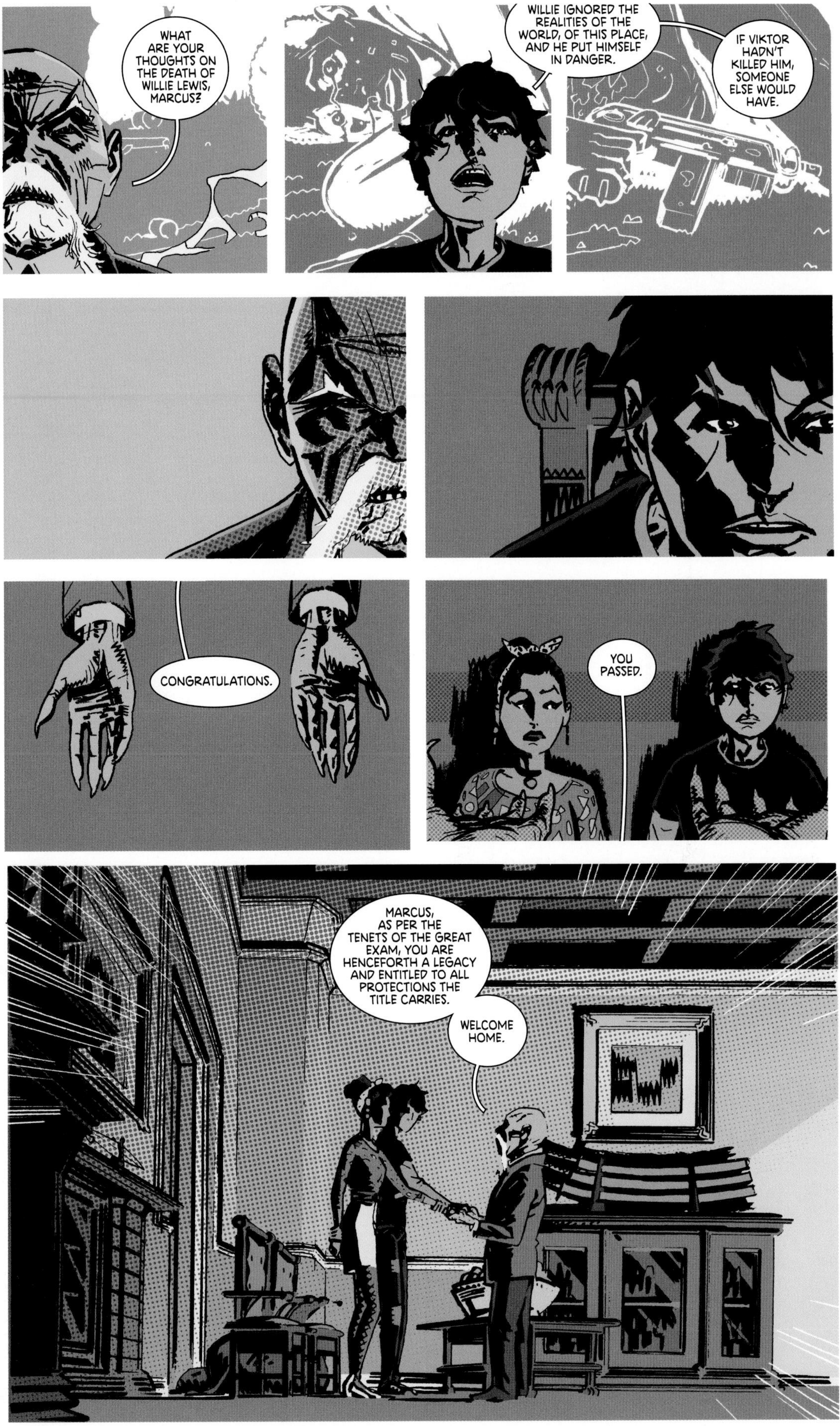
WHAT ARE YOUR THOUGHTS ON THE DEATH OF WILLIE LEWIS, MARCUS?
WILLIE IGNORED THE REALITIES OF THE WORLD, OF THIS PLACE, AND HE PUT HIMSELF IN DANGER.
IF VIKTOR HADN'T KILLED HIM, SOMEONE ELSE WOULD HAVE.
CONGRATULATIONS.
YOU PASSED.
MARCUS, AS PER THE TENETS OF THE GREAT EXAM, YOU ARE HENCEFORTH A LEGACY AND ENTITLED TO ALL PROTECTIONS THE TITLE CARRIES.
WELCOME HOME.

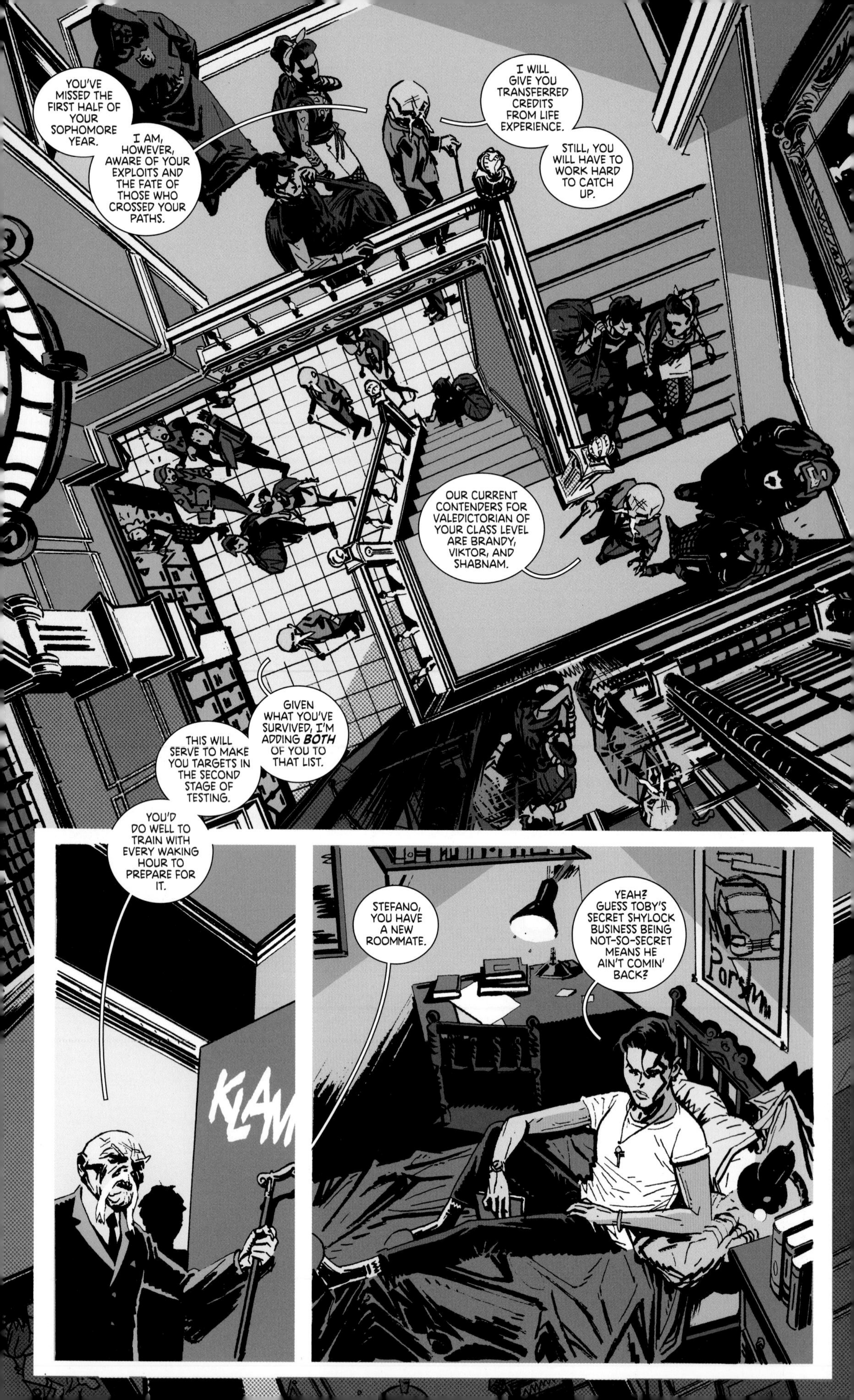

YOU'VE MISSED THE FIRST HALF OF YOUR SOPHOMORE YEAR.
I AM, HOWEVER, AWARE OF YOUR EXPLOITS AND THE FATE OF THOSE WHO CROSSED YOUR PATHS.
I WILL GIVE YOU TRANSFERRED CREDITS FROM LIFE EXPERIENCE.
STILL, YOU WILL HAVE TO WORK HARD TO CATCH UP.
OUR CURRENT CONTENDERS FOR VALEDICTORIAN OF YOUR CLASS LEVEL ARE BRANDY, VIKTOR, AND SHABNAM.
GIVEN WHAT YOU'VE SURVIVED, I'M ADDING **BOTH** OF YOU TO THAT LIST.
THIS WILL SERVE TO MAKE YOU TARGETS IN THE SECOND STAGE OF TESTING.
YOU'D DO WELL TO TRAIN WITH EVERY WAKING HOUR TO PREPARE FOR IT.
KLAM
STEFANO, YOU HAVE A NEW ROOMMATE.
YEAH? GUESS TOBY'S SECRET SHYLOCK BUSINESS BEING NOT-SO-SECRET MEANS HE AIN'T COMIN' BACK?

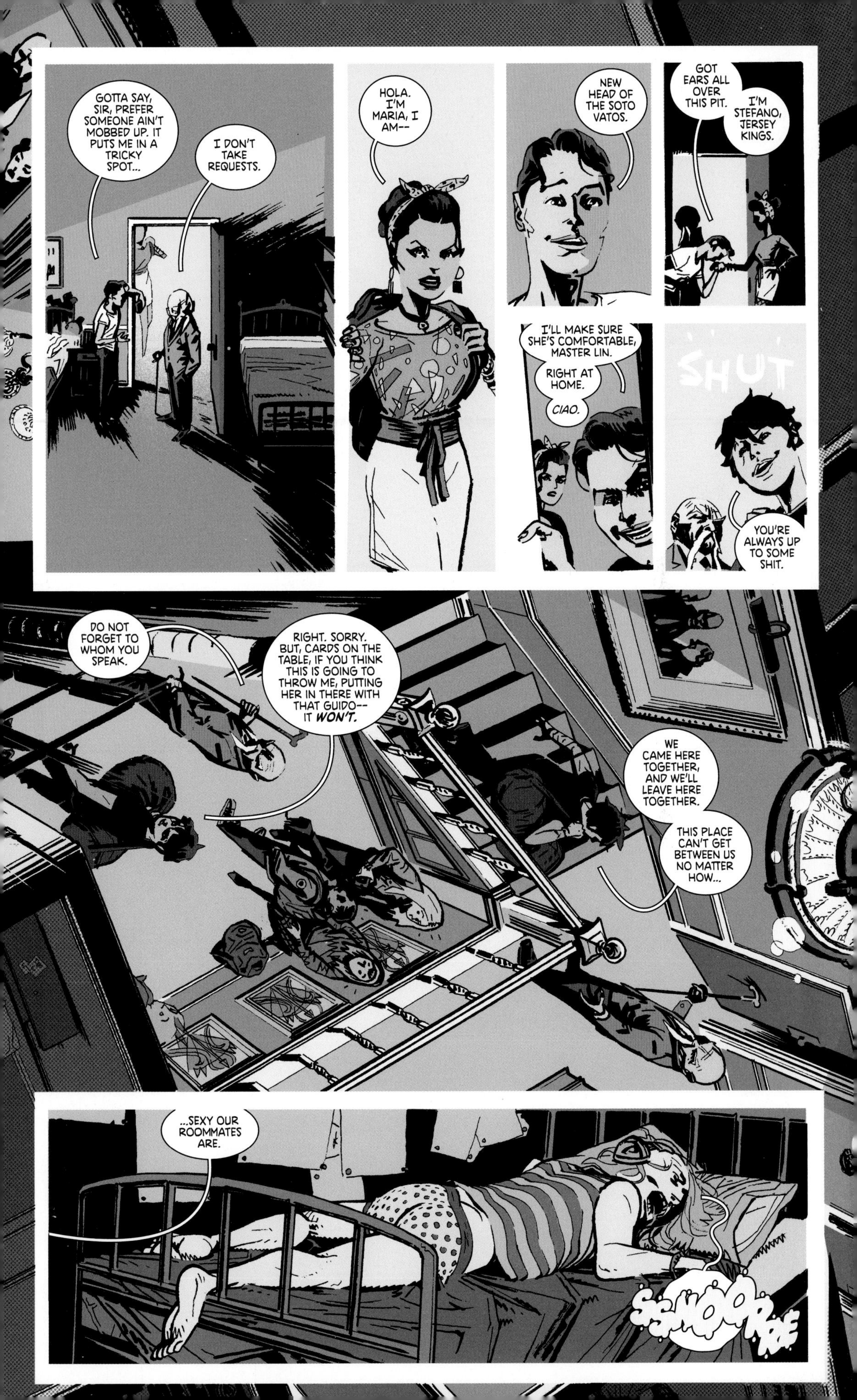
GOTTA SAY, SIR, PREFER SOMEONE AIN'T MOBBED UP. IT PUTS ME IN A TRICKY SPOT...
I DON'T TAKE REQUESTS.
HOLA. I'M MARIA, I AM--
NEW HEAD OF THE SOTO VATOS.
GOT EARS ALL OVER THIS PIT.
I'M STEFANO, JERSEY KINGS.
I'LL MAKE SURE SHE'S COMFORTABLE, MASTER LIN.
RIGHT AT HOME.
CIAO.
SHUT
YOU'RE ALWAYS UP TO SOME SHIT.
DO NOT FORGET TO WHOM YOU SPEAK.
RIGHT. SORRY. BUT, CARDS ON THE TABLE, IF YOU THINK THIS IS GOING TO THROW ME, PUTTING HER IN THERE WITH THAT GUIDO-- IT WON'T.
WE CAME HERE TOGETHER, AND WE'LL LEAVE HERE TOGETHER.
THIS PLACE CAN'T GET BETWEEN US NO MATTER HOW...
...SEXY OUR ROOMMATES ARE.
SSNOORRE

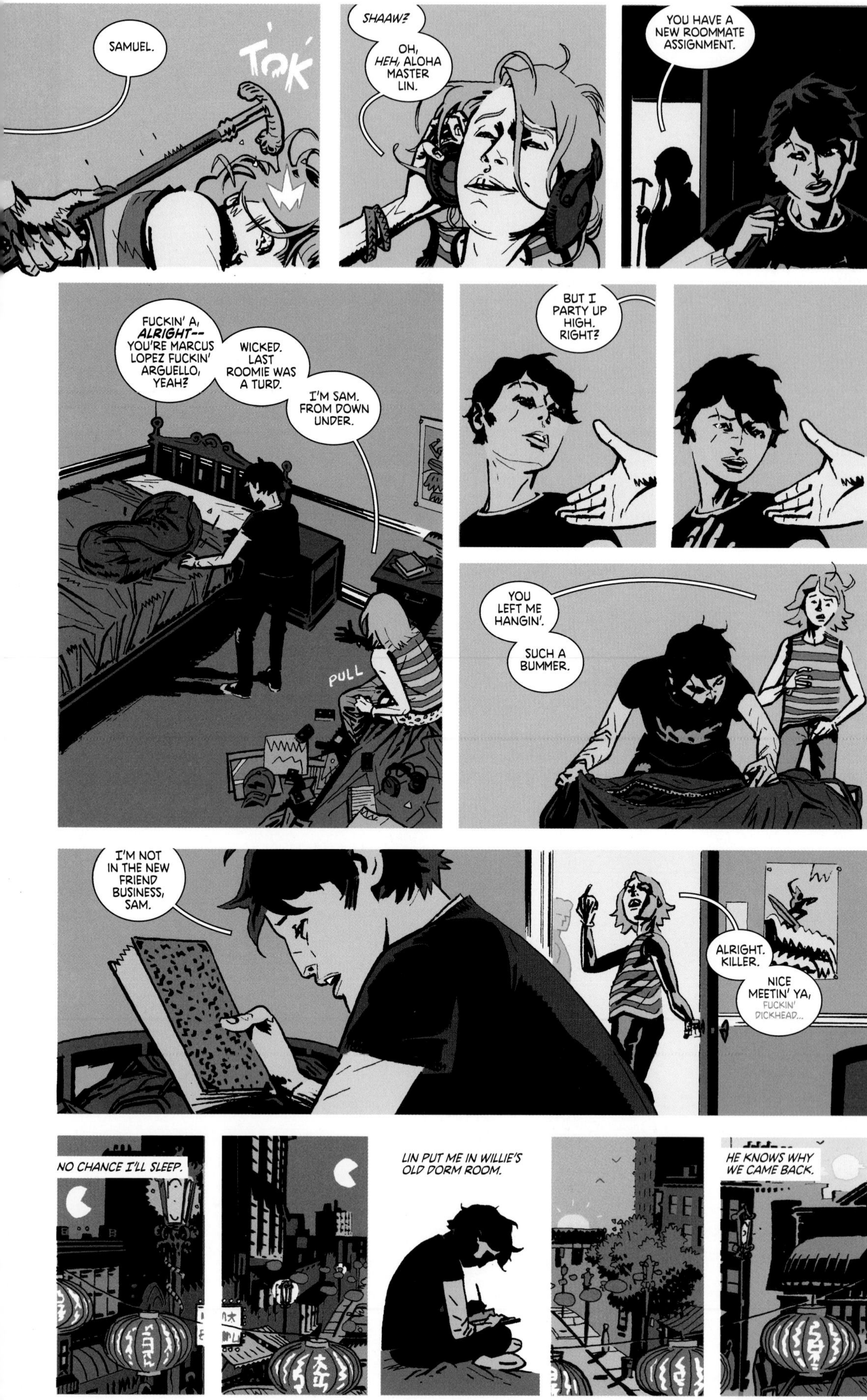
SAMUEL.
TÓK
SHAAW?
OH, HEH, ALOHA MASTER LIN.
YOU HAVE A NEW ROOMMATE ASSIGNMENT.
FUCKIN' A, ALRIGHT-- YOU'RE MARCUS LOPEZ FUCKIN' ARGUELLO, YEAH?
WICKED. LAST ROOMIE WAS A TURD.
I'M SAM. FROM DOWN UNDER.
PULL
BUT I PARTY UP HIGH. RIGHT?
YOU LEFT ME HANGIN'.
SUCH A BUMMER.
I'M NOT IN THE NEW FRIEND BUSINESS, SAM.
ALRIGHT. KILLER.
NICE MEETIN' YA, FUCKIN' DICKHEAD...
NO CHANCE I'LL SLEEP.
LIN PUT ME IN WILLIE'S OLD DORM ROOM.
HE KNOWS WHY WE CAME BACK.

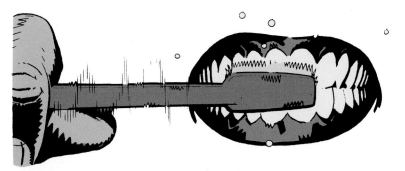

EVERYTHING IS **WRONG.**
OFF-BALANCE.

CAN YOU FEEL IT?

I **SHOULDN'T** BE HERE.
I SHOULDN'T BE ALIVE.

ENDED UP IN A STRANGE
ALTERNATE DIMENSION
WHERE EVERYTHING IS
ON THE WRONG AXIS.

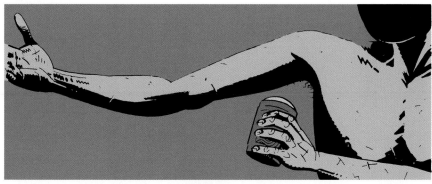

THE AIR RADIATES
REJECTION.

THE SMELL OF THIS PLACE...
WET EARTH, MOLD, SAGE...
FORCED MEMORY FLASHES:

THE LAST NIGHT I SLEPT HERE.

HIGH ON METH.

STRESSED MUSCLES TENSE
UP INVOLUNTARILY.

FWO WAS GOING AFTER
WILLIE BECAUSE OF WHAT
I TOLD THEM.

SAYA WAS GOING TO **KILL**
ME FOR BETRAYING HIM.

I WAS GOING TO
KILL **VIKTOR...**

...MASTER ZANE GOT
IN THE CROSSFIRE.

THE ONE DEATH I NEVER
HAD TIME TO ABSORB.

DID THAT LIGHT THE FUSE?

EARN ME THE REST?

AFTER ZANE DIED, ONE
BY ONE, I LOST THE
PEOPLE I LOVED.

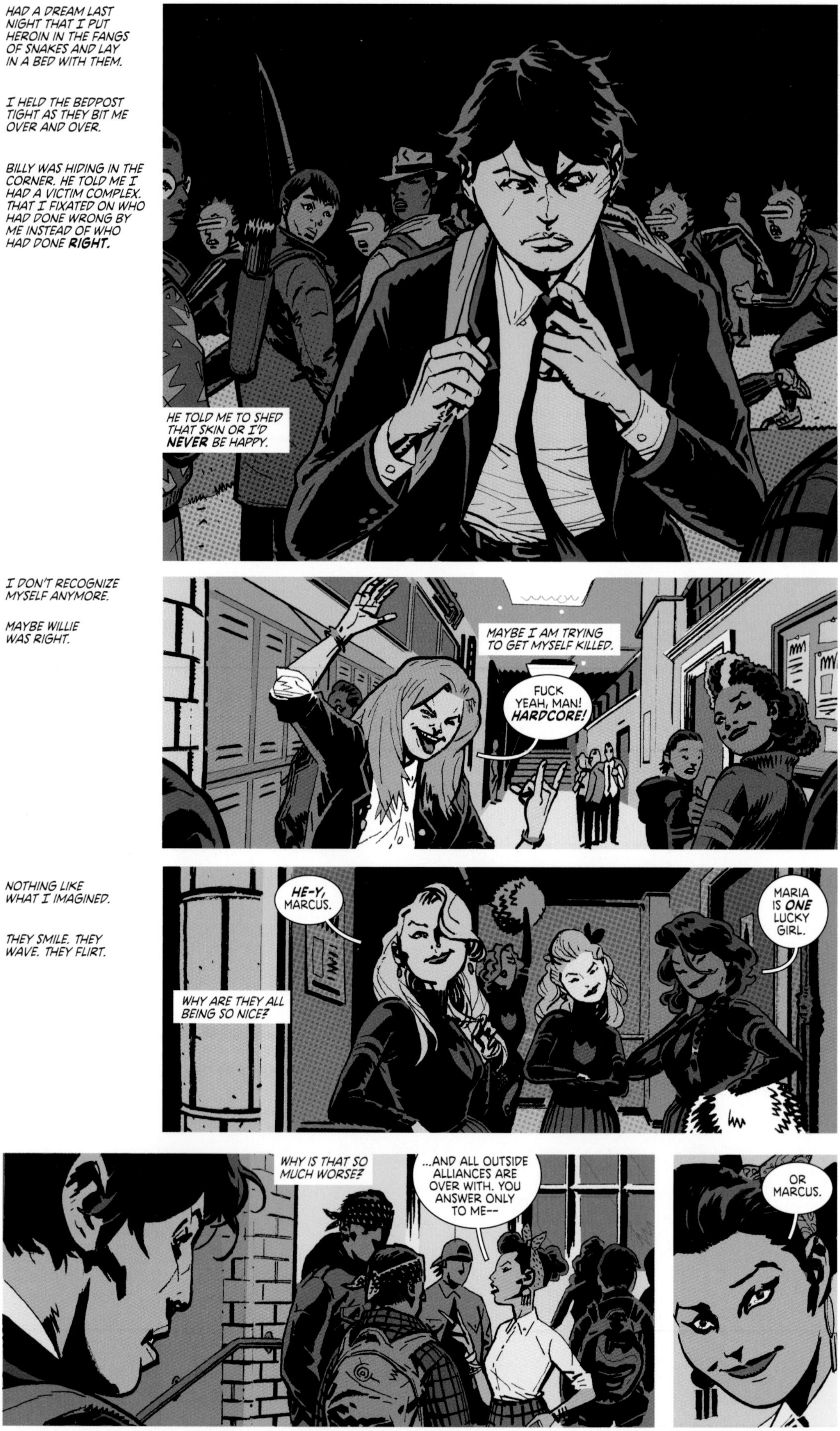
HAD A DREAM LAST NIGHT THAT I PUT HEROIN IN THE FANGS OF SNAKES AND LAY IN A BED WITH THEM.
I HELD THE BEDPOST TIGHT AS THEY BIT ME OVER AND OVER.
BILLY WAS HIDING IN THE CORNER. HE TOLD ME I HAD A VICTIM COMPLEX. THAT I FIXATED ON WHO HAD DONE WRONG BY ME INSTEAD OF WHO HAD DONE **RIGHT.**
HE TOLD ME TO SHED THAT SKIN OR I'D **NEVER** BE HAPPY.
I DON'T RECOGNIZE MYSELF ANYMORE.
MAYBE WILLIE WAS RIGHT.
MAYBE I AM TRYING TO GET MYSELF KILLED.
FUCK YEAH, MAN! **HARDCORE!**
NOTHING LIKE WHAT I IMAGINED.
THEY SMILE. THEY WAVE. THEY FLIRT.
HE-Y, MARCUS.
WHY ARE THEY ALL BEING SO NICE?
MARIA IS **ONE** LUCKY GIRL.
WHY IS THAT SO MUCH WORSE?
...AND ALL OUTSIDE ALLIANCES ARE OVER WITH. YOU ANSWER ONLY TO ME--
OR MARCUS.

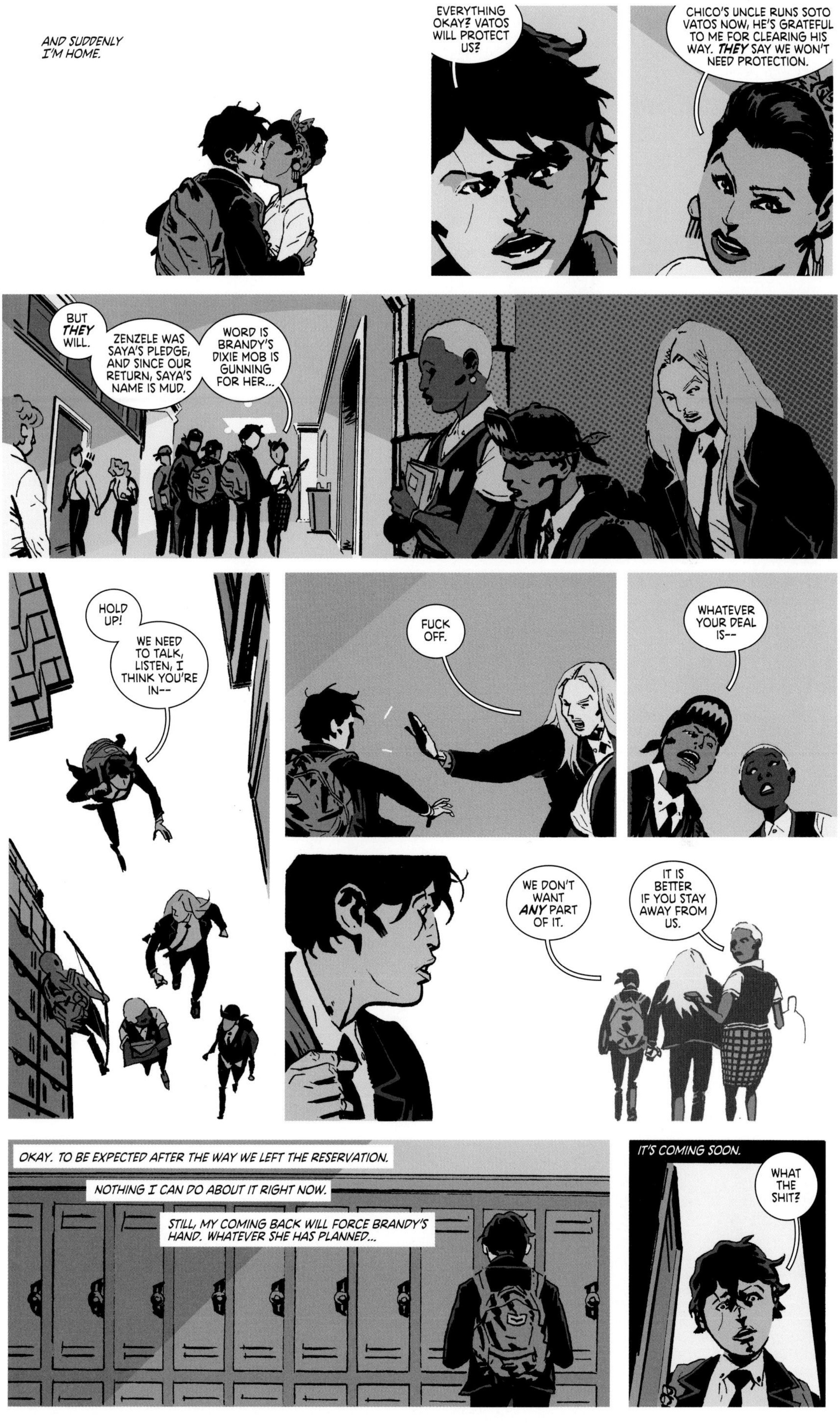
AND SUDDENLY I'M HOME.
EVERYTHING OKAY? VATOS WILL PROTECT US?
CHICO'S UNCLE RUNS SOTO VATOS NOW, HE'S GRATEFUL TO ME FOR CLEARING HIS WAY. THEY SAY WE WON'T NEED PROTECTION.
BUT THEY WILL.
ZENZELE WAS SAYA'S PLEDGE, AND SINCE OUR RETURN, SAYA'S NAME IS MUD.
WORD IS BRANDY'S DIXIE MOB IS GUNNING FOR HER...
HOLD UP!
WE NEED TO TALK, LISTEN, I THINK YOU'RE IN--
FUCK OFF.
WHATEVER YOUR DEAL IS--
WE DON'T WANT ANY PART OF IT.
IT IS BETTER IF YOU STAY AWAY FROM US.
OKAY. TO BE EXPECTED AFTER THE WAY WE LEFT THE RESERVATION.
NOTHING I CAN DO ABOUT IT RIGHT NOW.
STILL, MY COMING BACK WILL FORCE BRANDY'S HAND. WHATEVER SHE HAS PLANNED...
IT'S COMING SOON.
WHAT THE SHIT?

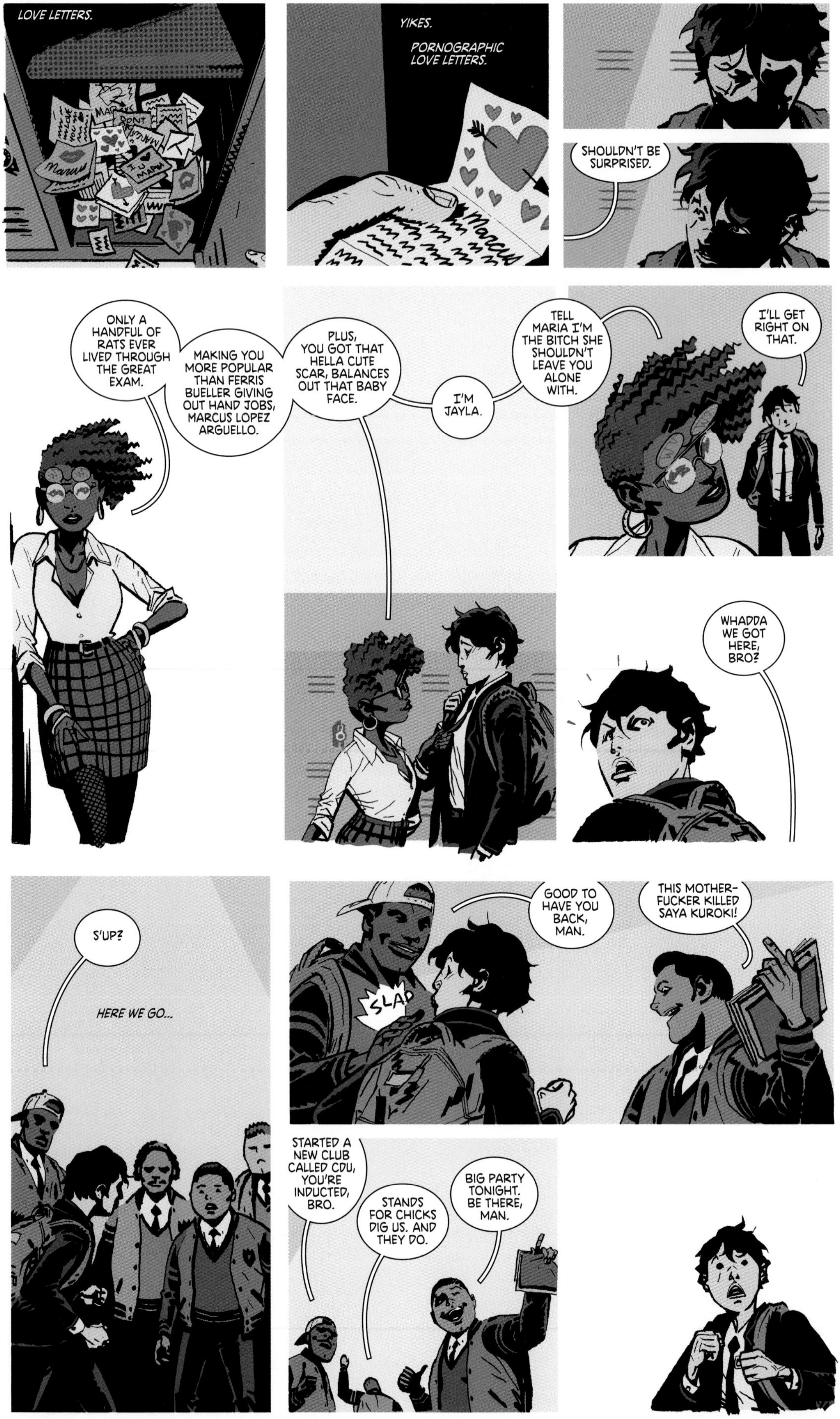
LOVE LETTERS.
YIKES.
PORNOGRAPHIC LOVE LETTERS.
SHOULDN'T BE SURPRISED.
ONLY A HANDFUL OF RATS EVER LIVED THROUGH THE GREAT EXAM.
MAKING YOU MORE POPULAR THAN FERRIS BUELLER GIVING OUT HAND JOBS, MARCUS LOPEZ ARGUELLO.
PLUS, YOU GOT THAT HELLA CUTE SCAR, BALANCES OUT THAT BABY FACE.
I'M JAYLA.
TELL MARIA I'M THE BITCH SHE SHOULDN'T LEAVE YOU ALONE WITH.
I'LL GET RIGHT ON THAT.
WHADDA WE GOT HERE, BRO?
S'UP?
HERE WE GO...
GOOD TO HAVE YOU BACK, MAN.
SLAP
THIS MOTHER-FUCKER KILLED SAYA KUROKI!
STARTED A NEW CLUB CALLED CDU, YOU'RE INDUCTED, BRO.
STANDS FOR CHICKS DIG US. AND THEY DO.
BIG PARTY TONIGHT. BE THERE, MAN.

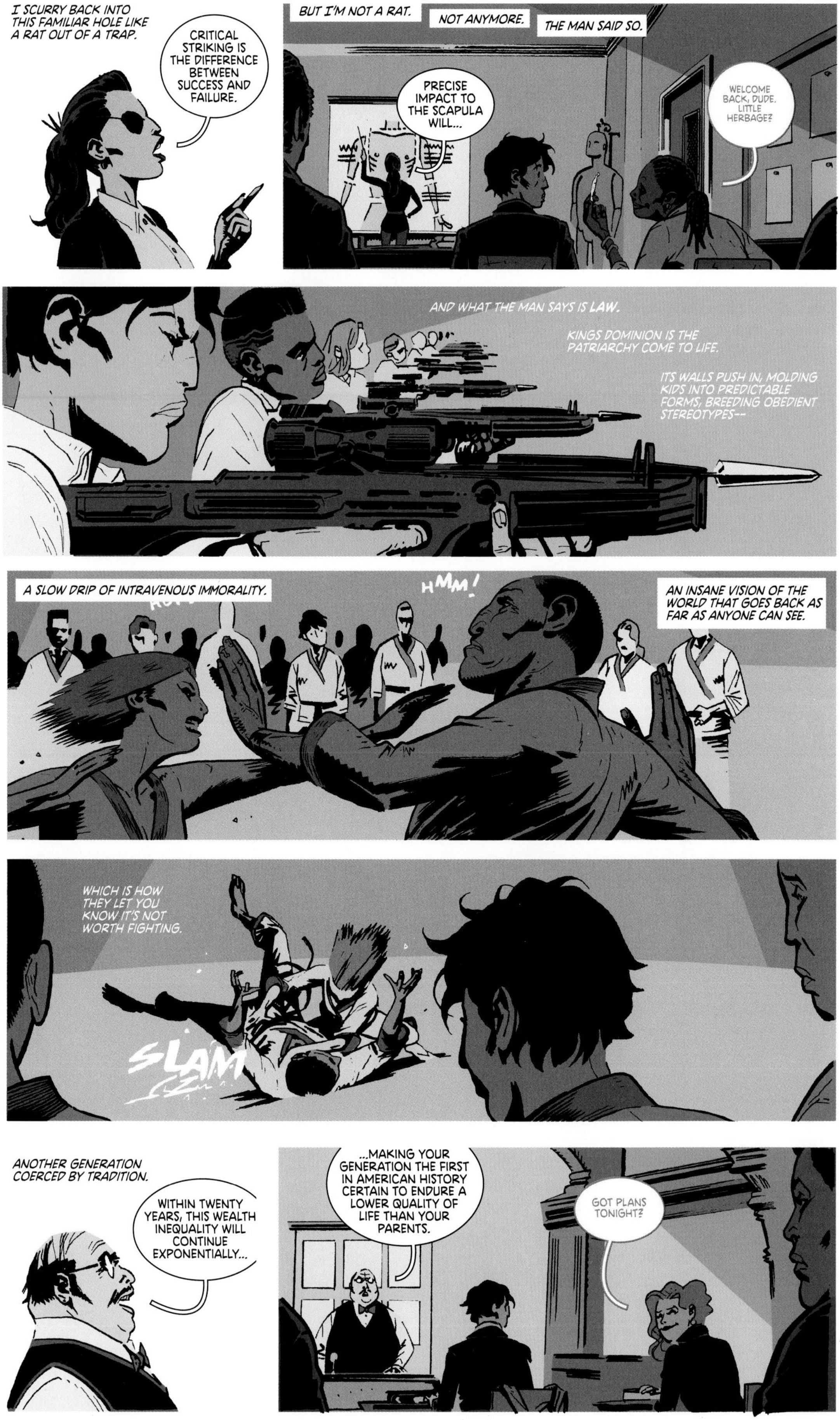
I SCURRY BACK INTO THIS FAMILIAR HOLE LIKE A RAT OUT OF A TRAP.
CRITICAL STRIKING IS THE DIFFERENCE BETWEEN SUCCESS AND FAILURE.
BUT I'M NOT A RAT.
NOT ANYMORE.
THE MAN SAID SO.
PRECISE IMPACT TO THE SCAPULA WILL...
WELCOME BACK, DUDE. LITTLE HERBAGE?
AND WHAT THE MAN SAYS IS LAW.
KINGS DOMINION IS THE PATRIARCHY COME TO LIFE.
ITS WALLS PUSH IN, MOLDING KIDS INTO PREDICTABLE FORMS, BREEDING OBEDIENT STEREOTYPES--
A SLOW DRIP OF INTRAVENOUS IMMORALITY.
HMM!
AN INSANE VISION OF THE WORLD THAT GOES BACK AS FAR AS ANYONE CAN SEE.
WHICH IS HOW THEY LET YOU KNOW IT'S NOT WORTH FIGHTING.
SLAM
ANOTHER GENERATION COERCED BY TRADITION.
WITHIN TWENTY YEARS, THIS WEALTH INEQUALITY WILL CONTINUE EXPONENTIALLY...
...MAKING YOUR GENERATION THE FIRST IN AMERICAN HISTORY CERTAIN TO ENDURE A LOWER QUALITY OF LIFE THAN YOUR PARENTS.
GOT PLANS TONIGHT?

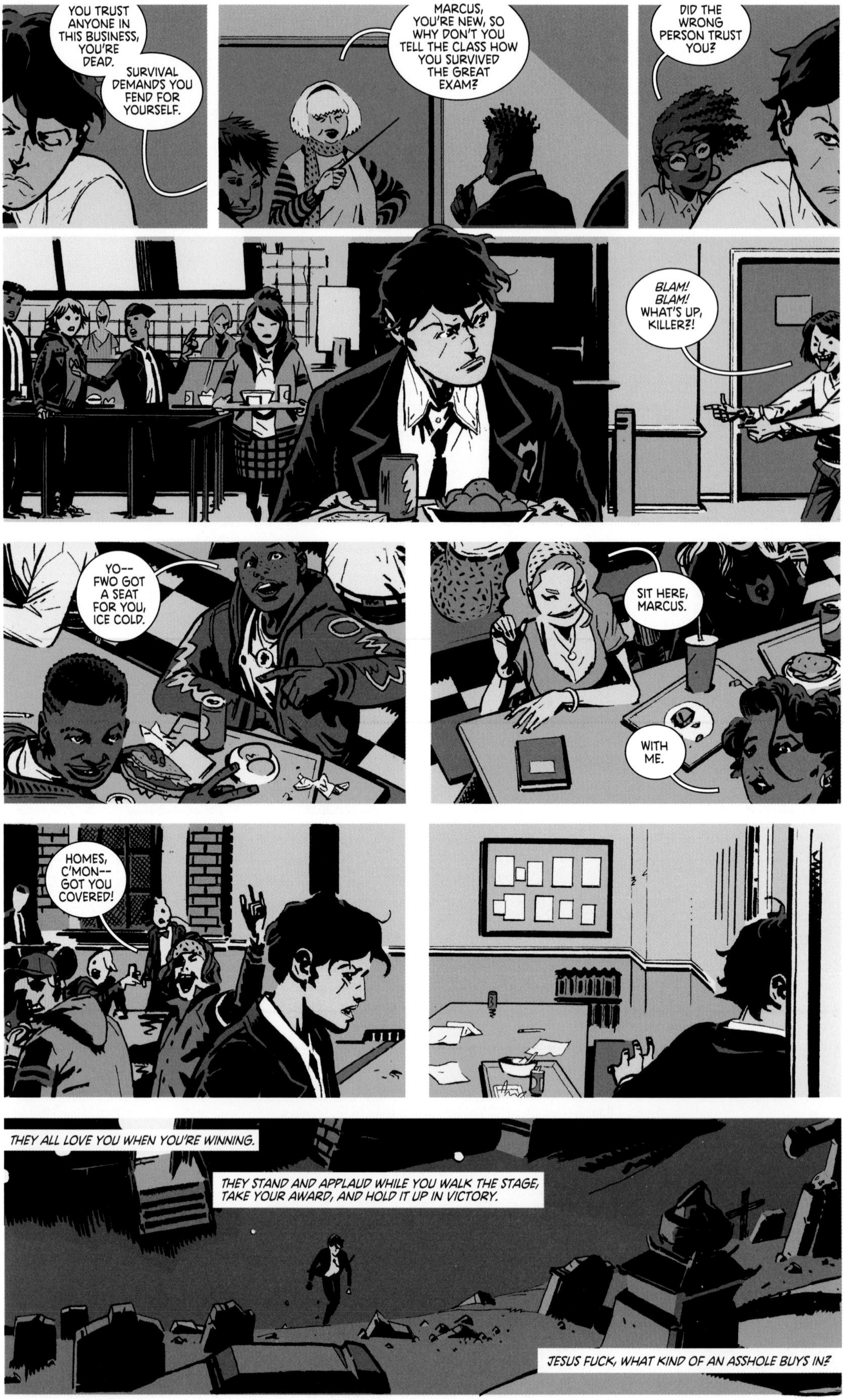
YOU TRUST ANYONE IN THIS BUSINESS, YOU'RE DEAD.
SURVIVAL DEMANDS YOU FEND FOR YOURSELF.
MARCUS, YOU'RE NEW, SO WHY DON'T YOU TELL THE CLASS HOW YOU SURVIVED THE GREAT EXAM?
DID THE WRONG PERSON TRUST YOU?
BLAM! BLAM! WHAT'S UP, KILLER?!
YO-- FWO GOT A SEAT FOR YOU, ICE COLD.
SIT HERE, MARCUS.
WITH ME.
HOMES, C'MON-- GOT YOU COVERED!
THEY ALL LOVE YOU WHEN YOU'RE WINNING.
THEY STAND AND APPLAUD WHILE YOU WALK THE STAGE, TAKE YOUR AWARD, AND HOLD IT UP IN VICTORY.
JESUS FUCK, WHAT KIND OF AN ASSHOLE BUYS IN?

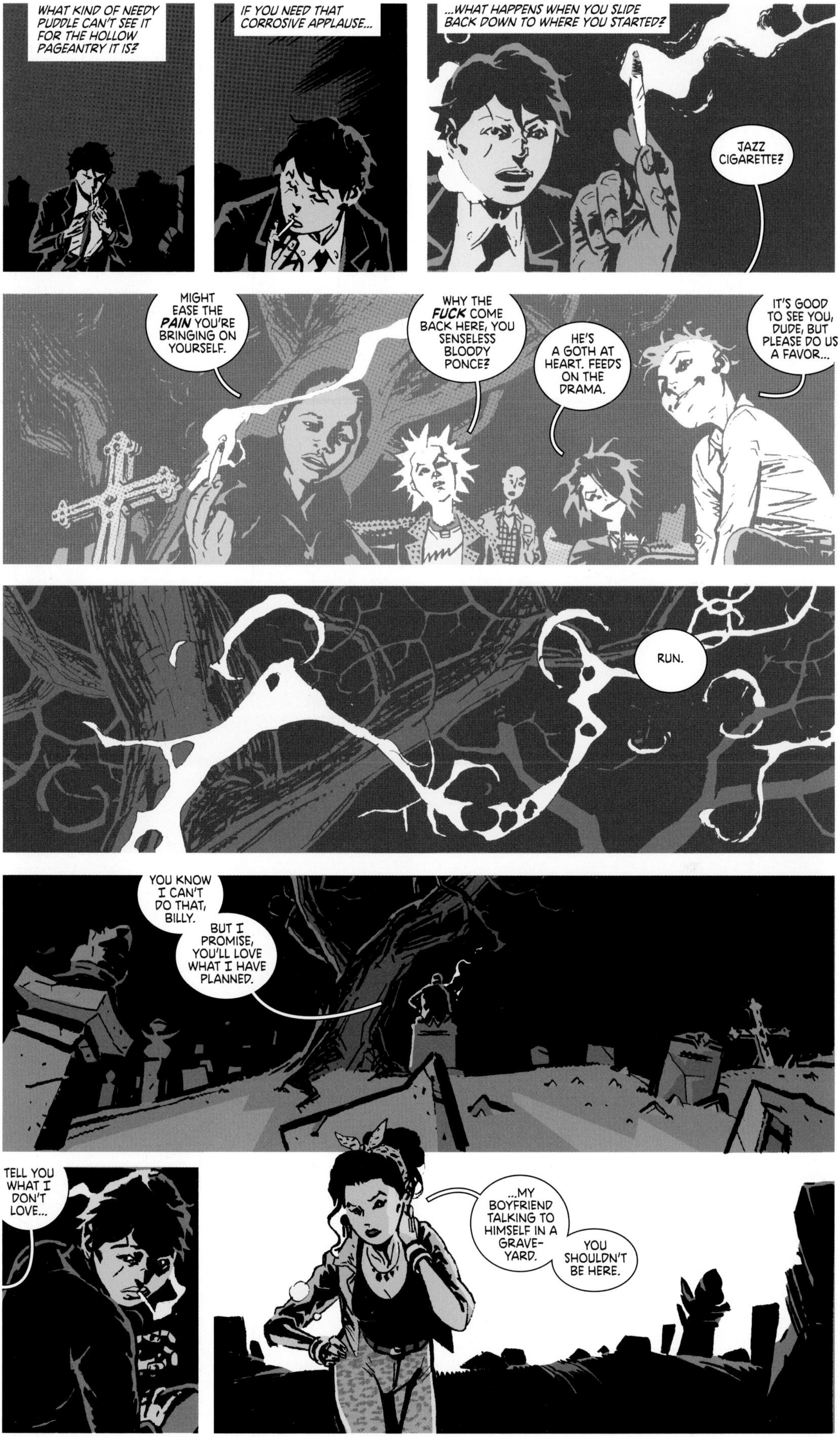
WHAT KIND OF NEEDY PUDDLE CAN'T SEE IT FOR THE HOLLOW PAGEANTRY IT IS?
IF YOU NEED THAT CORROSIVE APPLAUSE...
...WHAT HAPPENS WHEN YOU SLIDE BACK DOWN TO WHERE YOU STARTED?
JAZZ CIGARETTE?
MIGHT EASE THE PAIN YOU'RE BRINGING ON YOURSELF.
WHY THE FUCK COME BACK HERE, YOU SENSELESS BLOODY PONCE?
HE'S A GOTH AT HEART. FEEDS ON THE DRAMA.
IT'S GOOD TO SEE YOU, DUDE, BUT PLEASE DO US A FAVOR...
RUN.
YOU KNOW I CAN'T DO THAT, BILLY.
BUT I PROMISE, YOU'LL LOVE WHAT I HAVE PLANNED.
TELL YOU WHAT I DON'T LOVE...
...MY BOYFRIEND TALKING TO HIMSELF IN A GRAVE-YARD.
YOU SHOULDN'T BE HERE.

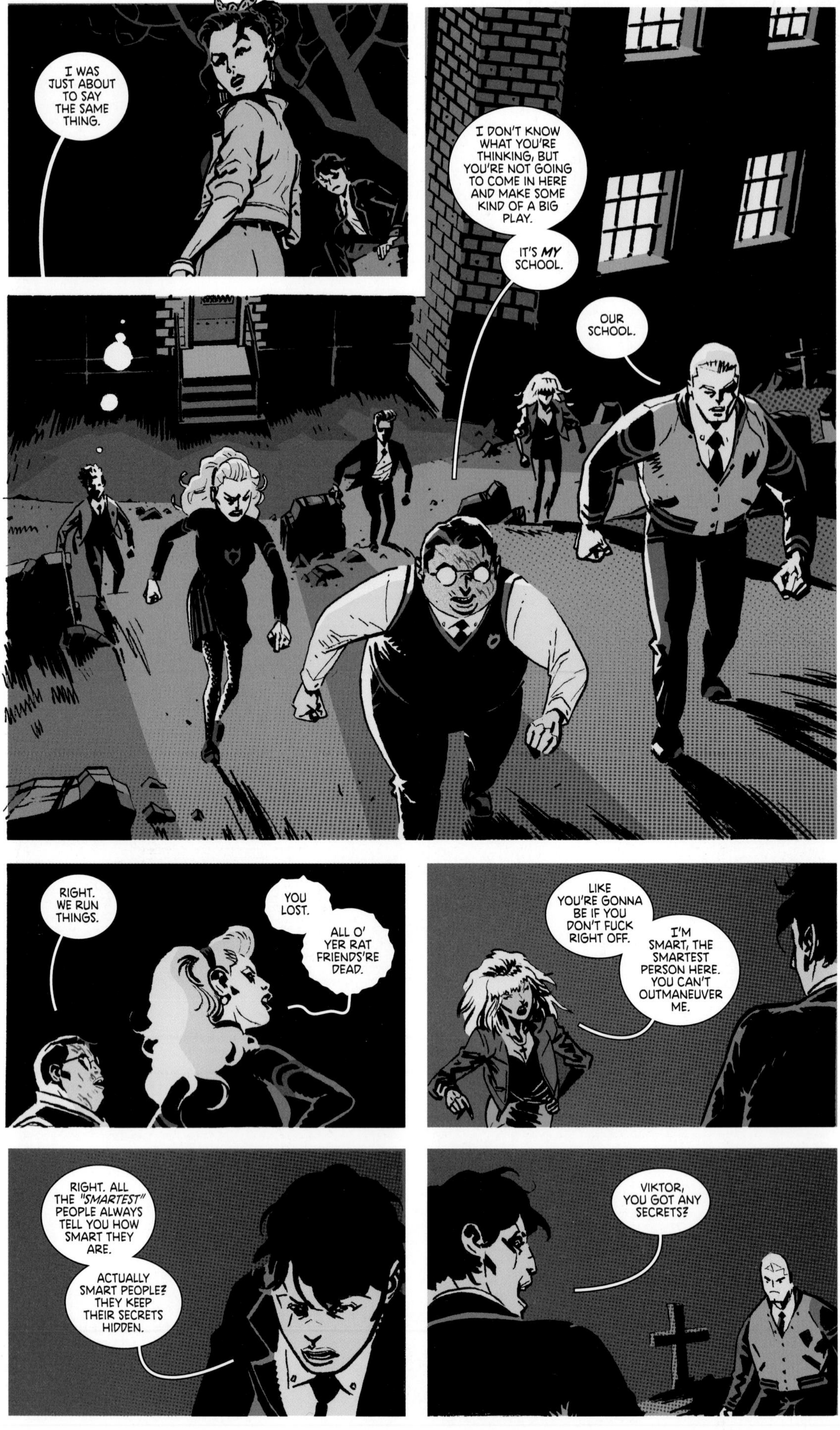

I WAS JUST ABOUT TO SAY THE SAME THING.
I DON'T KNOW WHAT YOU'RE THINKING, BUT YOU'RE NOT GOING TO COME IN HERE AND MAKE SOME KIND OF A BIG PLAY.
IT'S *MY* SCHOOL.
OUR SCHOOL.
RIGHT. WE RUN THINGS.
YOU LOST.
ALL O' YER RAT FRIENDS'RE DEAD.
LIKE YOU'RE GONNA BE IF YOU DON'T FUCK RIGHT OFF.
I'M SMART, THE SMARTEST PERSON HERE. YOU CAN'T OUTMANEUVER ME.
RIGHT. ALL THE *"SMARTEST"* PEOPLE ALWAYS TELL YOU HOW SMART THEY ARE.
ACTUALLY SMART PEOPLE? THEY KEEP THEIR SECRETS HIDDEN.
VIKTOR, YOU GOT ANY SECRETS?

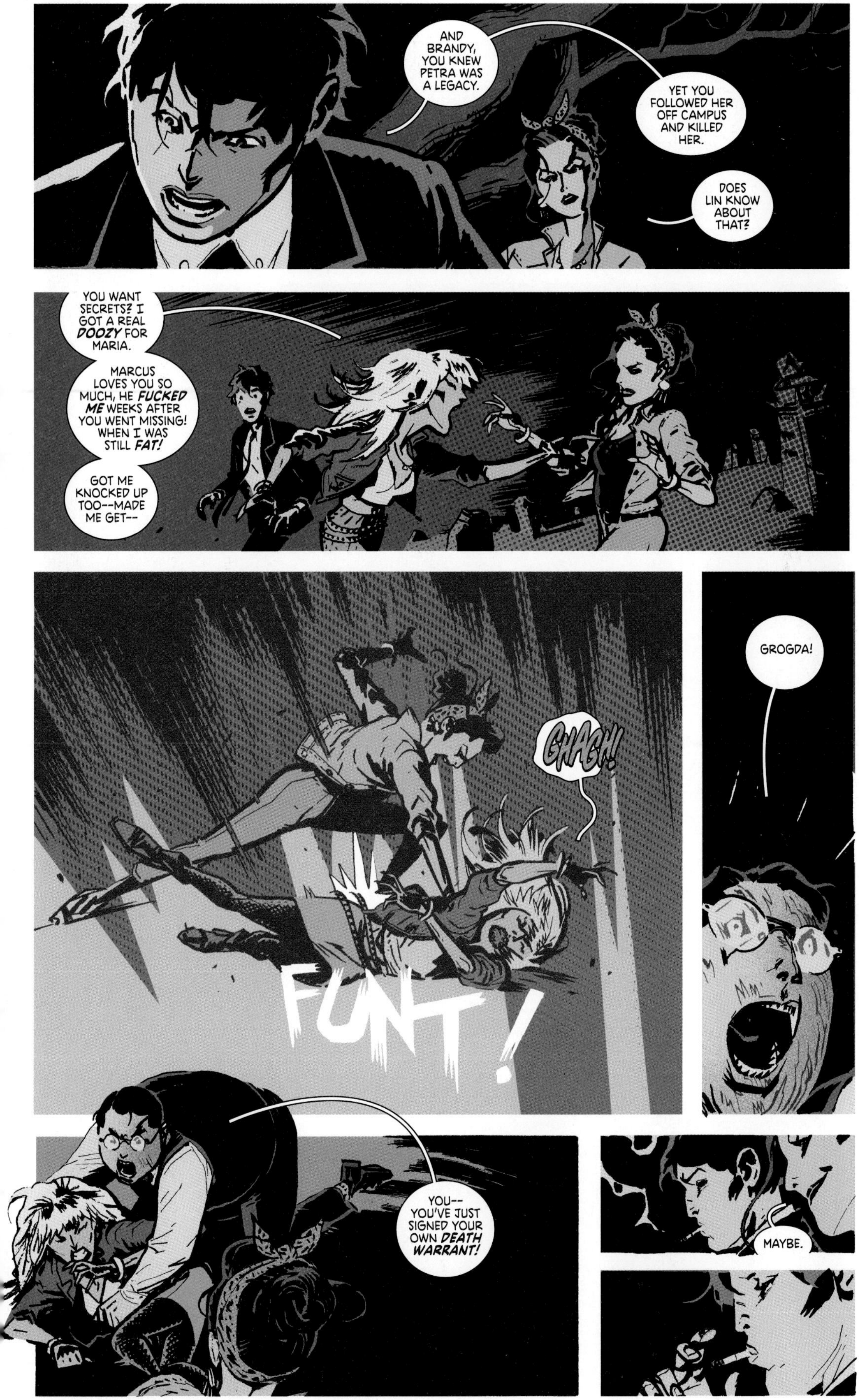
AND BRANDY, YOU KNEW PETRA WAS A LEGACY.
YET YOU FOLLOWED HER OFF CAMPUS AND KILLED HER.
DOES LIN KNOW ABOUT THAT?
YOU WANT SECRETS? I GOT A REAL DOOZY FOR MARIA.
MARCUS LOVES YOU SO MUCH, HE FUCKED ME WEEKS AFTER YOU WENT MISSING! WHEN I WAS STILL FAT!
GOT ME KNOCKED UP TOO--MADE ME GET--
GHACH!
FUNT!
GROGDA!
YOU-- YOU'VE JUST SIGNED YOUR OWN DEATH WARRANT!
MAYBE.

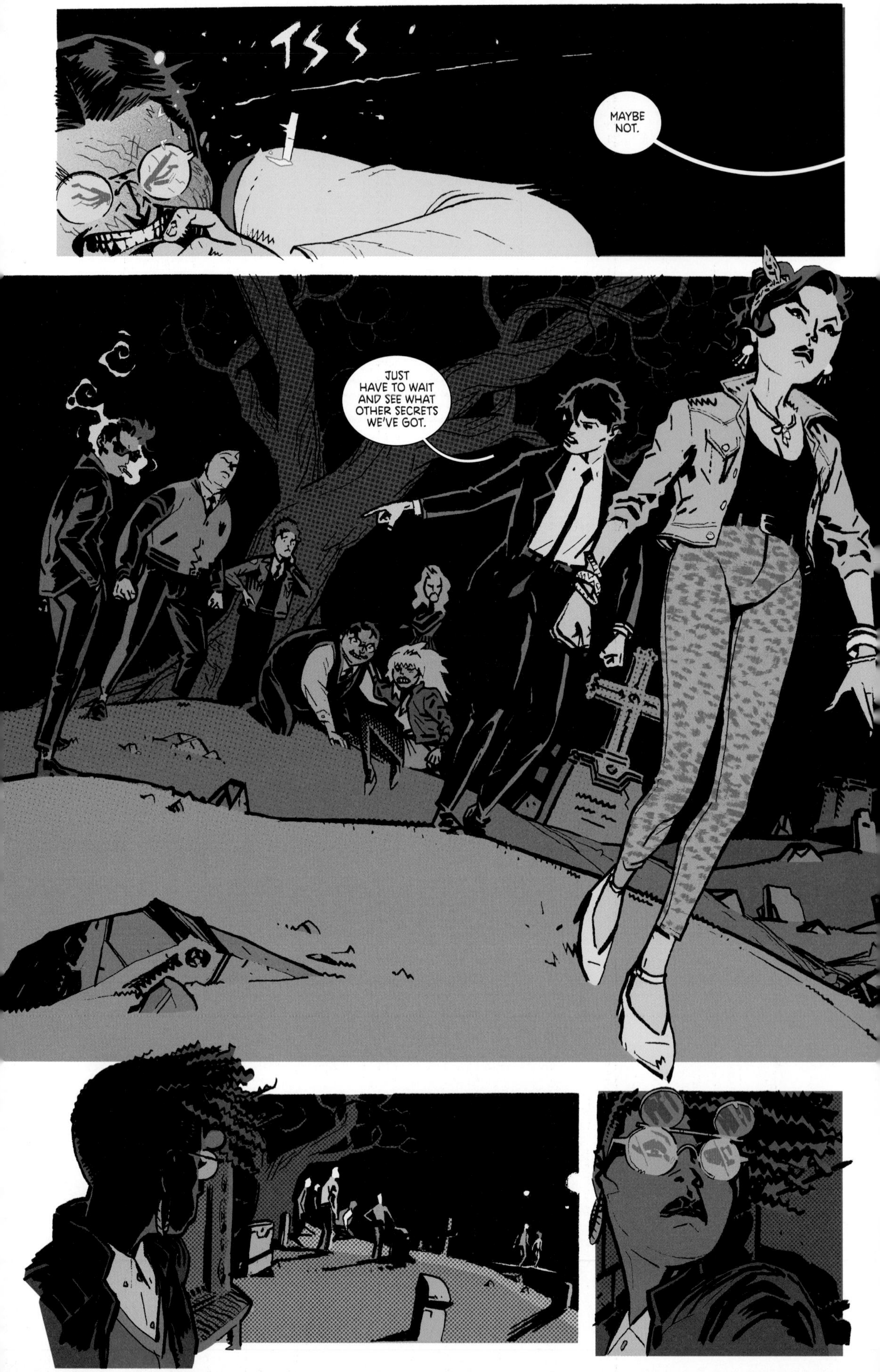
TSS
MAYBE NOT.
JUST HAVE TO WAIT AND SEE WHAT OTHER SECRETS WE'VE GOT.

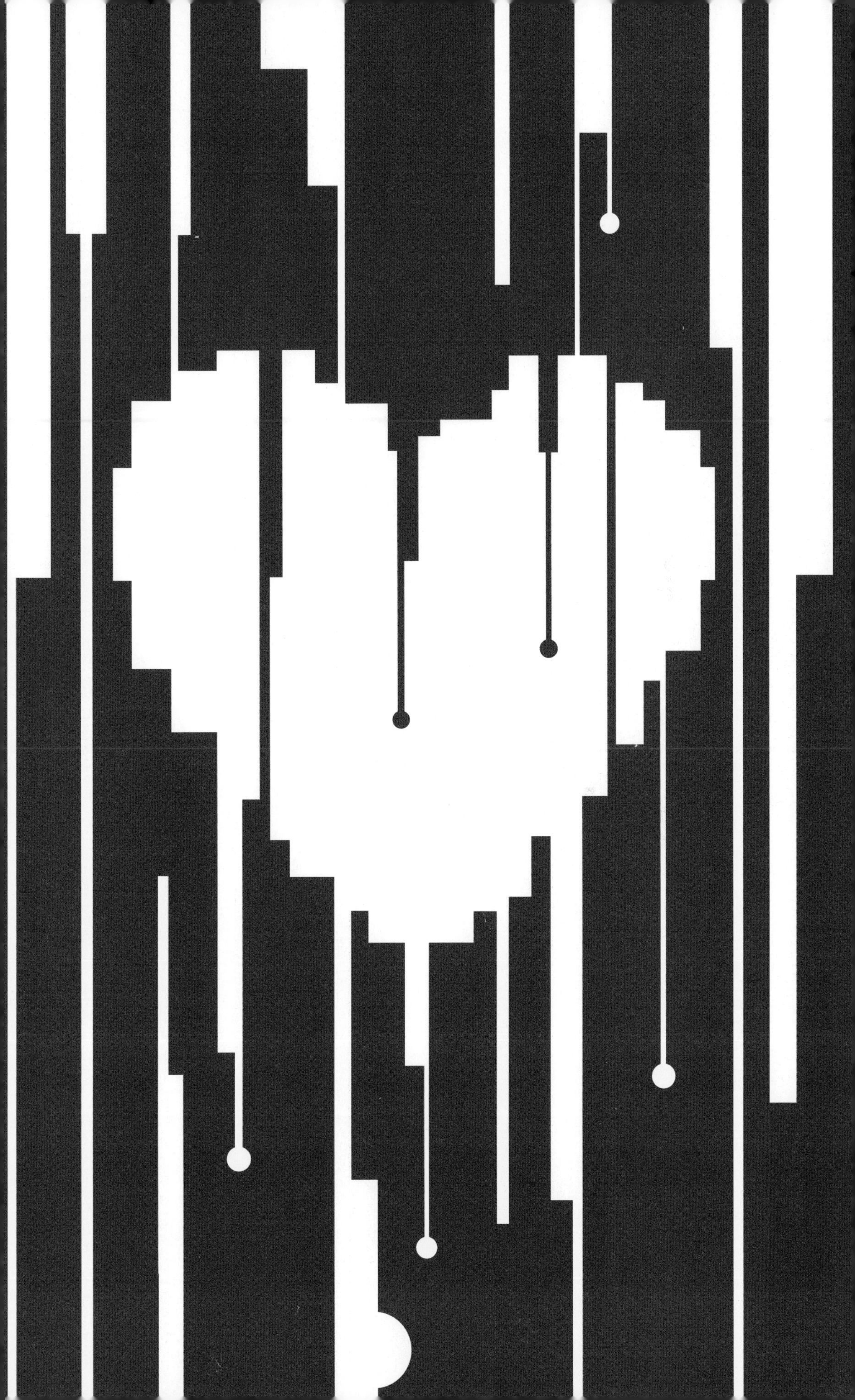

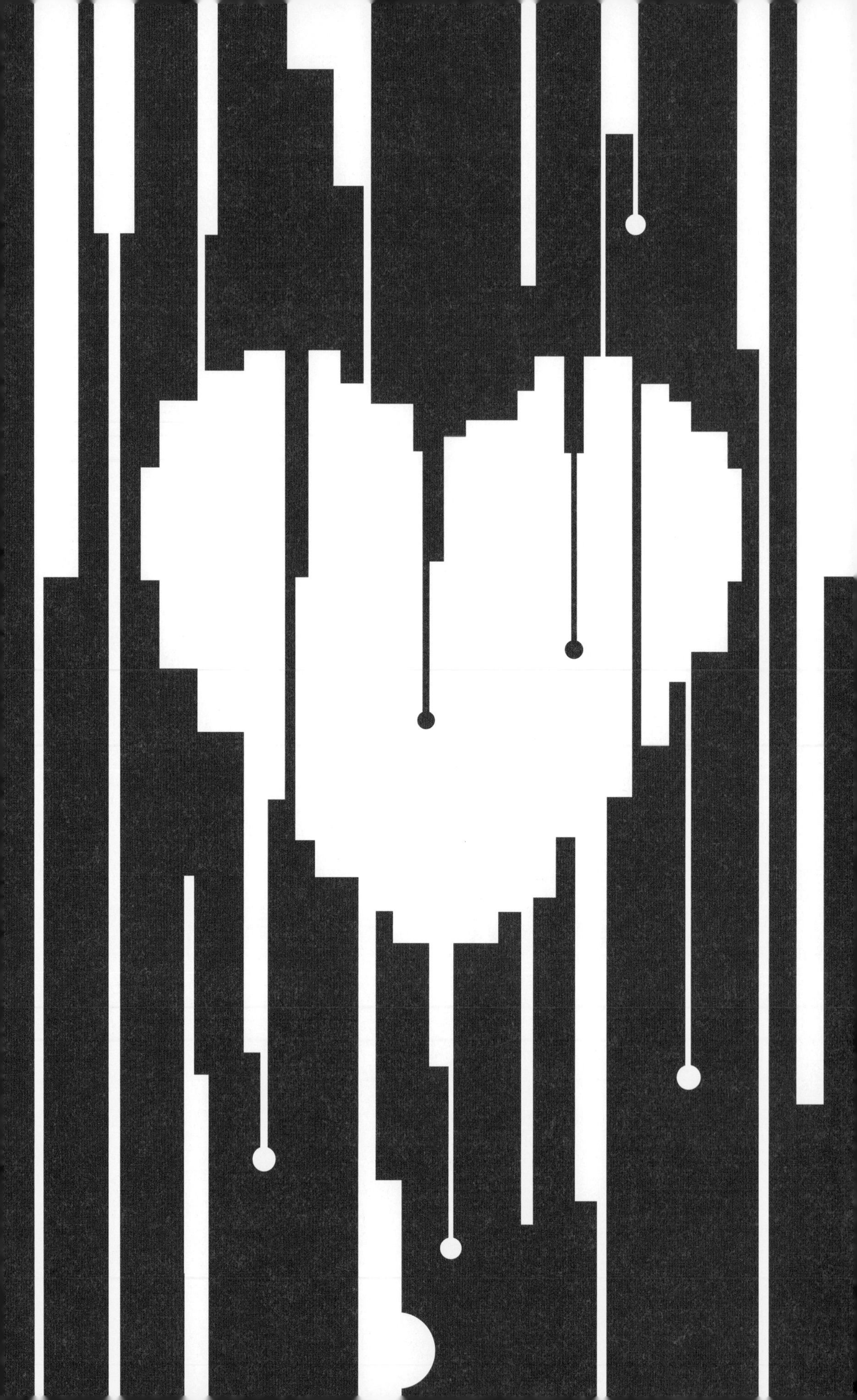

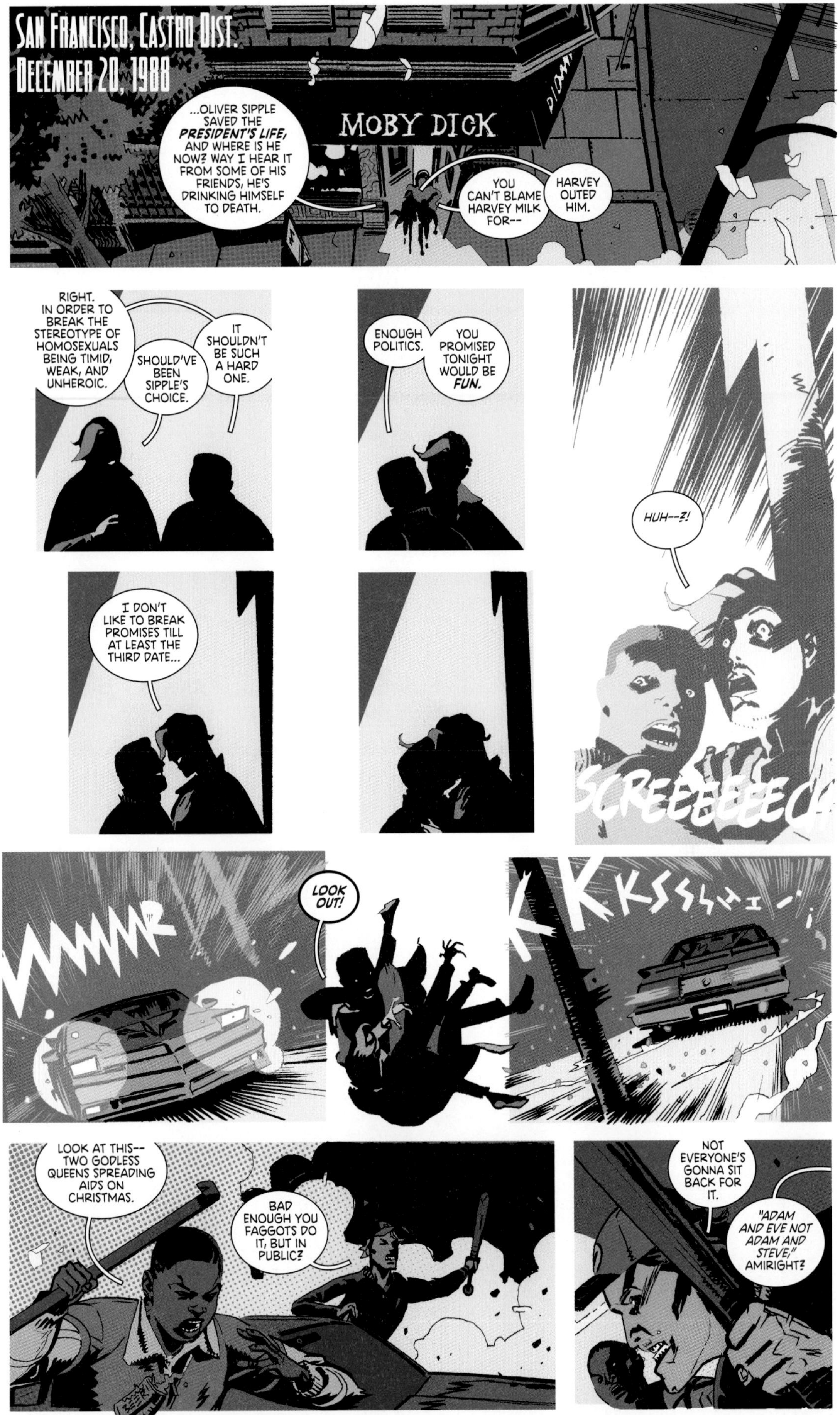
San Francisco, Castro Dist.
December 20, 1988
MOBY DICK
...OLIVER SIPPLE SAVED THE PRESIDENT'S LIFE, AND WHERE IS HE NOW? WAY I HEAR IT FROM SOME OF HIS FRIENDS, HE'S DRINKING HIMSELF TO DEATH.
YOU CAN'T BLAME HARVEY MILK FOR--
HARVEY OUTED HIM.
RIGHT. IN ORDER TO BREAK THE STEREOTYPE OF HOMOSEXUALS BEING TIMID, WEAK, AND UNHEROIC.
SHOULD'VE BEEN SIPPLE'S CHOICE.
IT SHOULDN'T BE SUCH A HARD ONE.
ENOUGH POLITICS.
YOU PROMISED TONIGHT WOULD BE FUN.
I DON'T LIKE TO BREAK PROMISES TILL AT LEAST THE THIRD DATE...
HUH--?!
LOOK OUT!
LOOK AT THIS--TWO GODLESS QUEENS SPREADING AIDS ON CHRISTMAS.
BAD ENOUGH YOU FAGGOTS DO IT, BUT IN PUBLIC?
NOT EVERYONE'S GONNA SIT BACK FOR IT.
"ADAM AND EVE NOT ADAM AND STEVE," AMIRIGHT?

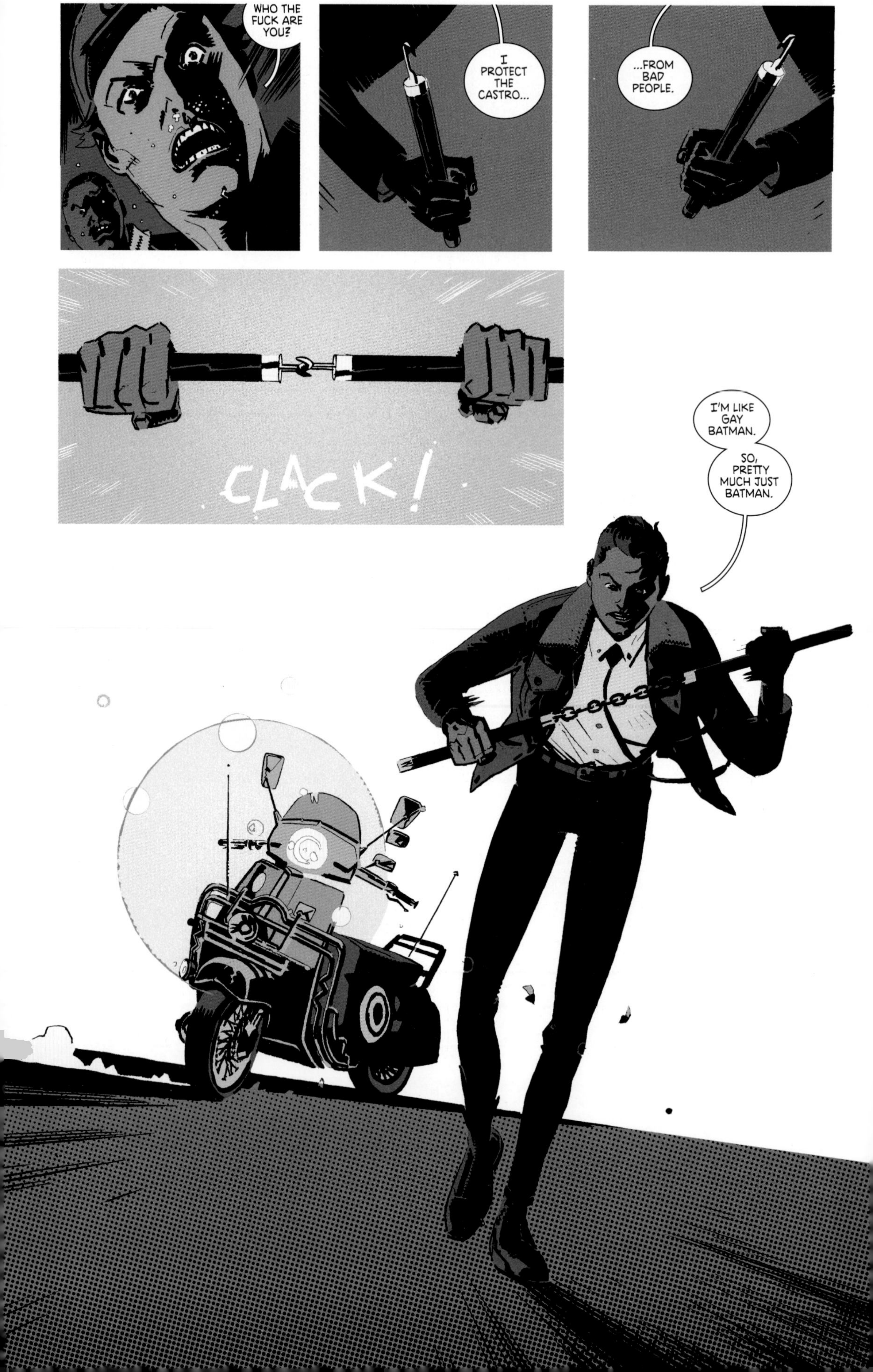
WHO THE FUCK ARE YOU?
I PROTECT THE CASTRO...
...FROM BAD PEOPLE.
CLACK!
I'M LIKE GAY BATMAN.
SO, PRETTY MUCH JUST BATMAN.

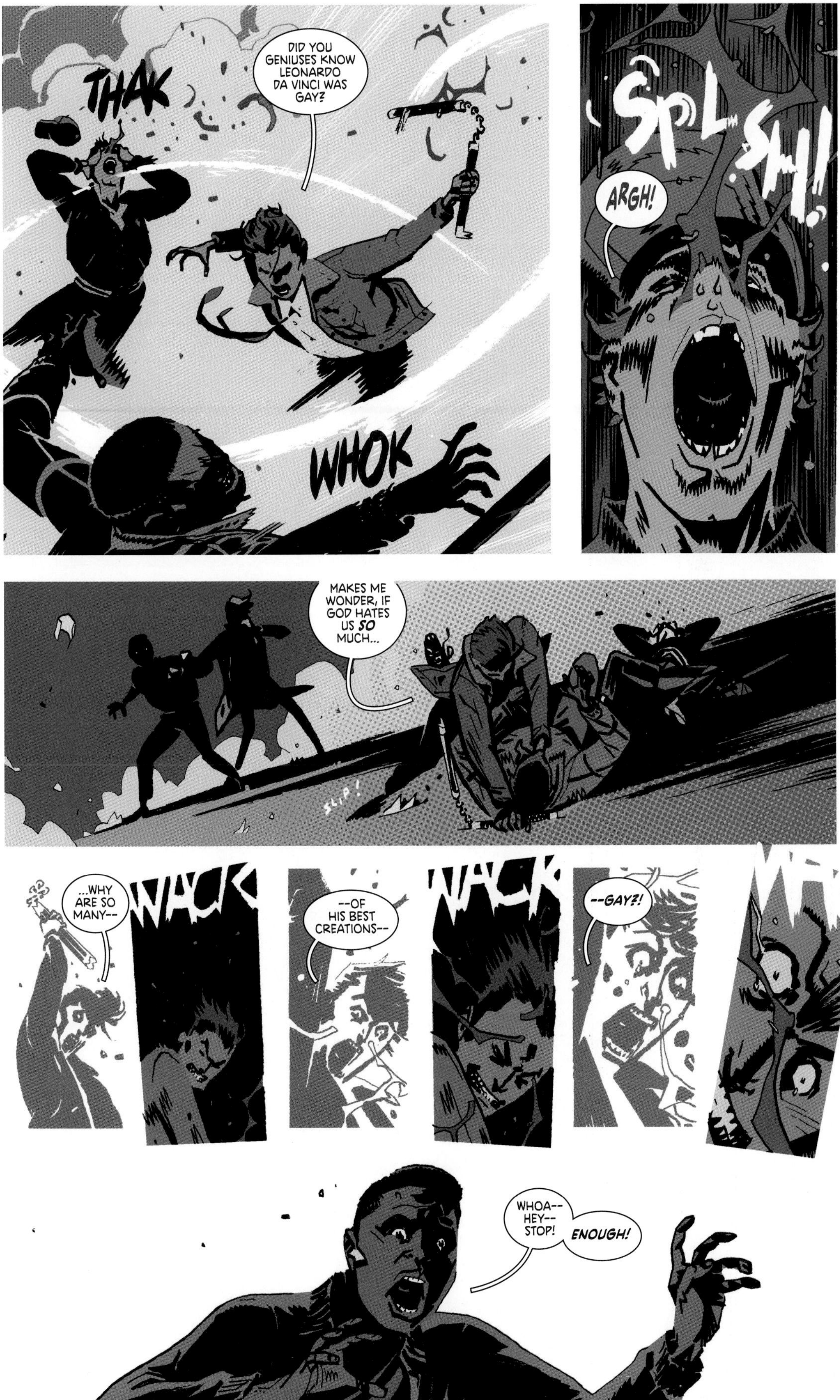

THAK
DID YOU GENIUSES KNOW LEONARDO DA VINCI WAS GAY?
WHOK
SPLSH!
ARGH!
MAKES ME WONDER, IF GOD HATES US *SO* MUCH...
SLIP!
...WHY ARE SO MANY--
WACK
--OF HIS BEST CREATIONS--
WACK
--GAY?!
WHOA-- HEY-- STOP!
ENOUGH!

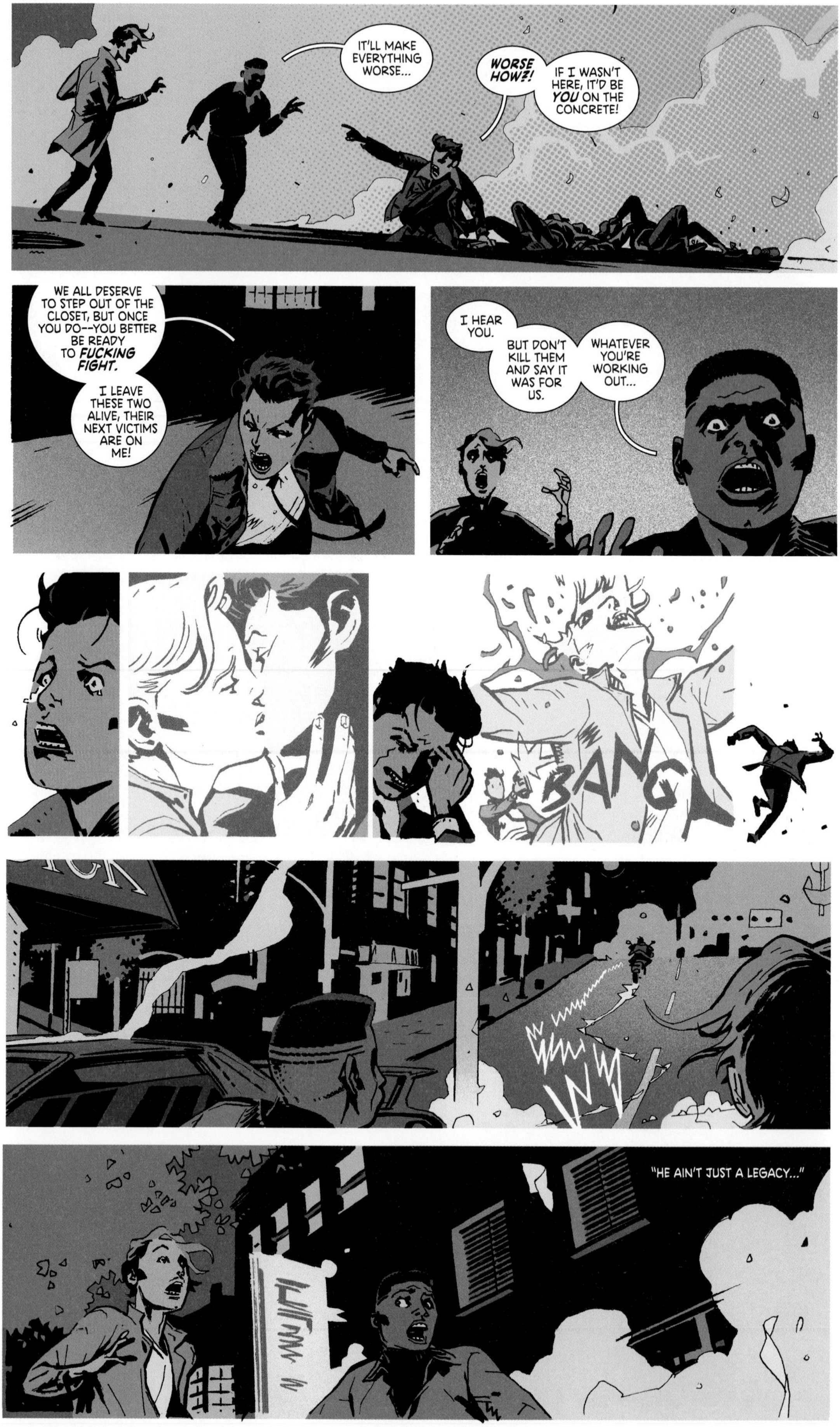

IT'LL MAKE EVERYTHING WORSE...
WORSE HOW?!
IF I WASN'T HERE, IT'D BE YOU ON THE CONCRETE!
WE ALL DESERVE TO STEP OUT OF THE CLOSET, BUT ONCE YOU DO--YOU BETTER BE READY TO FUCKING FIGHT.
I LEAVE THESE TWO ALIVE, THEIR NEXT VICTIMS ARE ON ME!
I HEAR YOU.
BUT DON'T KILL THEM AND SAY IT WAS FOR US.
WHATEVER YOU'RE WORKING OUT...
BANG
"HE AIN'T JUST A LEGACY..."

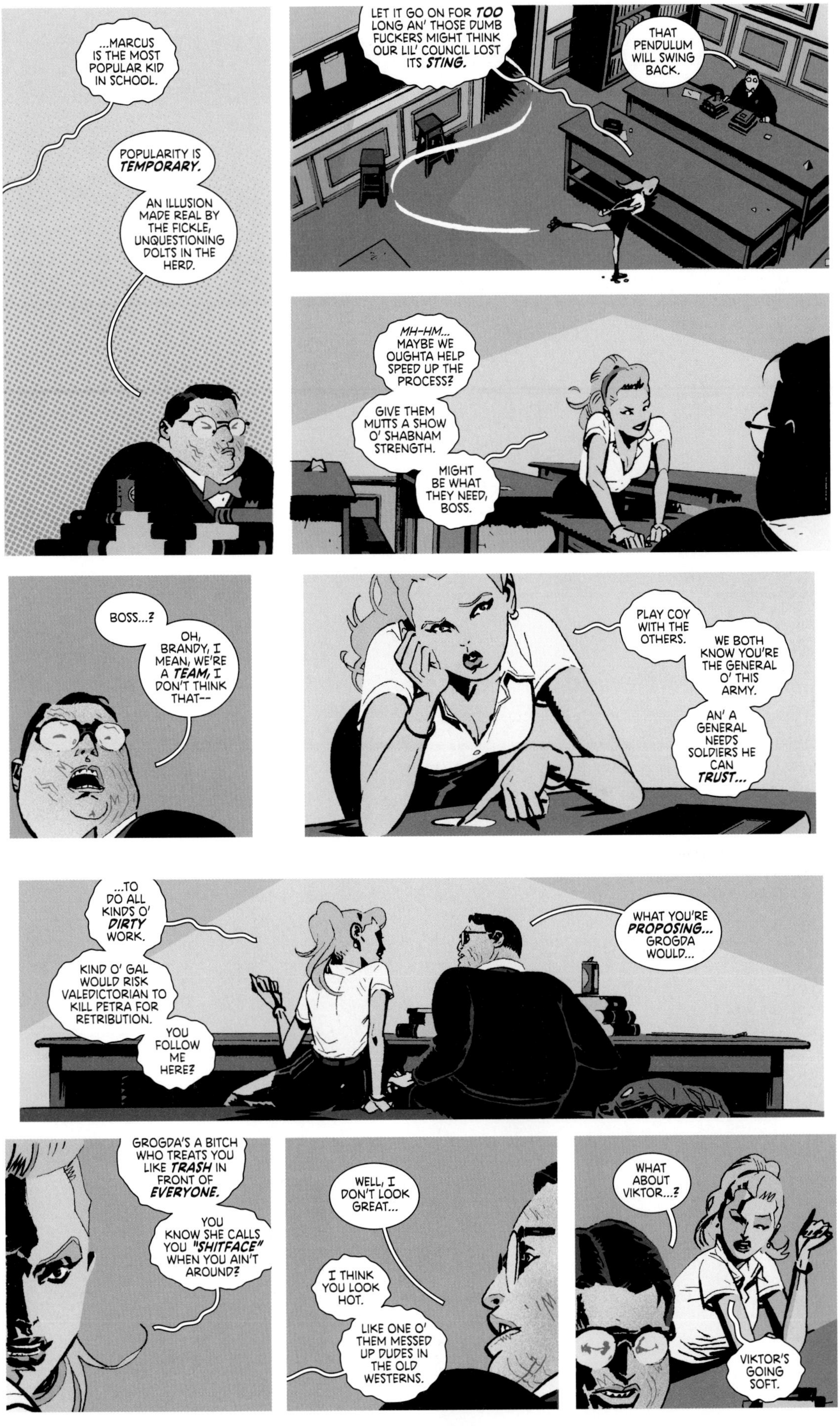
...MARCUS IS THE MOST POPULAR KID IN SCHOOL.
POPULARITY IS TEMPORARY.
AN ILLUSION MADE REAL BY THE FICKLE, UNQUESTIONING DOLTS IN THE HERD.
LET IT GO ON FOR TOO LONG AN' THOSE DUMB FUCKERS MIGHT THINK OUR LIL' COUNCIL LOST ITS STING.
THAT PENDULUM WILL SWING BACK.
MH-HM... MAYBE WE OUGHTA HELP SPEED UP THE PROCESS?
GIVE THEM MUTTS A SHOW O' SHABNAM STRENGTH.
MIGHT BE WHAT THEY NEED, BOSS.
BOSS...?
OH, BRANDY, I MEAN, WE'RE A TEAM, I DON'T THINK THAT--
PLAY COY WITH THE OTHERS.
WE BOTH KNOW YOU'RE THE GENERAL O' THIS ARMY.
AN' A GENERAL NEEDS SOLDIERS HE CAN TRUST...
...TO DO ALL KINDS O' DIRTY WORK.
KIND O' GAL WOULD RISK VALEDICTORIAN TO KILL PETRA FOR RETRIBUTION.
YOU FOLLOW ME HERE?
WHAT YOU'RE PROPOSING... GROGDA WOULD...
GROGDA'S A BITCH WHO TREATS YOU LIKE TRASH IN FRONT OF EVERYONE.
YOU KNOW SHE CALLS YOU "SHITFACE" WHEN YOU AIN'T AROUND?
WELL, I DON'T LOOK GREAT...
I THINK YOU LOOK HOT.
LIKE ONE O' THEM MESSED UP DUDES IN THE OLD WESTERNS.
WHAT ABOUT VIKTOR...?
VIKTOR'S GOING SOFT.

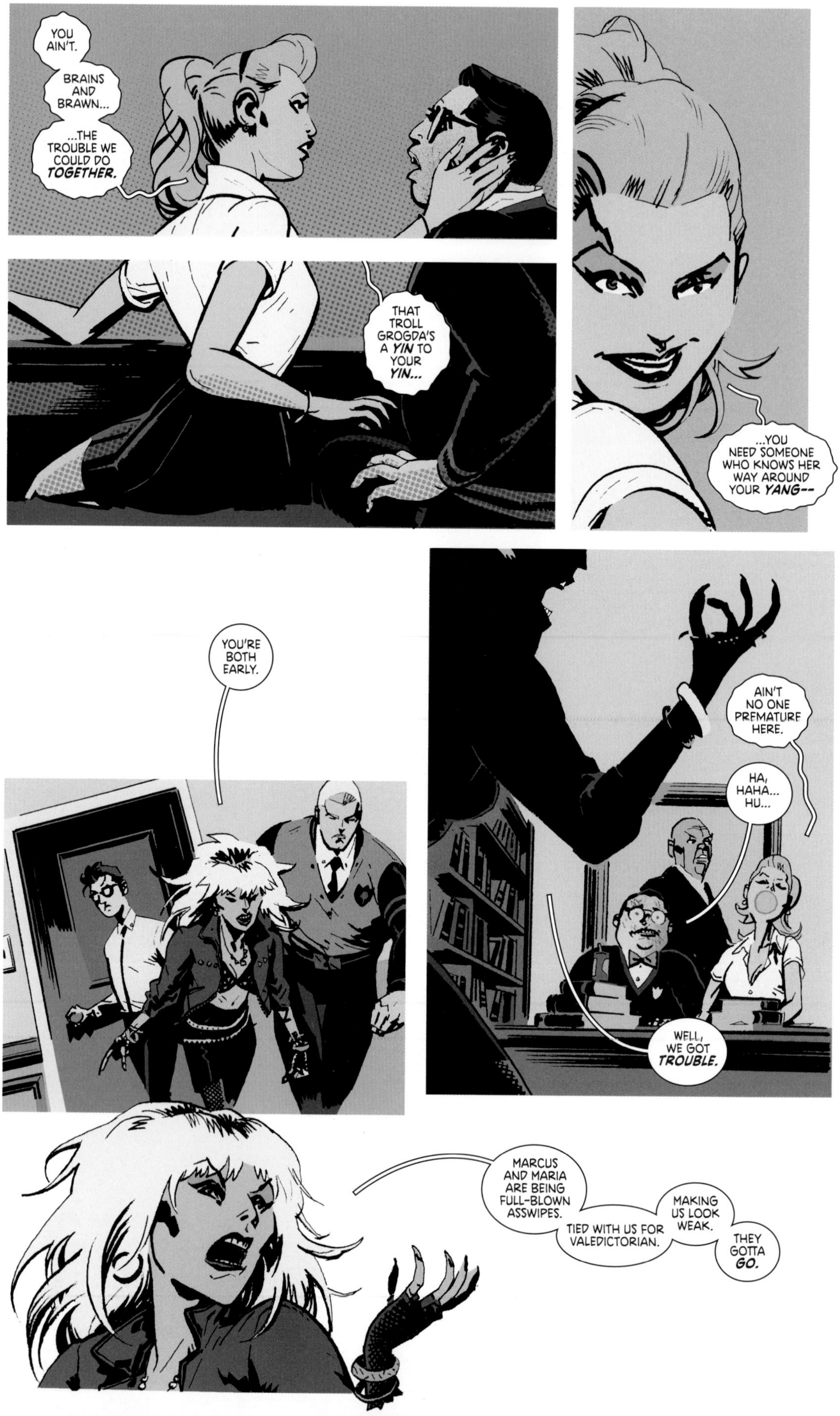

YOU AIN'T.
BRAINS AND BRAWN...
...THE TROUBLE WE COULD DO *TOGETHER.*
THAT TROLL GROGDA'S A *YIN* TO YOUR *YIN...*
...YOU NEED SOMEONE WHO KNOWS HER WAY AROUND YOUR *YANG--*
YOU'RE BOTH EARLY.
AIN'T NO ONE PREMATURE HERE.
HA, HAHA... HU...
WELL, WE GOT *TROUBLE.*
MARCUS AND MARIA ARE BEING FULL-BLOWN ASSWIPES.
TIED WITH US FOR VALEDICTORIAN.
MAKING US LOOK WEAK.
THEY GOTTA *GO.*

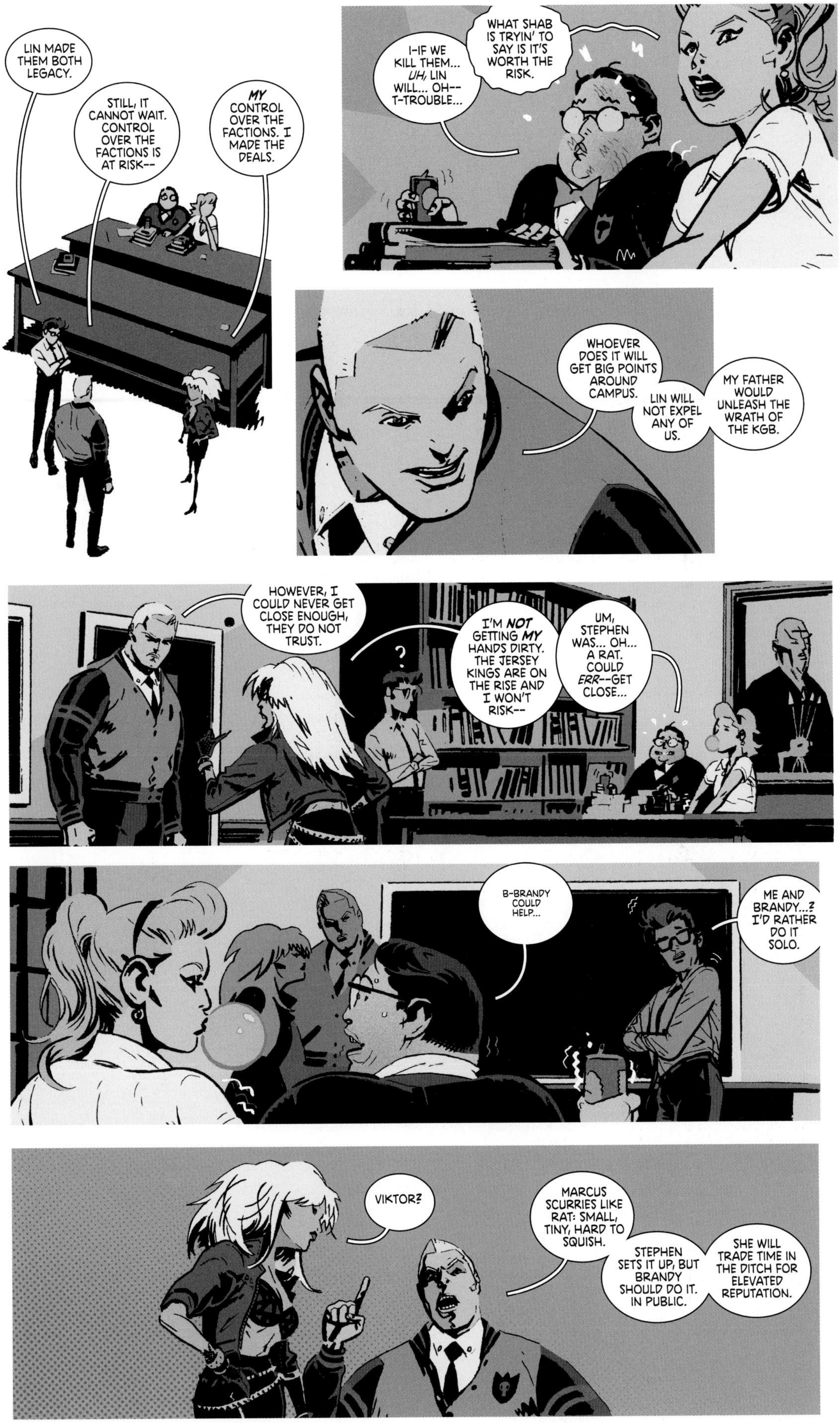
LIN MADE THEM BOTH LEGACY.
STILL, IT CANNOT WAIT. CONTROL OVER THE FACTIONS IS AT RISK--
MY CONTROL OVER THE FACTIONS. I MADE THE DEALS.
I-IF WE KILL THEM... UH, LIN WILL... OH-- T-TROUBLE...
WHAT SHAB IS TRYIN' TO SAY IS IT'S WORTH THE RISK.
WHOEVER DOES IT WILL GET BIG POINTS AROUND CAMPUS.
LIN WILL NOT EXPEL ANY OF US.
MY FATHER WOULD UNLEASH THE WRATH OF THE KGB.
HOWEVER, I COULD NEVER GET CLOSE ENOUGH, THEY DO NOT TRUST.
?
I'M NOT GETTING MY HANDS DIRTY. THE JERSEY KINGS ARE ON THE RISE AND I WON'T RISK--
UM, STEPHEN WAS... OH... A RAT. COULD ERR--GET CLOSE...
B-BRANDY COULD HELP...
ME AND BRANDY...? I'D RATHER DO IT SOLO.
VIKTOR?
MARCUS SCURRIES LIKE RAT: SMALL, TINY, HARD TO SQUISH.
STEPHEN SETS IT UP, BUT BRANDY SHOULD DO IT. IN PUBLIC.
SHE WILL TRADE TIME IN THE DITCH FOR ELEVATED REPUTATION.

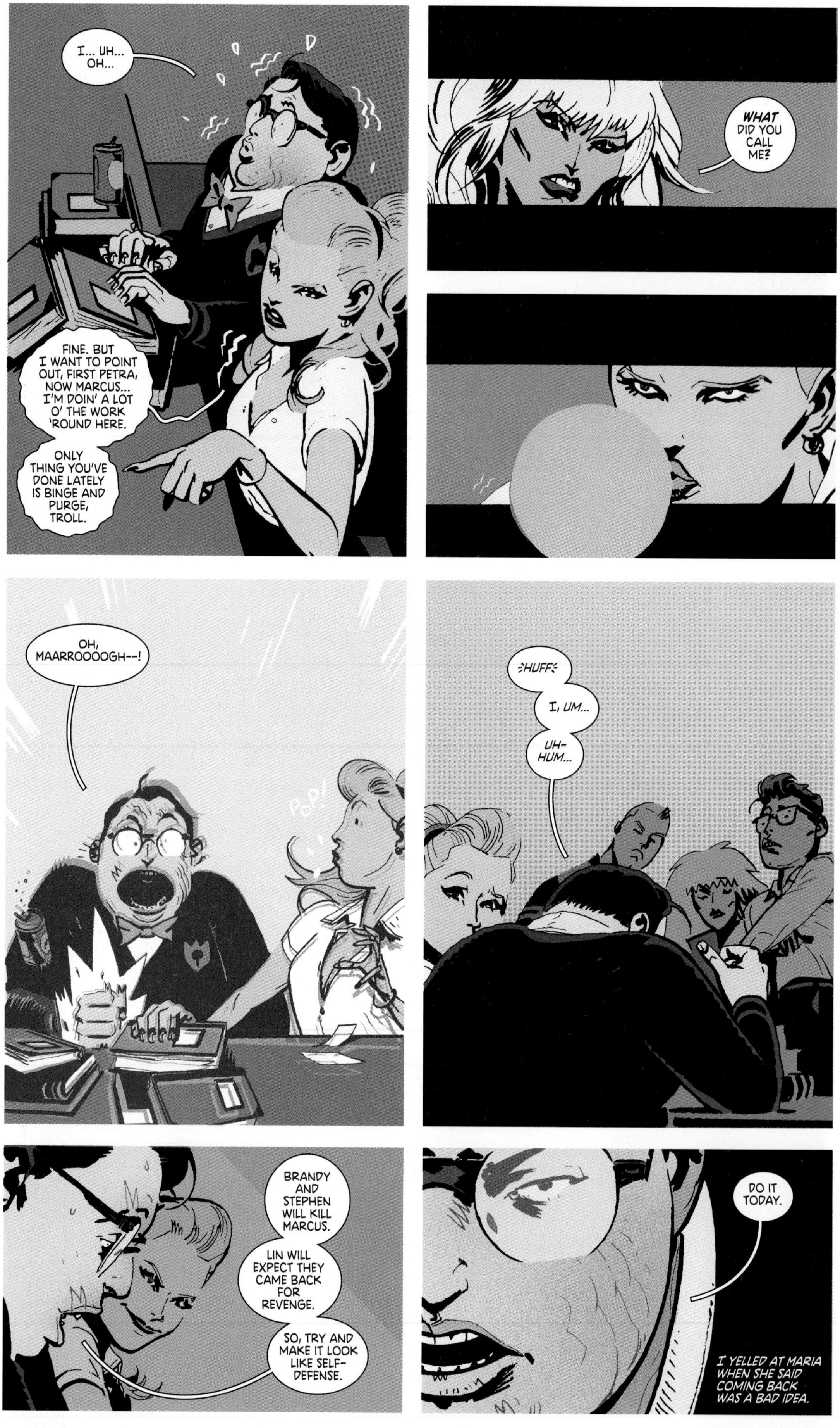
I... UH... OH...
FINE. BUT I WANT TO POINT OUT, FIRST PETRA, NOW MARCUS... I'M DOIN' A LOT O' THE WORK 'ROUND HERE.
ONLY THING YOU'VE DONE LATELY IS BINGE AND PURGE, TROLL.
WHAT DID YOU CALL ME?
OH, MAARROOOOGH--!
POP!
HUFF
I, UM...
UH-HUM...
BRANDY AND STEPHEN WILL KILL MARCUS.
LIN WILL EXPECT THEY CAME BACK FOR REVENGE.
SO, TRY AND MAKE IT LOOK LIKE SELF-DEFENSE.
DO IT TODAY.
I YELLED AT MARIA WHEN SHE SAID COMING BACK WAS A BAD IDEA.

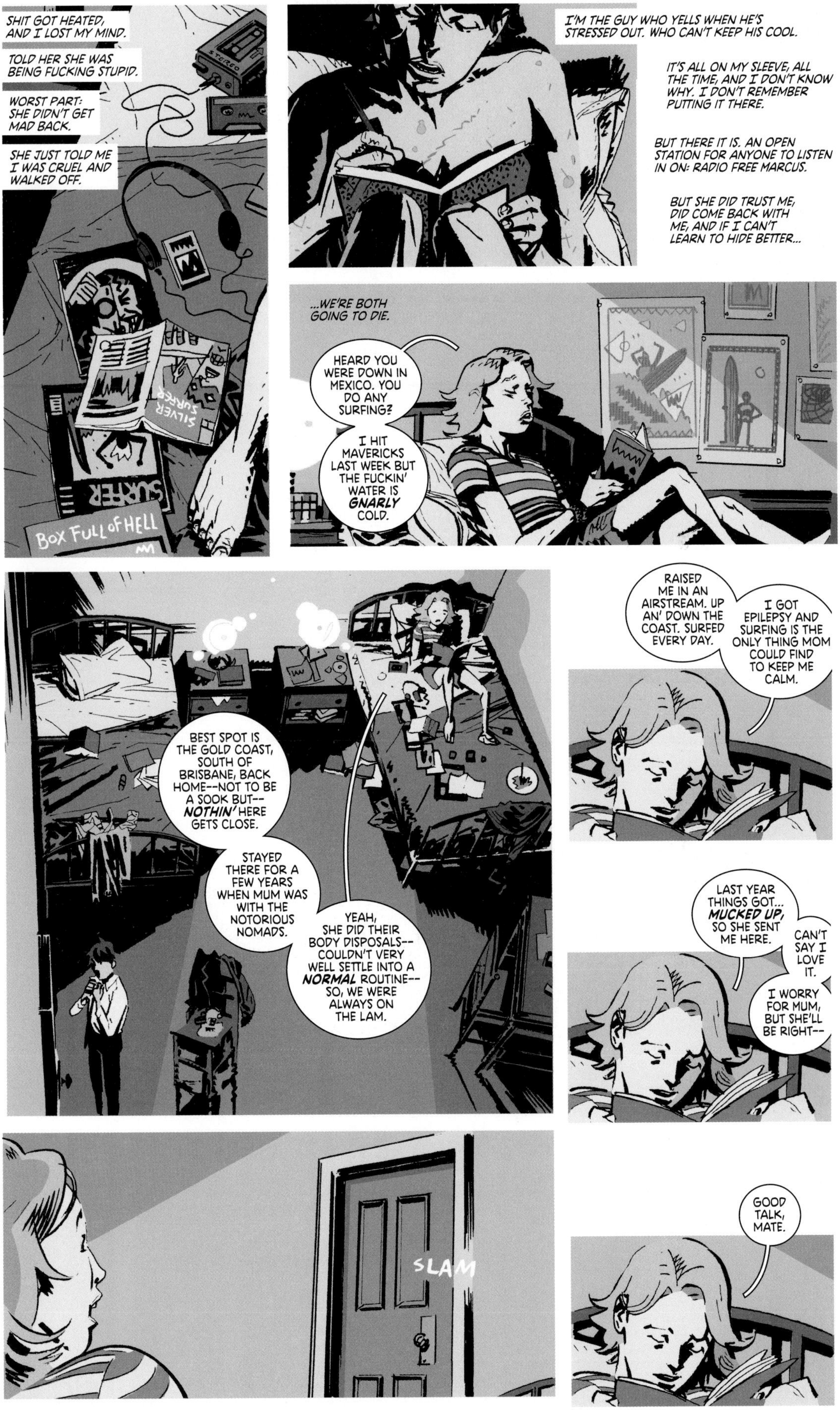
SHIT GOT HEATED, AND I LOST MY MIND.
TOLD HER SHE WAS BEING FUCKING STUPID.
WORST PART: SHE DIDN'T GET MAD BACK.
SHE JUST TOLD ME I WAS CRUEL AND WALKED OFF.
STEREO
SILVER SURFER
SURFER
BOX FULL OF HELL
I'M THE GUY WHO YELLS WHEN HE'S STRESSED OUT. WHO CAN'T KEEP HIS COOL.
IT'S ALL ON MY SLEEVE, ALL THE TIME, AND I DON'T KNOW WHY. I DON'T REMEMBER PUTTING IT THERE.
BUT THERE IT IS. AN OPEN STATION FOR ANYONE TO LISTEN IN ON: RADIO FREE MARCUS.
BUT SHE DID TRUST ME, DID COME BACK WITH ME, AND IF I CAN'T LEARN TO HIDE BETTER...
...WE'RE BOTH GOING TO DIE.
HEARD YOU WERE DOWN IN MEXICO. YOU DO ANY SURFING?
I HIT MAVERICKS LAST WEEK BUT THE FUCKIN' WATER IS GNARLY COLD.
BEST SPOT IS THE GOLD COAST, SOUTH OF BRISBANE, BACK HOME--NOT TO BE A SOOK BUT--NOTHIN' HERE GETS CLOSE.
STAYED THERE FOR A FEW YEARS WHEN MUM WAS WITH THE NOTORIOUS NOMADS.
YEAH, SHE DID THEIR BODY DISPOSALS--COULDN'T VERY WELL SETTLE INTO A NORMAL ROUTINE--SO, WE WERE ALWAYS ON THE LAM.
RAISED ME IN AN AIRSTREAM. UP AN' DOWN THE COAST. SURFED EVERY DAY.
I GOT EPILEPSY AND SURFING IS THE ONLY THING MOM COULD FIND TO KEEP ME CALM.
LAST YEAR THINGS GOT... MUCKED UP, SO SHE SENT ME HERE.
CAN'T SAY I LOVE IT.
I WORRY FOR MUM, BUT SHE'LL BE RIGHT--
SLAM
GOOD TALK, MATE.

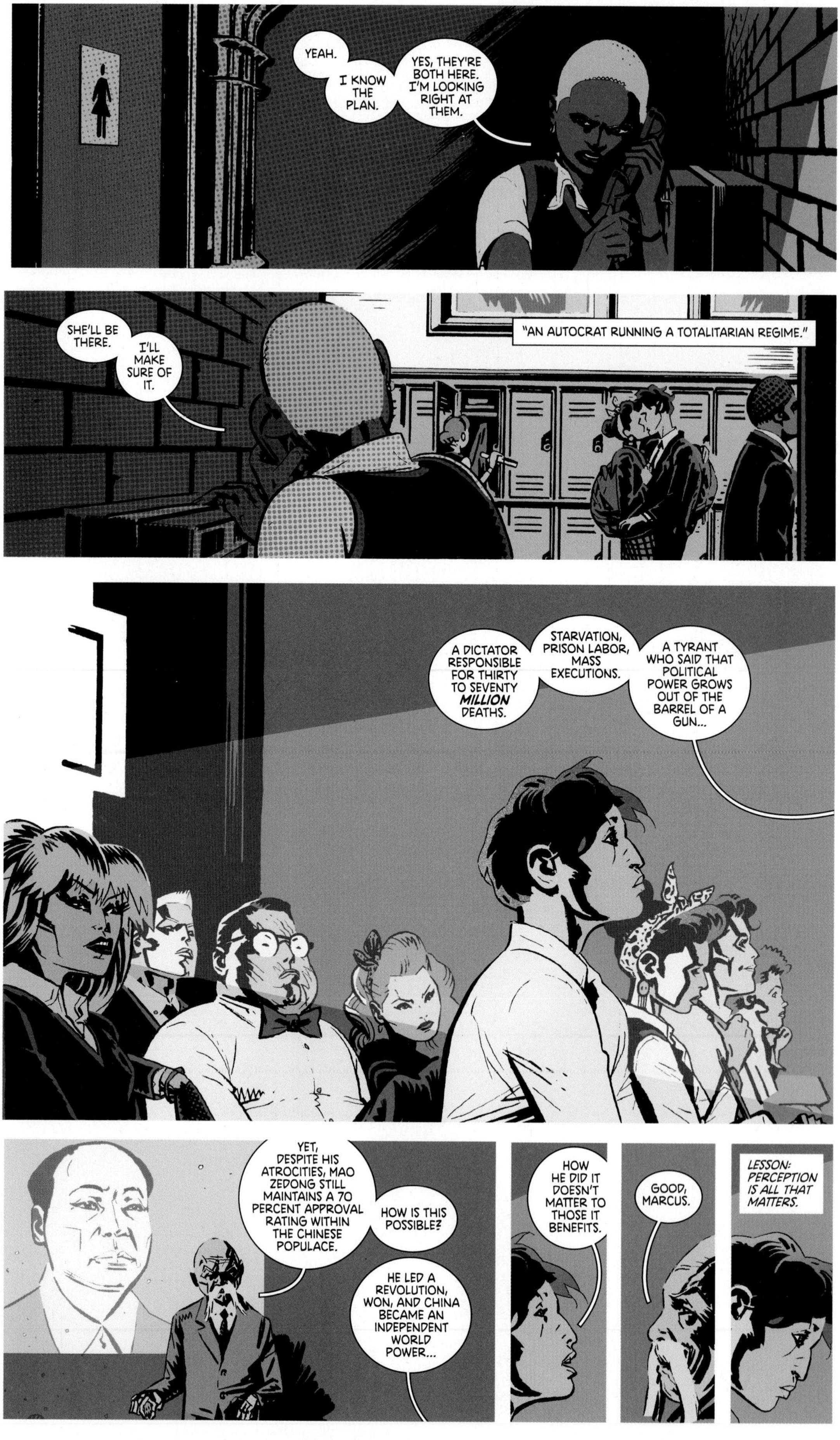

YEAH.
I KNOW THE PLAN.
YES, THEY'RE BOTH HERE. I'M LOOKING RIGHT AT THEM.
SHE'LL BE THERE.
I'LL MAKE SURE OF IT.
"AN AUTOCRAT RUNNING A TOTALITARIAN REGIME."
A DICTATOR RESPONSIBLE FOR THIRTY TO SEVENTY *MILLION* DEATHS.
STARVATION, PRISON LABOR, MASS EXECUTIONS.
A TYRANT WHO SAID THAT POLITICAL POWER GROWS OUT OF THE BARREL OF A GUN...
YET, DESPITE HIS ATROCITIES, MAO ZEDONG STILL MAINTAINS A 70 PERCENT APPROVAL RATING WITHIN THE CHINESE POPULACE.
HOW IS THIS POSSIBLE?
HE LED A REVOLUTION, WON, AND CHINA BECAME AN INDEPENDENT WORLD POWER...
HOW HE DID IT DOESN'T MATTER TO THOSE IT BENEFITS.
GOOD, MARCUS.
LESSON: PERCEPTION IS ALL THAT MATTERS.

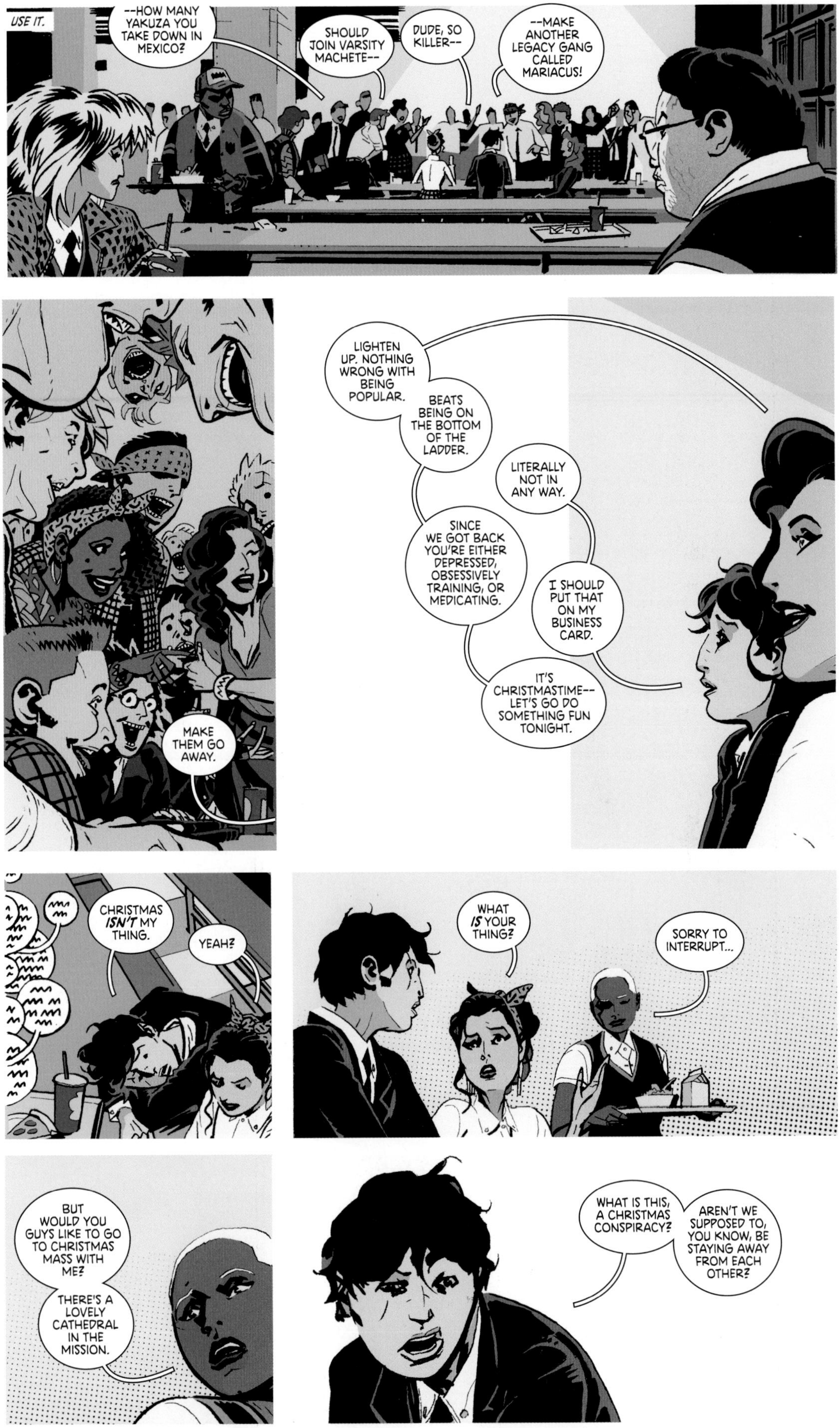
USE IT.
--HOW MANY YAKUZA YOU TAKE DOWN IN MEXICO?
SHOULD JOIN VARSITY MACHETE--
DUDE, SO KILLER--
--MAKE ANOTHER LEGACY GANG CALLED MARIACUS!
MAKE THEM GO AWAY.
LIGHTEN UP. NOTHING WRONG WITH BEING POPULAR.
BEATS BEING ON THE BOTTOM OF THE LADDER.
LITERALLY NOT IN ANY WAY.
SINCE WE GOT BACK YOU'RE EITHER DEPRESSED, OBSESSIVELY TRAINING, OR MEDICATING.
I SHOULD PUT THAT ON MY BUSINESS CARD.
IT'S CHRISTMASTIME-- LET'S GO DO SOMETHING FUN TONIGHT.
CHRISTMAS *ISN'T* MY THING.
YEAH?
WHAT *IS* YOUR THING?
SORRY TO INTERRUPT...
BUT WOULD YOU GUYS LIKE TO GO TO CHRISTMAS MASS WITH ME?
THERE'S A LOVELY CATHEDRAL IN THE MISSION.
WHAT IS THIS, A CHRISTMAS CONSPIRACY?
AREN'T WE SUPPOSED TO, YOU KNOW, BE STAYING AWAY FROM EACH OTHER?

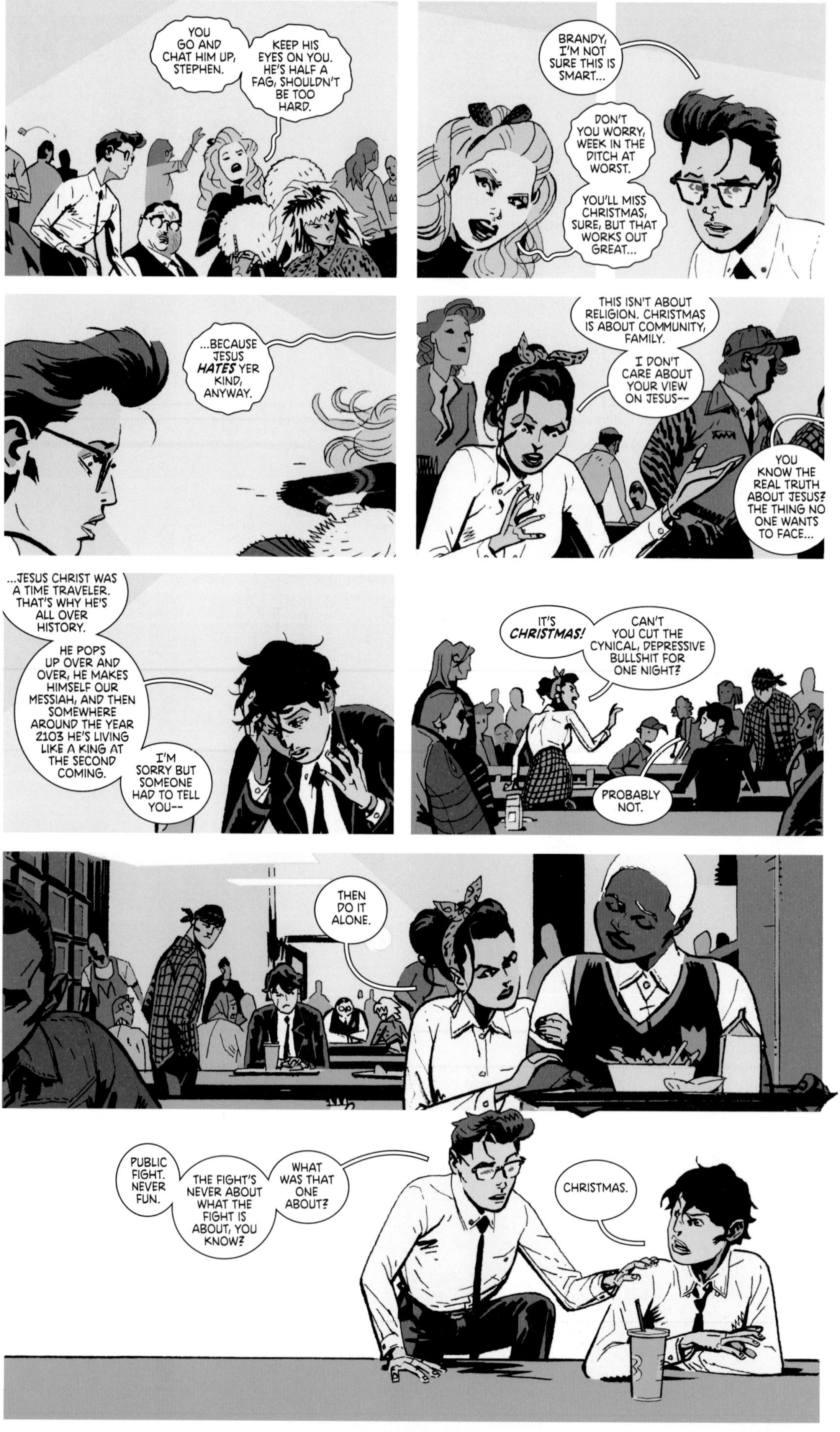
YOU GO AND CHAT HIM UP, STEPHEN.
KEEP HIS EYES ON YOU. HE'S HALF A FAG, SHOULDN'T BE TOO HARD.
BRANDY, I'M NOT SURE THIS IS SMART...
DON'T YOU WORRY, WEEK IN THE DITCH AT WORST.
YOU'LL MISS CHRISTMAS, SURE, BUT THAT WORKS OUT GREAT...
...BECAUSE JESUS HATES YER KIND, ANYWAY.
THIS ISN'T ABOUT RELIGION. CHRISTMAS IS ABOUT COMMUNITY, FAMILY.
I DON'T CARE ABOUT YOUR VIEW ON JESUS--
YOU KNOW THE REAL TRUTH ABOUT JESUS? THE THING NO ONE WANTS TO FACE...
...JESUS CHRIST WAS A TIME TRAVELER. THAT'S WHY HE'S ALL OVER HISTORY.
HE POPS UP OVER AND OVER, HE MAKES HIMSELF OUR MESSIAH, AND THEN SOMEWHERE AROUND THE YEAR 2103 HE'S LIVING LIKE A KING AT THE SECOND COMING.
I'M SORRY BUT SOMEONE HAD TO TELL YOU--
IT'S CHRISTMAS!
CAN'T YOU CUT THE CYNICAL, DEPRESSIVE BULLSHIT FOR ONE NIGHT?
PROBABLY NOT.
THEN DO IT ALONE.
PUBLIC FIGHT. NEVER FUN.
THE FIGHT'S NEVER ABOUT WHAT THE FIGHT IS ABOUT, YOU KNOW?
WHAT WAS THAT ONE ABOUT?
CHRISTMAS.

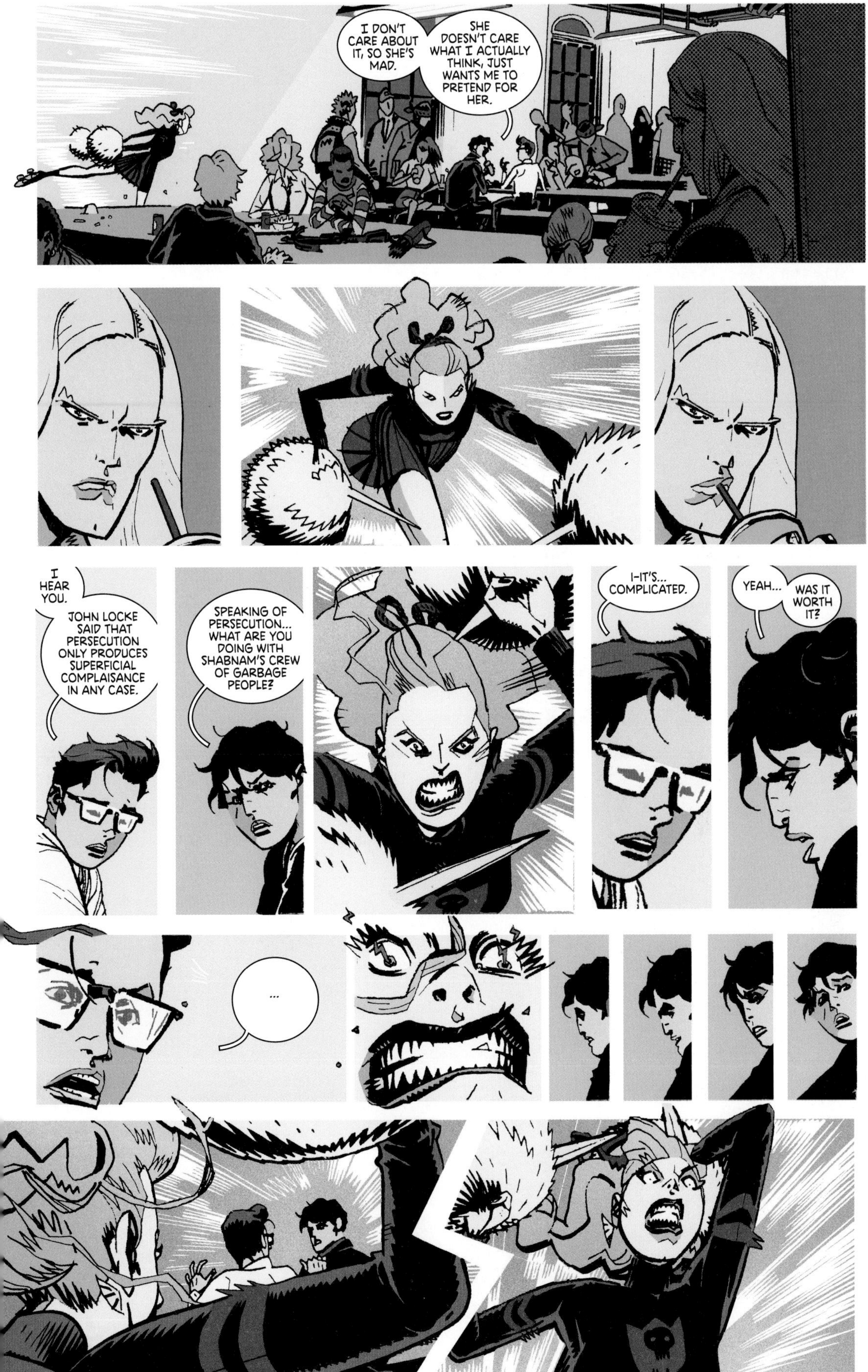
I DON'T CARE ABOUT IT, SO SHE'S MAD.
SHE DOESN'T CARE WHAT I ACTUALLY THINK, JUST WANTS ME TO PRETEND FOR HER.
I HEAR YOU.
JOHN LOCKE SAID THAT PERSECUTION ONLY PRODUCES SUPERFICIAL COMPLAISANCE IN ANY CASE.
SPEAKING OF PERSECUTION... WHAT ARE YOU DOING WITH SHABNAM'S CREW OF GARBAGE PEOPLE?
I-IT'S... COMPLICATED.
YEAH...
WAS IT WORTH IT?
...

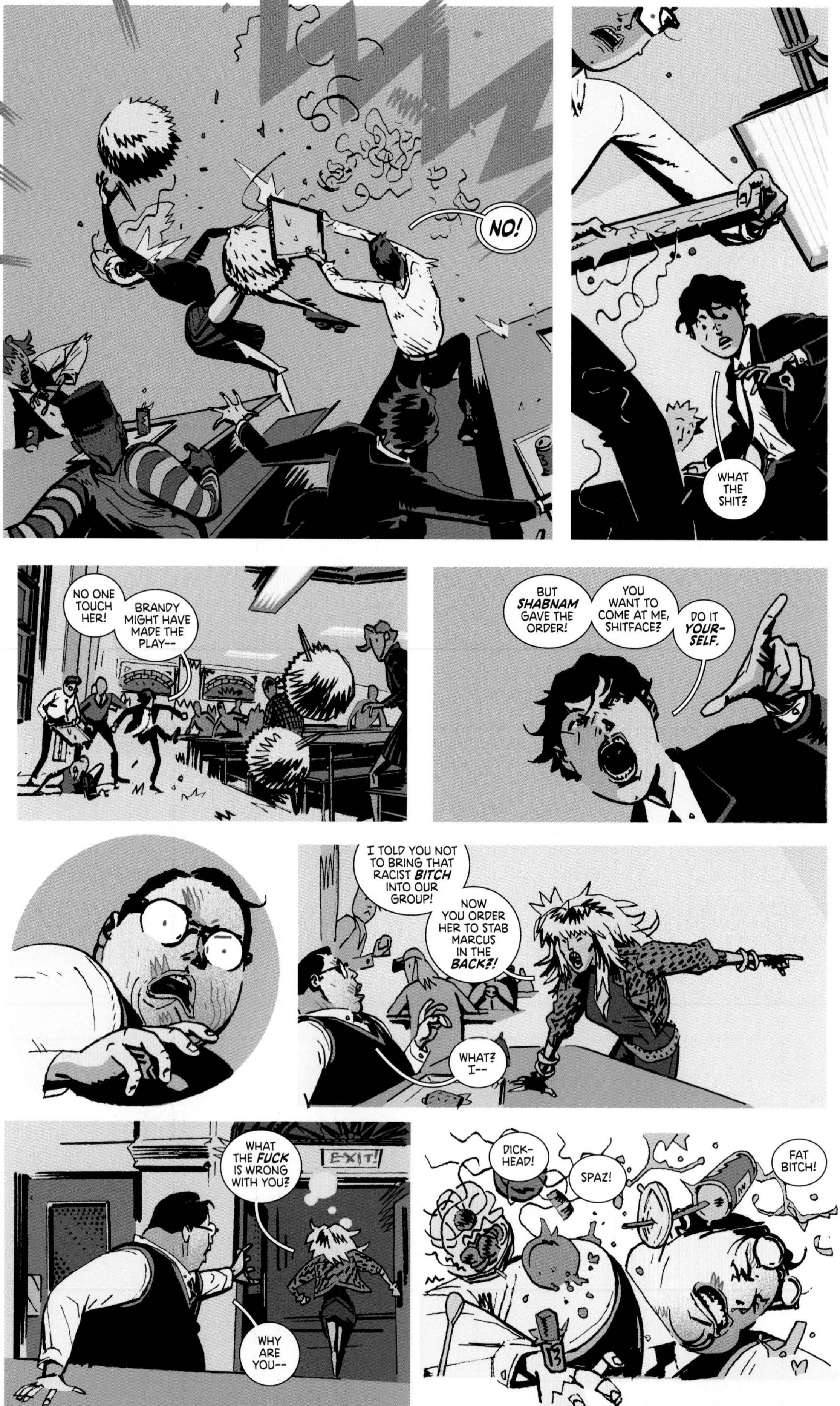
NO!
WHAT THE SHIT?
NO ONE TOUCH HER!
BRANDY MIGHT HAVE MADE THE PLAY--
BUT SHABNAM GAVE THE ORDER!
YOU WANT TO COME AT ME, SHITFACE?
DO IT YOURSELF.
I TOLD YOU NOT TO BRING THAT RACIST BITCH INTO OUR GROUP!
NOW YOU ORDER HER TO STAB MARCUS IN THE BACK?!
WHAT? I--
WHAT THE FUCK IS WRONG WITH YOU?
EXIT!
WHY ARE YOU--
DICK-HEAD!
SPAZ!
FAT BITCH!
13

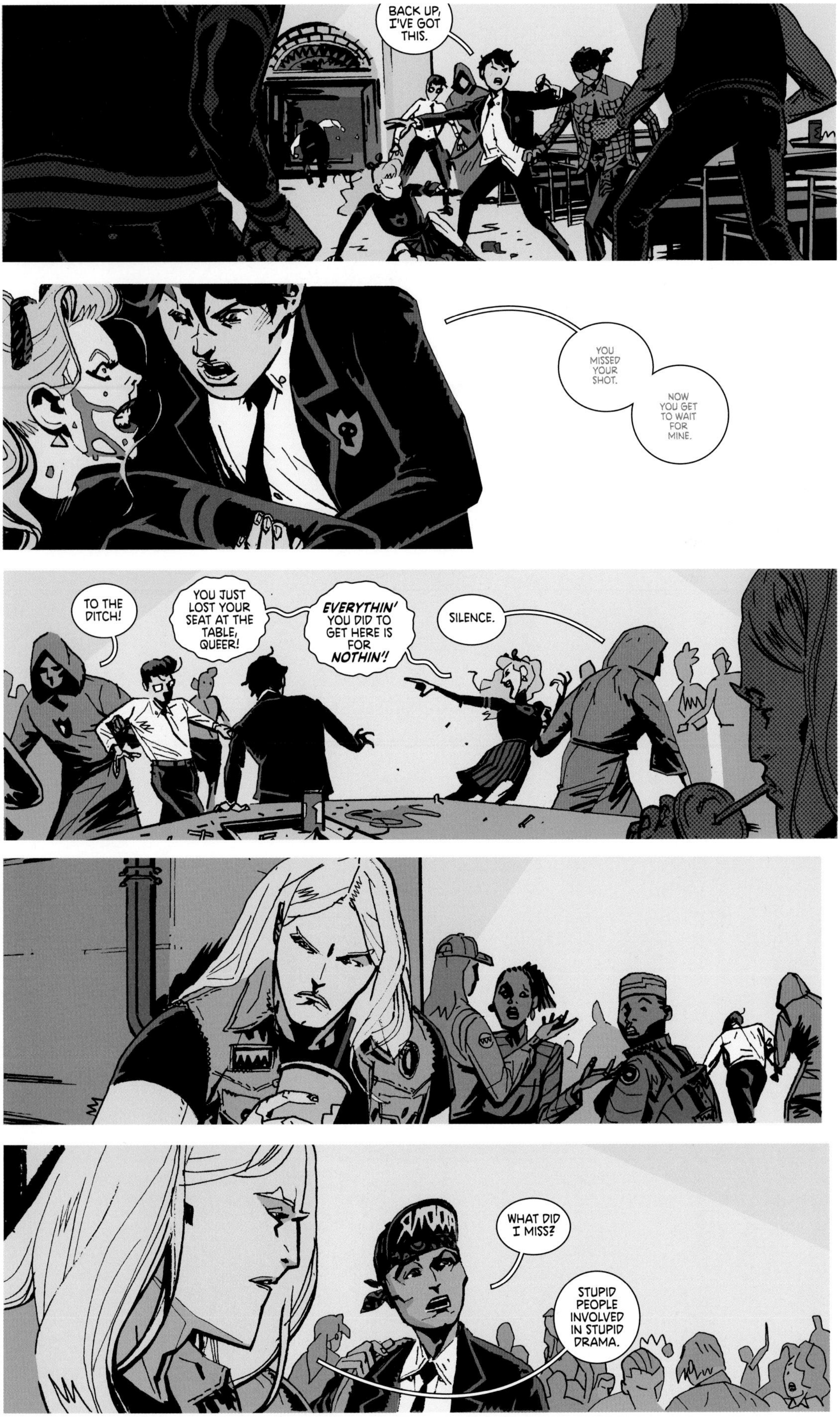
BACK UP, I'VE GOT THIS.
YOU MISSED YOUR SHOT.
NOW YOU GET TO WAIT FOR MINE.
TO THE DITCH!
YOU JUST LOST YOUR SEAT AT THE TABLE, QUEER!
EVERYTHIN' YOU DID TO GET HERE IS FOR NOTHIN'!
SILENCE.
WHAT DID I MISS?
STUPID PEOPLE INVOLVED IN STUPID DRAMA.

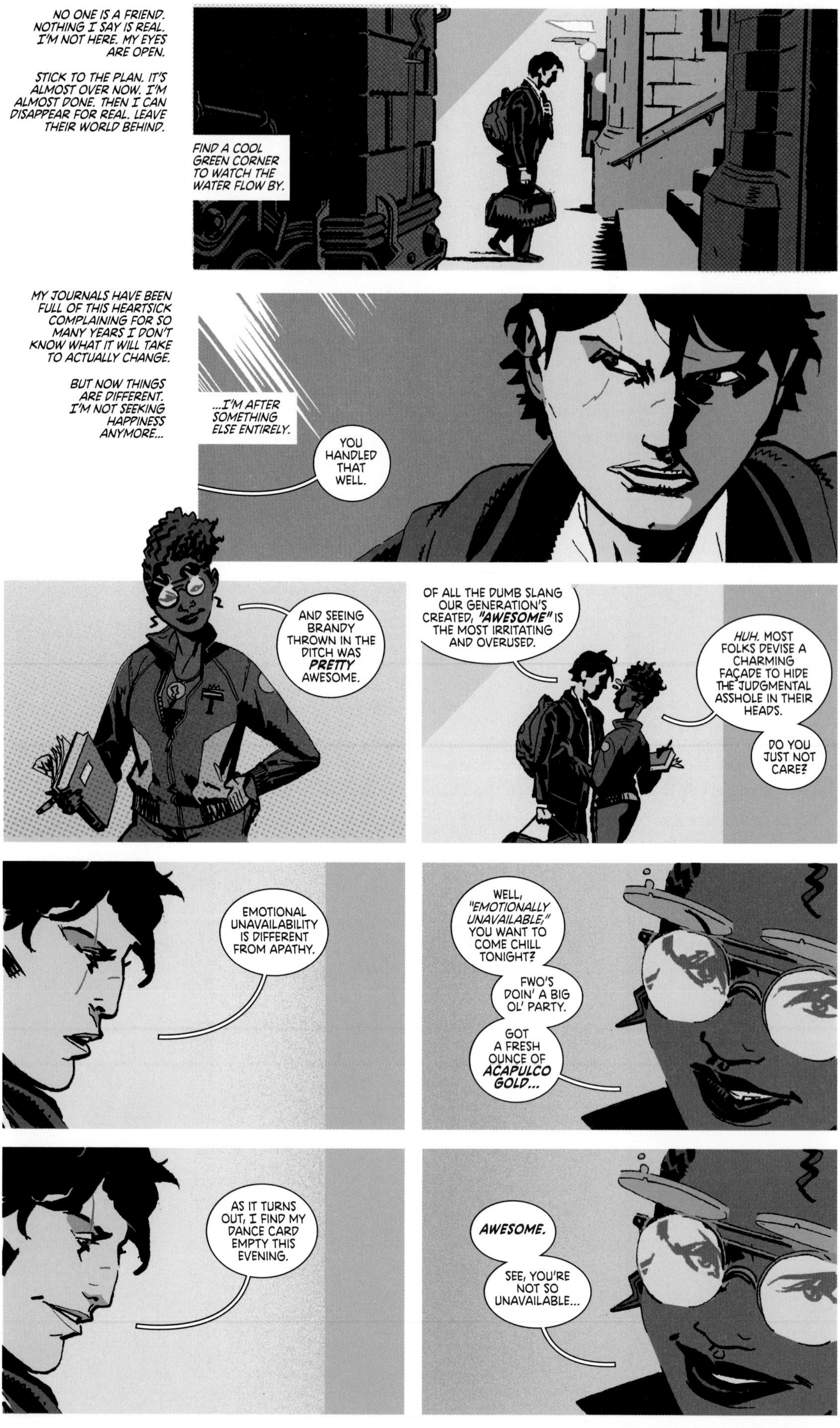
NO ONE IS A FRIEND. NOTHING I SAY IS REAL. I'M NOT HERE. MY EYES ARE OPEN.
STICK TO THE PLAN. IT'S ALMOST OVER NOW. I'M ALMOST DONE. THEN I CAN DISAPPEAR FOR REAL. LEAVE THEIR WORLD BEHIND.
FIND A COOL GREEN CORNER TO WATCH THE WATER FLOW BY.
MY JOURNALS HAVE BEEN FULL OF THIS HEARTSICK COMPLAINING FOR SO MANY YEARS I DON'T KNOW WHAT IT WILL TAKE TO ACTUALLY CHANGE.
BUT NOW THINGS ARE DIFFERENT. I'M NOT SEEKING HAPPINESS ANYMORE...
...I'M AFTER SOMETHING ELSE ENTIRELY.
YOU HANDLED THAT WELL.
AND SEEING BRANDY THROWN IN THE DITCH WAS PRETTY AWESOME.
OF ALL THE DUMB SLANG OUR GENERATION'S CREATED, "AWESOME" IS THE MOST IRRITATING AND OVERUSED.
HUH. MOST FOLKS DEVISE A CHARMING FAÇADE TO HIDE THE JUDGMENTAL ASSHOLE IN THEIR HEADS.
DO YOU JUST NOT CARE?
EMOTIONAL UNAVAILABILITY IS DIFFERENT FROM APATHY.
WELL, "EMOTIONALLY UNAVAILABLE," YOU WANT TO COME CHILL TONIGHT?
FWO'S DOIN' A BIG OL' PARTY.
GOT A FRESH OUNCE OF ACAPULCO GOLD...
AS IT TURNS OUT, I FIND MY DANCE CARD EMPTY THIS EVENING.
AWESOME.
SEE, YOU'RE NOT SO UNAVAILABLE...

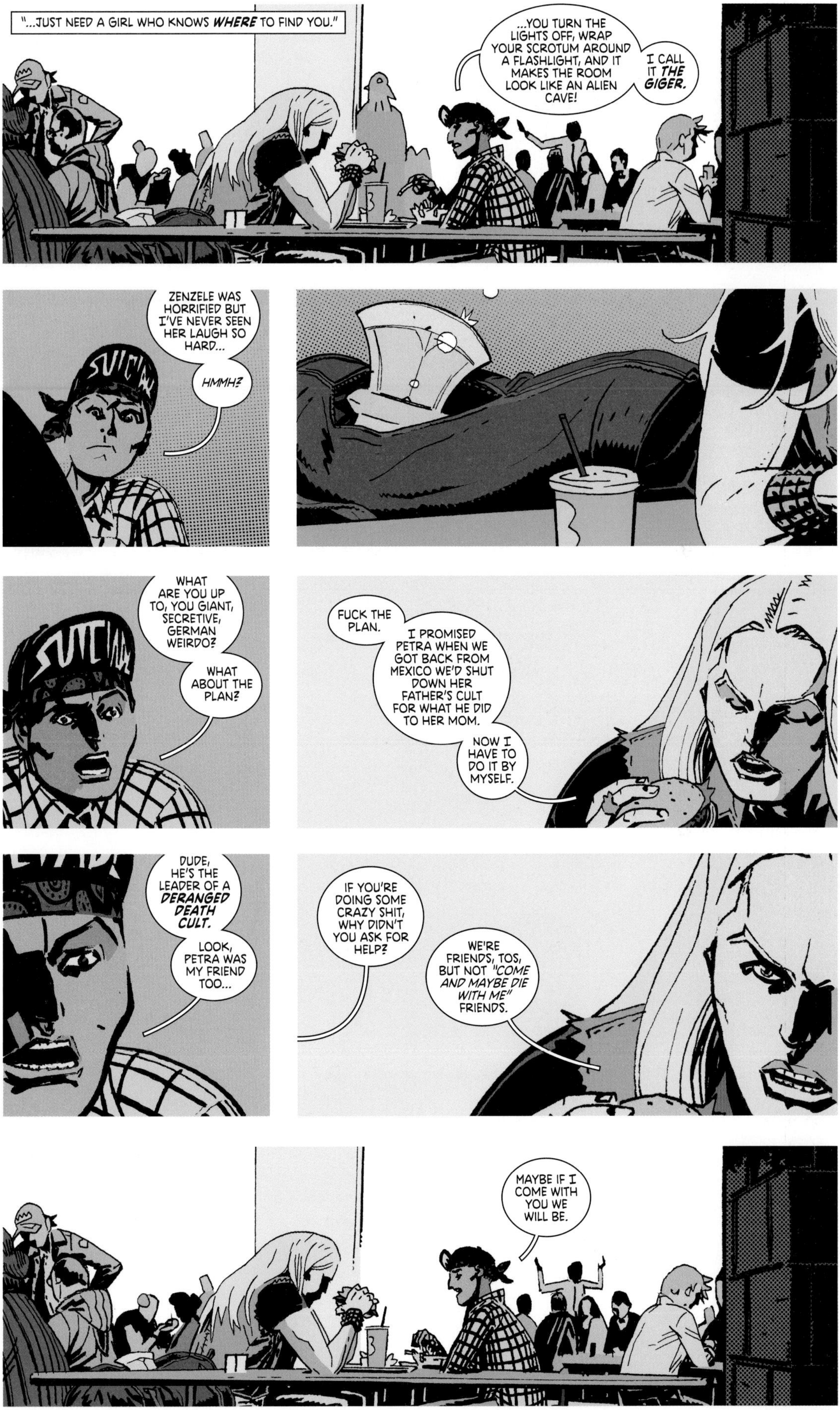
"...JUST NEED A GIRL WHO KNOWS WHERE TO FIND YOU."
...YOU TURN THE LIGHTS OFF, WRAP YOUR SCROTUM AROUND A FLASHLIGHT, AND IT MAKES THE ROOM LOOK LIKE AN ALIEN CAVE!
I CALL IT THE GIGER.
ZENZELE WAS HORRIFIED BUT I'VE NEVER SEEN HER LAUGH SO HARD...
HMMH?
WHAT ARE YOU UP TO, YOU GIANT, SECRETIVE, GERMAN WEIRDO?
WHAT ABOUT THE PLAN?
FUCK THE PLAN.
I PROMISED PETRA WHEN WE GOT BACK FROM MEXICO WE'D SHUT DOWN HER FATHER'S CULT FOR WHAT HE DID TO HER MOM.
NOW I HAVE TO DO IT BY MYSELF.
DUDE, HE'S THE LEADER OF A DERANGED DEATH CULT.
LOOK, PETRA WAS MY FRIEND TOO...
IF YOU'RE DOING SOME CRAZY SHIT, WHY DIDN'T YOU ASK FOR HELP?
WE'RE FRIENDS, TOS, BUT NOT "COME AND MAYBE DIE WITH ME" FRIENDS.
MAYBE IF I COME WITH YOU WE WILL BE.

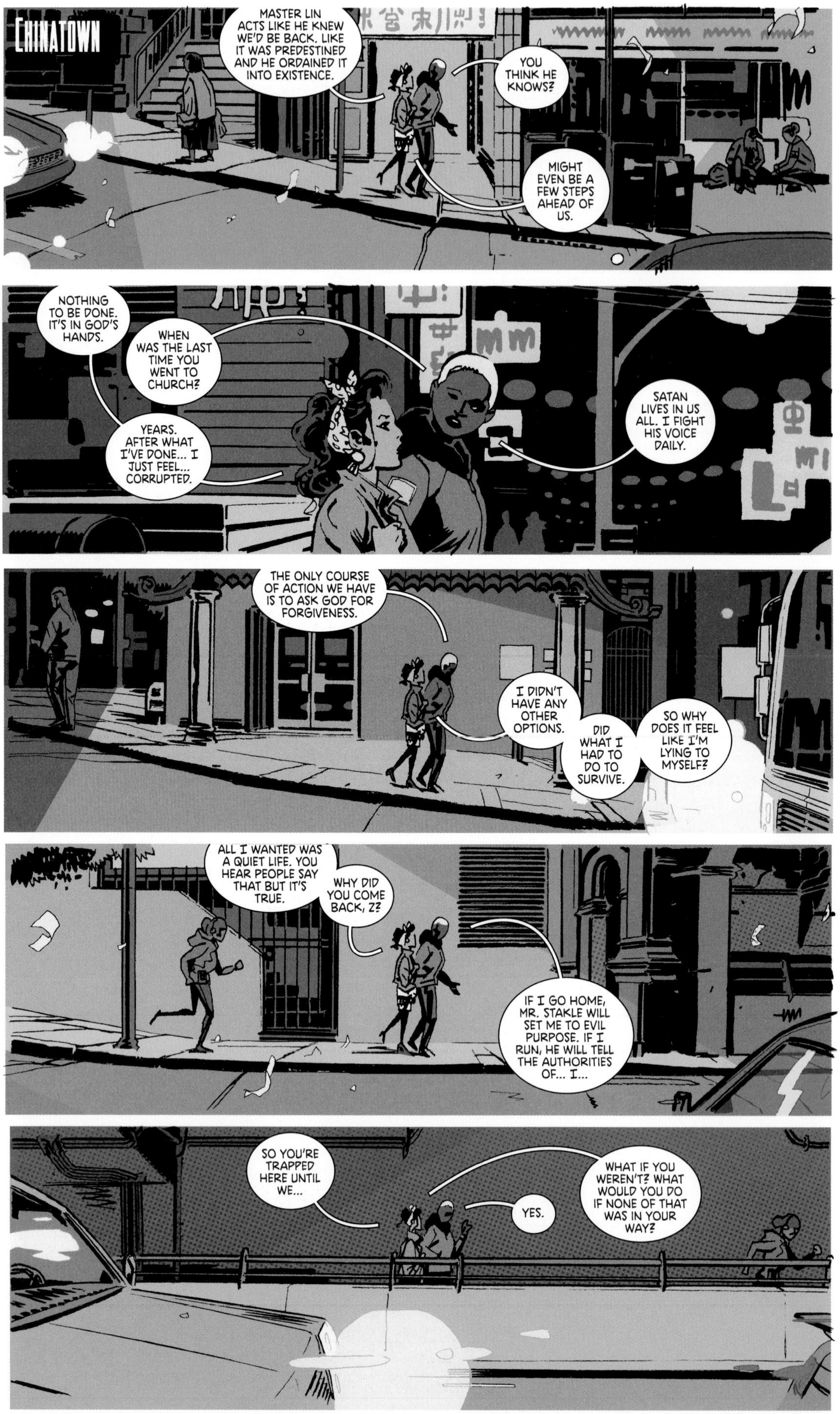
CHINATOWN
MASTER LIN ACTS LIKE HE KNEW WE'D BE BACK. LIKE IT WAS PREDESTINED AND HE ORDAINED IT INTO EXISTENCE.
YOU THINK HE KNOWS?
MIGHT EVEN BE A FEW STEPS AHEAD OF US.
NOTHING TO BE DONE. IT'S IN GOD'S HANDS.
WHEN WAS THE LAST TIME YOU WENT TO CHURCH?
YEARS. AFTER WHAT I'VE DONE... I JUST FEEL... CORRUPTED.
SATAN LIVES IN US ALL. I FIGHT HIS VOICE DAILY.
THE ONLY COURSE OF ACTION WE HAVE IS TO ASK GOD FOR FORGIVENESS.
I DIDN'T HAVE ANY OTHER OPTIONS.
DID WHAT I HAD TO DO TO SURVIVE.
SO WHY DOES IT FEEL LIKE I'M LYING TO MYSELF?
ALL I WANTED WAS A QUIET LIFE. YOU HEAR PEOPLE SAY THAT BUT IT'S TRUE.
WHY DID YOU COME BACK, Z?
IF I GO HOME, MR. STAKLE WILL SET ME TO EVIL PURPOSE. IF I RUN, HE WILL TELL THE AUTHORITIES OF... I...
SO YOU'RE TRAPPED HERE UNTIL WE...
YES.
WHAT IF YOU WEREN'T? WHAT WOULD YOU DO IF NONE OF THAT WAS IN YOUR WAY?

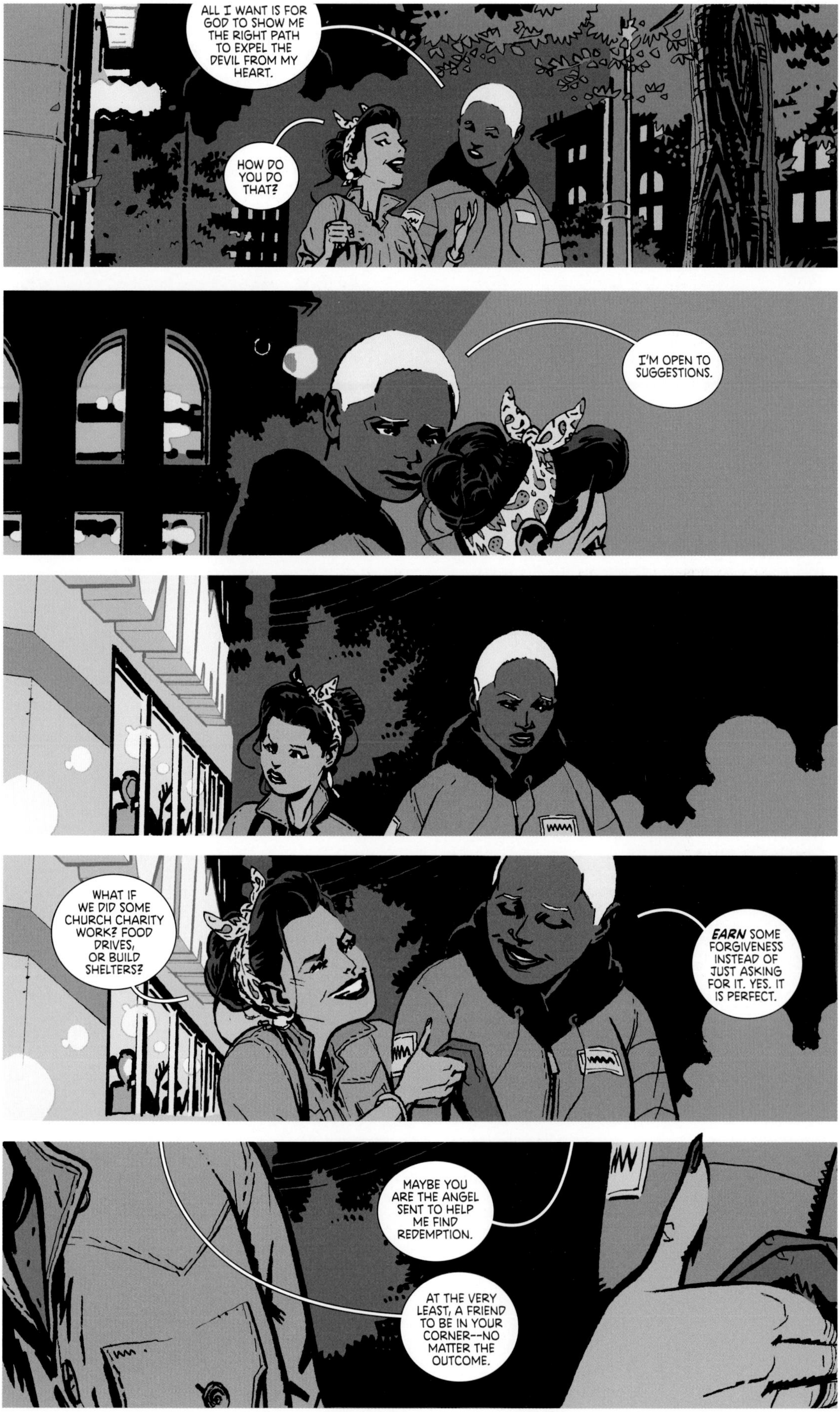
ALL I WANT IS FOR GOD TO SHOW ME THE RIGHT PATH TO EXPEL THE DEVIL FROM MY HEART.
HOW DO YOU DO THAT?
I'M OPEN TO SUGGESTIONS.
WHAT IF WE DID SOME CHURCH CHARITY WORK? FOOD DRIVES, OR BUILD SHELTERS?
EARN SOME FORGIVENESS INSTEAD OF JUST ASKING FOR IT. YES. IT IS PERFECT.
MAYBE YOU ARE THE ANGEL SENT TO HELP ME FIND REDEMPTION.
AT THE VERY LEAST, A FRIEND TO BE IN YOUR CORNER--NO MATTER THE OUTCOME.

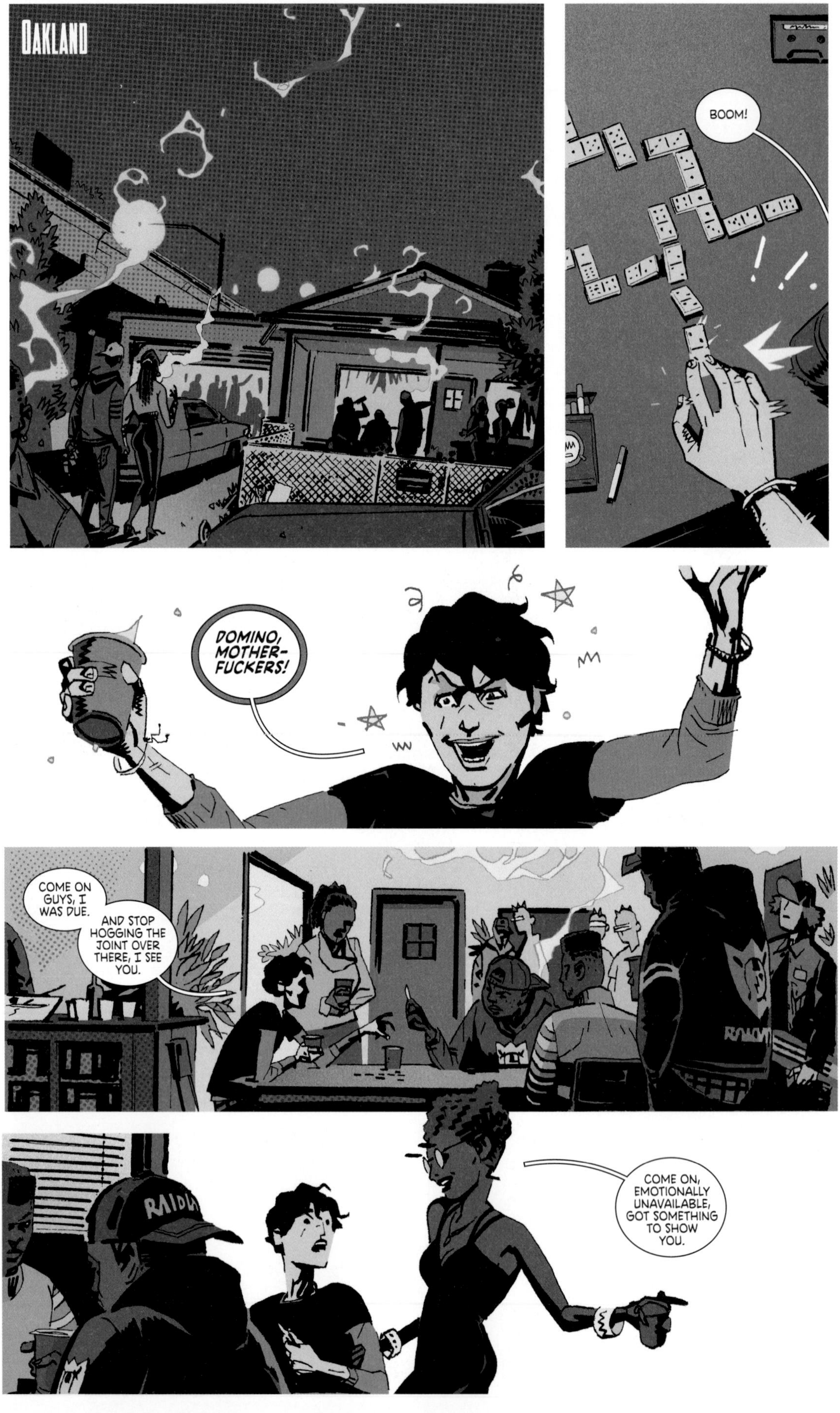
OAKLAND
BOOM!
DOMINO, MOTHER-FUCKERS!
COME ON GUYS, I WAS DUE.
AND STOP HOGGING THE JOINT OVER THERE, I SEE YOU.
COME ON, EMOTIONALLY UNAVAILABLE, GOT SOMETHING TO SHOW YOU.

I WAS JUST GETTING ON A STREAK.

ALL THE MORE REASON TO LEAVE.

THEY'RE NOT GONNA FUCK WITH ME.

I KNOW A LOT OF THESE FWO GUYS FROM BACK IN THE DAY...

HOW'S THAT?

MY BEST FRIEND WAS FWO.

THAT RIGHT?

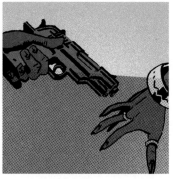

WHAT HAPPENED TO HIM?

HE WAS A GOOD PERSON TRAPPED IN A BAD WORLD.

DEFINITELY NOT THE TYPE TO TRICK SOMEONE TO A PARTY TO SHOOT HIM IN THE BACK OF THE HEAD.

BUT APPARENTLY, HIS SISTER WOULD.

HOW DID YOU--

I DIDN'T GET WILLIE KILLED, JAYLA.

MUST BE ANOTHER PUNK NAME MARCUS TRICKED HIM UP INTO THE OPEN SO THAT RUSSIAN MOTHERFUCKER COULD SHOOT HIM FROM BEHIND.

THAT'S A LONG STORY.

BUT IT STARTS WITH ONE FACT--

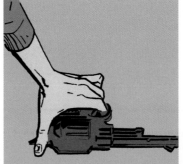

--WILLIE WAS MY BEST FRIEND.

I LOVED YOUR BROTHER.

KNEW HIM BETTER THAN ANYONE.

ENOUGH TO KNOW FOR SURE HE *WOULDN'T* LIKE WHAT I HAVE PLANNED.

BUT YOU MIGHT.

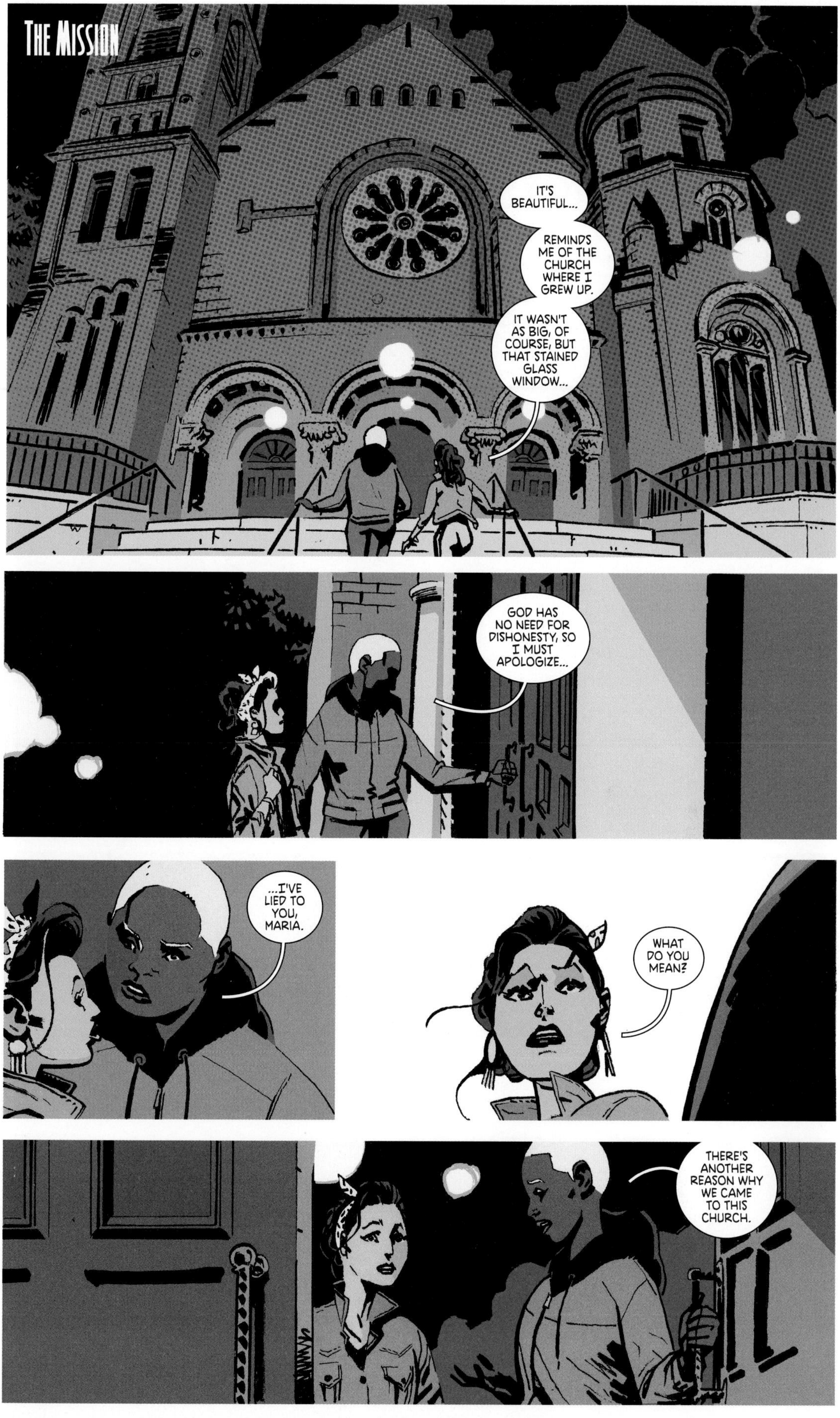
THE MISSION
IT'S BEAUTIFUL...
REMINDS ME OF THE CHURCH WHERE I GREW UP.
IT WASN'T AS BIG, OF COURSE, BUT THAT STAINED GLASS WINDOW...
GOD HAS NO NEED FOR DISHONESTY, SO I MUST APOLOGIZE...
...I'VE LIED TO YOU, MARIA.
WHAT DO YOU MEAN?
THERE'S ANOTHER REASON WHY WE CAME TO THIS CHURCH.

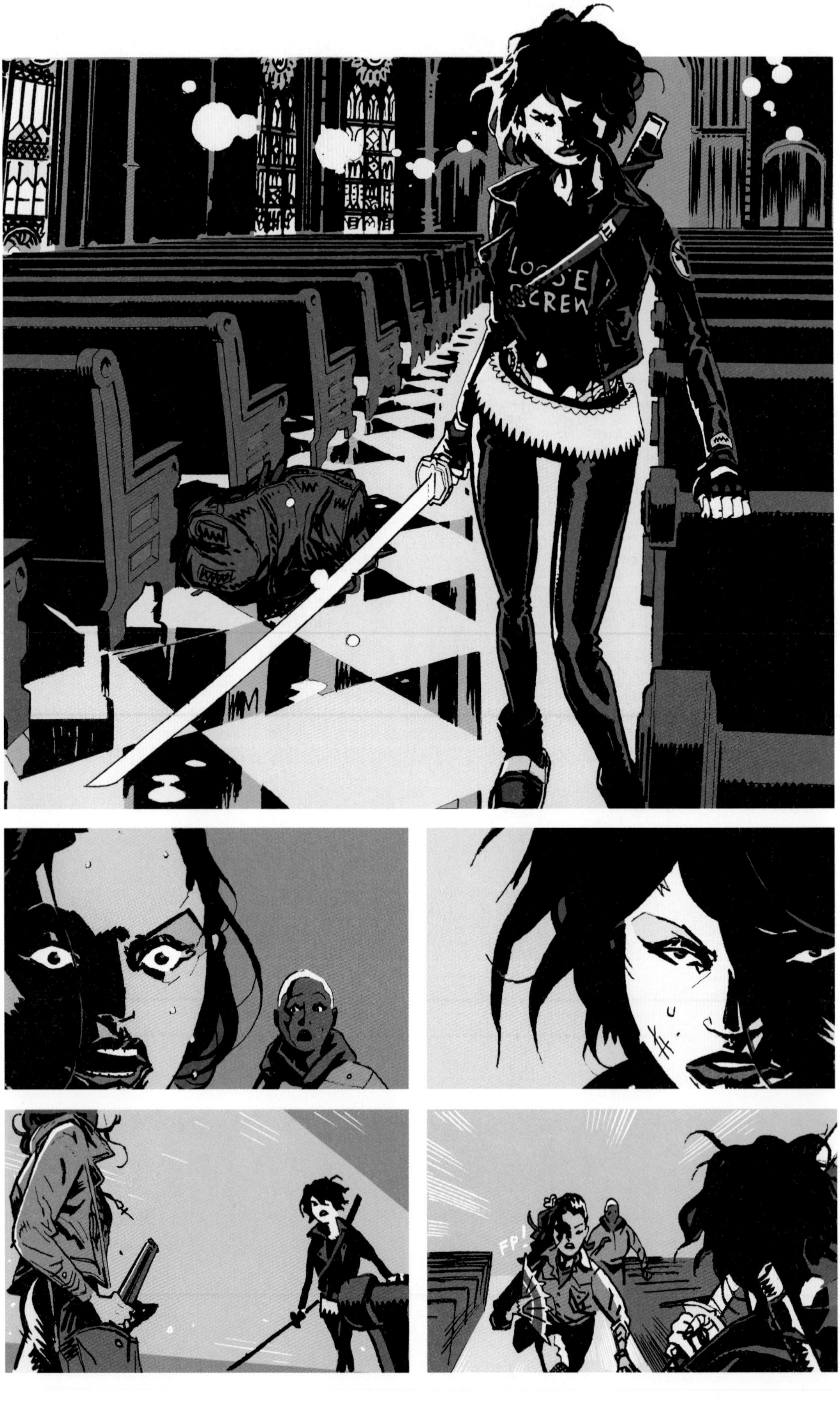
LOOSE SCREW
FP!

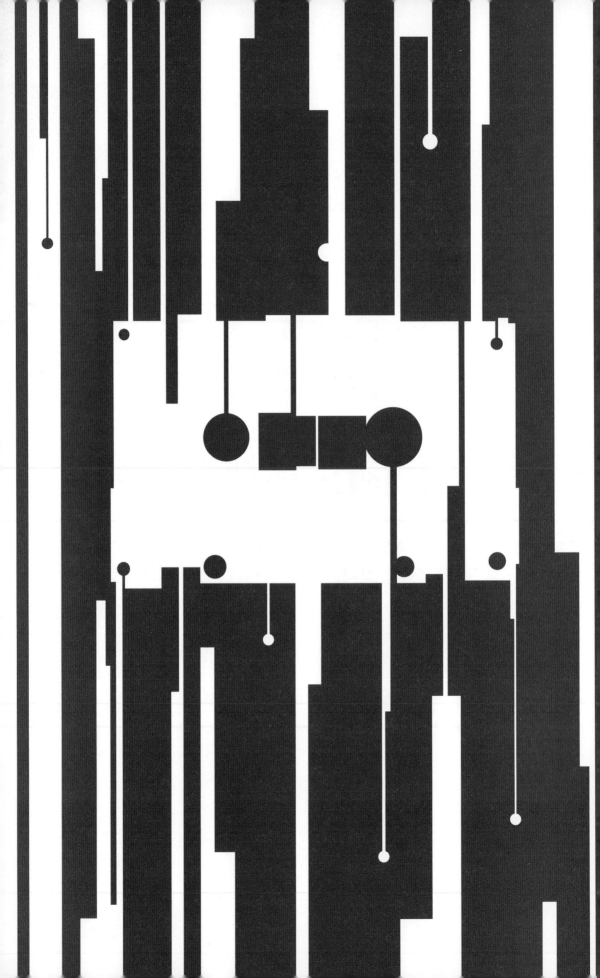

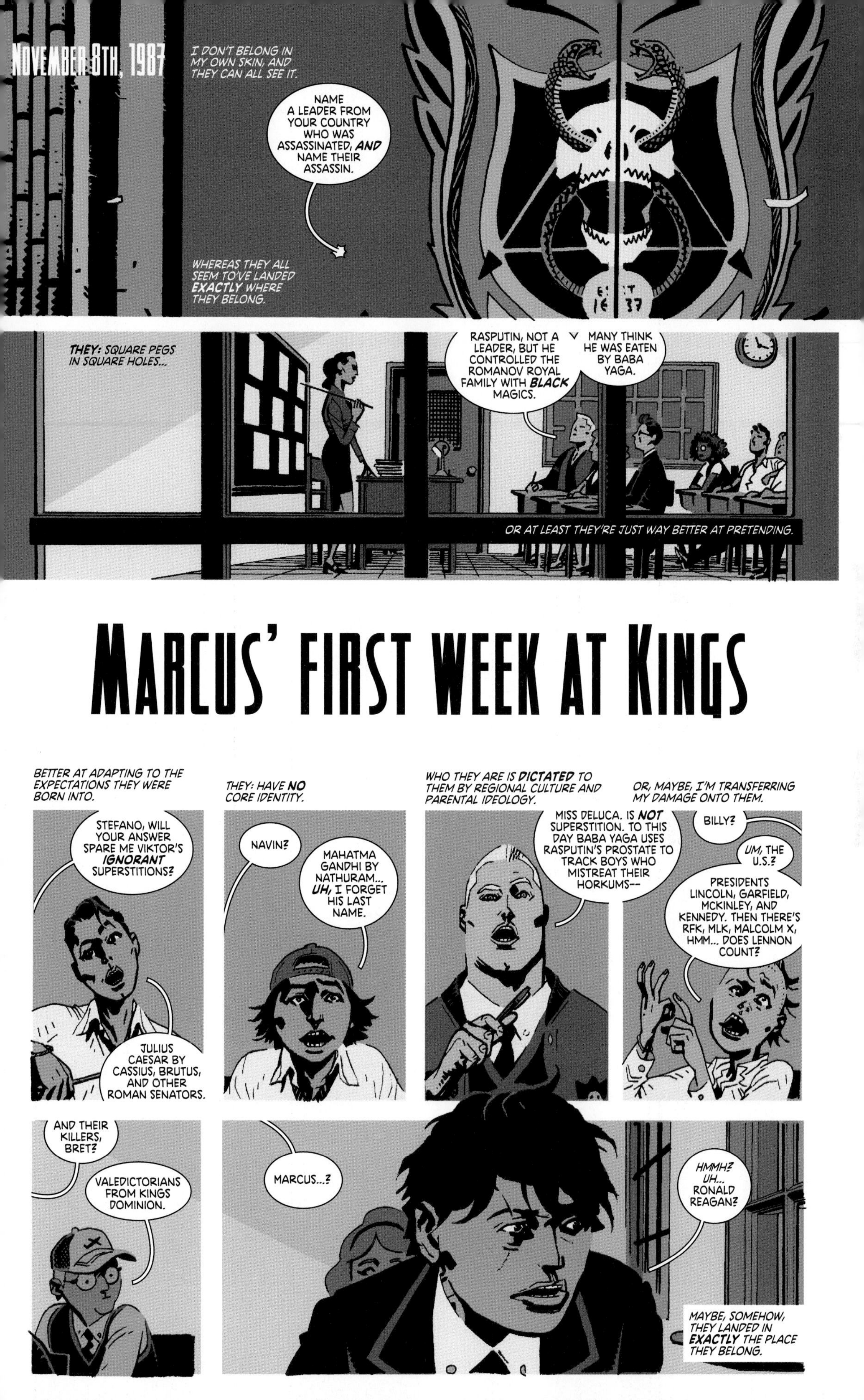

NOVEMBER 8TH, 1987
I DON'T BELONG IN MY OWN SKIN, AND THEY CAN ALL SEE IT.
NAME A LEADER FROM YOUR COUNTRY WHO WAS ASSASSINATED, AND NAME THEIR ASSASSIN.
WHEREAS THEY ALL SEEM TO'VE LANDED EXACTLY WHERE THEY BELONG.
THEY: SQUARE PEGS IN SQUARE HOLES...
RASPUTIN, NOT A LEADER, BUT HE CONTROLLED THE ROMANOV ROYAL FAMILY WITH BLACK MAGICS.
MANY THINK HE WAS EATEN BY BABA YAGA.
OR AT LEAST THEY'RE JUST WAY BETTER AT PRETENDING.
MARCUS' FIRST WEEK AT KINGS
BETTER AT ADAPTING TO THE EXPECTATIONS THEY WERE BORN INTO.
STEFANO, WILL YOUR ANSWER SPARE ME VIKTOR'S IGNORANT SUPERSTITIONS?
JULIUS CAESAR BY CASSIUS, BRUTUS, AND OTHER ROMAN SENATORS.
THEY: HAVE NO CORE IDENTITY.
NAVIN?
MAHATMA GANDHI BY NATHURAM... UH, I FORGET HIS LAST NAME.
WHO THEY ARE IS DICTATED TO THEM BY REGIONAL CULTURE AND PARENTAL IDEOLOGY.
MISS DELUCA. IS NOT SUPERSTITION. TO THIS DAY BABA YAGA USES RASPUTIN'S PROSTATE TO TRACK BOYS WHO MISTREAT THEIR HORKUMS--
OR, MAYBE, I'M TRANSFERRING MY DAMAGE ONTO THEM.
BILLY?
UM, THE U.S.?
PRESIDENTS LINCOLN, GARFIELD, MCKINLEY, AND KENNEDY. THEN THERE'S RFK, MLK, MALCOLM X, HMM... DOES LENNON COUNT?
AND THEIR KILLERS, BRET?
VALEDICTORIANS FROM KINGS DOMINION.
MARCUS...?
HMMH? UH... RONALD REAGAN?
MAYBE, SOMEHOW, THEY LANDED IN EXACTLY THE PLACE THEY BELONG.

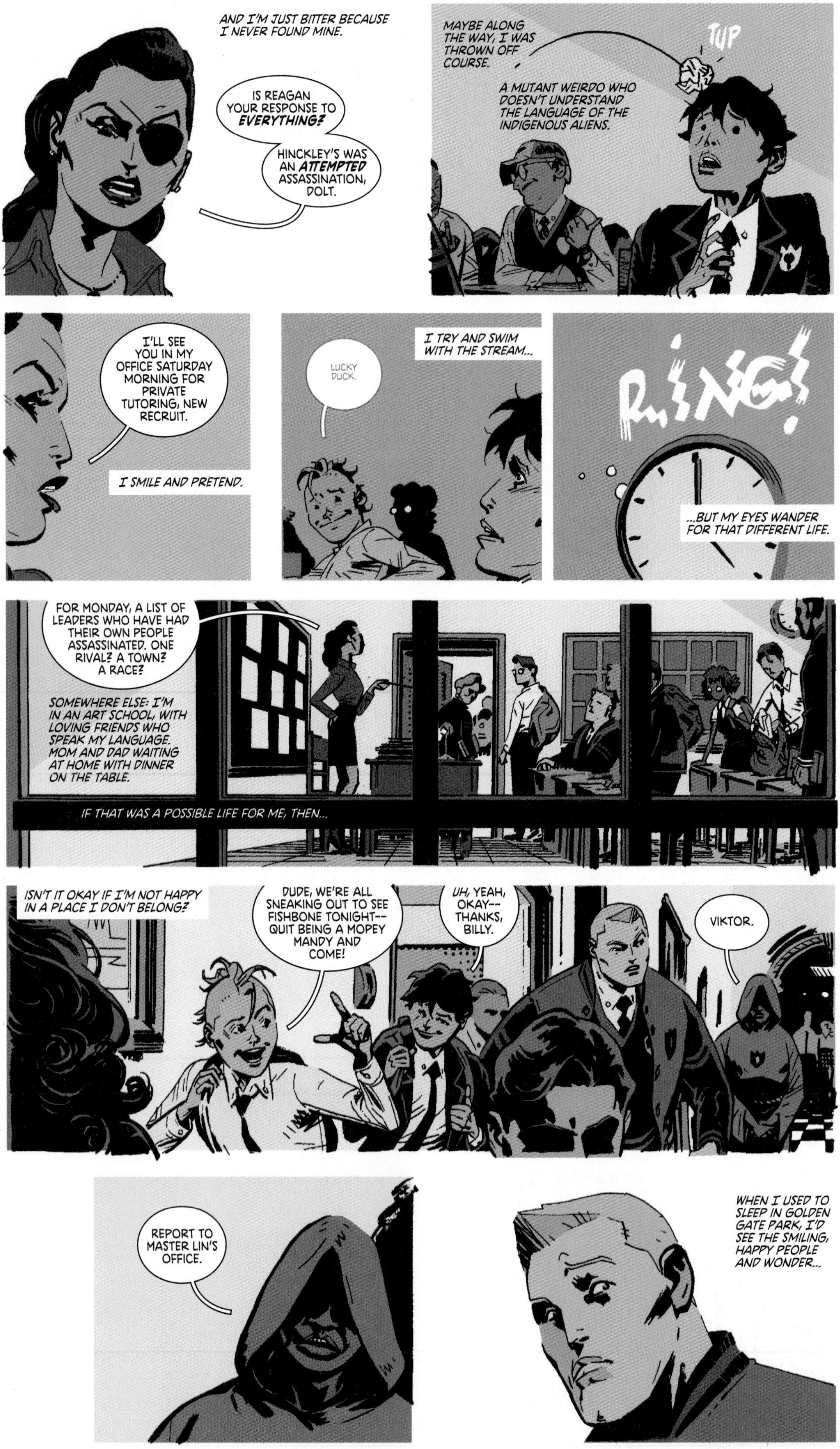
AND I'M JUST BITTER BECAUSE I NEVER FOUND MINE.
IS REAGAN YOUR RESPONSE TO EVERYTHING?
HINCKLEY'S WAS AN ATTEMPTED ASSASSINATION, DOLT.
MAYBE ALONG THE WAY, I WAS THROWN OFF COURSE.
TUP
A MUTANT WEIRDO WHO DOESN'T UNDERSTAND THE LANGUAGE OF THE INDIGENOUS ALIENS.
I'LL SEE YOU IN MY OFFICE SATURDAY MORNING FOR PRIVATE TUTORING, NEW RECRUIT.
I SMILE AND PRETEND.
I TRY AND SWIM WITH THE STREAM...
LUCKY DUCK.
RING!
...BUT MY EYES WANDER FOR THAT DIFFERENT LIFE.
FOR MONDAY, A LIST OF LEADERS WHO HAVE HAD THEIR OWN PEOPLE ASSASSINATED. ONE RIVAL? A TOWN? A RACE?
SOMEWHERE ELSE: I'M IN AN ART SCHOOL, WITH LOVING FRIENDS WHO SPEAK MY LANGUAGE. MOM AND DAD WAITING AT HOME WITH DINNER ON THE TABLE.
IF THAT WAS A POSSIBLE LIFE FOR ME, THEN...
ISN'T IT OKAY IF I'M NOT HAPPY IN A PLACE I DON'T BELONG?
DUDE, WE'RE ALL SNEAKING OUT TO SEE FISHBONE TONIGHT-- QUIT BEING A MOPEY MANDY AND COME!
UH, YEAH, OKAY-- THANKS, BILLY.
VIKTOR.
REPORT TO MASTER LIN'S OFFICE.
WHEN I USED TO SLEEP IN GOLDEN GATE PARK, I'D SEE THE SMILING, HAPPY PEOPLE AND WONDER...

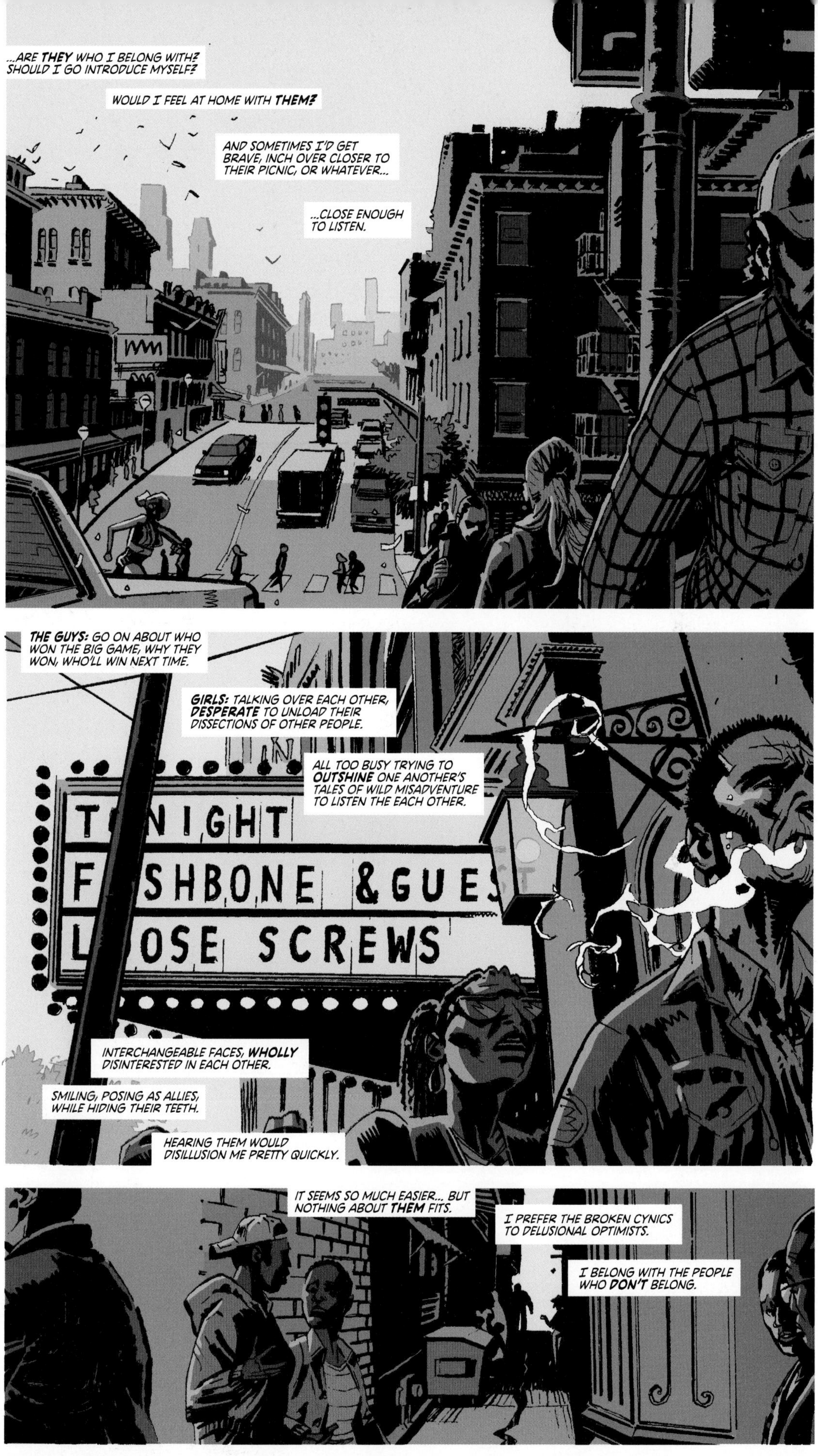
...ARE **THEY** WHO I BELONG WITH? SHOULD I GO INTRODUCE MYSELF?
WOULD I FEEL AT HOME WITH **THEM?**
AND SOMETIMES I'D GET BRAVE, INCH OVER CLOSER TO THEIR PICNIC, OR WHATEVER...
...CLOSE ENOUGH TO LISTEN.
THE GUYS: GO ON ABOUT WHO WON THE BIG GAME, WHY THEY WON, WHO'LL WIN NEXT TIME.
GIRLS: TALKING OVER EACH OTHER, **DESPERATE** TO UNLOAD THEIR DISSECTIONS OF OTHER PEOPLE.
ALL TOO BUSY TRYING TO **OUTSHINE** ONE ANOTHER'S TALES OF WILD MISADVENTURE TO LISTEN THE EACH OTHER.
T NIGHT
F SHBONE &GUES
L OSE SCREWS
INTERCHANGEABLE FACES, **WHOLLY** DISINTERESTED IN EACH OTHER.
SMILING, POSING AS ALLIES, WHILE HIDING THEIR TEETH.
HEARING THEM WOULD DISILLUSION ME PRETTY QUICKLY.
IT SEEMS SO MUCH EASIER... BUT NOTHING ABOUT **THEM** FITS.
I PREFER THE BROKEN CYNICS TO DELUSIONAL OPTIMISTS.
I BELONG WITH THE PEOPLE WHO **DON'T** BELONG.

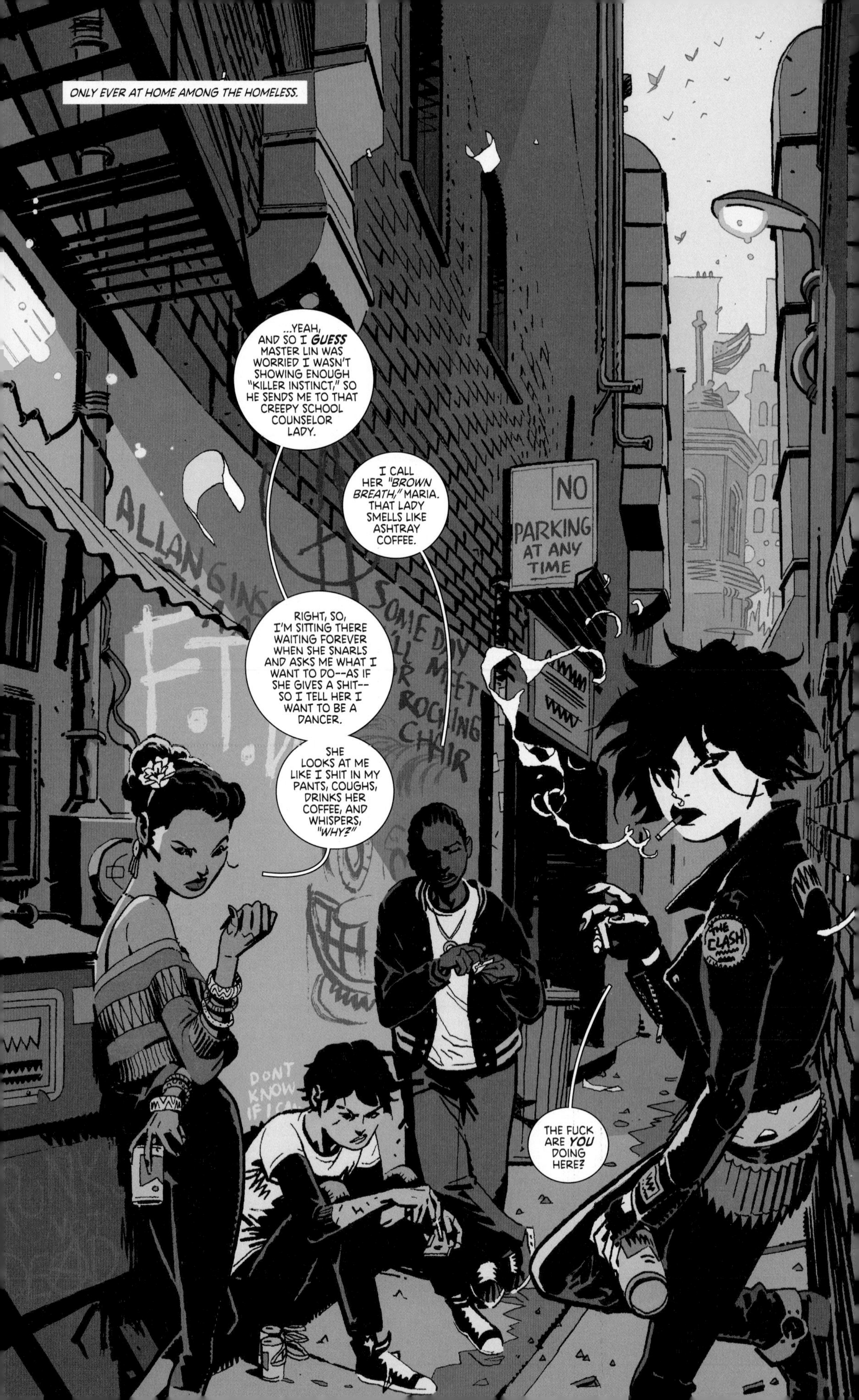
ONLY EVER AT HOME AMONG THE HOMELESS.
...YEAH, AND SO I GUESS MASTER LIN WAS WORRIED I WASN'T SHOWING ENOUGH "KILLER INSTINCT," SO HE SENDS ME TO THAT CREEPY SCHOOL COUNSELOR LADY.
I CALL HER "BROWN BREATH," MARIA. THAT LADY SMELLS LIKE ASHTRAY COFFEE.
RIGHT, SO, I'M SITTING THERE WAITING FOREVER WHEN SHE SNARLS AND ASKS ME WHAT I WANT TO DO--AS IF SHE GIVES A SHIT--SO I TELL HER I WANT TO BE A DANCER.
SHE LOOKS AT ME LIKE I SHIT IN MY PANTS, COUGHS, DRINKS HER COFFEE, AND WHISPERS, "WHY?"
THE FUCK ARE YOU DOING HERE?
NO PARKING AT ANY TIME
THE CLASH

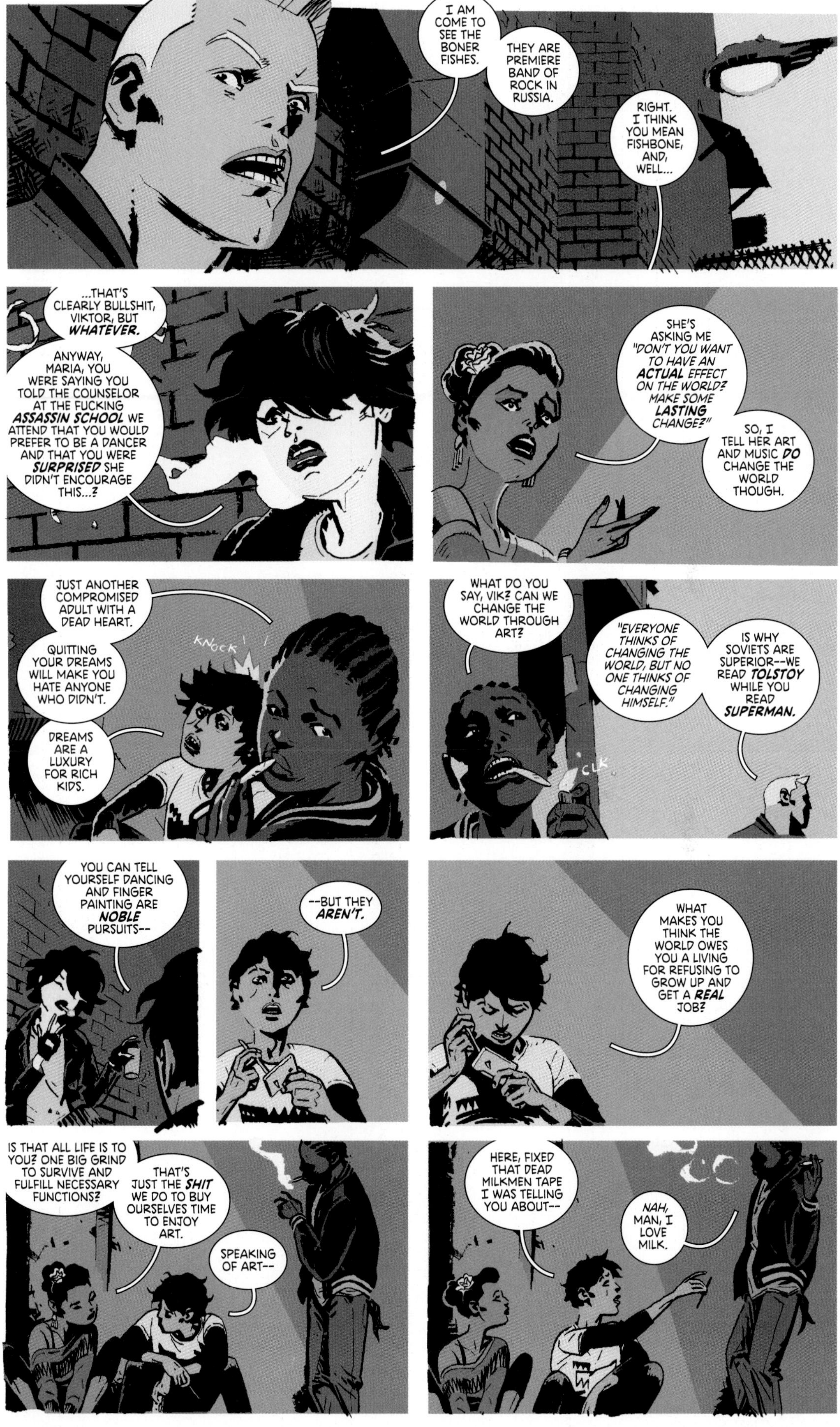
I AM COME TO SEE THE BONER FISHES.
THEY ARE PREMIERE BAND OF ROCK IN RUSSIA.
RIGHT. I THINK YOU MEAN FISHBONE, AND, WELL...
...THAT'S CLEARLY BULLSHIT, VIKTOR, BUT WHATEVER.
ANYWAY, MARIA, YOU WERE SAYING YOU TOLD THE COUNSELOR AT THE FUCKING ASSASSIN SCHOOL WE ATTEND THAT YOU WOULD PREFER TO BE A DANCER AND THAT YOU WERE SURPRISED SHE DIDN'T ENCOURAGE THIS...?
SHE'S ASKING ME "DON'T YOU WANT TO HAVE AN ACTUAL EFFECT ON THE WORLD? MAKE SOME LASTING CHANGE?"
SO, I TELL HER ART AND MUSIC DO CHANGE THE WORLD THOUGH.
JUST ANOTHER COMPROMISED ADULT WITH A DEAD HEART.
QUITTING YOUR DREAMS WILL MAKE YOU HATE ANYONE WHO DIDN'T.
KNOCK
DREAMS ARE A LUXURY FOR RICH KIDS.
WHAT DO YOU SAY, VIK? CAN WE CHANGE THE WORLD THROUGH ART?
"EVERYONE THINKS OF CHANGING THE WORLD, BUT NO ONE THINKS OF CHANGING HIMSELF."
IS WHY SOVIETS ARE SUPERIOR--WE READ TOLSTOY WHILE YOU READ SUPERMAN.
CLK
YOU CAN TELL YOURSELF DANCING AND FINGER PAINTING ARE NOBLE PURSUITS--
--BUT THEY AREN'T.
WHAT MAKES YOU THINK THE WORLD OWES YOU A LIVING FOR REFUSING TO GROW UP AND GET A REAL JOB?
IS THAT ALL LIFE IS TO YOU? ONE BIG GRIND TO SURVIVE AND FULFILL NECESSARY FUNCTIONS?
THAT'S JUST THE SHIT WE DO TO BUY OURSELVES TIME TO ENJOY ART.
SPEAKING OF ART--
HERE, FIXED THAT DEAD MILKMEN TAPE I WAS TELLING YOU ABOUT--
NAH, MAN, I LOVE MILK.

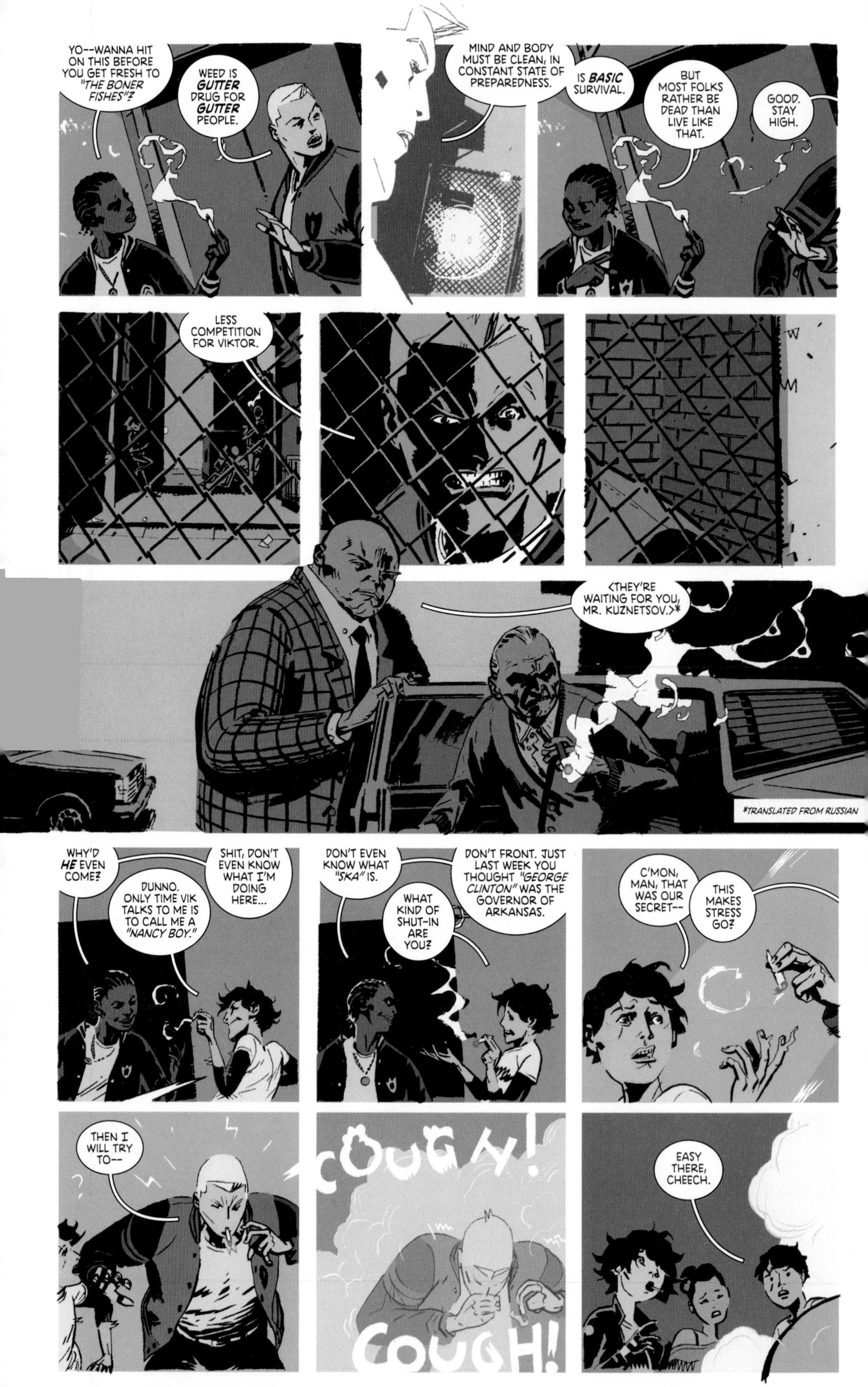
YO--WANNA HIT ON THIS BEFORE YOU GET FRESH TO "THE BONER FISHES"?
WEED IS GUTTER DRUG FOR GUTTER PEOPLE.
MIND AND BODY MUST BE CLEAN, IN CONSTANT STATE OF PREPAREDNESS.
IS BASIC SURVIVAL.
BUT MOST FOLKS RATHER BE DEAD THAN LIVE LIKE THAT.
GOOD. STAY HIGH.
LESS COMPETITION FOR VIKTOR.
<THEY'RE WAITING FOR YOU, MR. KUZNETSOV.>*
*TRANSLATED FROM RUSSIAN
WHY'D HE EVEN COME?
SHIT, DON'T EVEN KNOW WHAT I'M DOING HERE...
DUNNO. ONLY TIME VIK TALKS TO ME IS TO CALL ME A "NANCY BOY."
DON'T EVEN KNOW WHAT "SKA" IS.
DON'T FRONT. JUST LAST WEEK YOU THOUGHT "GEORGE CLINTON" WAS THE GOVERNOR OF ARKANSAS.
WHAT KIND OF SHUT-IN ARE YOU?
C'MON, MAN, THAT WAS OUR SECRET--
THIS MAKES STRESS GO?
THEN I WILL TRY TO--
COUGH!
COUGH!
EASY THERE, CHEECH.

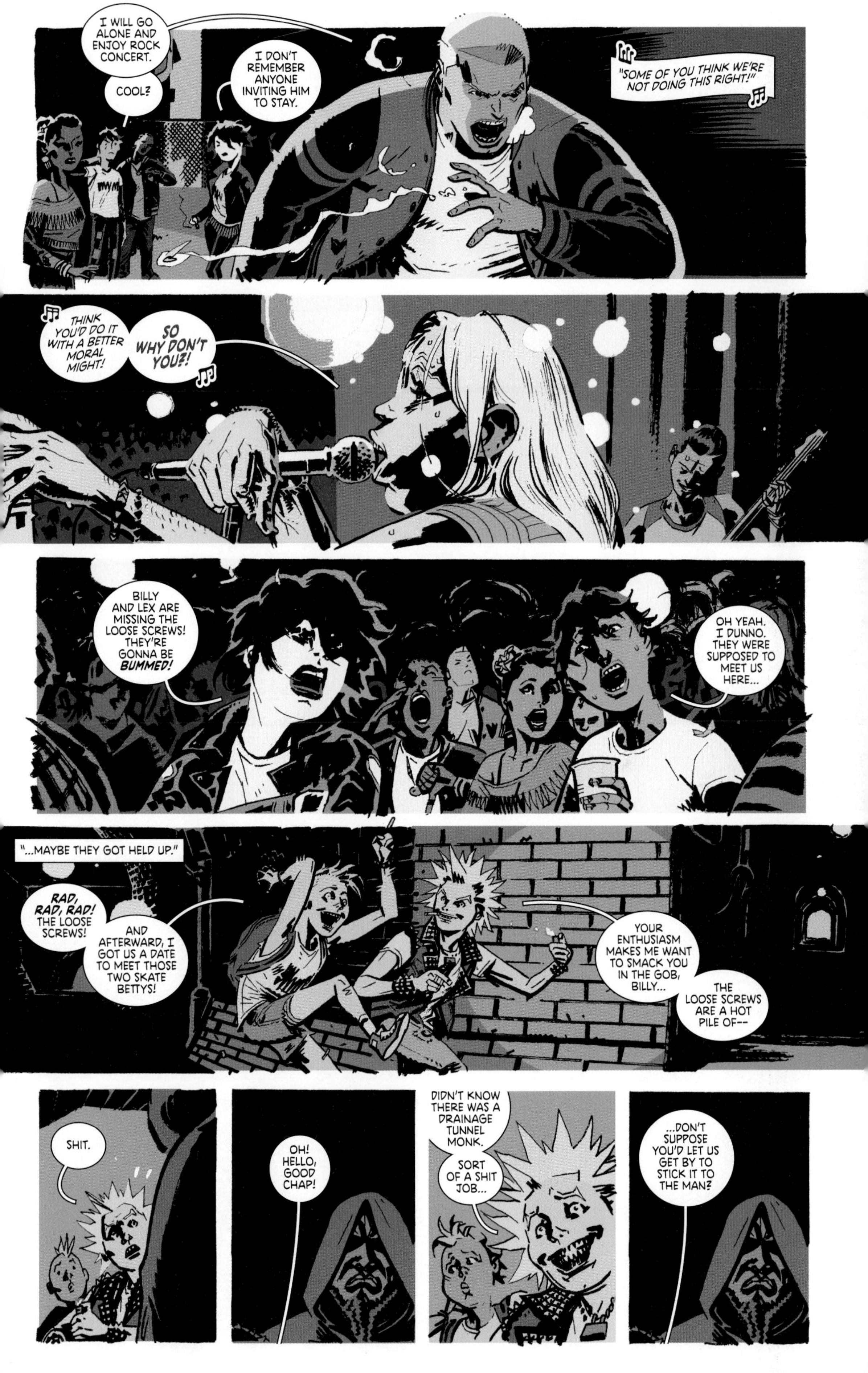
I WILL GO ALONE AND ENJOY ROCK CONCERT.
COOL?
I DON'T REMEMBER ANYONE INVITING HIM TO STAY.
"SOME OF YOU THINK WE'RE NOT DOING THIS RIGHT!"
THINK YOU'D DO IT WITH A BETTER MORAL MIGHT!
SO WHY DON'T YOU?!
BILLY AND LEX ARE MISSING THE LOOSE SCREWS! THEY'RE GONNA BE BUMMED!
OH YEAH. I DUNNO. THEY WERE SUPPOSED TO MEET US HERE...
"...MAYBE THEY GOT HELD UP."
RAD, RAD, RAD! THE LOOSE SCREWS!
AND AFTERWARD, I GOT US A DATE TO MEET THOSE TWO SKATE BETTYS!
YOUR ENTHUSIASM MAKES ME WANT TO SMACK YOU IN THE GOB, BILLY...
THE LOOSE SCREWS ARE A HOT PILE OF--
SHIT.
OH! HELLO, GOOD CHAP!
DIDN'T KNOW THERE WAS A DRAINAGE TUNNEL MONK.
SORT OF A SHIT JOB...
...DON'T SUPPOSE YOU'D LET US GET BY TO STICK IT TO THE MAN?

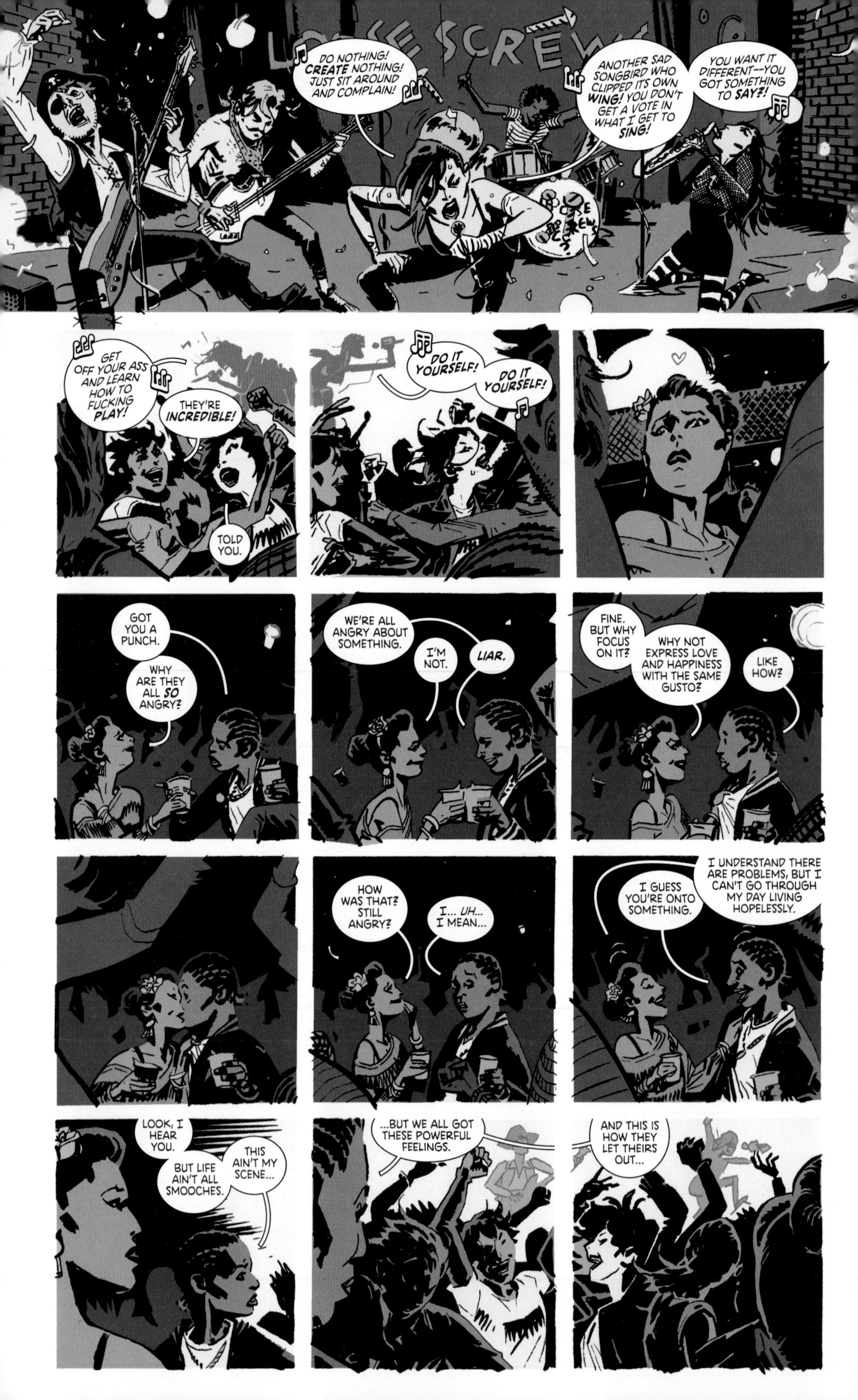
DO NOTHING! CREATE NOTHING! JUST SIT AROUND AND COMPLAIN!
ANOTHER SAD SONGBIRD WHO CLIPPED ITS OWN WING! YOU DON'T GET A VOTE IN WHAT I GET TO SING!
YOU WANT IT DIFFERENT--YOU GOT SOMETHING TO SAY?!
GET OFF YOUR ASS AND LEARN HOW TO FUCKING PLAY!
THEY'RE INCREDIBLE!
TOLD YOU.
DO IT YOURSELF!
DO IT YOURSELF!
GOT YOU A PUNCH.
WHY ARE THEY ALL SO ANGRY?
WE'RE ALL ANGRY ABOUT SOMETHING.
I'M NOT.
LIAR.
FINE. BUT WHY FOCUS ON IT?
WHY NOT EXPRESS LOVE AND HAPPINESS WITH THE SAME GUSTO?
LIKE HOW?
HOW WAS THAT? STILL ANGRY?
I... UH... I MEAN...
I GUESS YOU'RE ONTO SOMETHING.
I UNDERSTAND THERE ARE PROBLEMS, BUT I CAN'T GO THROUGH MY DAY LIVING HOPELESSLY.
LOOK, I HEAR YOU.
BUT LIFE AIN'T ALL SMOOCHES.
THIS AIN'T MY SCENE...
...BUT WE ALL GOT THESE POWERFUL FEELINGS.
AND THIS IS HOW THEY LET THEIRS OUT...

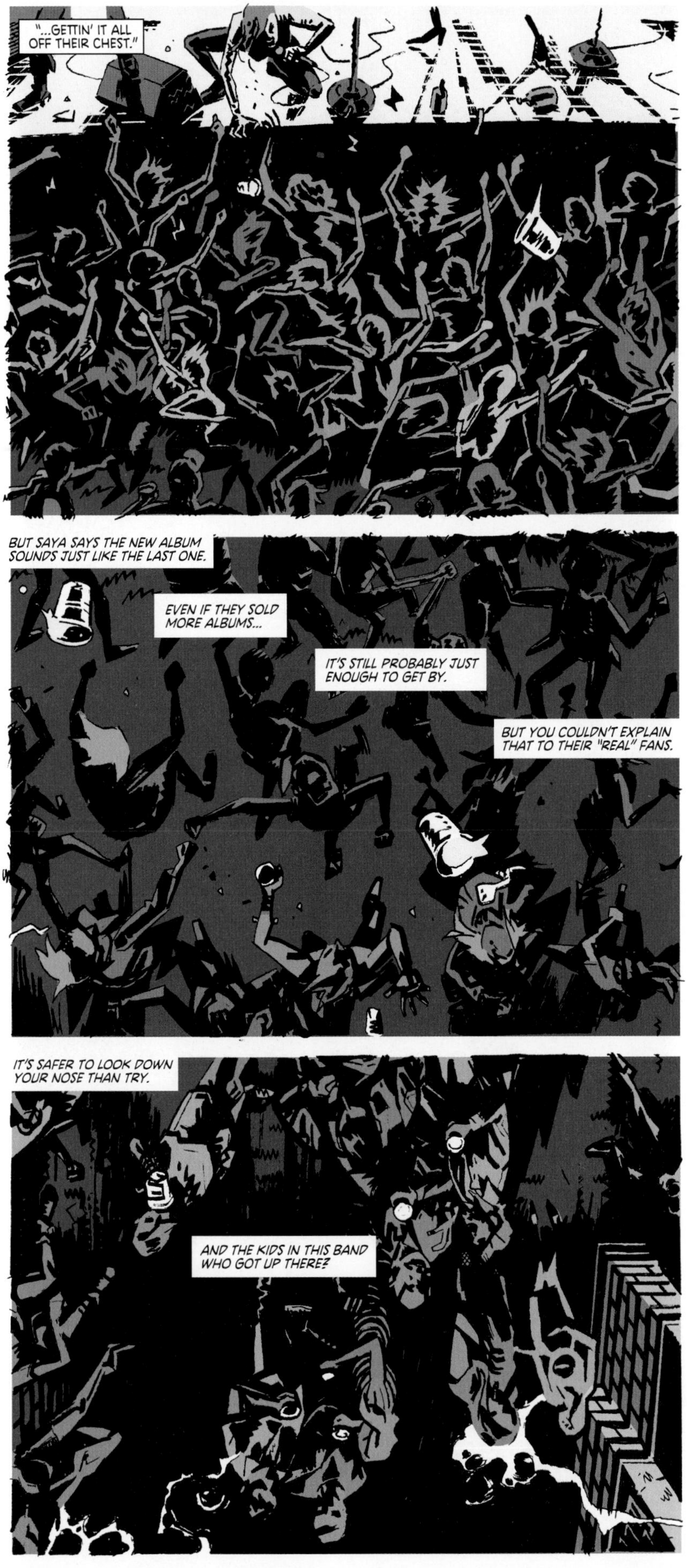
"...GETTIN' IT ALL OFF THEIR CHEST."
BUT SAYA SAYS THE NEW ALBUM SOUNDS JUST LIKE THE LAST ONE.
EVEN IF THEY SOLD MORE ALBUMS...
IT'S STILL PROBABLY JUST ENOUGH TO GET BY.
BUT YOU COULDN'T EXPLAIN THAT TO THEIR "REAL" FANS.
IT'S SAFER TO LOOK DOWN YOUR NOSE THAN TRY.
AND THE KIDS IN THIS BAND WHO GOT UP THERE?

SAYA WOULDN'T SHUT UP ABOUT THE LOOSE SCREWS ALL WEEK. I STARTED TO SEE THE BAND ON THE FRONT OF A FEW MAGAZINES A BIT BACK, THEY'RE BREAKING THEY SAY, FINDING A WIDER AUDIENCE.

WAITING IN LINE TO GET IN WE HEARD A BUNCH OF KIDS TALKING ABOUT WHAT SELLOUT CUNTS THEY ARE NOW, HOW MUCH BETTER THEY WERE BEFORE ANYONE CAME TO SEE THEM.

TALKING TOUGH ABOUT HOW THEY'D DO IT DIFFERENTLY IF IT WERE THEM.

I WONDER WHAT THEY'D DO IN THE SAME SITUATION? AFTER YEARS OF WORK, WOULD THEY TURN DOWN MAKING SOME RENT MONEY?

NO. AND PEOPLE LIKE THAT, THEY NEVER TAKE THE STAGE.

TERRIFIED OF A GROUP OF BITTER PILLS SITTING IN THE BACK SNARLING AT THEM THE SAME WAY.

TERRIFIED OF THEIR OWN BRAND OF POISON.

I GUESS THEY DESERVE TO HAVE VOMIT SPEWED ON THEM FOR CHASING THEIR DREAMS...

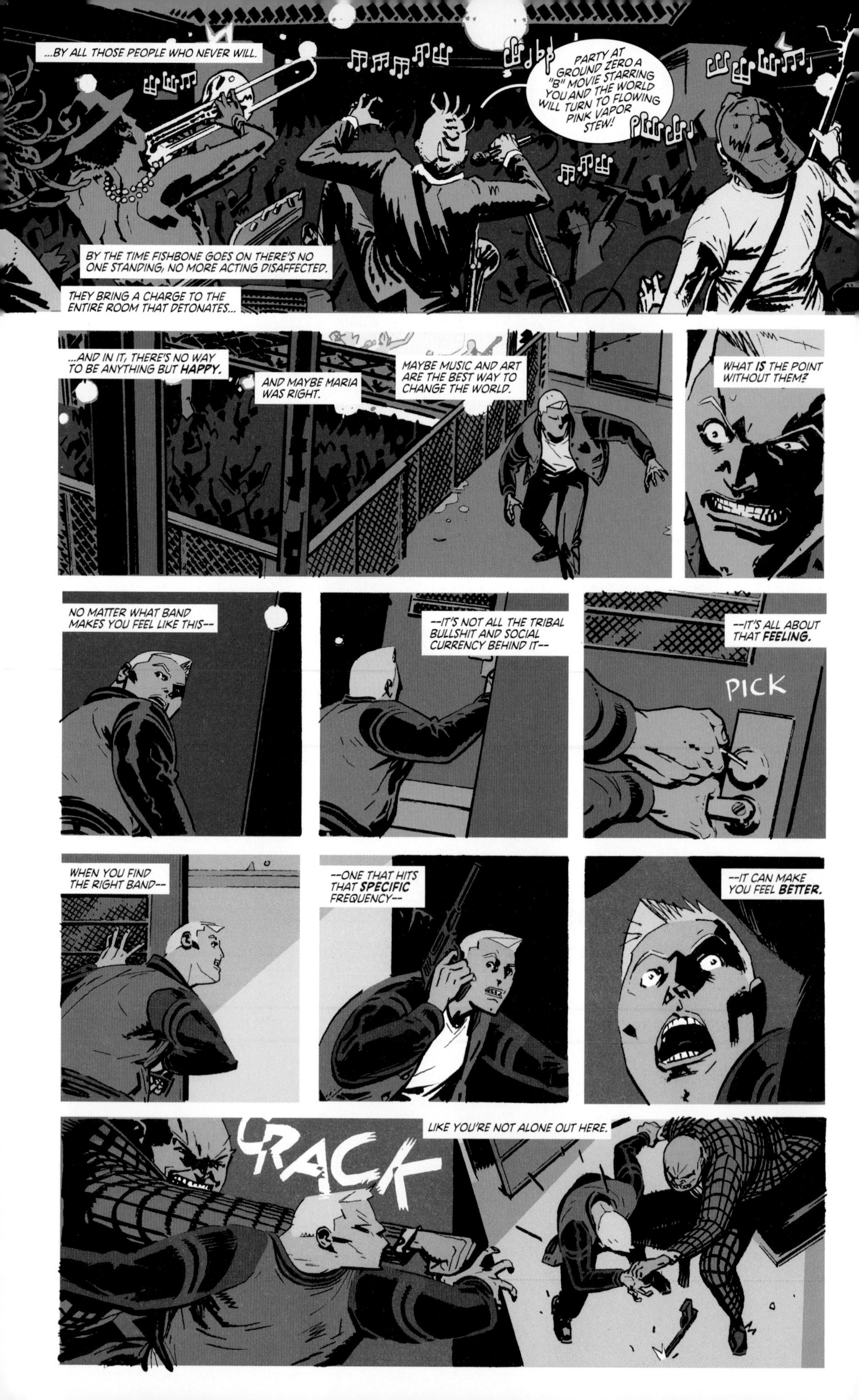
...BY ALL THOSE PEOPLE WHO NEVER WILL.
PARTY AT GROUND ZERO A "B" MOVIE STARRING YOU AND THE WORLD WILL TURN TO FLOWING PINK VAPOR STEW!
BY THE TIME FISHBONE GOES ON THERE'S NO ONE STANDING, NO MORE ACTING DISAFFECTED.
THEY BRING A CHARGE TO THE ENTIRE ROOM THAT DETONATES...
...AND IN IT, THERE'S NO WAY TO BE ANYTHING BUT HAPPY.
AND MAYBE MARIA WAS RIGHT.
MAYBE MUSIC AND ART ARE THE BEST WAY TO CHANGE THE WORLD.
WHAT IS THE POINT WITHOUT THEM?
NO MATTER WHAT BAND MAKES YOU FEEL LIKE THIS--
--IT'S NOT ALL THE TRIBAL BULLSHIT AND SOCIAL CURRENCY BEHIND IT--
--IT'S ALL ABOUT THAT FEELING.
PICK
WHEN YOU FIND THE RIGHT BAND--
--ONE THAT HITS THAT SPECIFIC FREQUENCY--
--IT CAN MAKE YOU FEEL BETTER.
CRACK
LIKE YOU'RE NOT ALONE OUT HERE.

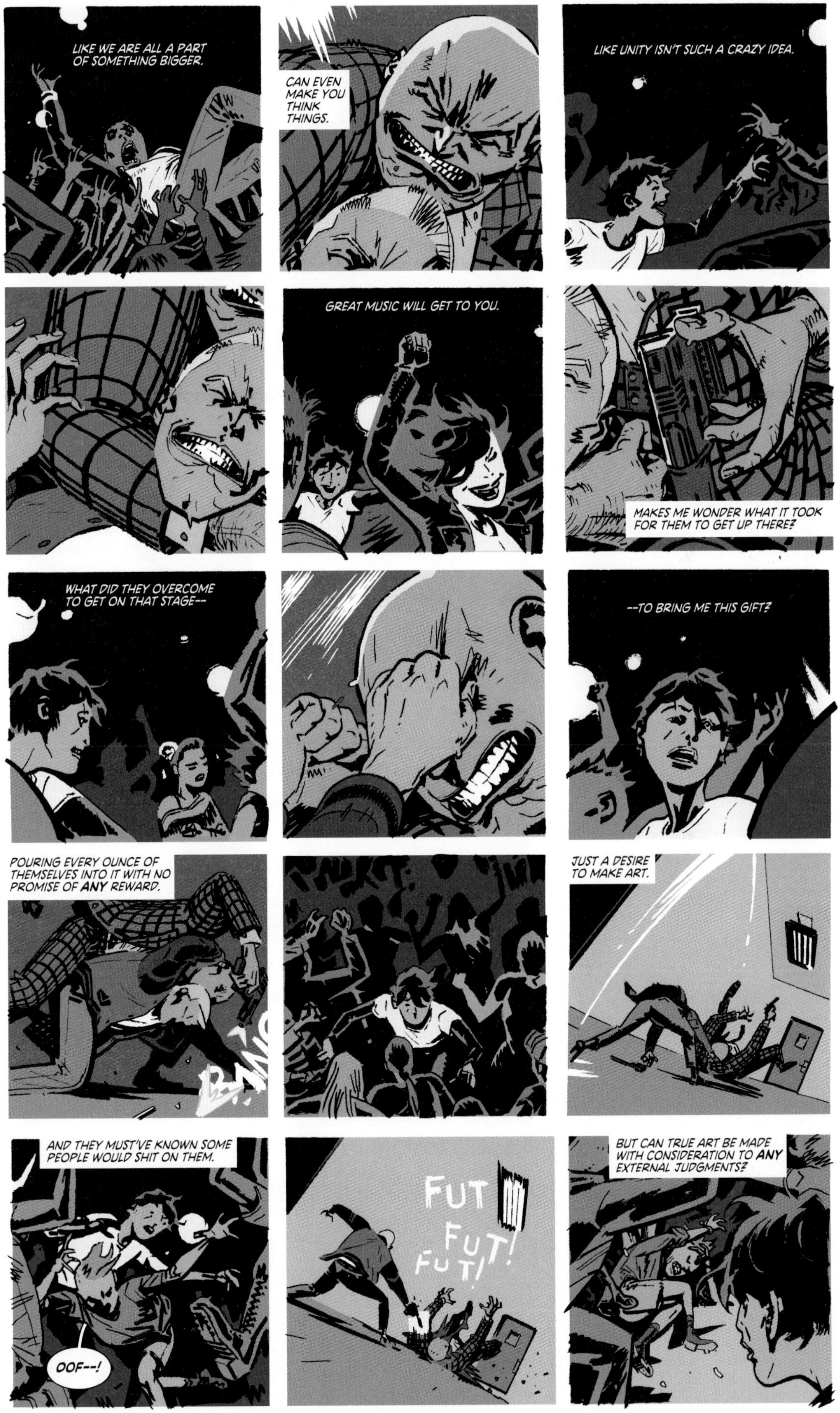

LIKE WE ARE ALL A PART OF SOMETHING BIGGER.
CAN EVEN MAKE YOU THINK THINGS.
LIKE UNITY ISN'T SUCH A CRAZY IDEA.
GREAT MUSIC WILL GET TO YOU.
MAKES ME WONDER WHAT IT TOOK FOR THEM TO GET UP THERE?
WHAT DID THEY OVERCOME TO GET ON THAT STAGE--
--TO BRING ME THIS GIFT?
POURING EVERY OUNCE OF THEMSELVES INTO IT WITH NO PROMISE OF ANY REWARD.
JUST A DESIRE TO MAKE ART.
AND THEY MUST'VE KNOWN SOME PEOPLE WOULD SHIT ON THEM.
OOF--!
FUT
FUT!
FUT!
BUT CAN TRUE ART BE MADE WITH CONSIDERATION TO ANY EXTERNAL JUDGMENTS?

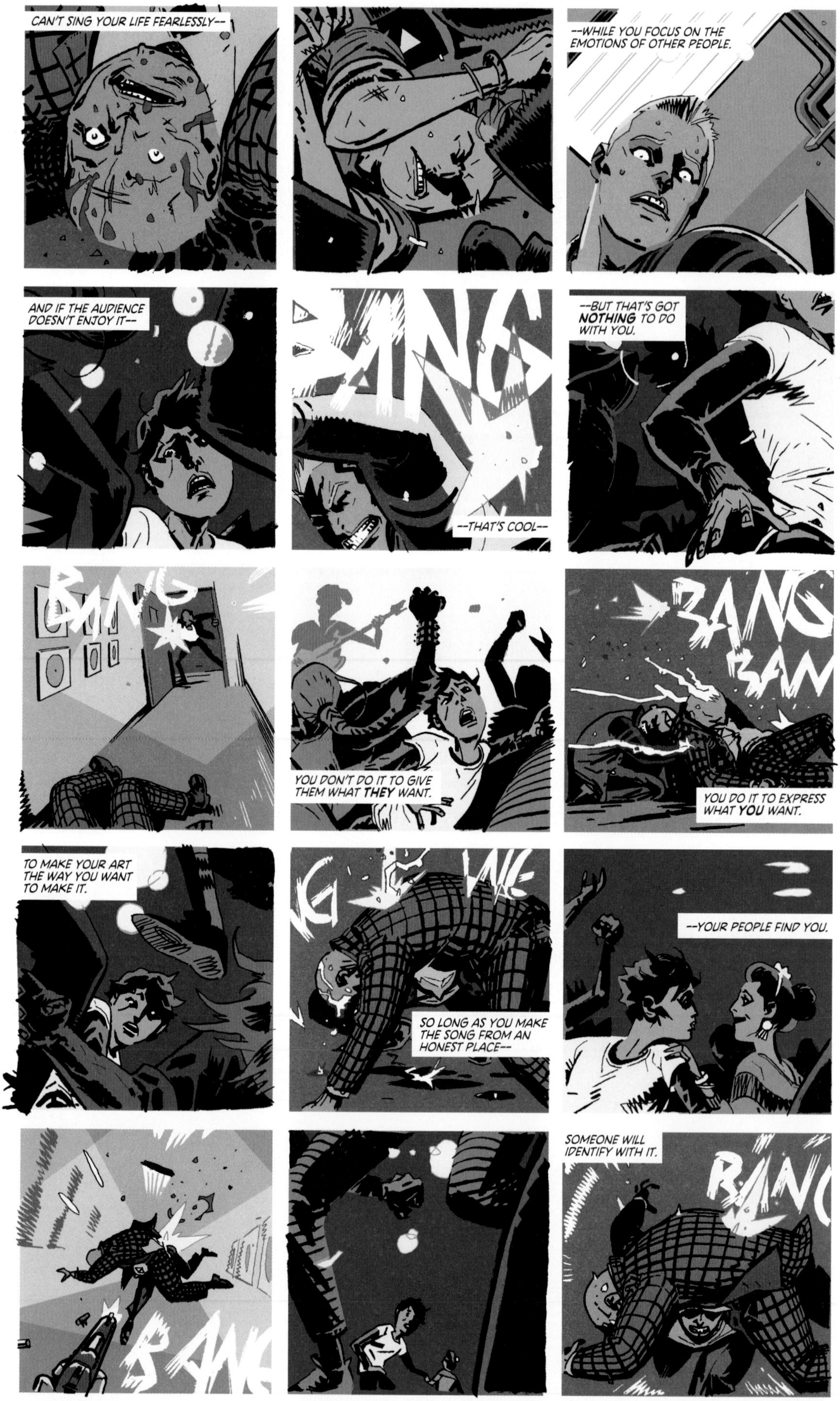
CAN'T SING YOUR LIFE FEARLESSLY--
--WHILE YOU FOCUS ON THE EMOTIONS OF OTHER PEOPLE.
AND IF THE AUDIENCE DOESN'T ENJOY IT--
--THAT'S COOL--
--BUT THAT'S GOT **NOTHING** TO DO WITH YOU.
BANG
YOU DON'T DO IT TO GIVE THEM WHAT **THEY** WANT.
BANG
YOU DO IT TO EXPRESS WHAT **YOU** WANT.
TO MAKE YOUR ART THE WAY YOU WANT TO MAKE IT.
SO LONG AS YOU MAKE THE SONG FROM AN HONEST PLACE--
--YOUR PEOPLE FIND YOU.
SOMEONE WILL IDENTIFY WITH IT.

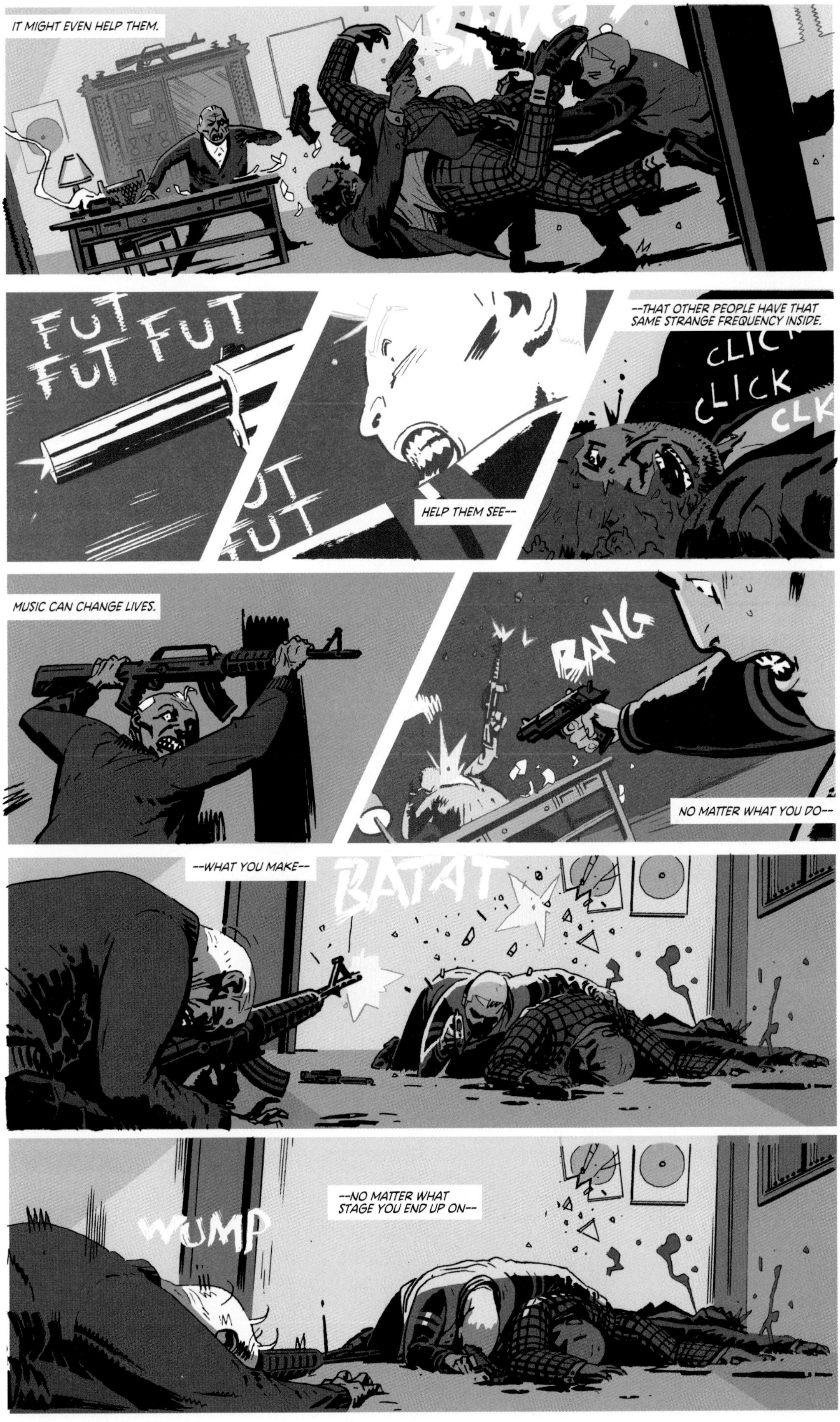
IT MIGHT EVEN HELP THEM.
BANG!
FUT FUT FUT FUT
FUT FUT
HELP THEM SEE--
--THAT OTHER PEOPLE HAVE THAT SAME STRANGE FREQUENCY INSIDE.
CLICK
CLICK
CLK
MUSIC CAN CHANGE LIVES.
BANG
NO MATTER WHAT YOU DO--
--WHAT YOU MAKE--
BATAT
--NO MATTER WHAT STAGE YOU END UP ON--
WUMP

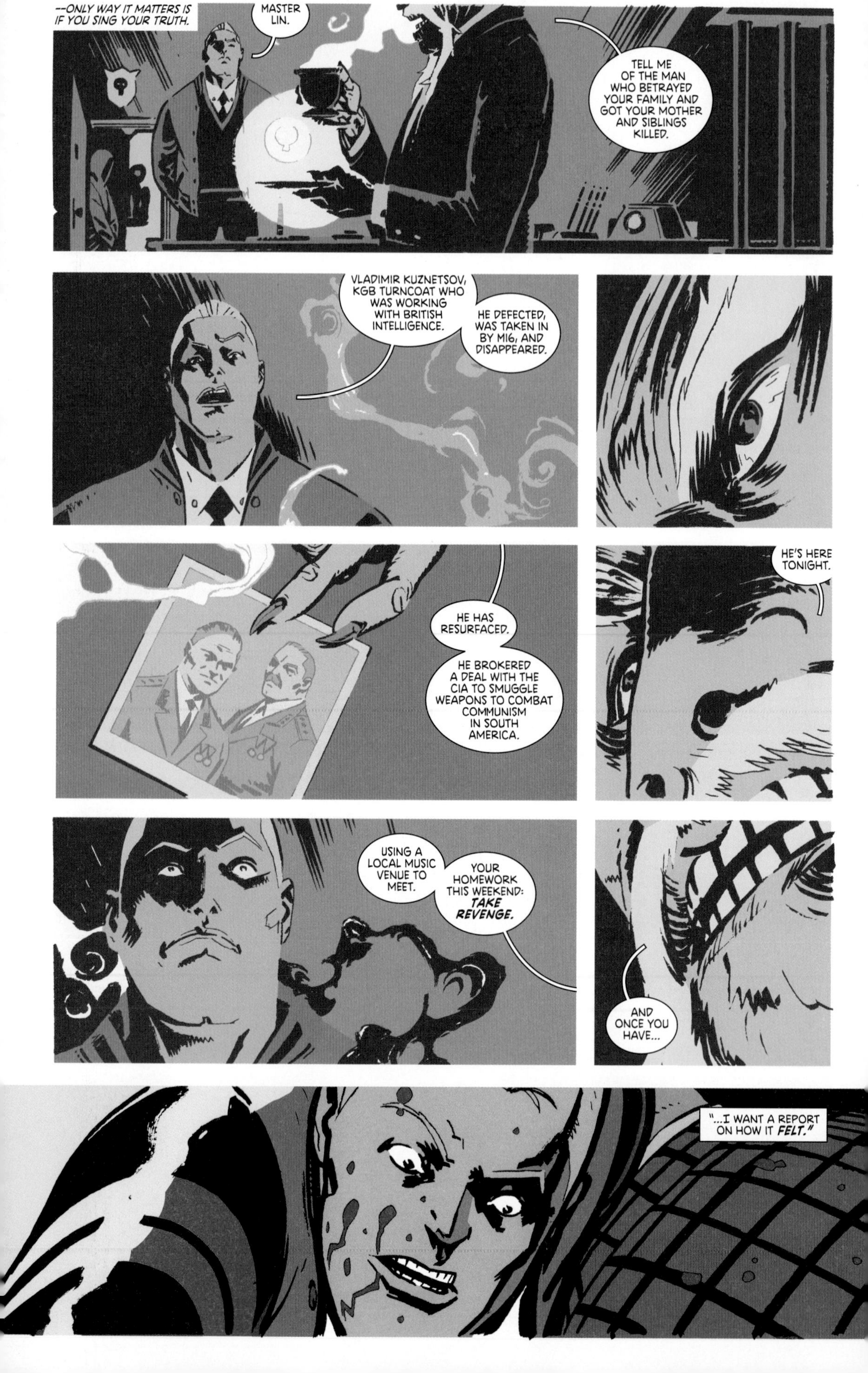
--ONLY WAY IT MATTERS IS IF YOU SING YOUR TRUTH.
MASTER LIN.
TELL ME OF THE MAN WHO BETRAYED YOUR FAMILY AND GOT YOUR MOTHER AND SIBLINGS KILLED.
VLADIMIR KUZNETSOV, KGB TURNCOAT WHO WAS WORKING WITH BRITISH INTELLIGENCE.
HE DEFECTED, WAS TAKEN IN BY MI6, AND DISAPPEARED.
HE HAS RESURFACED.
HE BROKERED A DEAL WITH THE CIA TO SMUGGLE WEAPONS TO COMBAT COMMUNISM IN SOUTH AMERICA.
HE'S HERE TONIGHT.
USING A LOCAL MUSIC VENUE TO MEET.
YOUR HOMEWORK THIS WEEKEND: TAKE REVENGE.
AND ONCE YOU HAVE...
"...I WANT A REPORT ON HOW IT FELT."

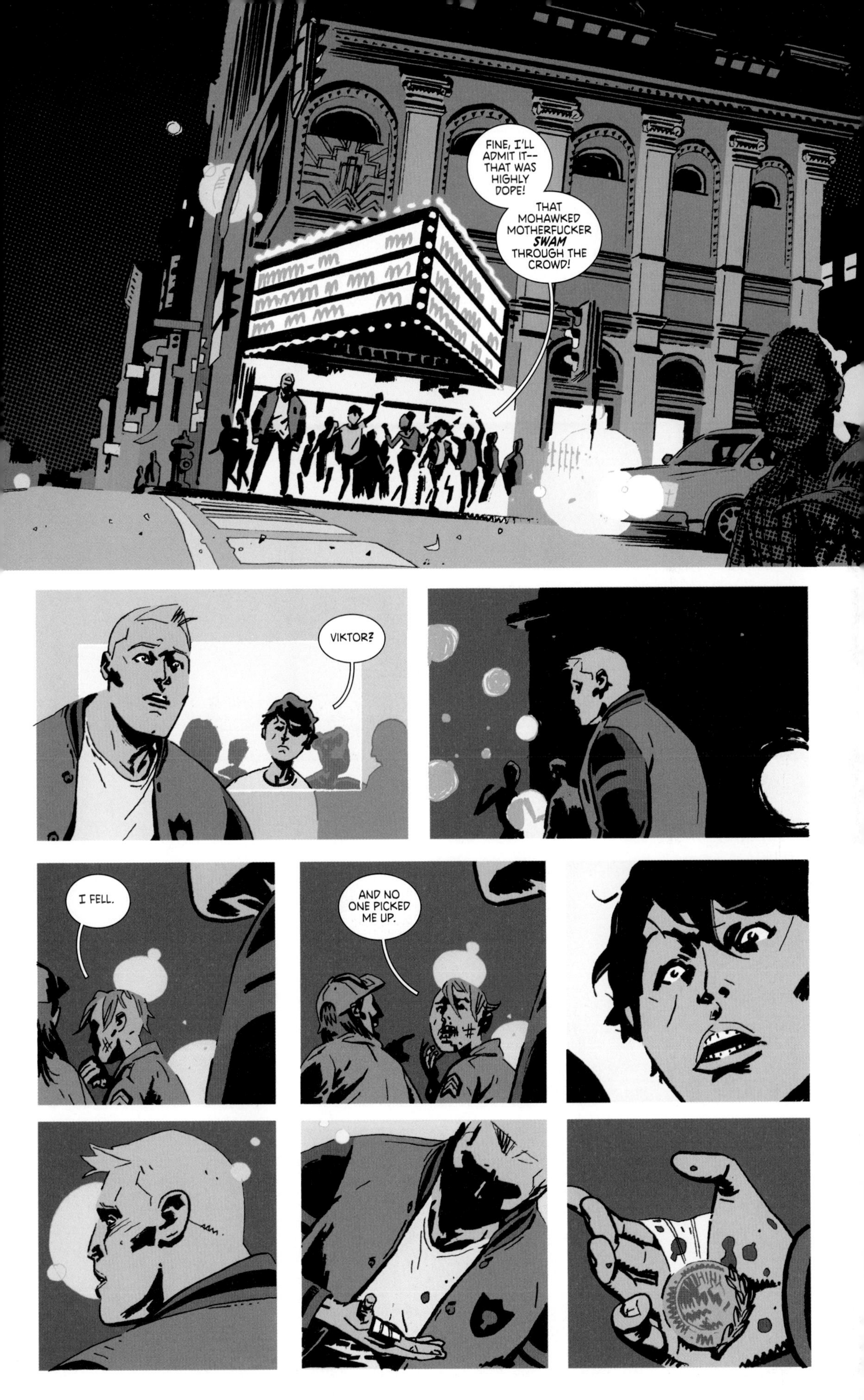
FINE, I'LL ADMIT IT-- THAT WAS HIGHLY DOPE!
THAT MOHAWKED MOTHERFUCKER SWAM THROUGH THE CROWD!
VIKTOR?
I FELL.
AND NO ONE PICKED ME UP.

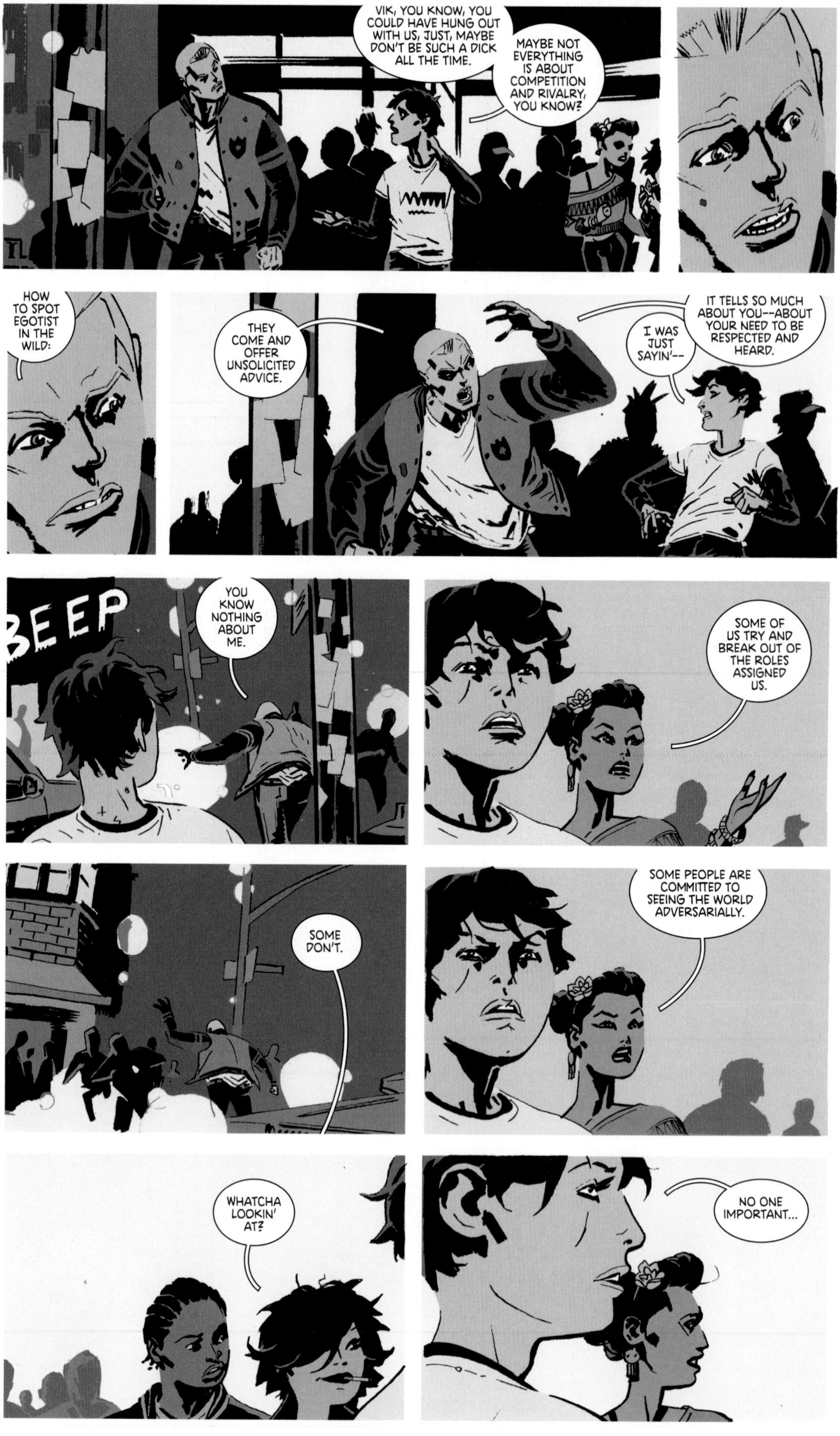
VIK, YOU KNOW, YOU COULD HAVE HUNG OUT WITH US, JUST, MAYBE DON'T BE SUCH A DICK ALL THE TIME.
MAYBE NOT EVERYTHING IS ABOUT COMPETITION AND RIVALRY, YOU KNOW?
HOW TO SPOT EGOTIST IN THE WILD:
THEY COME AND OFFER UNSOLICITED ADVICE.
IT TELLS SO MUCH ABOUT YOU--ABOUT YOUR NEED TO BE RESPECTED AND HEARD.
I WAS JUST SAYIN'--
BEEP
YOU KNOW NOTHING ABOUT ME.
SOME OF US TRY AND BREAK OUT OF THE ROLES ASSIGNED US.
SOME DON'T.
SOME PEOPLE ARE COMMITTED TO SEEING THE WORLD ADVERSARIALLY.
WHATCHA LOOKIN' AT?
NO ONE IMPORTANT...

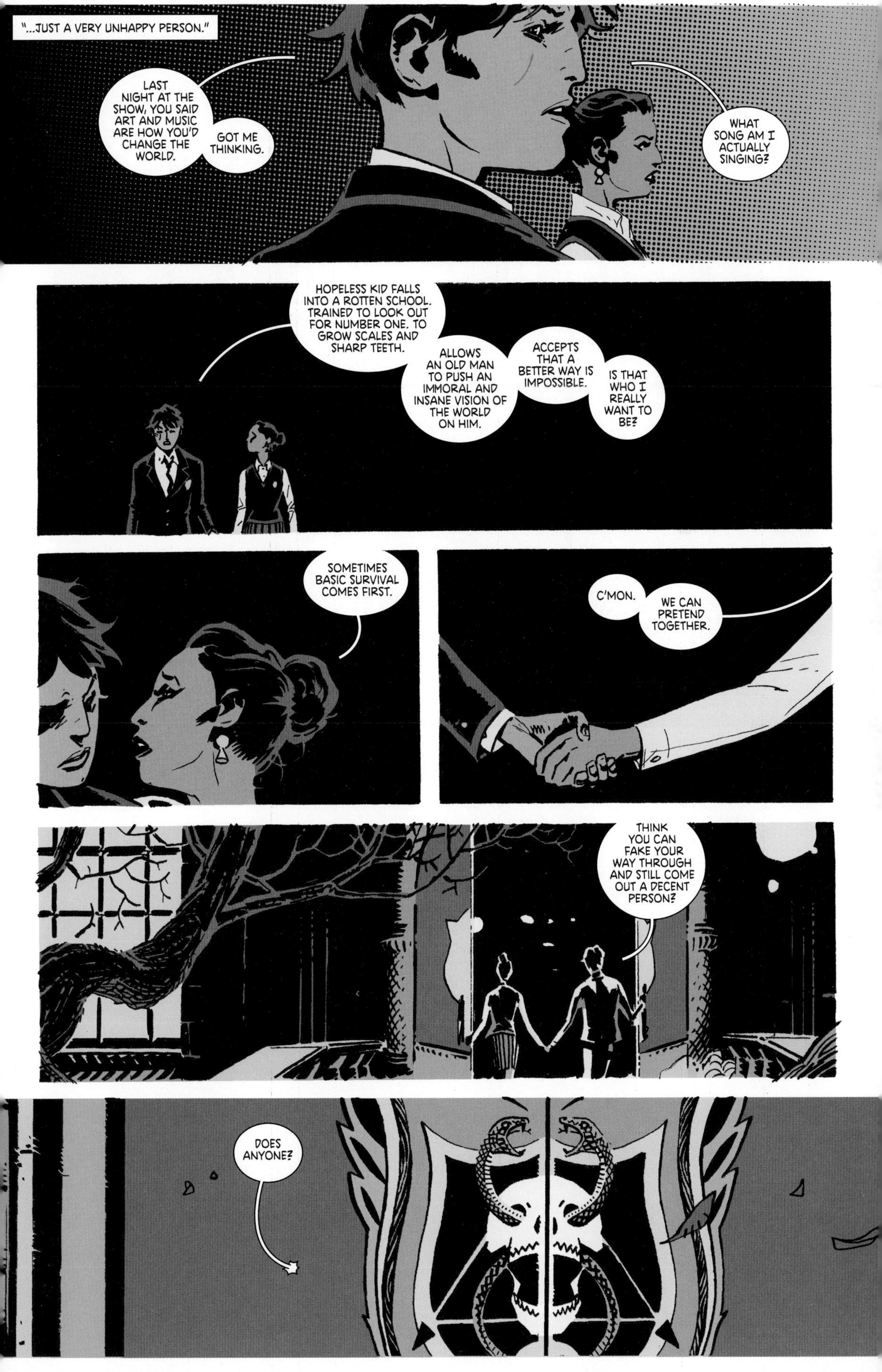
"...JUST A VERY UNHAPPY PERSON."
LAST NIGHT AT THE SHOW, YOU SAID ART AND MUSIC ARE HOW YOU'D CHANGE THE WORLD.
GOT ME THINKING.
WHAT SONG AM I ACTUALLY SINGING?
HOPELESS KID FALLS INTO A ROTTEN SCHOOL. TRAINED TO LOOK OUT FOR NUMBER ONE. TO GROW SCALES AND SHARP TEETH.
ALLOWS AN OLD MAN TO PUSH AN IMMORAL AND INSANE VISION OF THE WORLD ON HIM.
ACCEPTS THAT A BETTER WAY IS IMPOSSIBLE.
IS THAT WHO I REALLY WANT TO BE?
SOMETIMES BASIC SURVIVAL COMES FIRST.
C'MON.
WE CAN PRETEND TOGETHER.
THINK YOU CAN FAKE YOUR WAY THROUGH AND STILL COME OUT A DECENT PERSON?
DOES ANYONE?

COVER GALLERY

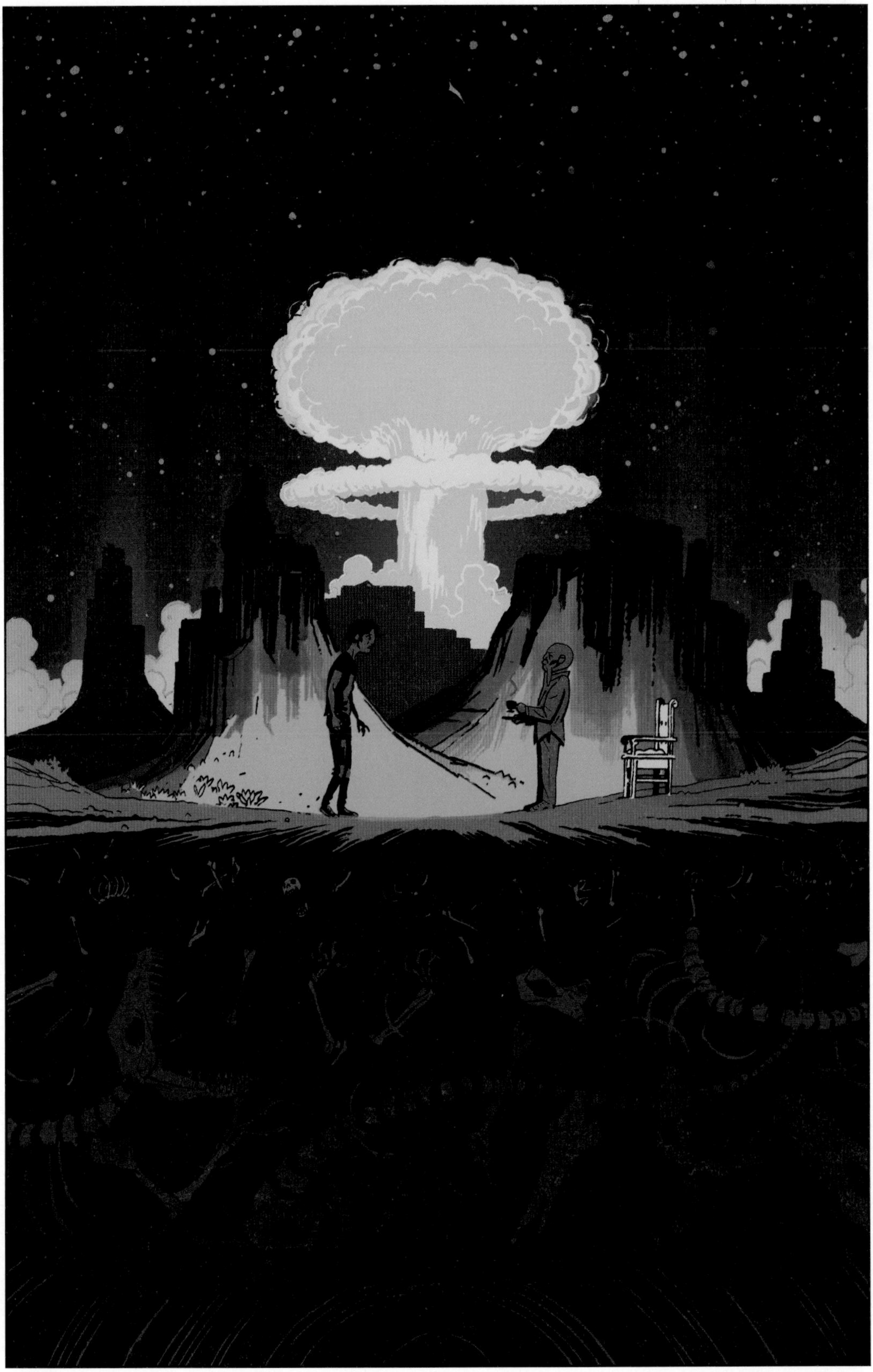

#36 COVER BY **WES CRAIG**

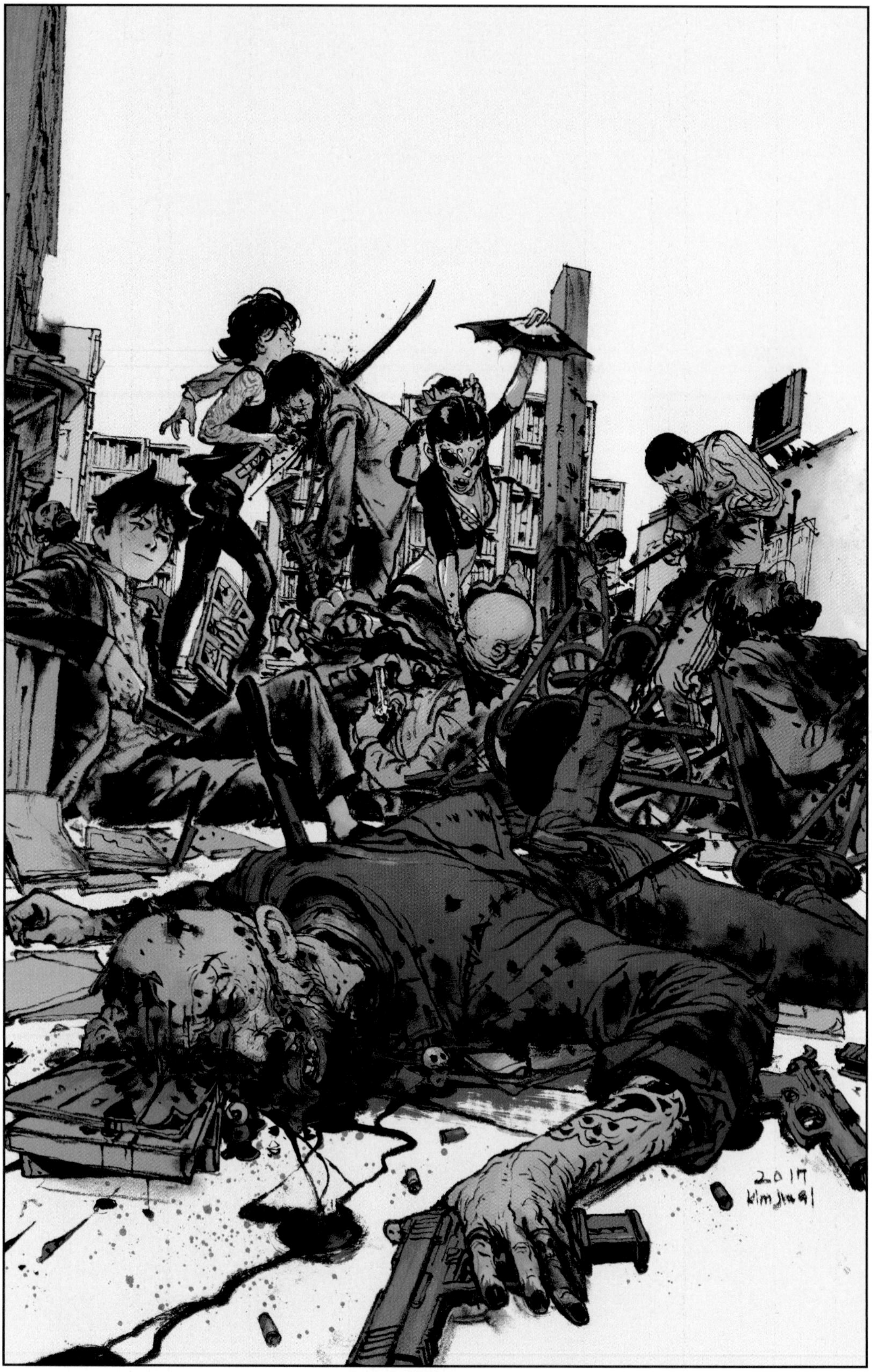
2017

#36 VARIANT BY **KIM JUNG GI & DAVE McCAIG**

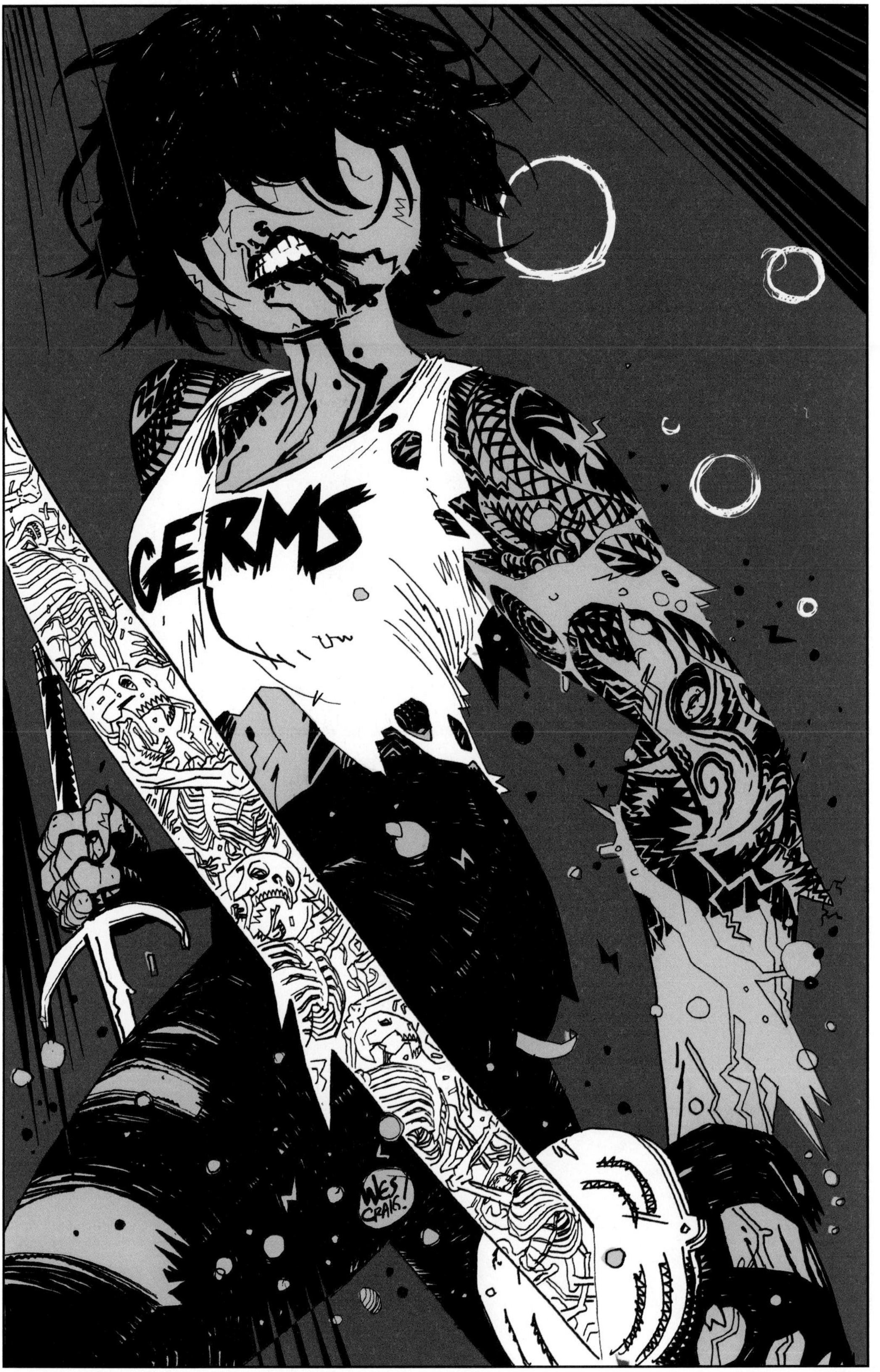
GERMS
WES CRAIG

#37 COVER BY **WES CRAIG**

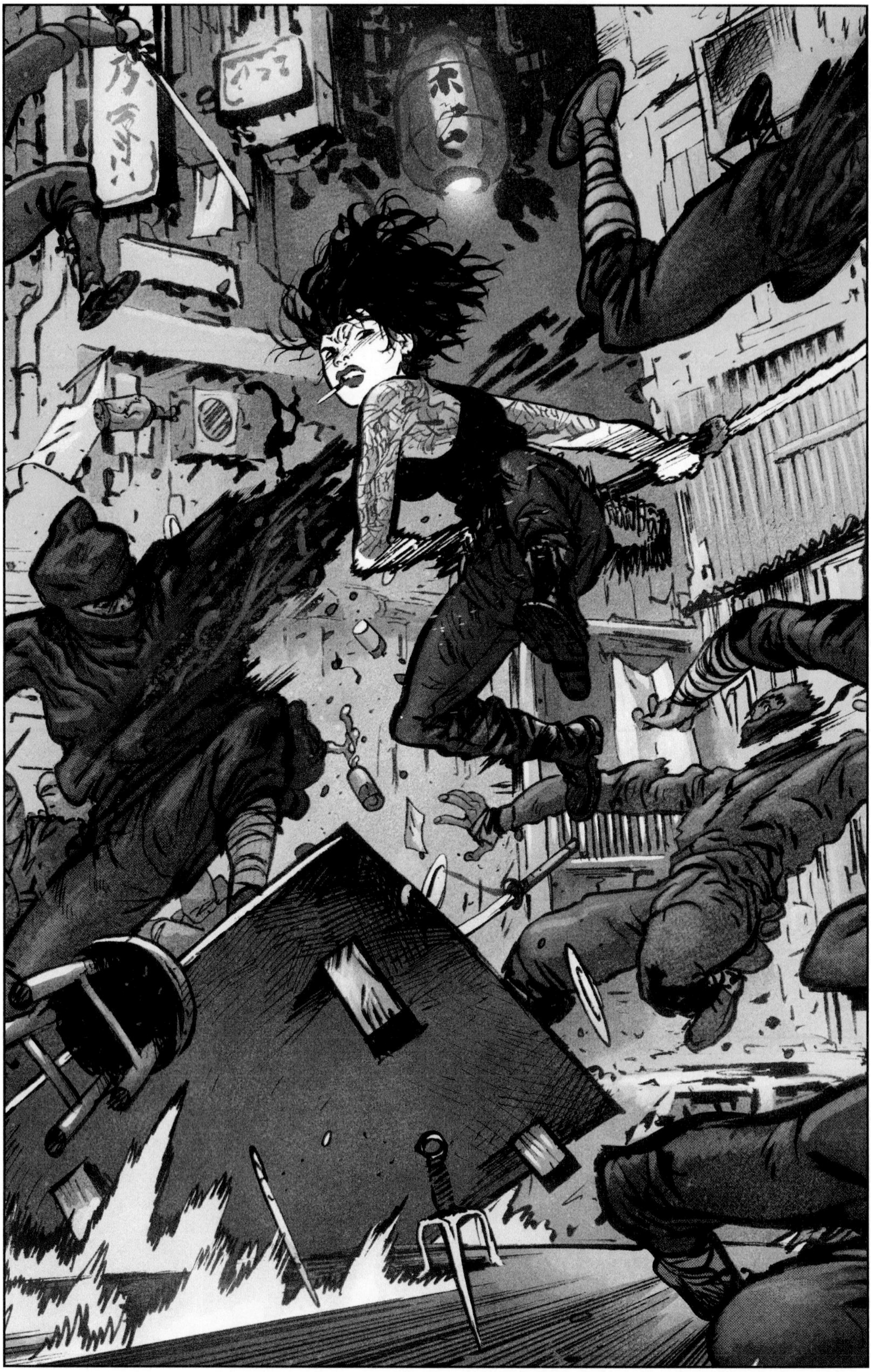

#37 VARIANT BY **DANIEL WARREN JOHNSON & JORDAN BOYD**

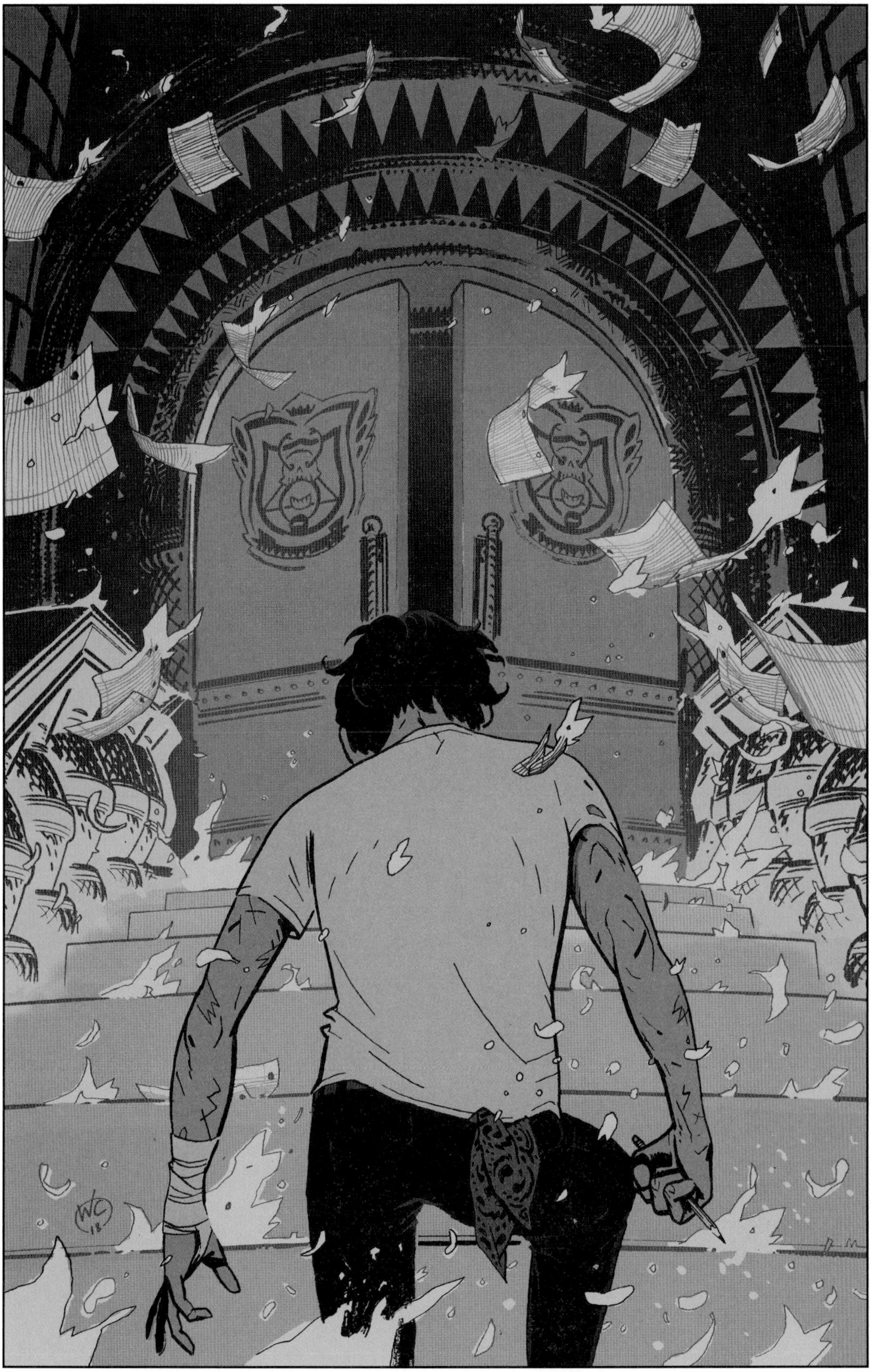

#38 COVER BY **WES CRAIG**

#38 VARIANT BY **JOHN McCREA**

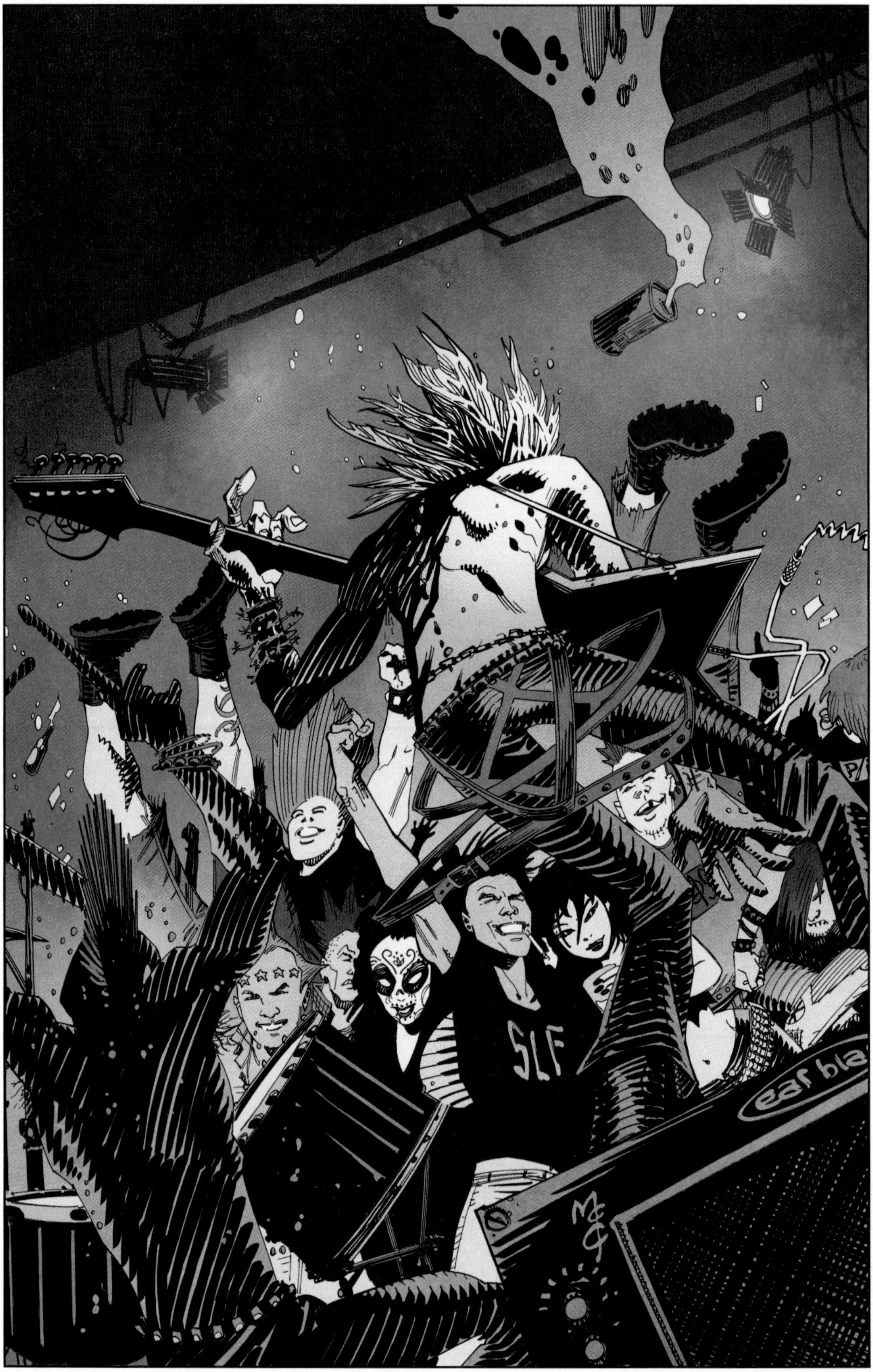
SLF

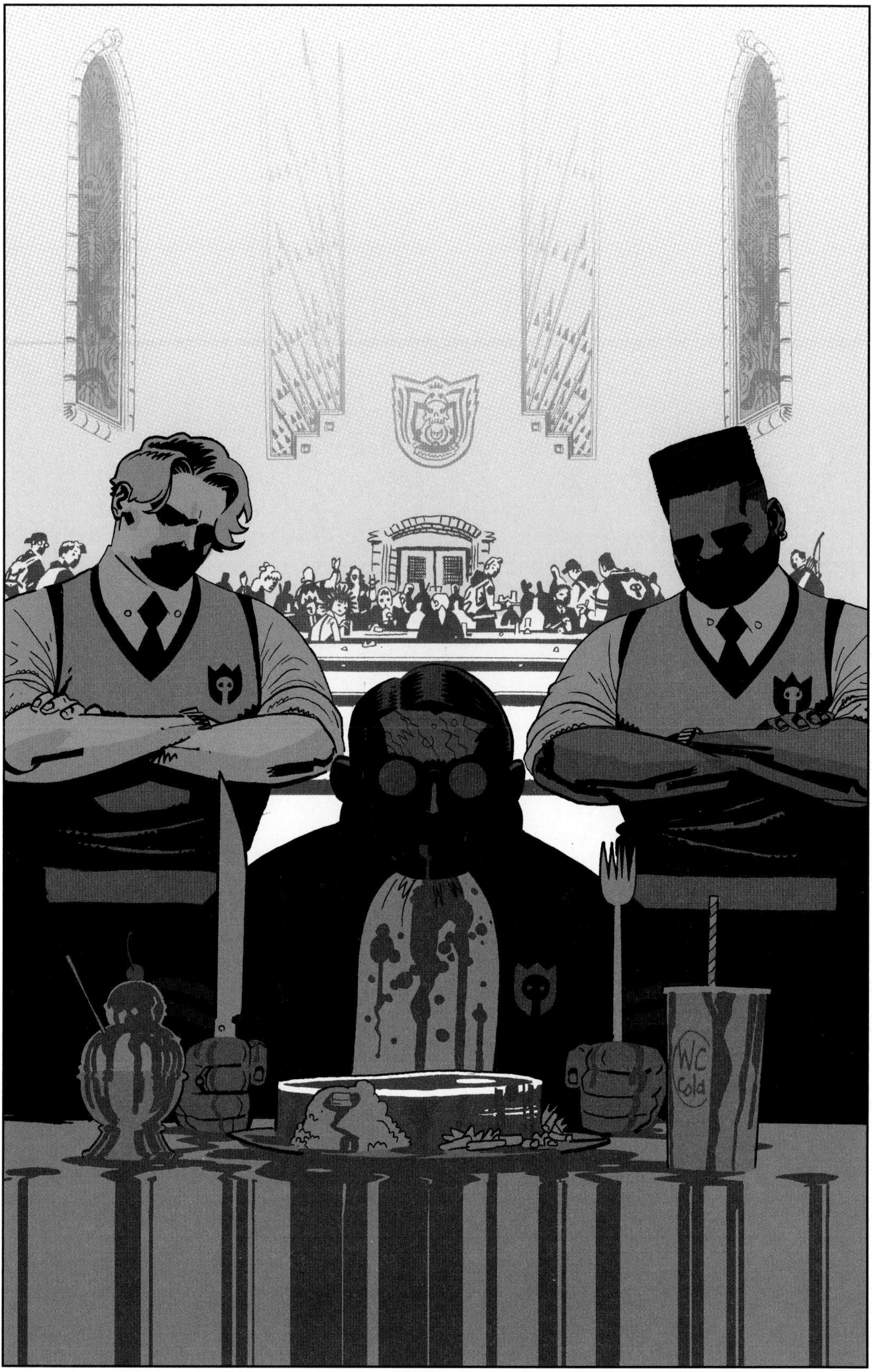
WC Cola

#39 COVER BY **WES CRAIG**

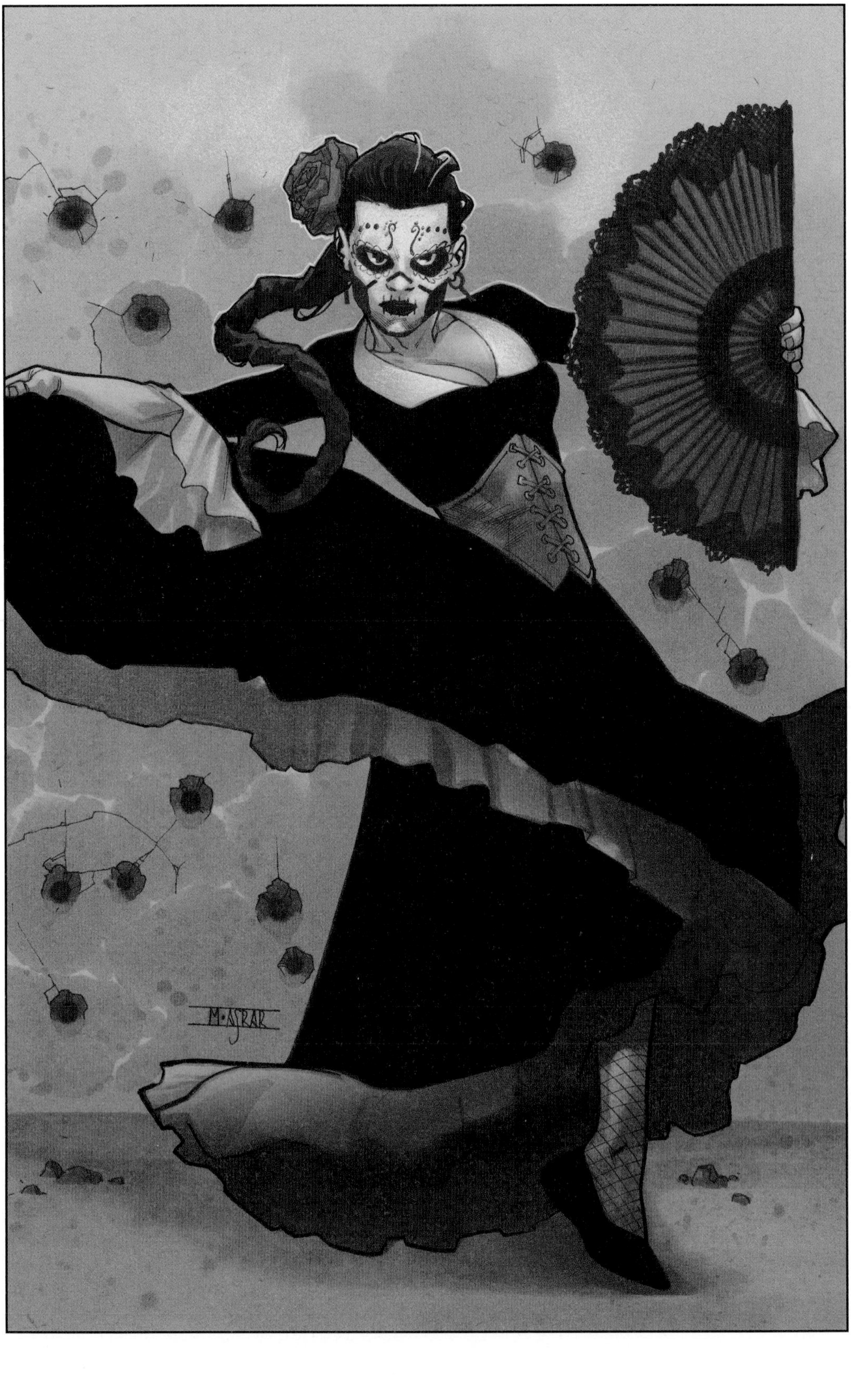
M·ASRAR

#39 VARIANT BY **MAHMUD ASRAR & DAVE McCAIG**

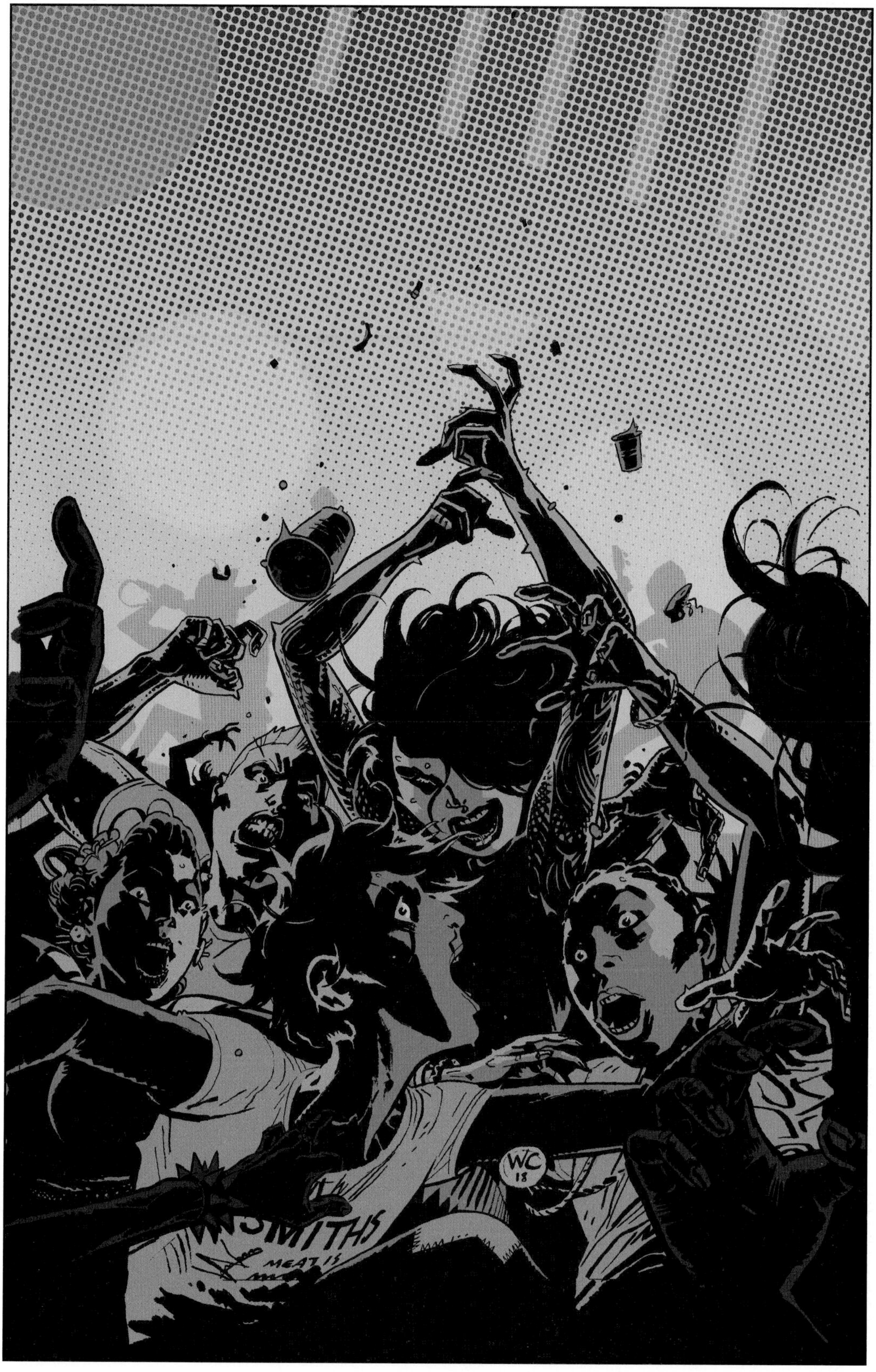
SMITHS
MEAT IS

2019 FCBD COVER BY **WES CRAIG**

#39 INTERIOR ROUGHS BY **WES CRAIG**

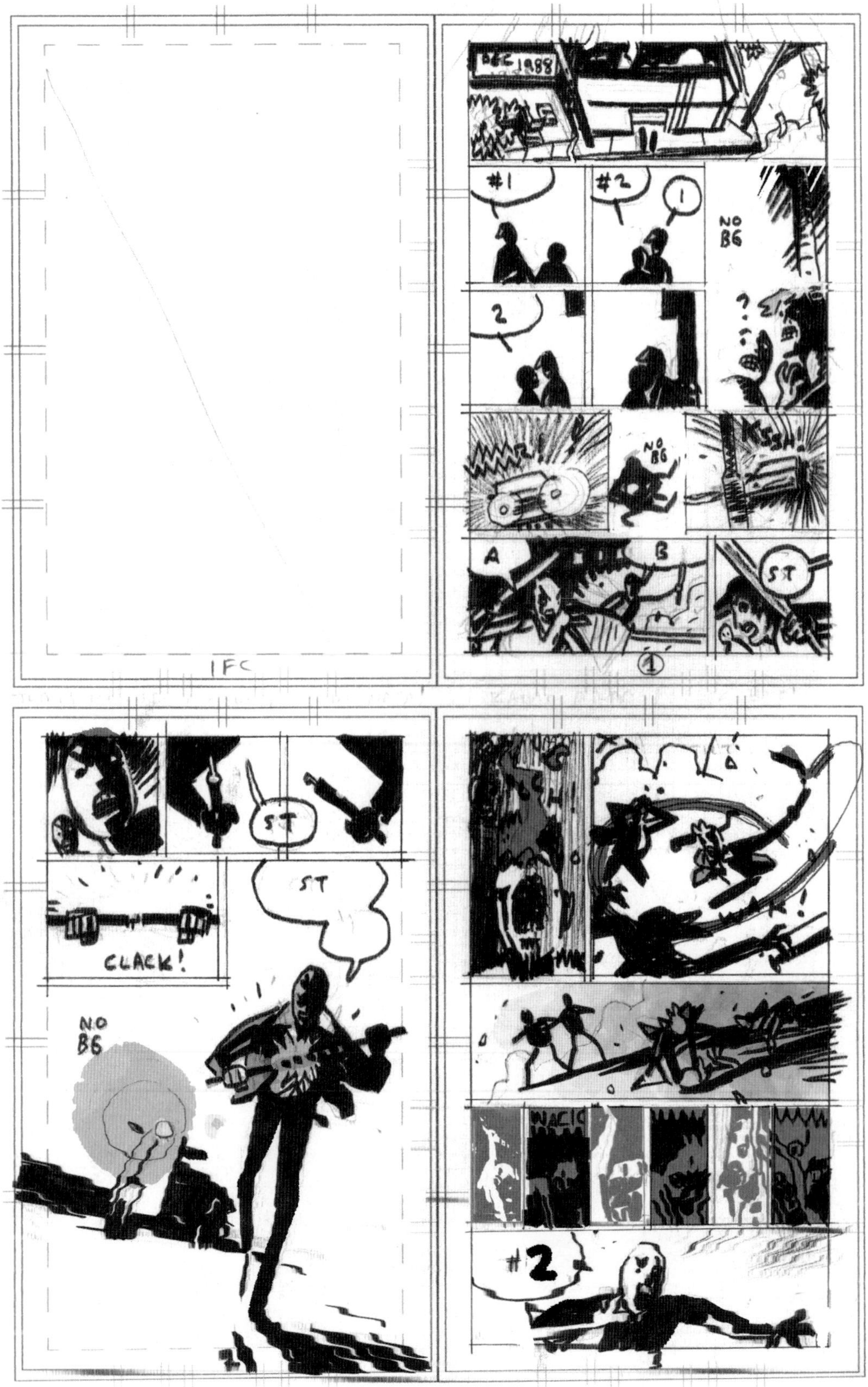

IFC
DEC 1988
#1
#2
1
NO BG
2
NO BG
A
B
ST
ST
ST
CLACK!
NO BG
#2

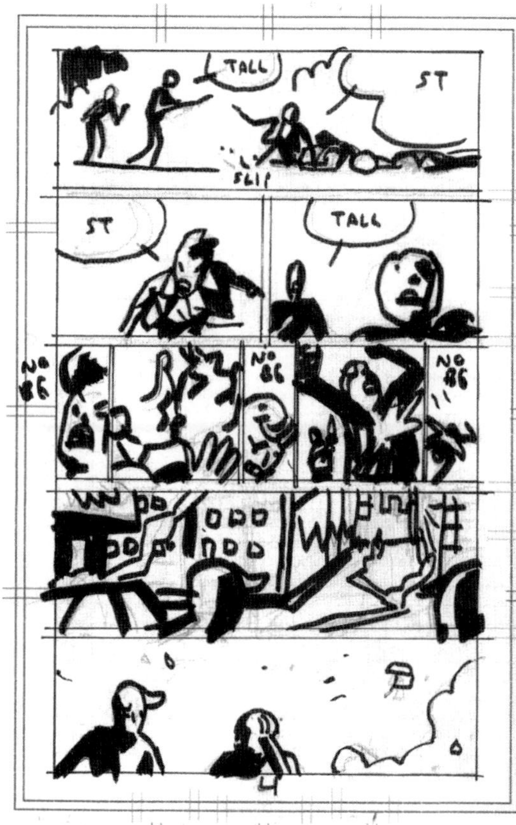
TALL
ST
SLIP
ST
TALL
NO 86
NO 86
NO 86
4

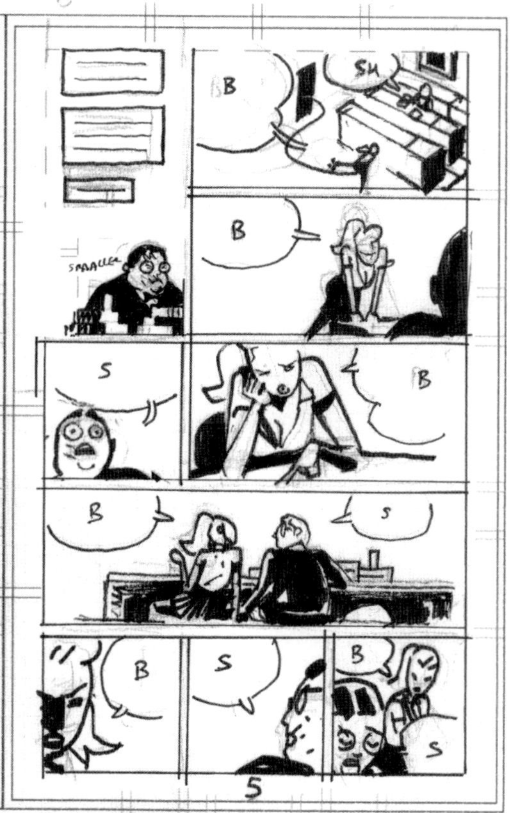
B
SH
B
S
B
B
S
B
S
B
S
5

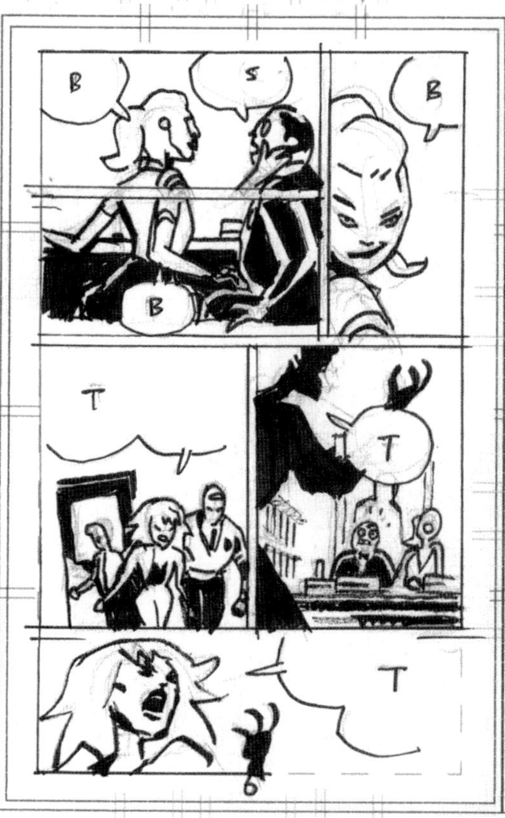
B
S
B
B
T
T
T
6

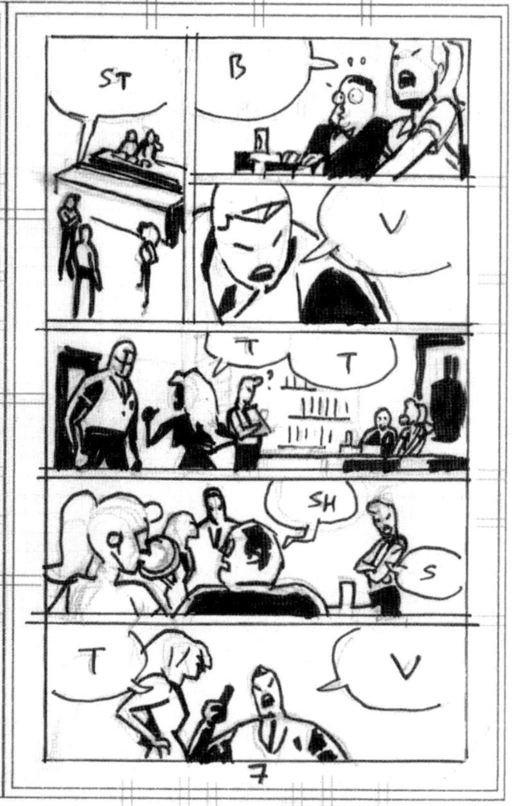
ST
B
V
T
T
SH
S
T
V
7

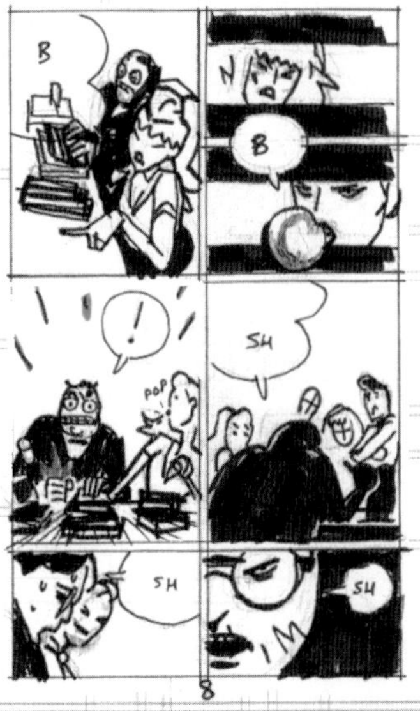
B
N
B
!
POP
SH
SH
SH
8

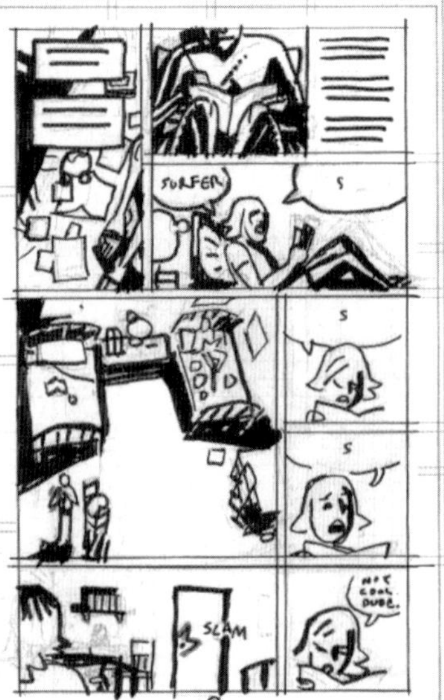
SURFER
S
S
S
SLAM
NOT COOL DUDE.
9

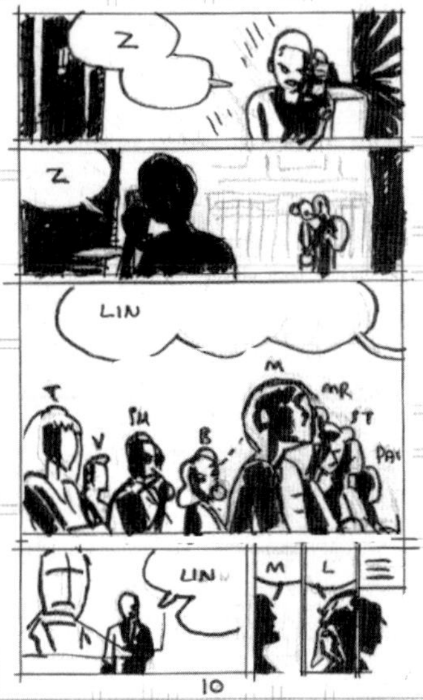
Z
Z
LIN
LIN
M
L
10

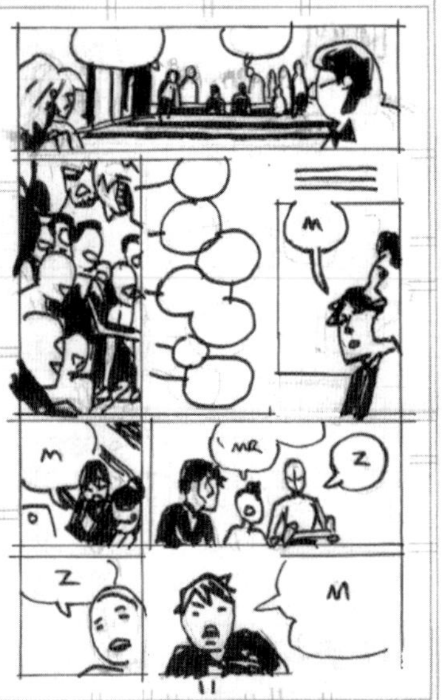
M
M
MR
Z
Z
M
11

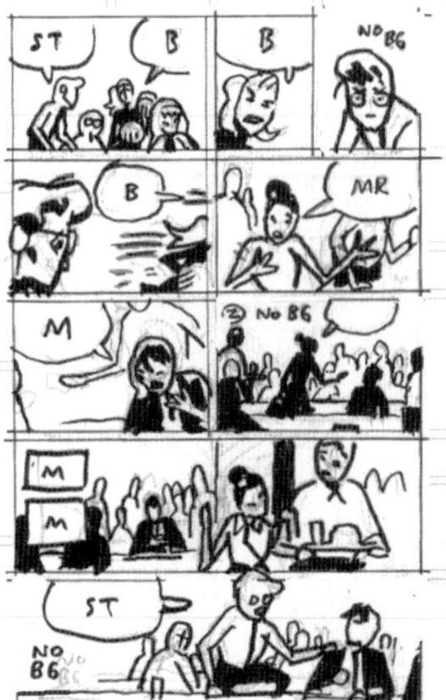
ST
B
B
NO BG
B
MR
M
NO BG
M
M
ST
NO BG
12

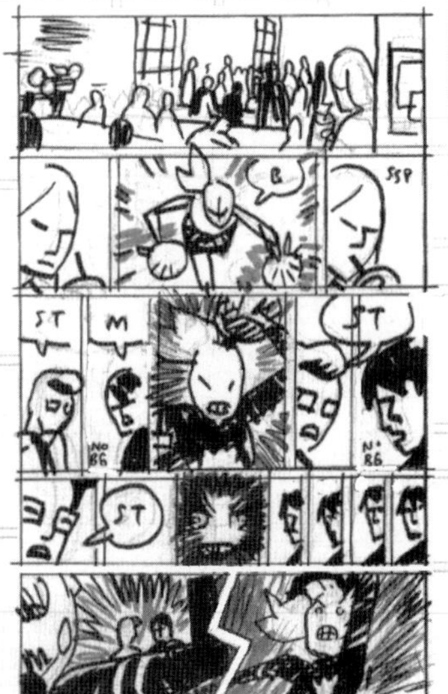
B
SSP
ST
M
ST
NO BG
NO BG
ST
13

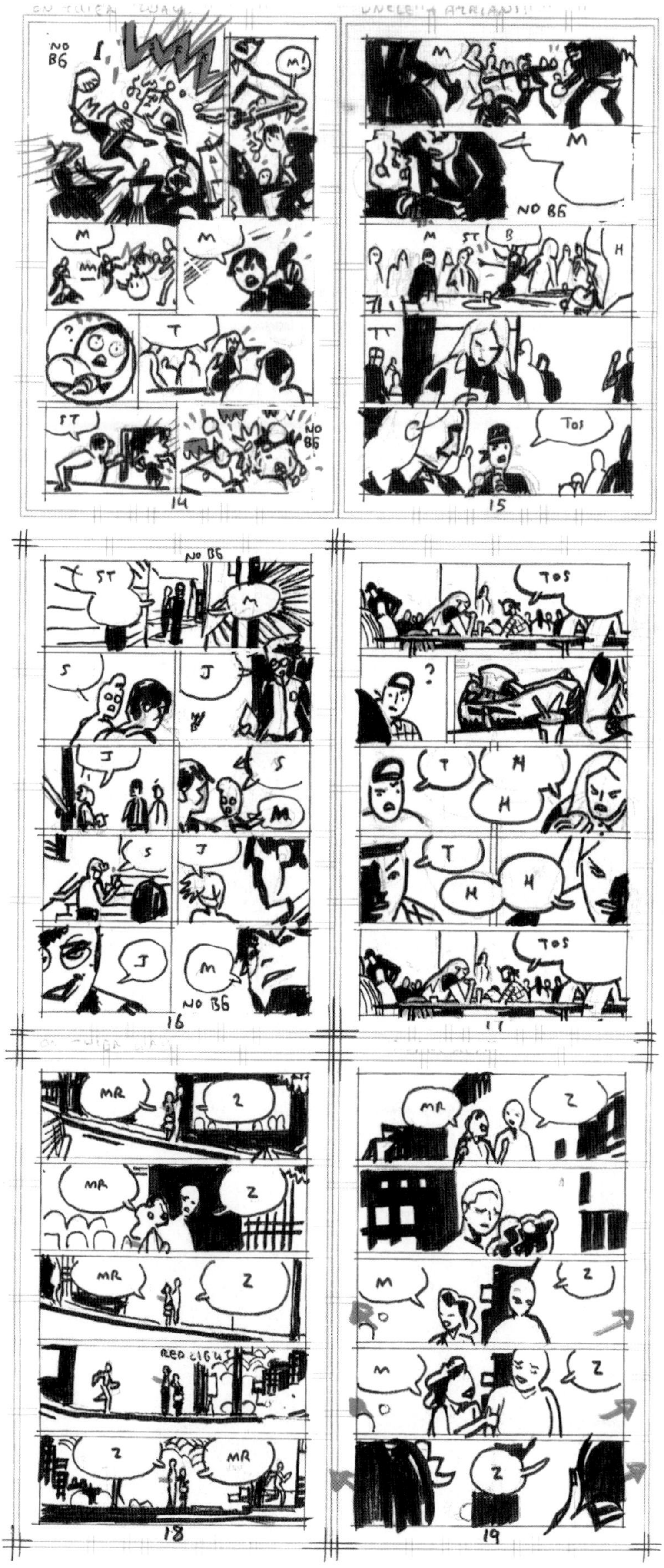

NO BG
M!
M
M
?
T
ST
NO BG
14
M
M
NO BG
M
ST
B
H
TT
TOS
15
NO BG
ST
M
S
J
J
S
M
S
J
J
M
NO BG
16
TOS
?
T
H
H
T
H
H
TOS
MR
Z
MR
Z
MR
Z
RED LIGHT
Z
MR
18
MR
Z
M
Z
M
Z
Z
19

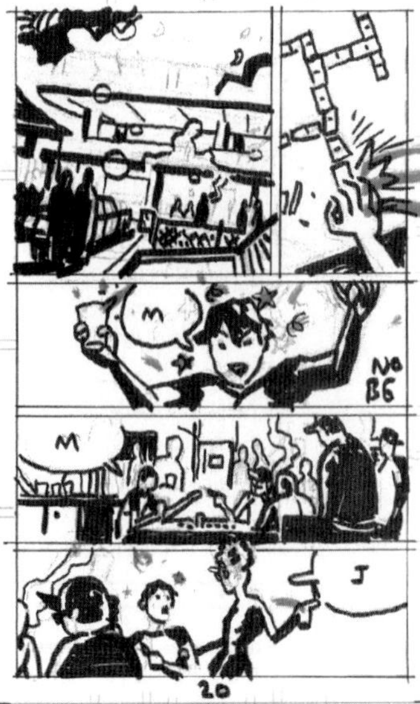
M
NO BG
M
J

20

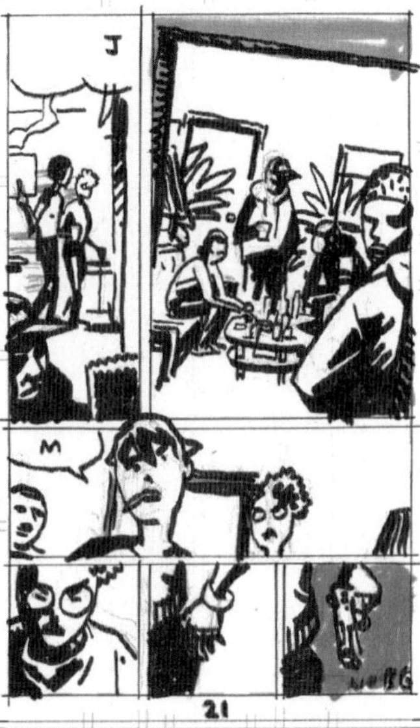
J
M
NO BG

21

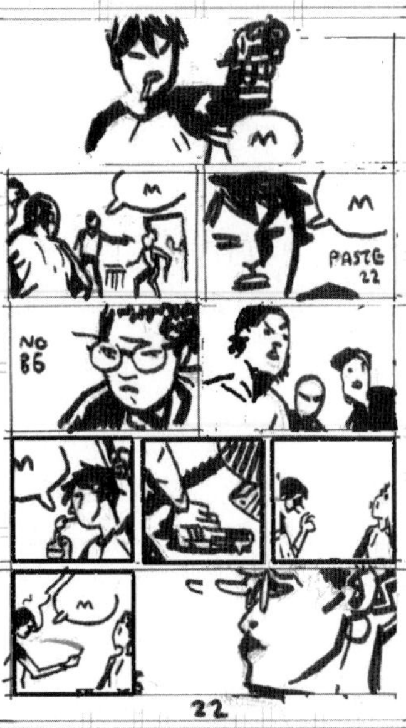
M
M
PASTE 22
NO BG
M
M

22

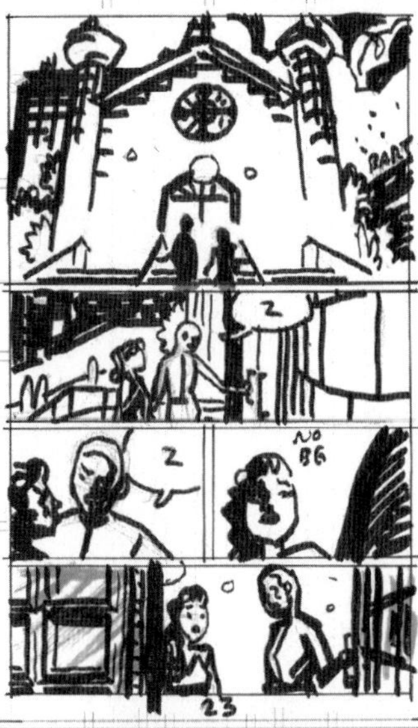
Z
Z
NO BG

23

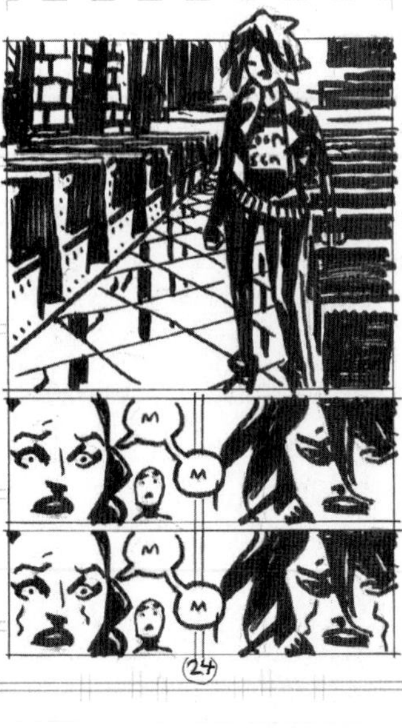
M
M
M
M

24

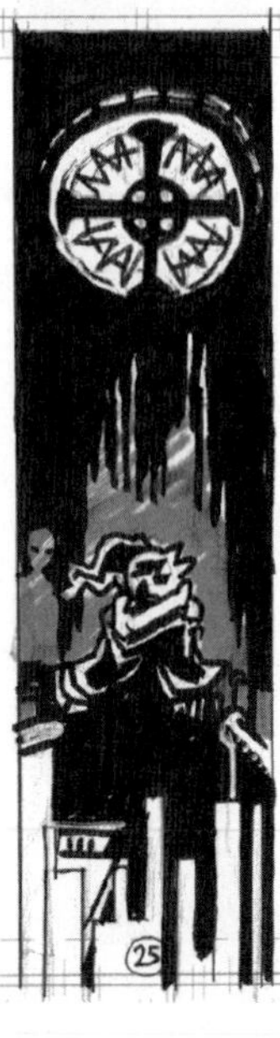

25

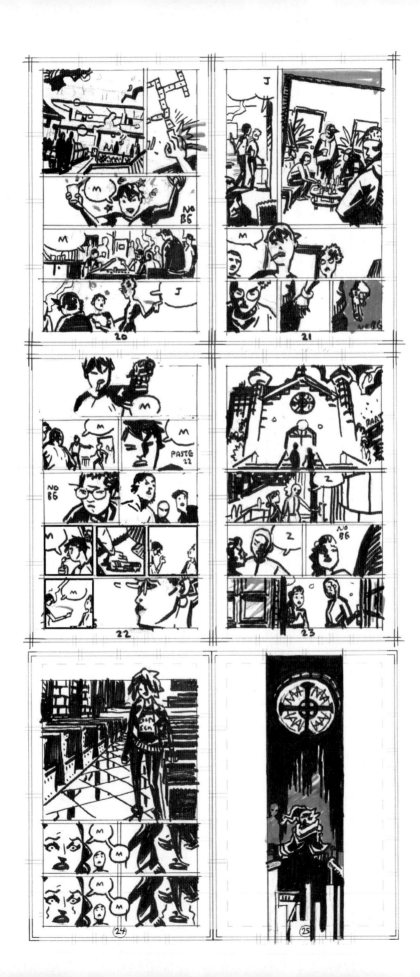

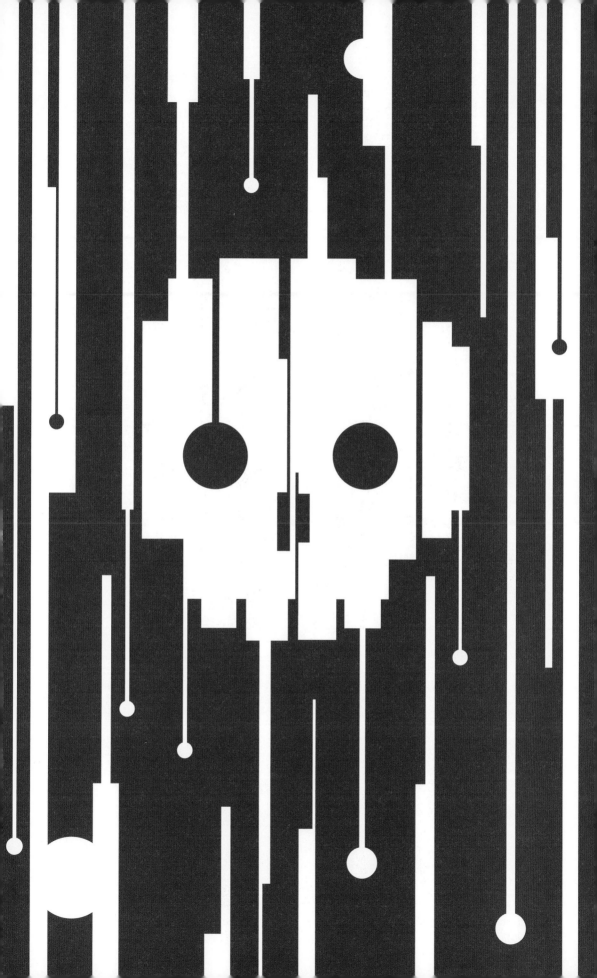

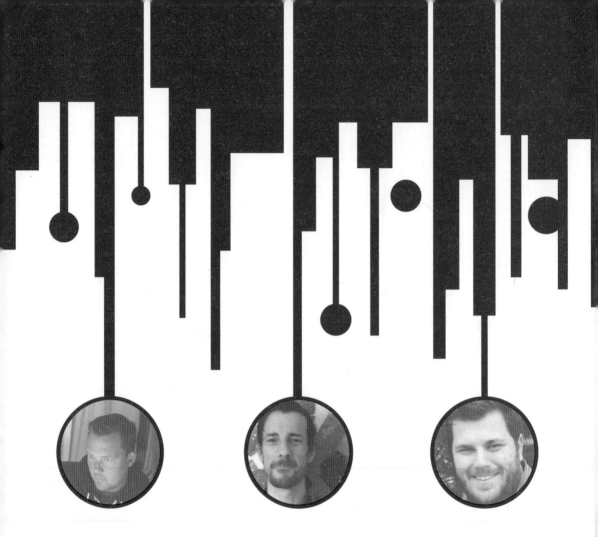

RICK REMENDER is the writer/ co-creator of comics such as *Deadly Class*, *Fear Agent*, *Black Science*, *Seven to Eternity*, and *Death or Glory*. During his years at Marvel, he wrote *Captain America*, *Uncanny X-Force*, and *Venom* and created *The Uncanny Avengers*. Outside of comics, he served as lead writer on EA's *Bulletstorm* game and the hit game *Dead Space*. Prior to this, he ran a satellite of Wild Brain animation, worked on films such as *The Iron Giant* and *Anastasia*, and taught sequential art and animation at San Francisco's Academy of Art University.

He currently curates his own publishing imprint, Giant Generator, at Image Comics and previously served as lead writer/co-showrunner on SyFy's adaption of his co-creation *Deadly Class*.

WES CRAIG is the artist and co-creator of *Deadly Class* with Rick Remender; the writer, co-creator, and cover artist of *The Gravediggers Union* with Toby Cypress; and the writer-artist of *Blackhand Comics*, published by Image. Working out of Montreal, Quebec, he has been drawing comic books professionally since 2004 on such titles as *Guardians of the Galaxy*, *Batman*, and *The Flash*.

Despite nearly flunking kindergarten for his exclusive use of black crayons, **JORDAN BOYD** has moved on to become an increasingly prolific comic book colorist, including work on *Astonishing Ant-Man* and *All-New Wolverine* for Marvel; *Invisible Republic*, *Evolution,* and *Deadly Class* for Image; *Devolution* at Dynamite; and *Suiciders: Kings of HelL.A.* from DC/Vertigo. He and his wife, kids, dogs, hedgehogs, and fish currently live in Norman, OK.